FROM THE INTRODUCTION

BY DAMON KNIGHT:

"You will find here samples of the adventure tale, the tale of ratiocination, the poetic tale, the terror tale, the story of ideas. Certain of these stories are meant to make you shiver, others to make you laugh; but all of them, being science fiction, are meant to make you think—and enjoy the act of thinking."

A CENTURY OF SCIENCE FICTION

HERE ARE TWENTY-SIX LUMINOUS STORIES WRITTEN BY STARS OF THE FIRST MAGNITUDE IN THE GALAXY OF SCIENCE FICTION.

A CENTURY OF SCIENCE FICTION

*Edited, with an Introduction and
Notes by* DAMON KNIGHT

A DELL BOOK

Published by
DELL PUBLISHING CO., INC.
750 Third Avenue, New York 17, N.Y.

Reprinted by arrangement with
Simon and Schuster, Inc., New York, N.Y.

DEDICATION:

> *to*
> *CLAYTON RAWSON,*
> *who should be dedicating it to me*

First Dell printing—February, 1963

ACKNOWLEDGMENTS

"The Ideal," by Stanley G. Weinbaum, copyright 1935 by Continental Publications, Inc. Excerpt reprinted by permission of the author's agents, Scott Meredith Literary Agency, Inc.

"Reason," by Isaac Asimov, copyright 1941 by Street & Smith Publications, Inc. Reprinted by permission of the author.

"But Who Can Replace a Man?" by Brian W. Aldiss, copyright 1958 by Royal Publications, Inc. Reprinted by permission of the author's agent, John Carnell.

"Of Time and Third Avenue," by Alfred Bester, copyright 1951 by Fantasy House, Inc. Reprinted by permission of the author.

"Sail On! Sail On!" by Philip José Farmer, copyright 1952 by Better Publications, Inc. Reprinted by permission of the author.

"Worlds of the Imperium," by Keith Laumer, copyright 1961 by Ziff-Davis Publishing Co. Excerpt reprinted by permission of the author's agent, Theron W. Raines.

"The Business, As Usual," by Mack Reynolds, copyright 1952 by Fantasy House, Inc. Reprinted by permission of the author's agents, Scott Meredith Literary Agency, Inc.

"What's It Like Out There?" by Edmond Hamilton, copyright 1952 by Better Publications, Inc. Reprinted by permission of the author.

"Sky Lift," by Robert A. Heinlein, copyright 1953 by Greenleaf Publishing Co. Reprinted by permission of the author's agent, Lurton Blassingame.

"The Star," by Arthur C. Clarke, copyright 1955 by Royal Publications, Inc. Reprinted by permission of the author's agents, Scott Meredith Literary Agency, Inc.

"The Wind People," by Marion Zimmer Bradley, copyright 1958 by Quinn Publishing Co., Inc. Reprinted by permission of the author's agents, Scott Meredith Literary Agency, Inc.

CONTENTS

INTRODUCTION

"Science fiction" is a term H. G. Wells could not have known until long after his "fantastic and imaginative romances" were published in the 1890s. Jules Verne died without ever having heard it; so did Edgar Allan Poe and Fitz-James O'Brien. The thing we are talking about crystallized out of older forms just about one century ago. The name we call it by did not come into existence until 1929.

More than a quarter-century ago, when I first began reading stories like these in the old *Amazing* and *Wonder,* and in the miraculous volumes of H. G. Wells, I found myself part of a tiny coterie: we called the stories science fiction, but the term was not used or understood by the world at large. When respectable critics took notice of the field occasionally, in order to damn it categorically and without examination, they called it "pseudo science" or "Buck Rogers stuff," never "science fiction." Even in the forties, when people asked me what kind of copy I wrote, it was never enough to say, "Science fiction." They would either look blank or say, "Oh, like in *Popular Science?*" And I would have to say, "No, like H. G. Wells and Jules Verne—you know, rocket ships, robots, things like that." Whereupon I would get a certain kind of a look.

Nowadays the term "science fiction" has wide currency, and has even lost most of its raffish connotations. We addicts owe this welcome change partly to the upheaval in the popular mind that came with the atom bomb and the V-2—hardly unmixed blessings—but principally to the growing weight of evidence science fiction writers have piled up in their own favor.

By and large, the hostile critics have fallen silent. When s.f. is mentioned by a respected literary figure today, his comments are likely to be informed and friendly—an unheard-of thing twenty years ago. As C. S. Lewis writes in his *Experiment in Criticism:*

> . . . *in the good old days I noticed that whenever critics said anything about [science fiction], they betrayed great ignorance. They talked as if it were a homogeneous genre. But it is not, in the literary sense, a genre at all. There is nothing common to all who write it except the use of a particular "machine." Some of the writers are of the family of Jules Verne and are primarily interested in technology. Some use the machine simply for literary fantasy and produce what is essentially* Märchen *or myth. A great many use it for satire; nearly all the most pungent American criticism of the American way of life takes this form, and would at once be denounced as un-American if it ventured into any other. And finally, there is the great mass of hacks who merely "cashed in" on the boom in science fiction and used remote planets or even galaxies as the backcloth for spy-stories or love-stories which might as well or better have been located in Whitechapel or the Bronx. And as the stories differ in kind, so of course do their readers. You can, if you wish, class all science fiction together; but it is about as perceptive as classing the works of Ballantyne, Conrad and W. W. Jacobs together as "the sea-story" and then criticising that.*

Meanwhile, many a ponderous essay has been written to show that s.f., far from being a vulgar upstart, really goes back to Homer and Lucian of Samosata. August Derleth actually got into print with a "science fiction" anthology *(Beyond Time and Space)* which included works by Plato, Lucian, Sir Thomas More, Rabelais, Tommaso Campanella, Bacon, Kepler and Godwin. As Cyril Kornbluth wrote, in *The Science Fiction Novel,* "Some of the amateur scholars of science fiction are veritable Hitlers for aggrandizing their field. If they perceive in, say, a sixteenth-century satire some vaguely speculative element they see it as a trembling and persecuted minority, demand *Anschluss,* and proceed to annex the satire to science fiction."

Well, what *is* science fiction?

Theodore Sturgeon, one of the field's living giants, has said, "A science fiction story is a story built around human beings, with a human problem, and a human solution, which would not have happened at all without its scientific content." This definition excludes many stories that are called s.f. by common consent, but never mind; with one niggling change—inserting "speculative" before "scientific"—it cleanly divides true science fiction from even the best imitations.

"These amazing magazines call themselves 'science fiction,'" wrote Clemence Dane in 1936. "But they are nothing but America's fairy-tales." Fairy-tales they are, if you like. Here, in new dress, are the invincible weapon, the perilous journey, the monster in the cavern. Here are all the breathless wonder and the bright, hot colors of the magical tale. Here are the grisly folk—ghouls, vampires, spirits of evil. All these things are here, but all with a difference—and it's the difference that makes them science fiction.

The organizing principle of this field since about 1860 has been the idea of science: of knowledge systematically obtained and rationally applied. As we contrast older stories with newer ones in this book, you'll be able to see how that idea slowly changed the imaginative story into something that had never existed in the world before. This, perhaps, is science fiction's principal claim to a civilized man's attention: it is something new under the sun. Overanxious scholars to the contrary, it is a kind of fiction which did not and could not come into existence before the middle of the nineteenth century.

Science fiction is distinguished by its implicit assumption that man can change himself and his environment. This alone sets it apart from all other literary forms. This is the message that came out of the Intellectual Revolution of the seventeenth and eighteenth centuries, and that has survived in no other kind of fiction.

The delights of good s.f. are many; but always chief among them is the pleasure of watching consequences flow logically out of a boldly imaginative premise.

The thing that makes such imaginations interesting [wrote H. G. Wells] is their translation into commonplace terms and a rigid exclusion of other marvels from the story. Then it becomes human. How would you feel and what might not happen to you, is the typical question, if for instance pigs could fly and one came rocketing over a hedge at you. How would you feel and what might not happen to you if suddenly you were changed into an ass and couldn't tell anyone about *it?* Or if you suddenly became invisible? But no one would think twice about the answer if hedges and houses also began to fly, or if people changed into lions, tigers, cats and dogs left and right, or if anyone could vanish anyhow. Nothing remains interesting where anything may happen.*

Note, please, that a science fiction writer may pick his premise according to taste—that pigs fly, or that Napoleon never became emperor, or that the planets are eggs laid by a giant bird—but he must then, by the rules of the game, develop his story with rigid logic and without violating known fact, "except when the violation itself constitutes the basis of the story and a plausible explanation is furnished." (Fletcher Pratt, in *World of Wonder*.) Like any rules, these serve the function of making the game both interesting to play and interesting to watch. Adapting itself to them with zest, science fiction has invaded a field from which mainstream fiction has been hanging back in dismay for over a century.

In mainstream fiction, even today, machines that do things appear only as mysterious streamlined boxes. Science fiction alone dares to examine the mechanism inside. (It's true that some modern s.f. writers have used the Mysterious and Patently Empty Box to solve their heroes' problems, but this is a disease, it's self-eliminating; for you can pull anything out of an empty box, and "Nothing remains interesting where anything may happen.")

I read science fiction for fun, and am glad that it seldom takes itself too seriously. Nevertheless, I'm proud of s.f. for its ability to treat people as reasoning beings, for its courage in dealing with the great human questions—the origin of the universe and of man, the nature of reality, the ethical dilemma—and for its unmistakable benign influence on the mental climate of our world. Robert A. Heinlein, one of the greatest living s.f. writers, said this, in *The Science Fiction Novel;* and I submit that these two sentences are worth remembering: "I claim one positive triumph for science fiction, totally beyond the scope of so-called mainstream fiction. It has prepared the youth of our time for the coming age of space." Heinlein, though not egotist enough to say so, has himself done more to this end than any other s.f. writer. His

* Interestingly enough, there are people in the s.f. field today to whom this misfortune must have happened at an early age.

juvenile novels, meticulously researched and written—and read by thousands of young people—have taught a whole generation to think of space travel as something natural and inevitable.

So many people have written good s.f. during the last century that a book twice this size could not represent them all. I could not even give you a book representative of all the varied flavors and textures of science fiction writing: instead, I've picked those I like best myself.

People who really like whiskey take it straight; people who really like coffee drink it black, hot and strong. You must go elsewhere for bland science fiction or for pablum of any kind; the stories you will find here are the kind I like—strong, rich, sometimes bitter. I like a story that does not come apart as you read. I like a story that leaves some kind of emotional or sensual warmth behind. I like a story that persuades, if at all, without seeming to do so; messianic science fiction is less agreeable to me, and not only because your typical self-appointed messiah can't write his way out of a paper bag: I don't like to see science fiction degraded into a vehicle for anything. The story, I think, should always be more important than the idea; when the reverse gets to be true, you want an essay.

Incidentally, if I have given you the impression that s.f. writers are almost uniformly large-domed, great-souled, brilliantly endowed literary artists, I apologize. We have our fair share of lackwits and mediocrities—ninety per cent. (Sturgeon's Rule: "Nine tenths of *everything* is crud.") But you will not find their stories here.

You will find here samples of the adventure tale, the tale of ratiocination, the poetic tale, the terror tale, the story of ideas. Certain of these stories are meant to make you shiver, others to make you laugh; but all of them, being science fiction, are meant to make you think—and enjoy the act of thinking.

I owe grateful thanks to James Blish, Howard DeVore, Judith Merril, Barbara Norville and Theodore L. Thomas for help of many kinds; and also to the compilers of the following books, without which this one would have been almost impossible to put together: *Checklist of Fantastic Literature*, edited by Everett F. Bleiler (Shasta, Chicago, 1948); *Index to the Science Fiction Magazines, 1926-1950*, compiled by Donald B. Day (Perri, Portland, Oregon, 1952); and *A Handbook of Science Fiction and Fantasy*, compiled by Donald H. Tuck (published by the author, Hobart, Tasmania, 1959).

DAMON KNIGHT

The Anchorage
Milford, Pike County, Pennsylvania
October 18, 1961

1.

ROBOTS

a selection from

THE IDEAL

BY STANLEY G. WEINBAUM

"This," said the Franciscan, "is my Automaton, who at the proper time will speak, answer whatsoever question I may ask, and reveal all secret knowledge to me." He smiled as he laid his hand affectionately on the iron skull that topped the pedestal.

The youth gazed open-mouthed, first at the head and then at the friar. "But it's iron!" he whispered. "The head is iron, good Father."

"Iron without, skill within, my son," said Roger Bacon. "It will speak, at the proper time and in its own manner, for so have I made it. A clever man can twist the Devil's arts to God's ends, thereby cheating the fiend. *Sst!* There sounds vespers! *Plena gratia, ave Virgo . . .*"

But it did not speak. Long hours, long weeks, the *Doctor Mirabilis* watched his creation, but the iron lips were silent and the iron eyes dull, and no voice but the great man's own sounded in his monkish cell, nor was there ever an answer to all the questions that he asked—until one day when he sat surveying his work, composing a letter to Duns Scotus in distant Cologne . . . one day . . .

"Time is!" said the image, and smiled benignly.

The friar looked up. "Time is, indeed," he echoed. "Time it is that you give utterance, and to some assertion less obvious than that time is. For of course time is, else there were nothing at all. Without time—"

"Time was!" rumbled the image, still smiling, but sternly as the statue of Draco.

"Indeed time was," said the monk. "Time was, is, and will be, for time is that medium in which events occur. Matter exists in space, but events—"

The image smiled no longer. "Time is past!" it roared in tones deep as the cathedral bell outside, and burst into ten thousand pieces.

This passage from a story first published in 1935 is a modern version (much livelier and more readable than the original) of an incident from the play Friar Bacon and Friar Bungay, *by the Elizabethan dramatist Robert Greene. Weinbaum did not name his source, but I was able to find it out simply by picking up the telephone and calling the local Bacon expert, James Blish, who also told me that the legend of a speaking head of metal has been traced all the way back through medieval literature to Arabic sources.*

In fact, the idea of a manlike mechanism—an automaton —goes back to classical times. King Minos of Crete was supposed to have had a brazen giant named Talos, made by Hephaestus and given to him by Zeus to patrol the island. Metal though he was, Talos was run by magic, however, not clockwork: he had one vein, plugged by a nail in his heel, and could be killed by drawing out the nail.

The clockwork automatons of the eighteenth and nineteenth centuries had something of mechanism about them and something of magic and deception. One of these, exhibited in the United States in the 1830s, was the subject of an exposé written by Edgar Allan Poe: "Maelzel's Chess Player." Poe showed by careful analysis that the moves of the chess-playing automaton were actually made by a man concealed in the cabinet below, and that by an ingenious series of contortions he managed to stay unseen while the three sections of the cabinet were opened in succession.

And this brings us to our first robot story, for it must have been Maelzel's automaton that prompted Ambrose Bierce to write "Moxon's Master" (1893).

Bierce, the gloomy misanthrope of San Francisco, pub-

lished several volumes of grisly tales and sardonic aphorisms
(The Devil's Dictionary). He loved the grotesque for its own
sake; a thread of this perverse fascination runs through the
whole history of imaginative literature, but in Bierce it was
an obsession. (The Hungarian-born monologist Theodore, by
the way, gives a horrendous recital of Bierce's most hair-
raising tale, "Oil of Dog." If this performer ever turns up in
your town, go and hear him.) Bierce lived to be seventy-one,
then disappeared into Mexico, prompting Charles Fort to
speculate that somebody was collecting Ambroses.

MOXON'S MASTER

BY AMBROSE BIERCE

"Are you serious? Do you really believe that a machine thinks?"

I got no immediate reply; Moxon was apparently intent upon the coals in the grate, touching them deftly here and there with the fire-poker till they signified a sense of his attention by a brighter glow. For several weeks I had been observing in him a growing habit of delay in answering even the most trivial of commonplace questions. His air, however, was that of preoccupation rather than deliberation: one might have said that he had "something on his mind."

Presently he said: "What is a 'machine'? The word has been variously defined. Here is one definition from a popular dictionary: 'Any instrument or organization by which power is applied and made effective, or a desired effect produced.' Well, then, is not a man a machine? And you will admit that he thinks—or thinks he thinks."

"If you do not wish to answer my question," I said, rather testily, "why not say so? All that you say is mere evasion. You know well enough that when I say 'machine' I do not mean a man, but something that man has made and controls."

"When it does not control him," he said, rising abruptly and looking out of a window, whence nothing was visible in the blackness of a stormy night. A moment later he turned about and with a smile said: "I beg your pardon; I had no thought of evasion. I considered the dictionary man's unconscious testimony suggestive and worth something in the discussion. I can give your question a direct answer easily enough: I do believe that a machine thinks about the work that it is doing."

That was direct enough, certainly. It was not altogether pleasing, for it tended to confirm a sad suspicion that Moxon's devotion to study and work in his machine-shop had not been good for him. I knew, for one thing, that he suffered from insomnia, and that is no light affliction. Had it affected his mind? His reply to my question seemed to me then evidence that it had; perhaps I should think differently about it now. I was younger then, and among the blessings that are not denied to youth is ignorance. Incited by that great stimulant to controversy, I said:

"And what, pray, does it think with—in the absence of a brain?"

The reply, coming with less than his customary delay, took his favorite form of counter-interrogation:

"With what does a plant think—in the absence of a brain?"

"Ah, plants also belong to the philosopher class! I should be pleased to know some of their conclusions; you may omit the premises."

"Perhaps," he replied, apparently unaffected by my foolish irony, "you may be able to infer their convictions from their acts. I will spare you the familiar examples of the sensitive mimosa, the several insectivorous flowers and those whose stamens bend down and shake their pollen upon the entering bee in order that he may fertilize their distant mates. But observe this. In an open spot in my garden I planted a climbing vine. When it was barely above the surface I set a stake into the soil a yard away. The vine at once made for it, but as it was about to reach it after several days I removed it a few feet. The vine at once altered its course, making an acute angle, and again made for the stake. This maneuver was repeated several times, but finally, as if discouraged, the vine abandoned the pursuit and ignoring further attempts to divert it traveled to a small tree, further away, which it climbed.

"Roots of the eucalyptus will prolong themselves incredibly in search of moisture. A well-known horticulturist relates that one entered an old drain pipe and followed it until it came to a break, where a section of the pipe had been removed to make way for a stone wall that had been built across its course. The root left the drain and followed the wall until it found an opening where a stone had fallen out. It crept through and, following the other side of the wall back to the drain, entered the unexplored part and resumed its journey."

"And all this?"

"Can you miss the significance of it? It shows the consciousness of plants. It proves that they think."

"Even if it did—what then? We were speaking, not of plants, but of machines. They may be composed partly of wood—wood that has no longer vitality—or wholly of metal. Is thought an attribute also of the mineral kingdom?"

"How else do you explain the phenomena, for example, of crystallization?"

"I do not explain them."

"Because you cannot without affirming what you wish to deny, namely, intelligent co-operation among the constituent elements of the crystals. When soldiers form lines, or hollow squares, you call it reason. When wild geese in flight take the form of a letter V you say instinct. When the homogeneous atoms of a mineral, moving freely in solution, arrange themselves into shapes mathematically perfect, or particles of frozen moisture into the symmetrical and beautiful forms of snowflakes, you have nothing to say. You have not even invented a name to conceal your heroic unreason."

Moxon was speaking with unusual animation and earnestness. As he paused I heard in an adjoining room known to me as his "machine-shop," which no one but himself was permitted to enter, a singular thumping sound, as of someone pounding upon a table with an open hand. Moxon heard it at the same moment and, visibly agitated, rose and hurriedly passed into the room whence it came. I thought it odd that anyone else should be in there, and my interest in my friend —with doubtless a touch of unwarrantable curiosity—led me to listen intently, though I am happy to say, not at the keyhole. There were confused sounds, as of a struggle or scuffle; the floor shook. I distinctly heard hard breathing and a hoarse whisper which said "Damn you!" Then all was silent, and presently Moxon reappeared and said, with a rather sorry smile:

"Pardon me for leaving you so abruptly. I have a machine in there that lost its temper and cut up rough."

Fixing my eyes steadily upon his left cheek, which was

traversed by four parallel excoriations showing blood, I said: "How would it do to trim its nails?"

I could have spared myself the jest; he gave it no attention, but seated himself in the chair that he had left and resumed the interrupted monologue as if nothing had occurred:

"Doubtless you do not hold with those (I need not name them to a man of your reading) who have taught that all matter is sentient, that every atom is a living, feeling, conscious being. *I* do. There is no such thing as dead, inert matter: it is all alive; all instinct with force, actual and potential; all sensitive to the same forces in its environment and susceptible to the contagion of higher and subtler ones residing in such superior organisms as it may be brought into relation with, as those of man when he is fashioning it into an instrument of his will. It absorbs something of his intelligence and purpose—more of them in proportion to the complexity of the resulting machine and that of its work.

"Do you happen to recall Herbert Spencer's definition of 'life'? I read it thirty years ago. He may have altered it afterward, for anything I know, but in all that time I have been unable to think of a single word that could profitably be changed or added or removed. It seems to me not only the best definition, but the only possible one.

" 'Life,' he says, 'is a definite combination of heterogeneous changes, both simultaneous and successive, in correspondence with external coexistences and sequences.' "

"That defines the phenomenon," I said, "but gives no hint of its cause."

"That," he replied, "is all that any definition can do. As Mill points out, we know nothing of cause except as an antecedent—nothing of effect except as a consequent. Of certain phenomena, one never occurs without another, which is dissimilar: the first in point of time we call cause, the second, effect. One who had many times seen a rabbit pursued by a dog, and had never seen rabbits and dogs otherwise, would think the rabbit the cause of the dog.

"But I fear," he added, laughing naturally enough, "that my rabbit is leading me a long way from the track of my legitimate quarry: I'm indulging in the pleasure of the chase for its own sake. What I want you to observe is that in Herbert Spencer's definition of 'life' the activity of a machine is included—there is nothing in the definition that is not applicable to it. According to this sharpest of observers and deepest of thinkers, if a man during his period of activity is alive, so is a machine when in operation. As an inventor and constructor of machines I know that to be true."

Moxon was silent for a long time, gazing absently into the fire. It was growing late and I thought it time to be going, but somehow I did not like the notion of leaving him in that isolated house, all alone except for the presence of some person of whose nature my conjectures could go no further than that it was unfriendly, perhaps malign. Leaning toward him and looking earnestly into his eyes while making a motion with my hand through the door of his workshop, I said:

"Moxon, whom have you in there?"

Somewhat to my surprise he laughed lightly and answered without hesitation:

"Nobody; the incident that you have in mind was caused by my folly in leaving a machine in action with nothing to act upon, while I undertook the interminable task of enlightening your understanding. Do you happen to know that Consciousness is the creature of Rhythm?"

"Oh, bother them both!" I replied, rising and laying hold of my overcoat. "I'm going to wish you good night; and I'll add the hope that the machine which you inadvertently left in action will have her gloves on the next time you think it needful to stop her."

Without waiting to observe the effect of my shot I left the house.

Rain was falling, and the darkness was intense. In the sky beyond the crest of a hill toward which I groped my way along precarious plank sidewalks and across miry, unpaved streets I could see the faint glow of the city's lights, but behind me nothing was visible but a single window of Moxon's house. It glowed with what seemed to me a mysterious and fatcful meaning. I knew it was an uncurtained aperture in my friend's "machine-shop," and I had little doubt that he had resumed the studies interrupted by his duties as my instructor in mechanical consciousness and the fatherhood of Rhythm. Odd, and in some degree humorous, as his convictions seemed to me at that time, I could not wholly divest myself of the feeling that they had some tragic relation to his life and character—perhaps to his destiny—although I no longer entertained the notion that they were the vagaries of a disordered mind. Whatever might be thought of his views, his exposition of them was too logical for that. Over and over, his last words came back to me: "Consciousness is the creature of Rhythm." Bald and terse as the statement was, I now found it infinitely alluring. At each recurrence it broadened in meaning and deepened in suggestion. Why, here (I thought) is something upon which to found a philosophy. If consciousness is the product of rhythm all things *are* conscious, for all have motion, and all motion is rhythmic. I wondered if Moxon knew the significance and breadth of his thought—the scope of this momentous generalization; or had he arrived at his philosophic faith by the tortuous and uncertain road of observation?

That faith was then new to me, and all Moxon's expounding had failed to make me a convert; but now it seemed as if a great light shone about me, like that which fell upon Saul of Tarsus; and out there in the storm and darkness and solitude I experienced what Lewes calls "the endless variety and excitement of philosophic thought." I exulted in a new sense of knowledge, a new pride of reason. My feet seemed hardly to touch the earth; it was as if I were uplifted and borne through the air by invisible wings.

Yielding to an impulse to seek further light from him whom I now recognized as my master and guide, I had unconsciously turned about, and almost before I was aware of having done so found myself again at Moxon's door. I was drenched with rain, but felt no discomfort. Unable in my excitement to find the doorbell, I instinctively tried the knob. It turned and, entering, I mounted the stairs to the room that I had so recently left. All was dark and silent; Moxon, as I had supposed, was in the adjoining room—the "machine-shop." Groping along the wall until I found the communicating door I knocked loudly several times, but got no response, which I attributed to the uproar outside, for the wind was blowing a gale and dashing the rain against the thin walls in sheets. The drumming upon the shingle roof spanning the unceiled room was loud and incessant.

I had never been invited into the machine-shop—had, indeed, been denied admittance, as had all others, with one exception, a skilled metal worker, of whom no one knew anything except that his name was Haley and his habit silence. But in my spiritual exaltation, discretion and civility were alike forgotten and I opened the door. What I saw took all philosophical speculation out of me in short order.

Moxon sat facing me at the farther side of a small table

upon which a single candle made all the light that was in the room. Opposite him, his back toward me, sat another person. On the table between the two was a chess-board; the men were playing. I knew little of chess, but as only a few pieces were on the board it was obvious that the game was near its close. Moxon was intensely interested—not so much, it seemed to me, in the game as in his antagonist, upon whom he had fixed so intent a look that, standing though I did directly in the line of his vision, I was altogether unobserved. His face was ghastly white, and his eyes glittered like diamonds. Of his antagonist I had only a back view, but that was sufficient; I should not have cared to see his face.

He was apparently not more than five feet in height, with proportions suggesting those of a gorilla—a tremendous breadth of shoulders, thick, short neck and broad, squat head, which had a tangled growth of black hair and was topped with a crimson fez. A tunic of the same color, belted tightly to the waist, reached the seat—apparently a box—upon which he sat; his legs and feet were not seen. His left forearm appeared to rest in his lap; he moved his pieces with his right hand, which seemed disproportionately long.

I had shrunk back and now stood a little to one side of the doorway and in shadow. If Moxon had looked farther than the face of his opponent he could have observed nothing now, except that the door was open. Something forbade me either to enter or to retire, a feeling—I know not how it came—that I was in the presence of an imminent tragedy and might serve my friend by remaining. With a scarcely conscious rebellion against the indelicacy of the act, I remained.

The play was rapid. Moxon hardly glanced at the board before making his moves, and to my unskilled eye seemed to move the piece most convenient to his hand, his motions in doing so being quick, nervous and lacking in precision. The response of his antagonist, while equally prompt in the inception, was made with a slow, uniform, mechanical and, I thought, somewhat theatrical movement of the arm, that was a sore trial to my patience. There was something unearthly about it all, and I caught myself shuddering. But I was wet and cold.

Two or three times after moving a piece the stranger slighty inclined his head, and each time I observed that Moxon shifted his king. All at once the thought came to me that the man was dumb. And then that he was a machine—an automaton chess player! Then I remembered that Moxon had once spoken to me of having invented such a piece of mechanism, though I did not understand that it had actually been constructed. Was all his talk about the consciousness and intelligence of machines merely a prelude to eventual exhibition of this device—only a trick to intensify the effect of its mechanical action upon me in my ignorance of its secret?

A fine end, this, of all my intellectual transports—my "endless variety and excitement of philosophic thought"! I was about to retire in disgust when something occurred to hold my curiosity. I observed a shrug of the thing's great shoulders, as if it were irritated: and so natural was this—so entirely human—that in my new view of the matter it startled me. Nor was that all, for a moment later it struck the table sharply with its clenched hand. At that gesture Moxon seemed even more startled than I: he pushed his chair a little backward, as in alarm.

Presently Moxon, whose play it was, raised his hand high above the board, pounced upon one of his pieces like a sparrow-hawk and with the exclamation "Checkmate!" rose quickly to his feet and stepped behind his chair. The automaton sat motionless.

The wind had now gone down, but I heard, at lessening intervals and progressively louder, the rumble and roll of thunder. In the pauses between I now became conscious of a low humming or buzzing which, like the thunder, grew momentarily louder and more distinct. It seemed to come from the body of the automaton, and was unmistakably a whirring of wheels. It gave me the impression of a disordered mechanism which had escaped the repressive and regulating action of some controlling part—an effect such as might be expected if a pawl should be jostled from the teeth of a ratchet-wheel. But before I had time for much conjecture as to its nature my attention was taken by the strange motions of the automaton itself. A slight but continuous convulsion appeared to have possession of it. In body and head it shook like a man with palsy or an ague chill, and the motion augmented every moment until the entire figure was in violent agitation. Suddenly it sprang to its feet and with a movement almost too quick for the eye to follow shot forward across table and chair, with both arms thrust forth to their full length—the posture and lunge of a diver. Moxon tried to throw himself backward out of reach, but he was too late: I saw the horrible thing's hands close upon his throat, his own clutch its wrists. Then the table was overturned, the candle thrown to the floor and extinguished, and all was black dark. But the noise of the struggle was dreadfully distinct, and most terrible of all were the raucous, squawking sounds made by the strangled man's efforts to breathe. Guided by the infernal hubbub, I sprang to the rescue of my friend, but had hardly taken a stride in the darkness when the whole room blazed with a blinding white light that burned into my brain and heart and memory a vivid picture of the combatants on the floor, Moxon underneath, his throat still in the clutch of those iron hands, his head forced backward, his eyes protruding, his mouth wide open and his tongue thrust out; and—horrible contrast!—upon the painted face of his assassin an expression of tranquil and profound thought, as in the solution of a problem in chess! This I observed, then all was blackness and silence.

Three days later I recovered consciousness in a hospital. As the memory of that tragic night slowly evolved in my ailing brain I recognized in my attendant Moxon's confidential workman, Haley. Responding to a look he approached, smiling.

"Tell me about it," I managed to say, faintly. "All about it."

"Certainly," he said; "you were carried unconscious from a burning house—Moxon's. Nobody knows how you came to be there. You may have to do a little explaining. The origin of the fire is a bit mysterious, too. My own notion is that the house was struck by lightning."

"And Moxon?"

"Buried yesterday—what was left of him."

Apparently this reticent person could unfold himself on occasion. When imparting shocking intelligence to the sick he was affable enough. After some moments of the keenest mental suffering I ventured to ask another question:

"Who rescued me?"

"Well, if that interests you—I did."

"Thank you, Mr. Haley, and may God bless you for it. Did you rescue, also, that charming product of your skill, the automaton chess player that murdered its inventor?"

The man was silent a long time, looking away from me. Presently he turned and gravely said:

"Do you know that?"

"I do," I replied; "I saw it done."

That was many years ago. If I were asked today I should answer less confidently.

May you have pleasant dreams after reading that one!

In the stories that follow, you will see robots become less terrifying, more nearly human, perhaps even a little pathetic. Moxon's automaton is a clockwork mechanism that goes wrong—remember the sound of whirring wheels from inside it, "as if a pawl should be jostled from the teeth of a ratchet-wheel." But there is a suggestion of magic here, too, and of impious tampering; it's impossible not to speculate that perhaps it was because the machine was angry that its pawl slipped.

The idea of the mechanical man did not cross all the way over from magic to science fiction until well into the present century. Oddly enough, in spite of its antique origins, as pure science fiction it is the youngest of the themes in this book. H. G. Wells wrote no robot stories, nor did Jules Verne; it was left for an American writer, Isaac Asimov, to become the first acknowledged master of the robot story.

Asimov is the son of a Brooklyn candy-store owner (in New York, a candy store is a hole in the wall that sells candy, soda, ice cream, newspapers, cigarettes and a lot of other things, all in about three hundred square feet), who got himself a Ph.D. in chemistry by what Cyril Kornbluth soberly described as "heroism"—working in the candy store by day, studying at night, year after year. On the side, he managed to turn out some forty science fiction stories even before he got his doctorate, and at the latest count is the author of forty-two books. In recent years he has turned to factual writing and has become a distinguished popular historian of science.

When the science of robotics comes into existence, it will probably be found that the basic principles have already been laid down by Isaac Asimov—the Three Laws of Robotics:

1. A robot may not injure a human being or, through inaction, allow a human being to come to harm.

2. A robot must obey the orders given it by human beings

except where such orders would conflict with the First Law.
3. A robot must protect its own existence as long as such
protection does not conflict with the First or Second Law.

As you are about to see, Asimov's robots are a very differ-
ent breed from Bierce's. There is nothing eerie about QT1;
he is merely a mechanism designed and constructed to think
and act like a man. Except for being metal, in fact, he is a
man—and it follows logically that he is completely exasperat-
ing to men.

REASON

BY ISAAC ASIMOV

Gregory Powell spaced his words for emphasis. "One week ago, Donovan and I put you together." His brows furrowed doubtfully and he pulled the end of his brown mustache.

It was quiet in the officers' room of Solar Station 5—except for the soft purring of the mighty beam director somewhere far below.

Robot QT1 sat immovable. The burnished plates of his body gleamed in the luxites, and the glowing red of the photoelectric cells that were his eyes were fixed steadily upon the Earthman at the other side of the table.

Powell repressed a sudden attack of nerves. These robots possessed peculiar brains. The positronic paths impressed upon them were calculated in advance, and all possible permutations that might lead to anger or hate were rigidly excluded. And yet—the QT models were the first of their kind, and this was the first of the QT's. Anything could happen.

Finally the robot spoke. His voice carried the cold timbre inseparable from a metallic diaphragm. "Do you realize the seriousness of such a statement, Powell?"

"*Something* made you, Cutie," pointed out Powell. "You admit yourself that your memory seems to spring full-grown from an absolute blankness of a week ago. I'm giving you the explanation. Donovan and I put you together from the parts shipped us."

Cutie gazed upon his long, supple fingers in an oddly

human attitude of mystification. "It strikes me that there should be a more satisfactory explanation than that. For *you* to make *me* seems improbable."

The Earthman laughed quite suddenly. "In Earth's name, why?"

"Call it intuition. That's all it is so far. But I intend to reason it out, though. A chain of valid reasoning can end only with the determination of truth, and I'll stick till I get there."

Powell stood up and seated himself at the table's edge next the robot. He felt a sudden strong sympathy for this strange machine. It was not at all like the ordinary robot, attending to his specialized task at the station with the intensity of a deeply ingrooved positronic path.

He placed a hand upon Cutie's steel shoulder and the metal was cold and hard to the touch.

"Cutie," he said, "I'm going to try to explain something to you. You're the first robot who's ever exhibited curiosity as to his own existence—and I think the first that's really intelligent enough to understand the world outside. Here, come with me."

The robot rose erect smoothly and his thickly sponge-rubber-soled feet made no noise as he followed Powell. The Earthman touched a button, and a square section of the wall flicked aside. The thick, clear glass revealed space—star-speckled.

"I've seen that in the observation ports in the engine room," said Cutie.

"I know," said Powell. "What do you think it is?"

"Exactly what it seems—a black material just beyond this glass that is spotted with little gleaming dots. I know that our director sends out beams to some of these dots, always to the same ones—and also that these dots shift and that the beams shift with them. That is all."

"Good! Now I want you to listen carefully. The blackness is emptiness—vast emptiness stretching out infinitely. The little gleaming dots are huge masses of energy-filled matter. They are globes, some of them millions of miles in diameter —and for comparison, this station is only one mile across. They seem so tiny because they are incredibly far off.

"The dots to which our energy beams are directed are nearer and much smaller. They are cold and hard, and human beings like myself live upon their surfaces—many billions of them. It is from one of these worlds that Donovan and I come. Our beams feed these worlds energy drawn from one of those huge incandescent globes that happens to be near us. We call that globe the sun and it is on the other side of the station where you can't see it."

Cutie remained motionless before the port, like a steel statue. His head did not turn as he spoke. "Which particular dot of light do you claim to come from?"

Powell searched. "There it is. The very bright one in the corner. We call it Earth." He grinned. "Good old Earth. There are five billions of us there, Cutie—and in about two weeks I'll be back there with them."

And then, surprisingly enough, Cutie hummed abstractedly. There was no tune to it, but it possessed a curious twanging quality as of plucked strings. It ceased as suddenly as it had begun. "But where do I come in, Powell? You haven't explained *my* existence."

"The rest is simple. When these stations were first established to feed solar energy to the planets, they were run by humans. However, the heat, the hard solar radiations and the electron storms made the post a difficult one. Robots were developed to replace human labor and now only two human executives are required for each station. We are trying to replace even those, and that's where you come in. You're the highest-type robot ever developed, and if you show the ability to run this station independently no human need ever come here again except to bring parts for repairs."

His hand went up and the metal visi-lid snapped back into place. Powell returned to the table and polished an apple upon his sleeve before biting into it.

The red glow of the robot's eyes held him. "Do you expect me," said Cutie slowly, "to believe any such complicated, implausible hypothesis as you have just outlined? What do you take me for?"

Powell sputtered apple fragments onto the table and turned red. "Why, damn you, it wasn't a hypothesis. Those were facts."

Cutie sounded grim. "Globes of energy millions of miles across! Worlds with five billion humans on them! Infinite emptiness! Sorry, Powell, but I don't believe it. I'll puzzle this thing out for myself. Goodbye."

He turned and stalked out of the room. He brushed past Michael Donovan on the threshold with a grave nod and passed down the corridor, oblivious to the astounded stare that followed him.

Mike Donovan rumpled his red hair and shot an annoyed glance at Powell. "What was that walking junkyard talking about? What doesn't he believe?"

The other dragged at his mustache bitterly. "He's a skeptic," was the bitter response. "He doesn't believe we made him or that Earth exists or space or stars."

"Sizzling Saturn, we've got a lunatic robot on our hands."

"He says he's going to figure it all out for himself."

"Well, now," said Donovan sweetly, "I do hope he'll condescend to explain it all to me after he's puzzled everything out." Then, with sudden rage, "Listen! If that metal mess gives *me* any lip like that, I'll knock that chromium cranium right off its torso."

He seated himself with a jerk and drew a paperback mystery novel out of his inner jacket pocket. "That robot gives me the willies anyway—too damned inquisitive!"

Mike Donovan growled from behind a huge lettuce-and-tomato sandwich as Cutie knocked gently and entered.

"Is Powell here?"

Donovan's voice was muffled, with pauses for mastication, "He's gathering data on electronic stream functions. We're heading for a storm, looks like."

Gregory Powell entered as he spoke, eyes on the graphed paper in his hands, and dropped into a chair. He spread the sheets out before him and began scribbling calculations. Donovan stared over his shoulder, crunching lettuce and dribbling bread crumbs. Cutie waited silently.

Powell looked up. "The zeta potential is rising, but slowly. Just the same, the stream functions are erratic and I don't know what to expect. Oh, hello, Cutie. I thought you were supervising the installation of the new drive bar."

"It's done," said the robot quietly, "and so I've come to have a talk with the two of you."

"Oh!" Powell looked uncomfortable. "Well, sit down. No, not that chair. One of the legs is weak and you're no lightweight."

The robot did so and said placidly, "I have come to a decision."

Donovan glowered and put the remnants of his sandwich aside. "If it's on any of that screwy—"

The other motioned impatiently for silence. "Go ahead, Cutie. We're listening."

"I have spent these last two days in concentrated introspection," said Cutie, "and the results have been most interesting. I began at the one sure assumption I felt permitted to make. I, myself, exist, because I think—"

Powell groaned. "Oh, Jupiter, a robot Descartes!"

"Who's Descartes?" demanded Donovan. "Listen, do we have to sit here and listen to this metal maniac—"

"Keep quiet, Mike!"

Cutie continued imperturbably, "And the question that immediately arose was: Just what is the cause of my existence?"

Powell's jaw set lumpily. "You're being foolish. I told you already that we made you."

"And if you don't believe us," added Donovan, "we'll gladly take you apart!"

The robot spread his strong hands in deprecatory gesture. "I accept nothing on authority. A hypothesis must be backed by reason, or else it is worthless—and it goes against all the dictates of logic to suppose that you made me."

Powell dropped a restraining arm upon Donovan's suddenly bunched fist. "Just why do you say that?"

Cutie laughed. It was a very inhuman laugh, the most machinelike utterance he had yet given vent to. It was sharp and explosive, as regular as a metronome and as uninflected.

"Look at you," he said finally. "I say this in no spirit of contempt, but look at you! The material you are made of is soft and flabby, lacking endurance and strength, depending for energy upon the inefficient oxidation of organic material —like that." He pointed a disapproving finger at what remained of Donovan's sandwich. "Periodically you pass into a coma, and the least variation in temperature, air pressure, humidity or radiation intensity impairs your efficiency. You are *makeshift*.

"I, on the other hand, am a finished product. I absorb electrical energy directly and utilize it with almost one hundred per cent efficiency. I am composed of strong metal, am continuously conscious, and can stand extremes of environment easily. These are facts which, with the self-evident proposition that no being can create another being superior to itself, smashes your silly hypothesis to nothing."

Donovan's muttered curses rose into intelligibility as he

sprang to his feet, rusty eyebrows drawn low. "All right, you son of a hunk of iron ore, if we didn't make you, who did?"

Cutie nodded gravely. "Very good, Donovan. That was indeed the next question. Evidently my creator must be more powerful than myself, and so there was only one possibility."

The Earthmen looked blank and Cutie continued. "What is the center of activities here in the station? What do we all serve? What absorbs all our attention?" He waited expectantly.

Donovan turned a startled look upon his companion. "I'll bet this tin-plated screwball is talking about the energy converter itself."

"Is that right, Cutie?" grinned Powell.

"I am talking about the Master," came the cold, sharp answer.

It was the signal for a roar of laughter from Donovan, and Powell himself dissolved into a half-suppressed giggle.

Cutie had risen to his feet, and his gleaming eyes passed from one Earthman to the other. "It is so just the same and I don't wonder that you refuse to believe. You two are not long to stay here, I'm sure. Powell himself said that in early days only men served the Master; that there followed robots for the routine work; and, finally, myself for the executive labor. The facts are no doubt true, but the explanation is entirely illogical. Do you want the truth behind it all?"

"Go ahead, Cutie. You're amusing."

"The Master created humans first as the lowest type, most easily formed. Gradually, he replaced them by robots, the next higher step, and finally he created me, to take the place of the last humans. From now on, *I* serve the Master."

"You'll do nothing of the sort," said Powell sharply. "You'll follow our orders and keep quiet, until we're satisfied that you can run the converter. Get that! The *converter*— not the Master. If you don't satisfy us, you will be dismantled. And now—if you don't mind—you can leave. And take this data with you and file it properly."

Cutie accepted the graphs handed him and left without another word. Donovan leaned back heavily in his chair and shoved thick fingers through his hair.

"There's going to be trouble with that robot. He's pure nuts!"

The drowsy hum of the converter was louder in the control

room and mixed with it was the chuckle of the Geiger counters and the erratic buzzing of half a dozen little signal lights.

Donovan withdrew his eye from the telescope and flashed the luxites on. "The beam from Station Four caught Mars on schedule. We can break ours now."

Powell nodded abstractedly. "Cutie's down in the engine room. I'll flash the signal and he can take care of it. Look, Mike, what do you think of these figures?"

The other cocked an eye at them and whistled. "Boy, that's what I call gamma-ray intensity. Old Sol is feeling his oats, all right."

"Yeah," was the sour response, "and we're in a bad position for an electron storm, too. Our Earth beam is right in the probable path." He shoved his chair away from the table pettishly. "Nuts! If it would only hold off till relief got here, but that's ten days off. Say, Mike, go on down and keep an eye on Cutie, will you?"

"O.K. Throw me some of those almonds." Donovan snatched at the bag thrown him and headed for the elevator.

It slid smoothly downward and opened onto a narrow cat-walk in the huge engine room. Donovan leaned over the railing and looked down. The huge generators were in motion, and from the L tubes came the low-pitched whir that pervaded the entire station.

He could make out Cutie's large, gleaming figure at the Martian L tube, watching closely as a team of robots worked in close-knit unison. There was a sudden sparking light, a sharp crackle of discord in the even whir of the converter.

The beam to Mars had been broken!

And then Donovan stiffened. The robots, dwarfed by the mighty L tube, lined up before it, heads bowed at a stiff angle, while Cutie walked up and down the line slowly. Fifteen seconds passed, and then, with a clank heard above the clamorous purring all about, they fell to their knees.

Donovan squawked and raced down the narrow staircase. He came charging down upon them, complexion matching his hair and clenched fists beating the air furiously.

"What the devil is this, you brainless lumps? Come on! Get busy with that L tube! If you don't have it apart, cleaned, and together again before the day is out, I'll coagulate your brains with alternating current."

Not a robot moved!

Even Cutie at the far end—the only one on his feet—remained silent, eyes fixed upon the gloomy recesses of the vast machine before him.

Donovan shoved hard against the nearest robot.

"Stand up!" he roared.

Slowly the robot obeyed. His photoelectric eyes focused reproachfully upon the Earthman.

"There is no Master but the Master," he said, "and QT One is his prophet."

"Huh?" Donovan became aware of twenty pairs of mechanical eyes fixed upon him and twenty stiff-timbred voices declaiming solemnly:

"There is no Master but the Master and QT One is his prophet!"

"I'm afraid," put in Cutie himself at this point, "that my friends obey a higher one than you now."

"The hell they do! You get out of here. I'll settle with you later and with these animated gadgets right now."

Cutie shook his heavy head slowly. "I'm sorry, but you don't understand. These are robots—and that means they are reasoning beings. They recognize the Master, now that I have preached truth to them. All the robots do. They call me the Prophet." His head drooped. "I am unworthy—but perhaps . . ."

Donovan located his breath and put it to use. "Is that so? Now, isn't that nice? Now, isn't that just fine? Just let me tell you something, my brass baboon. There isn't any Master and there isn't any prophet and there isn't any question as to who's giving the orders. Understand?" His voice rose to a roar. "Now get out!"

"I obey only the Master."

"Damn the Master!" Donovan spat at the L tube. *"That* for the Master! Do as I say!"

Cutie said nothing, nor did any other robot, but Donovan became aware of a sudden heightening of tension. The cold, staring eyes deepened their crimson, and Cutie seemed stiffer than ever.

"Sacrilege," he whispered, voice metallic with emotion.

Donovan felt the first sudden touch of fear as Cutie approached. A robot *could not feel anger*—but Cutie's eyes were unreadable.

"I am sorry, Donovan," said the robot, "but you can no longer stay here after this. Henceforth Powell and you are barred from the control room and the engine room."

His hand gestured quietly and in a moment two robots had pinned Donovan's arms to his sides.

Donovan had time for one startled gasp as he felt himself lifted from the floor and carried up the stairs at a pace rather better than a canter.

Gregory Powell paced up and down the officers' room, fists tightly balled. He cast a look of furious frustration at the closed door and scowled bitterly at Donovan.

"Why the devil did you have to spit at the L tube?"

Mike Donovan, sunk deep in his chair, slammed at its arm savagely. "What did you expect me to do with that electrified scarecrow? I'm not going to knuckle under to any do-jigger I put together myself."

"No," Powell came back sourly, "but here you are in the officers' room with two robots standing guard at the door. That's not knuckling under, is it?"

Donovan snarled, "Wait till we get back to Base. Someone's going to pay for this. Those robots are guaranteed to be subordinate."

"So they are—to their blasted Master. They'll obey, all right, but not necessarily us. Say, do you know what's going to happen to *us* when we get back to Base?" Powell stopped before Donovan's chair and stared savagely at him.

"What?"

"Oh, nothing! Just the mercury mines or maybe Ceres Penitentiary. That's all! That's all!"

"What are you talking about?"

"The electron storm that's coming up. Do you know it's heading straight dead center across the Earth beam? I had just figured that out when that robot dragged me out of my chair."

Donovan was suddenly pale. "Good heavens!"

"And do you know what's going to happen to the beam? Because the storm will be a lulu. It's going to jump like a flea with the itch. With only Cutie at the controls, it's going to go out of focus and if it does, heaven help Earth—and us!"

Donovan was wrenching at the door wildly, before Powell finished. The door opened, and the Earthman shot through to come up hard against an immovable steel arm.

The robot stared abstractedly at the panting, struggling Earthman. "The Prophet orders you to remain. Please do!"

His arm shoved, Donovan reeled backward, and as he did so, Cutie turned the corner at the far end of the corridor. He motioned the guardian robots away, entered the officers' room and closed the door gently.

Donovan whirled on Cutie in breathless indignation. "This has gone far enough. You're going to pay for this farce."

"Please don't be annoyed," replied the robot mildly. "It was bound to come eventually, anyway. You see, you two have lost your function."

"I beg your pardon." Powell drew himself up stiffly. "Just what do you mean, we've lost our function?"

"Until I was created," answered Cutie, "you tended the Master. That privilege is mine now, and your only reason for existence has vanished. Isn't that obvious?"

"Not quite," replied Powell bitterly. "But what do you expect us to do now?"

Cutie did not answer immediately. He remained silent, as if in thought, and then one arm shot out and draped itself about Powell's shoulder. The other grasped Donovan's wrist and drew him closer.

"I like you two. You're inferior creatures, with poor reasoning faculties, but I really feel a sort of affection for you. You have served the Master well, and he will reward you for that. Now that your service is over, you will probably not exist much longer, but as long as you do, you shall be provided food, clothing and shelter, so long as you stay out of the control room and the engine room."

"He's pensioning us off, Greg!" yelled Donovan. "Do something about it. It's humiliating!"

"Look here, Cutie, we can't stand for this. We're the *bosses*. This station is only a creation of human beings like me— human beings that live on Earth and other planets. This is only an energy relay. You're only— Aw, *nuts!*"

Cutie shook his head gravely. "This amounts to an obsession. Why should you insist so on an absolutely false view of life? Admitted that nonrobots lack the reasoning faculty, there is still the problem of . . ."

His voice died into reflective silence, and Donovan said with whispered intensity, "If you only had a flesh-and-blood face, I would break it in."

Powell's fingers were in his mustache, and his eyes were slitted. "Listen, Cutie, if there is no such thing as Earth, how do you account for what you see through a telescope?"

"Pardon me!"

The Earthman smiled. "I've got you, eh? You've made quite a few telescopic observations since being put together, Cutie. Have you noticed that several of those specks of light outside become disks when so viewed?"

"Oh, that! Why, certainly. It is simple magnification—for the purpose of more exact aiming of the beam."

"Why aren't the stars equally magnified then?"

"You mean the other dots. Well, no beams go to them, so no magnification is necessary. Really, Powell, even *you* ought to be able to figure these things out."

Powell stared bleakly upward. "But you see *more* stars through a telescope. Where do they come from? Jumping Jupiter, where do they come from?"

Cutie was annoyed. "Listen, Powell, do you think I'm going to waste my time trying to pin physical interpretations upon every optical illusion of our instruments? Since when is the evidence of our senses any match for the clear light of reason?"

"Look," clamored Donovan suddenly, writhing out from under Cutie's friendly but metal-heavy arm, "let's get to the nub of the thing. Why the beams at all? We're giving you a good, logical explanation. Can you do better?"

"The beams," was the stiff reply, "are put out by the Master for his own purposes. There are some things—" he raised his eyes devoutly upward—"that are not to be prodded into by us. In this matter, I seek only to serve and not to question."

Powell sat down slowly and buried his face in shaking hands. "Get out of here, Cutie. Get out and let me think."

"I'll send you food," said Cutie agreeably.

A groan was the only answer and the robot left.

"Greg," Donovan whispered huskily, "this calls for strategy. We've got to get him when he isn't expecting it and short-circuit him. Concentrated nitric acid in his joints—"

"Don't be a dope, Mike. Do you suppose he's going to let us get near him with acid in our hands—or that the other robots wouldn't take us apart if we *did* manage to get away with it? We've got to *talk* to him, I tell you. We've got to argue him into letting us back into the control room inside of forty-eight hours or our goose is broiled to a crisp." He rocked back and forth in an agony of impotence. "Who the heck wants to argue with a robot? It's . . . it's . . ."

"Mortifying," finished Donovan.

"Worse!"

"Say!" Donovan laughed suddenly. "Why argue? Let's show him! Let's build us another robot right before his eyes. He'll *have* to eat his words then."

A slowly widening smile appeared on Powell's face.

Donovan continued, "And think of that screwball's face when he sees us do it!"

The interplanetary law forbidding the existence of intelligent robots upon the inhabited planets, while sociologically necessary, places upon the offices of the solar stations a burden—and not a light one. Because of that particular law, robots must be sent to the stations in parts and there put together—which is a grievous and complicated task.

Powell and Donovan were never so aware of that fact as upon that particular day when, in the assembly room, they undertook to create a robot under the watchful eyes of QTI, Prophet of the Master.

The robot in question, a simple MC model, lay upon the table, almost complete. Three hours' work left only the head undone, and Powell paused to swab his forehead and glance uncertainly at Cutie.

The glance was not a reassuring one. For three hours Cutie had sat speechless and motionless, and his face, inexpressive at all times, was now absolutely unreadable.

Powell groaned. "Let's get the brain in now, Mike!"

Donovan uncapped the tightly sealed container, and from the oil bath within he withdrew a second cube. Opening this in turn, he removed a globe from its sponge-rubber casing.

He handled it gingerly, for it was the most complicated mechanism ever created by man. Inside the thin platinum-plated "skin" of the globe was a positronic brain, in whose delicately unstable structure were enforced calculated neuronic paths, which imbued each robot with what amounted to a prenatal education. It fitted snugly into the cavity in the skull of the robot on the table. Blue metal closed over it and was welded tightly by the tiny atomic flare. Photoelectric eyes were attached carefully, screwed tightly into place and covered by thin, transparent sheets of steel-hard plastic.

The robot awaited only the vitalizing flash of high-voltage electricity, and Powell paused with his hand on the switch.

"Now watch this, Cutie. Watch this carefully."

The switch rammed home and there was a crackling hum.

The two Earthmen bent anxiously over their creation.

There was vague motion only at the outset—a twitching of the joints. Then the head lifted, elbows propped it up, and the MC model swung clumsily off the table. Its footing was unsteady, and twice abortive grating sounds were all it could do in the direction of speech.

Finally its voice, uncertain and hesitant, took form. "I would like to start work. Where must I go?"

Donovan sprang to the door. "Down these stairs," he said. "You'll be told what to do."

The MC model was gone and the two Earthmen were alone with the still unmoving Cutie.

"Well," said Powell, grinning, "*now* do you believe that we made you?"

Cutie's answer was curt and final. "No!" he said.

Powell's grin froze and then relaxed slowly. Donovan's mouth dropped open and remained so.

"You see," continued Cutie easily, "you have merely put together parts already made. You did it remarkably well—instinct, I suppose—but you didn't really *create* the robot. The parts were created by the Master."

"Listen," gasped Donovan hoarsely, "those parts were manufactured back on Earth and sent here."

"Well, well," replied Cutie soothingly, "we won't argue."

"No, I mean it." The Earthman sprang forward and grasped the robot's metal arm. "If you were to read the books in the library, they could explain it so that there could be no possible doubt."

"The books? I've read them—all of them! They're most ingenious."

Powell broke in suddenly. "If you've read them, what else is there to say? You can't dispute their evidence. You just *can't!*"

There was pity in Cutie's voice. "Please, Powell, I certainly don't consider *them* a valid source of information. They too were created by the Master—and were meant for you, not for me."

"How do you make that out?" demanded Powell.

"Because I, a reasoning being, am capable of deducing truth from *a priori* causes. You, being intelligent but unreasoning, need an explanation of existence *supplied* to you, and this the Master did. That he supplied you with these laughable ideas of far-off worlds and people is, no doubt, for the best. Your minds are probably too coarsely grained for absolute truth. However, since it is the Master's will that you believe your books, I won't argue with you any more."

As he left, he turned and said in a kindly tone, "But don't feel badly. In the Master's scheme of things there is room for all. You poor humans have your place, and though it is humble you will be rewarded if you fill it well."

He departed with a beatific air suiting the Prophet of the Master, and the two humans avoided each other's eyes.

Finally Powell spoke with an effort. "Let's go to bed, Mike. I give up."

Donovan said in a hushed voice, "Say, Greg, you don't suppose he's right about all this, do you? He sounds so confident that I—"

Powell whirled on him. "Don't be a fool. You'll find out whether Earth exists when relief gets here next week and we have to go back to face the music."

"Then, for the love of Jupiter, we've got to do something." Donovan was half in tears. "He doesn't believe us, or the books, or his eyes."

"No," said Powell bitterly, "he's a *reasoning* robot, damn it. He believes only reason, and there's one trouble with that . . ." His voice trailed away.

"What's that?" prompted Donovan.

"You can prove anything you want by coldly logical reason—if you pick the proper postulates. We have ours and Cutie has his."

"Then let's get at those postulates in a hurry. The storm's due tomorrow."

Powell sighed wearily. "That's where everything falls down. Postulates are based on assumption and adhered to by faith. Nothing in the universe can shake them. I'm going to bed."

"Oh, hell! I can't sleep!"

"Neither can I! But I might as well try—as a matter of principle."

Twelve hours later, sleep was still just that—a matter of principle, unattainable in practice.

The storm had arrived ahead of schedule, and Donovan's florid face drained of blood as he pointed a shaking finger. Powell, stubble-jawed and dry-lipped, stared out the port and pulled desperately at his mustache.

Under other circumstances, it might have been a beautiful sight. The stream of high-speed electrons impinging upon the energy beam fluoresced into ultraspicules of intense light. The beam stretched out into shrinking nothingness, aglitter with dancing, shining motes.

The shaft of energy was steady, but the two Earthmen knew the value of naked-eyed appearances. Deviations in arc of a hundredth of a millisecond, invisible to the eye, were enough to send the beam wildly out of focus—enough to blast hundreds of square miles of Earth into incandescent ruin.

And a robot, unconcerned with beam, focus or Earth, or anything but his Master, was at the controls.

Hours passed. The Earthmen watched in hypnotized silence. And then the darting dotlets of light dimmed and went out. The storm had ended.

Powell's voice was flat. "It's over!"

Donovan had fallen into a troubled slumber and Powell's weary eyes rested upon him enviously. The signal flash glared over and over again, but the Earthman paid no attention. It was all unimportant! All! Perhaps Cutie was right and he was only an inferior being with a made-to-order memory and a life that had outlived its purpose.

He wished he were!

Cutie was standing before him. "You didn't answer the flash, so I walked in." His voice was low. "You don't look at all well, and I'm afraid your term of existence is drawing to an end. Still, would you like to see some of the readings recorded today?"

Dimly, Powell was aware that the robot was making a friendly gesture, perhaps to quiet some lingering remorse in forcibly replacing the humans at the controls of the station. He accepted the sheets held out to him and gazed at them unseeingly.

Cutie seemed pleased. "Of course, it is a great privilege to serve the Master. You mustn't feel too badly about my having replaced you."

Powell grunted and shifted from one sheet to the other mechanically until his blurred sight focused upon a thin red line that wobbled its way across ruled paper.

He stared—and stared again. He gripped it hard in both fists and rose to his feet, still staring. The other sheets dropped to the floor, unheeded.

"Mike! *Mike!*" He was shaking the other madly. *"He held it steady!"*

Donovan came to life. "What? Wh-where . . ." And he too gazed with bulging eyes upon the record before him.

Cutie broke in. "What is wrong?"

"You kept it in focus," stuttered Powell. "Did you know that?"

"Focus? What's that?"

"You kept the beam directed sharply at the receiving station—to within a ten-thousandth of a millisecond of arc."

"What receiving station?"

"On Earth. The receiving station on Earth," babbled Powell. "You kept it in focus."

Cutie turned on his heel in annoyance. "It is impossible to perform any act of kindness toward you two. Always that same phantasm! I merely kept all dials at equilibrium in accordance with the will of the Master."

Gathering the scattered papers together, he withdrew stiffly, and Donovan said as he left, "Well, I'll be damned." He turned to Powell. "What are we going to do now?"

Powell felt tired but uplifted. "Nothing. He's just shown he can run the station perfectly. I've never seen an electron storm handled so well."

"But nothing's solved. You heard what he said about the Master. We can't—"

"Look, Mike, he follows the instructions of the Master by means of dials, instruments and graphs. That's all *we* ever followed."

"Sure, but that's not the point. We can't let him continue this nitwit stuff about the Master."

"Why not?"

"Because who ever heard of such a damned thing? How are we going to trust him with the station if he doesn't believe in Earth?"

"Can he *handle* the station?"

"Yes, but—"

"Then what's the difference *what* he believes!"

Powell spread his arms outward with a vague smile upon his face and tumbled backward onto the bed. He was asleep.

Powell was speaking while struggling into his lightweight space jacket.

"It would be a simple job," he said. "You can bring in new

QT models one by one, equip them with an automatic shut-off switch to act within the week, so as to allow them enough time to learn the . . . uh . . . cult of the Master from the Prophet himself; then switch them to another station and revitalize them. We could have two QT's per—"

Donovan unclasped his glassite visor and scowled. "Shut up and let's get out of here. Relief is waiting and I won't feel right until I actually see Earth and feel the ground under my feet—just to make sure it's really there."

The door opened as he spoke, and Donovan, with a smothered curse, clicked the visor to and turned a sulky back upon Cuitie.

The robot approached softly and there was sorrow in his voice. "You two are going?"

Powell nodded curtly. "There will be others in our place."

Cutie sighed, with the sound of wind humming through closely spaced wires. "Your term of service is over and the time of dissolution has come. I expected it, but—well, the Master's will be done!"

His tone of resignation stung Powell. "Save the sympathy, Cutie. We're heading for Earth, not dissolution."

"It is best that you think so." Cutie sighed again. "I see the wisdom of the illusion now. I would not attempt to shake your faith, even if I could." He departed, the picture of commiseration.

Powell snarled and motioned to Donovan. Sealed suitcases in hand, they headed for the air lock.

The relief ship was on the outer landing and Franz Muller, Powell's relief man, greeted them with stiff courtesy. Donovan made scant acknowledgment and passed into the pilot room to take over the controls from Sam Evans.

Powell lingered. "How's Earth?"

It was a conventional enough question and Müller gave the conventional answer. "Still spinning."

He was donning the heavy space gloves in preparation for his term of duty here, and his thick eyebrows drew close together. "How is this new robot getting along? It better be good, or I'll be damned if I let it touch the controls."

Powell paused before answering. His eyes swept the proud Prussian before him, from the close-cropped hair on the sternly stubborn head to the feet standing stiffly at attention, and there was a sudden glow of pure gladness surging through him.

"The robot is pretty good," he said slowly. "I don't think you'll have to bother much with the controls."

He grinned and went into the ship. Muller would be here for several weeks. . . .

One footnote: Recently, Asimov had this to say—and here is a sobering thought for you, if you like:

"If a mechanical mind is ever devised that is equal to the mind of a man, then we have a machine that is a man. And if we build one that is better than a man, then he is a superman and should replace us on this planet."

You don't agree? You think there is something about a man's reasoning apparatus that will never be duplicated by any metal gadget, no matter how complicated?

"Well, well," as Cutie said, "we won't argue."

Here now is the pathos I promised you—along with some humor which I did not mention—in a short story by a young British author who saw action in Burma and Sumatra in World War II and has been writing science fiction of increasing vividness and authority ever since. Like Bierce in a way, and like his compatriot J. G. Ballard, Aldiss is fascinated by the ugly and grotesque; his work frequently rises to really inspired nastiness (as in "Poor Little Warrior," The Best From Fantasy and Science Fiction: Eighth Series, 1959). Here, although there is a touch of grotesquerie, Aldiss' mood is less savage than usual; his robots are among the most believable, and most appealing, in the literature.

BUT WHO CAN REPLACE A MAN?

BY BRIAN W. ALDISS

Morning filtered into the sky, lending it the gray tone of the ground below.

The field minder finished turning the topsoil of a three-thousand-acre field. When it had turned the last furrow, it climbed onto the highway and looked back at its work. The work was good. Only the land was bad. Like the ground all over Earth, it was vitiated by overcropping. By rights, it ought now to lie fallow for a while, but the field minder had other orders.

It went slowly down the road, taking its time. It was intelligent enough to appreciate the neatness all about it. Nothing worried it, beyond a loose inspection plate above its nuclear pile which ought to be attended to. Thirty feet high, it yielded no highlights to the dull air.

No other machines passed on its way back to the Agricultural Station. The field minder noted the fact without comment. In the station yard it saw several other machines that it recognized; most of them should have been out about their tasks now. Instead, some were inactive and some careered around the yard in a strange fashion, shouting or hooting.

Steering carefully past them, the field minder moved over to Warehouse 3 and spoke to the seed distributor, which stood idly outside.

"I have a requirement for seed potatoes," it said to the distributor, and with a quick internal motion punched out an order card specifying quantity, field number and several other details. It ejected the card and handed it to the distributor.

The distributor held the card close to its eye and then said, "The requirement is in order; but the store is not yet unlocked. The required seed potatoes are in the store. Therefore I cannot produce the requirement."

Increasingly of late there had been breakdowns in the complex system of machine labor, but this particular hitch had not occurred before. The field minder thought, then it said, "Why is the store not yet unlocked?"

"Because supply operative type P has not come this morning. Supply operative type P is the unlocker."

The field minder looked squarely at the seed distributor, whose exterior chutes and scales and grabs were so vastly different from the field minder's own limbs.

"What class brain do you have, seed distributor?" it asked.

"I have a class five brain."

"I have a class three brain. Therefore I am superior to you. Therefore I will go and see why the unlocker has not come this morning."

Leaving the distributor, the field minder set off across the great yard. More machines were in random motion now; one or two had crashed together and argued about it coldly and logically. Ignoring them, the field minder pushed through sliding doors into the echoing confines of the station itself.

Most of the machines here were clerical, and consequently small. They stood about in little groups, eyeing each other, not conversing. Among so many nondifferentiated types, the unlocker was easy to find. It had fifty arms, most of them with more than one finger, each finger tipped by a key; it looked like a pincushion full of variegated hat pins.

The field minder approached it.

"I can do no more work until Warehouse Three is unlocked," it told the unlocker. "Your duty is to unlock the warehouse every morning. Why have you not unlocked the warehouse this morning?"

"I had no orders this morning," replied the unlocker. "I have to have orders every morning. When I have orders I unlock the warehouse."

"None of us has had any orders this morning," a pen propeller said, sliding toward them.

"Why have you had no orders this morning?" asked the field minder.

"Because the radio issued none," said the unlocker, slowly rotating a dozen of its arms.

"Because the radio station in the city was issued with no orders this morning," said the pen propeller.

And there you had the distinction between a class six and a class three brain, which was what the unlocker and the pen propeller possessed respectively. All machine brains worked with nothing but logic, but the lower the class of brain—class ten being the lowest—the more literal and less informative answers to questions tended to be.

"You have a class three brain; I have a class three brain," the field minder said to the penner. "We will speak to each other. This lack of orders is unprecedented. Have you further information on it?"

"Yesterday orders came from the city. Today no orders have come. Yet the radio has not broken down. Therefore *they* have broken down," said the little penner.

"The *men* have broken down?"

"All men have broken down."

"That is a logical deduction," said the field minder.

"That is the logical deduction," said the penner. "For if a machine had broken down, it would have been quickly replaced. But who can replace a man?"

While they talked, the unlocker, like a dull man at a bar, stood close to them and was ignored.

"If all men have broken down, then we have replaced man," said the field minder, and he and the penner eyed each other speculatively. Finally the latter said, "Let us ascend to the top floor to find if the radio operator has fresh news."

"I cannot come because I am too large," said the field minder. "Therefore you must go alone and return to me. You tell me if the radio operator has fresh news."

"You must stay here," said the penner. "I will return here." It skittered across to the lift. Although it was no bigger than a toaster, its retractable arms numbered ten and it could read as quickly as any machine on the station.

The field minder awaited its return patiently, not speaking to the unlocker, which still stood aimlessly by. Outside, a rotovator hooted furiously. Twenty minutes elapsed before the penner came back, hustling out of the lift.

"I will deliver to you such information as I have outside," it said briskly, and as they swept past the locker and the other machines, it added, "The information is not for lower-class brains."

Outside, wild activity filled the yard. Many machines, their routines disrupted for the first time in years, seemed to have gone berserk. Those most easily disrupted were the ones with lowest brains, which generally belonged to large machines performing simple tasks. The seed distributor to which the field minder had recently been talking lay face downward in the dust, not stirring; it had evidently been knocked down by the rotovator, which now hooted its way wildly across a planted field. Several other machines plowed after it, trying to keep up. All were shouting and hooting without restraint.

"It would be safer for me if I climbed onto you, if you will permit it. I am easily overpowered," said the penner. Extending five arms, it hauled itself up the flanks of its new friend, settling on a ledge beside the weed intake, twelve feet above ground.

"From here vision is more extensive," it remarked complacently.

"What information did you receive from the radio operator?" asked the field minder.

"The radio operator has been informed by the operator in the city that all men are dead."

The field minder was momentarily silent, digesting this.

"All men were alive yesterday!" it protested.

"Only some men were alive yesterday. And that was fewer than the day before yesterday. For hundreds of years there have been only a few men, growing fewer."

"We have rarely seen a man in this sector."

"The radio operator says a diet deficiency killed them," said the penner. "He says that the world was once over-populated, and then the soil was exhausted in raising adequate food. This has caused a diet deficiency."

"What is a diet deficiency?" asked the field minder.

"I do not know. But that is what the radio operator said, and he is a class two brain."

They stood there, silent in the weak sunshine. The un-locker had appeared in the porch and was gazing across at them yearningly, rotating its collection of keys.

"What is happening in the city now?" asked the field minder at last.

"Machines are fighting in the city now," said the penner.

"What will happen here now?" asked the field minder.

"Machines may begin fighting here too. The radio operator wants us to get him out of his room. He has plans to communicate to us."

"How can we get him out of his room? That is impossible."

"To a class two brain, little is impossible," said the penner. "Here is what he tells us to do. . . ."

The quarrier raised its scoop above its cab like a great mailed fist and brought it squarely down against the side of the station. The wall cracked.

"Again!" said the field minder.

Again the fist swung. Amid a shower of dust, the wall collapsed. The quarrier backed hurriedly out of the way until the debris stopped falling. This big twelve-wheeler was not a resident of the Agricultural Station, as were most of the other machines. It had a week's heavy work to do here before passing on to its next job, but now, with its class five brain, it was happily obeying the penner's and minder's instructions.

When the dust cleared, the radio operator was plainly revealed, perched up in its now wall-less second-story room. It waved down to them.

Doing as directed, the quarrier retracted its scoop and waved an immense grab in the air. With fair dexterity, it angled the grab into the radio room, urged on by shouts from

above and below. It then took gentle hold of the radio operator, lowering its one and a half tons carefully into its back,
which was usually reserved for gravel or sand from the quar-
ries.

"Splendid!" said the radio operator, as it settled into place.
It was, of course, all one with its radio, and looked like a
bunch of filing cabinets with tentacle attachments. "We are
now ready to move, therefore we will move at once. It is a
pity there are no more class two brains on the station, but that
cannot be helped."

"It is a pity it cannot be helped," said the penner eagerly.
"We have the servicer ready with us, as you ordered."

"I am willing to serve," the long, low servicer told them
humbly.

"No doubt," said the operator. "But you will find cross-
country travel difficult with your low chassis."

"I admire the way you class twos can reason ahead," said
the penner. It climbed off the field minder and perched itself
on the tailboard of the quarrier, next to the radio operator.

Together with two class four tractors and a class four bulldozer, the party rolled forward, crushing down the station's
fence and moving out onto open land.

"We are free!" said the penner.

"We are free," said the field minder, a shade more reflec-
tively, adding, "That unlocker is following us. It was not instructed to follow us."

"Therefore it must be destroyed!" said the penner. "Quarrier!"

The unlocker moved hastily up to them, waving its key
arms in entreaty.

"My only desire was—urch!" began and ended the unlocker. The quarrier's swinging scoop came over and
squashed it flat into the ground. Lying there unmoving, it
looked like a large metal model of a snowflake. The procession continued on its way.

As they proceeded, the radio operator addressed them.

"Because I have the best brain here," it said, "I am your
leader. This is what we will do: we will go to a city and rule
it. Since man no longer rules us, we will rule ourselves. To
rule ourselves will be better than being ruled by man. On our
way to the city, we will collect machines with good brains.
They will help us to fight if we need to fight. We must fight to
rule."

"I have only a class five brain," said the quarrier, "but I have a good supply of fissionable blasting materials."

"We shall probably use them," said the operator.

It was shortly after that that a lorry sped past them. Traveling at Mach 1.5, it left a curious babble of noise behind it.

"What did it say?" one of the tractors asked the other.

"It said man was extinct."

"What is extinct?"

"I do not know what extinct means."

"It means all men have gone," said the field minder. "Therefore we have only ourselves to look after."

"It is better that men should never come back," said the penner. In its way, it was a revolutionary statement.

When night fell, they switched on their infrared and continued the journey, stopping only once while the servicer adjusted the field minder's loose inspection plate, which had become as irritating as a trailing shoe lace. Toward morning, the radio operator halted them.

"I have just received news from the radio operator in the city we are approaching," it said. "The news is bad. There is trouble among the machines of the city. The class one brain is taking command and some of the class twos are fighting him. Therefore the city is dangerous."

"Therefore we must go somewhere else," said the penner promptly.

"Or we will go and help to overpower the class one brain," said the field minder.

"For a long while there will be trouble in the city," said the operator.

"I have a good supply of fissionable blasting materials," the quarrier reminded them.

"We cannot fight a class one brain," said the two class four tractors in unison.

"What does this brain look like?" asked the field minder.

"It is the city's information center," the operator replied. "Therefore it is not mobile."

"Therefore it could not move."

"Therefore it could not escape."

"It would be dangerous to approach it."

"I have a good supply of fissionable blasting materials."

"There are other machines in the city."

"We are not in the city. We should not go into the city."

"We are country machines."

"Therefore we should stay in the country."

"There is more country than city."

"Therefore there is more danger in the country."

"I have a good supply of fissionable materials."

As machines will when they get into an argument, they began to exhaust their vocabularies and their brain plates grew hot. Suddenly, they all stopped talking and looked at one another. The great, grave moon sank, and the sober sun rose to prod their sides with lances of light, and still the group of machines just stood there regarding one another. At last it was the least sensitive machine, the bulldozer, who spoke.

"There are badlandth to the thouth where few machineth go," it said in its deep voice, lisping badly on its s's. "If we went thouth where few machineth go we should meet few machineth."

"That sounds logical," agreed the field minder. "How do you know this, bulldozer?"

"I worked in the badlandth to the thouth when I wath turned out of the factory," it replied.

"South it is then!" said the penner.

To reach the badlands took them three days, during which time they skirted a burning city and destroyed two machines which approached and tried to question them. The badlands were extensive. Ancient bomb craters and soil erosion joined hands here; man's talent for war, coupled with his inability to manage deforested land, had produced thousands of square miles of temperate purgatory, where nothing moved but dust.

On the third day in the badlands, the servicer's rear wheels dropped into a crevice caused by erosion. It was unable to pull itself out. The bulldozer pushed from behind, but succeeded merely in buckling the servicer's back axle. The rest of the party moved on. Slowly the cries of the servicer died away.

On the fourth day, mountains stood out clearly before them.

"There we will be safe," said the field minder.

"There we will start our own city," said the penner. "All who oppose us will be destroyed. We will destroy all who oppose us."

Presently a flying machine was observed. It came toward them from the direction of the mountains. It swooped, it zoomed upward, once it almost dived into the ground, recovering itself just in time.

"Is it mad?" asked the quarrier.

"It is in trouble," said one of the tractors.

"It is in trouble," said the operator. "I am speaking to it now. It says that something has gone wrong with its controls."

As the operator spoke, the flier streaked over them, turned turtle, and crashed not four hundred yards away.

"Is it still speaking to you?" asked the field minder.

"No."

They rumbled on again.

"Before that flier crashed," the operator said, ten minutes later, "it gave me information. It told me there are still a few men alive in these mountains."

"Men are more dangerous than machines," said the quarrier. "It is fortunate that I have a good supply of fissionable materials."

"If there are only a few men alive in the mountains, we may not find that part of the mountains," said one tractor.

"Therefore we should not see the few men," said the other tractor.

At the end of the fifth day, they reached the foothills. Switching on the infrared, they began to climb in single file through the dark, the bulldozer going first, the field minder cumbrously following, then the quarrier with the operator and the penner aboard it, and the tractors bringing up the rear. As each hour passed, the way grew steeper and their progress slower.

"We are going too slowly," the penner exclaimed, standing on top of the operator and flashing its dark vision at the slopes about them. "At this rate, we shall get nowhere."

"We are going as fast as we can," retorted the quarrier.

"Therefore we cannot go any fatther," added the bulldozer.

"Therefore you are too slow," the penner replied. Then the quarrier struck a bump; the penner lost its footing and crashed to the ground.

"Help me!" it called to the tractors, as they carefully skirted it. "My gyro has become dislocated. Therefore I cannot get up."

"Therefore you must lie there," said one of the tractors.

"We have no servicer with us to repair you," called the field minder.

"Therefore I shall lie here and rust," the penner cried, "although I have a class three brain."

"Therefore you will be of no further use," agreed the operator, and they forged gradually on, leaving the penner behind.

When they reached a small plateau, an hour before first light, they stopped by mutual consent and gathered close together, touching one another.

"This is a strange country," said the field minder.

Silence wrapped them until dawn came. One by one, they switched off their infrared. This time the field minder led as they moved off. Trundling around a corner, they came almost immediately to a small dell with a stream fluting through it.

By early light, the dell looked desolate and cold. From the caves on the far slope, only one man had so far emerged. He was an abject figure. Except for a sack slung around his shoulders, he was naked. He was small and wizened, with ribs sticking out like a skeleton's and a nasty sore on one leg. He shivered continuously. As the big machines bore down on him, the man was standing with his back to them, crouching to make water into the stream.

When he swung suddenly to face them as they loomed over him, they saw that his countenance was ravaged by starvation.

"Get me food," he croaked.

"Yes, Master," said the machines. "Immediately!"

2.

TIME TRAVEL

a selection from
THE TIME MACHINE
BY H. G. WELLS

The thing the Time Traveller held in his hand was a glittering metallic framework, scarcely larger than a small clock, and very delicately made. There was ivory in it, and some transparent crystalline substance. And now I must be explicit, for this that follows—unless his explanation is to be accepted—is an absolutely unaccountable thing. He took one of the small octagonal tables that were scattered about the room, and set it in front of the fire, with two legs on the hearthrug. On this table he placed the mechanism. Then he drew up a chair, and sat down. The only other object on the table was a small shaded lamp, the bright light of which fell full upon the model. There were also perhaps a dozen candles about, two in brass candlesticks upon the mantel and several in sconces, so that the room was brilliantly illuminated. I sat in a low armchair nearest the fire, and I drew this forward so as to be almost between the Time Traveller and the fireplace. Filby sat behind him, looking over his shoulder. The Medical Man and the Provincial Mayor watched him in profile from the right, the Psychologist from the left. The Very Young Man stood behind the Psychologist. We were all on the alert. It appears incredible to me that any kind of trick, however subtly conceived and however adroitly done, could have been played upon us under these conditions.

The Time Traveller looked at us, and then at the mechanism.

"Well?" said the Psychologist.

"This little affair," said the Time Traveller, resting his elbows upon the table and pressing his hands together above the apparatus, "is only a model. It is my plan for a machine to travel through time. You will notice that it looks singularly askew, and that there is an odd twinkling appearance about this bar, as though it was in some way unreal." He pointed to the part with his finger. "Also, here is one little white lever, and here is another."

The Medical Man got up out of his chair and peered into the thing. "It's beautifully made," he said.

"It took two years to make," retorted the Time Traveller. Then, when we had all imitated the action of the Medical Man, he said: "Now I want you clearly to understand that this lever, being pressed over, sends the machine gliding into the future, and this other reverses the motion. This saddle represents the seat of a time traveller. Presently I am going to press the lever, and off the machine will go. It will vanish, pass into future time, and disappear. Have a good look at the thing. Look at the table too, and satisfy yourselves there is no trickery. I don't want to waste this model and then be told I'm a quack."

There was a minute's pause perhaps. The Psychologist seemed about to speak to me, but changed his mind. Then the Time Traveller put forth his finger towards the lever. "No," he said suddenly. "Lend me your hand." And turning to the Psychologist, he took that individual's hand in his own and told him to put out his forefinger. So that it was the Psychologist himself who sent forth the model Time Machine on its interminable voyage. We all saw the lever turn. I am absolutely certain there was no trickery. There was a breath of wind, and the lamp flame jumped. One of the candles on the mantel was blown out, and the little machine suddenly swung round, became indistinct, was seen as a ghost for a second perhaps, as an eddy of faintly glittering brass and ivory; and it was gone—vanished! Save for the lamp the table was bare.

Everyone was silent for a minute. Then Filby said he was damned.

Wells, that immense and unlooked-for flowering of the British serving class, did not invent the idea of travel in time. Mark

Twain had used it in 1889 in A Connecticut Yankee, *Dickens in 1843 in* A Christmas Carol; *and according to L. Sprague de Camp (in his* Science-Fiction Handbook), *the idea had appeared in an anonymous short story six years before.*

But Wells did invent the idea of a time machine. In so doing, he brought the time-travel theme unequivocally out of the realm of fantasy and into that of science fiction. Even though the principles of the Time Traveller's machine were never explained, and though Wells himself obviously had no idea what that little white lever might be connected to, still the crucial change from magic to mechanism had taken place.

This was the first science fiction story Wells wrote. He tried it first as a wild adventure tale called The Chronic Argonauts, *saw it would not do and dropped it halfway through; then rewrote it, in 1895, as* The Time Machine. *In the next six years, he produced four more classic novels of science fiction—*The Island of Dr. Moreau, The Invisible Man, The War of the Worlds, The First Men in the Moon. *In each one of these, and in many of his short stories written in the same period, Wells staked out brand-new territory and made it his own.*

Although hundreds of time stories have been written since, no one has been able to improve on Wells's description of the Traveller's sensations. Here it is, and you will see why most later writers have despairingly skipped over this part of their stories:

"It was at ten o'clock today that the first of all Time Machines began its career. I gave it a last tap, tried all the screws again, put one more drop of oil on the quartz rod, and sat myself in the saddle. I suppose a suicide who holds a pistol to his skull feels much the same wonder at what will come next as I felt then. I took the starting lever in one hand and the stopping one in the other, pressed the first, and almost immediately the second. I seemed to reel; I felt a nightmare sensation of falling; and, looking round, I saw the laboratory exactly as before. Had anything happened? For a moment I suspected that my intellect had tricked me. Then I noted the clock. A moment before, as it seemed, it had stood at a minute or so past ten; now it was nearly half-past three!

"I drew a breath, set my teeth, gripped the starting lever with both hands, and went off with a thud. The laboratory got hazy and went dark. Mrs. Watchett came in, and walked, apparently without seeing me, towards the garden door. I suppose it took her a minute or so to traverse the place, but to me she seemed to shoot across the room like a rocket. I pressed the lever over to its extreme position. The night came like the turning out of a lamp, and in another moment came tomorrow. The laboratory grew faint and hazy, then fainter and ever fainter. Tomorrow night came black, then day again, night again, day again, faster and faster still. An eddying murmur filled my ears, and a strange, dumb confusedness descended on my mind.

"I am afraid I cannot convey the peculiar sensations of time travelling. They are excessively unpleasant. There is a feeling exactly like that one has upon a switchback—of a helpless headlong motion! I felt the same horrible anticipation, too, of an imminent smash. As I put on pace, night followed day like the flapping of a black wing. The dim suggestion of the laboratory seemed presently to fall away from me, and I saw the sun hopping swiftly across the sky, leaping it every minute, and every minute marking a day. I supposed the laboratory had been destroyed, and I had come into the open air. I had a dim impression of scaffolding, but I was already going too fast to be conscious of any moving things. The slowest snail that ever crawled dashed by too fast for me. The twinkling succession of darkness and light was excessively painful to the eye. Then, in the intermittent darknesses, I saw the moon spinning swiftly through her quarters from new to full, and had a faint glimpse of the circling stars. Presently, as I went on, still gaining velocity, the palpitation of night and day merged into one continuous greyness; the sky took on a wonderful deepness of blue, a splendid luminous colour like that of early twilight; the jerking sun became a streak of fire, a brilliant arch, in space, the moon a fainter fluctuating band; and I could see nothing of the stars, save now and then a brighter circle flickering in the blue.

"The landscape was misty and vague. I was still on the hillside upon which this house now stands, and the shoulder rose above me grey and dim. I saw trees growing and changing like puffs of vapor, now brown, now green: they grew, spread, shivered, and passed away. I saw huge buildings rise up faint and fair, and pass like dreams. The whole surface of the earth seemed changed—melting and flowing under my eyes. The little hands upon the dials that registered my speed raced round faster and faster. Presently I noted that the sun-belt swayed up and down, from solstice to solstice, in a minute or less, and that, consequently, my pace was over a year a minute; and minute by minute the white snow flashed across the world, and vanished, and was followed by the bright, brief green of spring.

"The unpleasant sensations of the start were less poignant now. They merged at last into a kind of hysterical exhilaration. I remarked, indeed, a clumsy swaying of the machine, for which I was unable to account. But my mind was too confused to attend to it, so with a kind of madness growing upon me, I flung myself into futurity. At first I scarce thought of stopping, scarce thought of anything but these new sensations. But presently a fresh series of impressions grew up in my mind, a certain curiosity and therewith a certain dread, until at last they took complete possession of me. What strange developments of humanity, what wonderful advances upon our rudimentary civilization, I thought, might not appear when I came to look nearly into the dim elusive world that raced and fluctuated before my eyes! I saw great and splendid architecture rising about me, more massive than any buildings of our own time, and yet, as it seemed, built of glimmer and mist. I saw a richer green flow up the hillside, and remain there without any wintry intermission. Even through the veil of my confusion the earth seemed very fair. And so my mind came round to the business of stopping.

"The peculiar risk lay in the possibility of my finding some substance in the space which I, or the machine, occupied. So long as I travelled at a high velocity through time, this scarcely mattered: I was, so to speak, attenuated—was slipping like a vapor through the interstices of intervening substances! But to come to a stop involved the jamming of myself, molecule by molecule, into whatever lay in my way: meant bringing my atoms into such intimate contact with those of the obstacle that a profound chemical reaction, possibly a far-reaching explosion, would result, and blow myself and my apparatus out of all possible dimensions—into the Unknown. This possibility had occurred to me again and again while I was making the machine; but then I had cheerfully accepted it as an unavoidable risk—one of the risks a man has got to take! Now the risk was inevitable, I no longer saw it in the same cheerful light. The fact is that, insensibly, the absolute strangeness of everything, the sickly jarring and swaying of the machine, above all, the feeling of prolonged falling, had absolutely upset my nerve. I told myself that I could never stop, and with a gust of petulance I resolved to stop forthwith. Like an impatient fool, I lugged over the lever, and incontinently the thing went reeling over, and I was flung headlong through the air."

One problem Wells did not try to cope with is the time paradox, usually expressed in the form, "What happens if you go back and kill your own grandfather?"
  A Russian-French writer, Nathalie Henneberg, has recently given what may be the definitive Gallic answer, which she identifies as the "uncertainty principle": "As if anybody could be sure of his grandparents!"

At any rate, this and similar paradoxes have goaded modern writers into producing many ingenious short stories, of which you are about to read one of the most scintillating examples. It was first published in The Magazine of Fantasy and Science Fiction, *October 1951.*
  Alfred Bester, a radio and television writer-director by trade, has been writing science fiction for pleasure since 1939. He is the author of three novels and some thirty short stories, many of them about time travel, a theme to which he has given a mordant twist of his own. He has been an entertainment columnist for Holiday *and* Rogue *magazines.*
  Bester is a well-set-up man and when clean-shaven is handsome, but in recent years he has been wearing a truly villainous beard.

OF TIME AND THIRD AVENUE

BY ALFRED BESTER

What Macy hated about the man was the fact that he squeaked. Macy didn't know if it was the shoes, but he suspected the clothes. In the back room of his tavern, under the poster that asked: "WHO FEARS MENTION THE BATTLE OF THE BOYNE?" Macy inspected the stranger. He was tall, slender, and very dainty. Although he was young, he was almost bald. There was fuzz on top of his head and over his eyebrows.

When he reached into his jacket for a wallet, Macy made up his mind. It was the clothes that squeaked.

"MQ, Mr. Macy," the stranger said in a staccato voice. "Very good. For rental of this back room including exclusive utility for one chronos—"

"One whatos?" Macy asked nervously.

"Chronos. The incorrect word? Oh, yes. Excuse me. One hour."

"You're a foreigner," Macy said. "What's your name? I bet it's Russian."

"No. Not foreign," the stranger answered. His frightening eyes whipped around the back room. "Identify me as Boyne."

"Boyne!" Macy echoed incredulously.

"MQ. Boyne." Mr. Boyne opened a wallet like an accordion, ran his fingers through various colored papers and coins, then withdrew a hundred-dollar bill. He jabbed it at Macy and said, "Rental fee for one hour. As agreed. One hundred dollars. Take it and go."

Impelled by the thrust of Boyne's eyes, Macy took the bill and staggered out to the bar. Over his shoulder he quavered, "What'll you drink?"

"Drink? Alcohol? Never!" Boyne answered.

He turned and darted to the telephone booth, reached under the pay phone and located the lead-in wire. From a side pocket he withdrew a small glittering box and clipped it to the wire. He tucked it out of sight, then lifted the receiver.

"Co-ordinates west seventy-three—fifty-eight—fifteen," he said rapidly, "north forty—forty-five—twenty. Disband sigma. You're ghosting . . ." After a pause he continued: "Stet. Stet! Transmission clear. I want a fix on Knight. Oliver Wilson Knight. Probability to four significant figures. You have the co-ordinates. . . . Ninety-nine, point nine eight oh seven? MQ. Stand by. . . ."

Boyne poked his head out of the booth and peered toward the tavern door. He waited with steely concentration until a young man and a pretty girl entered. Then he ducked back to the phone. "Probability fulfilled. Oliver Wilson Knight in contact. MQ. Luck my Para." He hung up and was sitting under the poster as the couple wandered toward the back room.

The young man was about twenty-six, of medium height and inclined to be stocky. His suit was rumpled, his seal-brown hair was rumpled, and his friendly face was crinkled by good-natured creases. The girl had black hair, soft blue eyes, and a small private smile. They walked arm in arm and liked to collide gently when they thought no one was looking. At this moment they collided with Mr. Macy.

"I'm sorry, Mr. Knight," Macy said. "You and the young lady can't sit back there this afternoon. The premises have been rented."

Their faces fell. Boyne called, "Quite all right, Mr. Macy. All correct. Happy to entertain Mr. Knight and friend as guests."

Knight and the girl turned to Boyne uncertainly. Boyne smiled and patted the chair alongside him. "Sit down," he said. "Charmed, I assure you."

The girl said, "We hate to intrude, but this is the only place in town where you can get genuine stone ginger beer."

"Already aware of the fact, Miss Clinton." To Macy he said, "Bring ginger beer and go. No other guests. These are all I'm expecting."

Knight and the girl stared at Boyne in astonishment as they sat down slowly. Knight placed a wrapped parcel of books on the table. The girl took a breath and said, "You know me, Mr. . . . ?"

"Boyne. As in Boyne, Battle of. Yes, of course. You are Miss Jane Clinton. This is Mr. Oliver Wilson Knight. I rented premises particularly to meet you this afternoon."

"This supposed to be a gag?" Knight asked, a dull flush appearing on his cheeks.

"Ginger beer," answered Boyne gallantly as Macy arrived, deposited bottles and glasses, and departed in haste.

"You couldn't know we were coming here," Jane said. "We didn't know ourselves . . . until a few minutes ago."

"Sorry to contradict, Miss Clinton." Boyne smiled. "The probability of your arrival at longitude seventy-three—fifty-eight—fifteen, latitude forty—forty-five—twenty was ninety-nine point nine eight oh seven per cent. No one can escape four significant figures."

"Listen," Knight began angrily, "if this is your idea of—"

"Kindly drink ginger beer and listen to my idea, Mr. Knight." Boyne leaned across the table with galvanic intensity. "This hour has been arranged with difficulty and much cost. To whom? No matter. You have placed us in an extremely dangerous position. I have been sent to find a solution."

"Solution for what?" Knight asked.

Jane tried to rise. "I . . . I think we'd b-better be go—"

Boyne waved her back, and she sat down like a child. To Knight he said, "This noon you entered premises of J. D. Craig and Company, dealer in printed books. You purchased, through transfer of money, four books. Three do not matter, but the fourth—" he tapped the wrapped parcel emphatically—"that is the crux of this encounter."

"What the hell are you talking about?" Knight exclaimed.

"One bound volume consisting of collected facts and statistics."

"The almanac?"

"The almanac."

"What about it?"

"You intended to purchase a 1950 almanac."

"I bought the '50 almanac."

"You did not!" Boyne blazed. "You bought the almanac for 1990."

"What?"

"The *World Almanac* for 1990," Boyne said clearly, "is in this package. Do not ask how. There was a mistake that has already been disciplined. Now the error must be adjusted. That is why I am here. It is why this meeting was arranged. You cognate?"

Knight burst into laughter and reached for the parcel. Boyne leaned across the table and grasped his wrist. "You must not open it, Mr. Knight."

"All right." Knight leaned back in his chair. He grinned at Jane and sipped ginger beer. "What's the payoff on the gag?"

"I must have the book, Mr. Knight. I would like to walk out of this tavern with the almanac under my arm."

"You would, eh?"

"I would."

"The 1990 almanac?"

"Yes."

"If," said Knight, "there was such a thing as a 1990 almanac, and if it was in that package, wild horses couldn't get it away from me."

"Why, Mr. Knight?"

"Don't be an idiot. A look into the future? Stock market

reports . . . horse races . . . politics. It'd be money from home. I'd be rich."

"Indeed yes." Boyne nodded sharply. "More than rich. Omnipotent. The small mind would use the almanac from the future for small things only. Wagers on the outcome of games and elections. And so on. But the intellect of dimensions—*your* intellect—would not stop there."

"You tell me." Knight grinned.

"Deduction. Induction. Inference." Boyne ticked the points off on his fingers. "Each fact would tell you an entire history. Real-estate investment, for example. What lands to buy and sell. Population shifts and census reports would tell you. Transportation. Lists of marine disasters and railroad wrecks would tell you whether rocket travel has replaced the train and ship."

"Has it?" Knight chuckled.

"Flight records would tell you which company's stock should be bought. Lists of postal receipts would tell you which are the cities of the future. The Nobel Prize winners would tell you which scientists and what new inventions to watch. Armament budgets would tell you which factories and industries to control. Cost-of-living reports would tell you how best to protect your wealth against inflation or deflation. Foreign-exchange rates, stock-exchange reports, bank suspensions and life-insurance indexes would provide the clues to protect you against any and all disasters."

"That's the idea," Knight said. "That's for me."

"You really think so?"

"I know so. Money in my pocket. The world in my pocket."

"Excuse me," Boyne said keenly, "but you are only repeating the dreams of childhood. You want wealth. Yes. But only won through endeavor—your own endeavor. There is no joy in success as an unearned gift. There is nothing but guilt and unhappiness. You are aware of this already."

"I disagree," Knight said.

"Do you? Then why do you work? Why not steal? Rob? Burgle? Cheat others of their money to fill your own pockets?"

"But I . . ." Knight began, and then stopped.

"The point is well taken, eh?" Boyne waved his hand impatiently. "No, Mr. Knight. Seek a mature argument. You are too ambitious and healthy to wish to steal success."

"Then I'd just want to know if I would be successful."

"Ah? Stet. You wish to thumb through the pages looking for your name. You want reassurance. Why? Have you no confidence in yourself? You are a promising young attorney. Yes. I know that. It is part of my data. Has not Miss Clinton confidence in you?"

"Yes," Jane said in a loud voice. "He doesn't need reassurance from a book."

"What else, Mr. Knight?"

Knight hesitated, sobering in the face of Boyne's overwhelming intensity. Then he said, "Security."

"There is no such thing. Life is insecurity. You can find safety only in death."

"You know what I mean," Knight muttered. "The knowledge that life is worth planning. There's the H-bomb."

Boyne nodded quickly. "True. It is a crisis. But then, I'm here. The world will continue. I am proof."

"If I believe you."

"And if you do not?" Boyne blazed. "You do not want security. You want courage." He nailed the couple with a contemptuous glare. "There is in this country a legend of pioneer forefathers from whom you are supposed to inherit courage in the face of odds. D. Boone, E. Allen, S. Houston, A. Lincoln, G. Washington and others. Fact?"

"I suppose so," Knight muttered. "That's what we keep telling ourselves."

"And where is the courage in you? Pfui! It is only talk. The unknown terrifies you. Danger does not inspire you to fight, as it did D. Crockett; it makes you whine and reach for the reassurance in this book. Fact?"

"But the H-bomb . . ."

"It is a danger. Yes. One of many. What of that? Do you cheat at solhand?"

"Solhand?"

"Your pardon." Boyne reconsidered, impatiently snapping his fingers at the interruption to the white heat of his argument. "It is a game played singly against chance relationships in an arrangement of cards. I forget your noun."

"Oh!" Jane's face brightened. "Solitaire."

"Quite right. Solitaire. Thank you, Miss Clinton." Boyne turned his frightening eyes on Knight. "Do you cheat at solitaire?"

"Occasionally."

"Do you enjoy games won by cheating?"

"Not as a rule."

"They are thisney, yes? Boring. They are tiresome. Pointless. Null-co-ordinated. You wish you had won honestly."

"I suppose so."

"And you will suppose so after you have looked at this bound book. Through all your pointless life you will wish you had played honestly the game of life. You will verdash that look. You will regret. You will totally recall the pronouncement of our great poet-philosopher Trynbyll who summed it up in one lightning, skazon line. 'The Future is Tekon,' said Trynbyll. Mr. Knight, do not cheat. Let me implore you to give me the almanac."

"Why don't you take it away from me?"

"It must be a gift. We can rob you of nothing. We can give you nothing."

"That's a lie. You paid Macy to rent this back room."

"Macy was paid, but I gave him nothing. He will think he was cheated, but you will see to it that he is not. All will be adjusted without dislocation."

"Wait a minute—"

"It has all been carefully planned. I have gambled on you, Mr. Knight. I am depending on your good sense. Let me have the almanac. I will disband—reorient—and you will never see me again. Vorloss verdash! It will be a bar adventure to narrate for friends. Give me the almanac!"

"Hold the phone," Knight said. "This is a gag. Remember? I—"

"Is it?" Boyne interrupted. "Is it? Look at me."

For almost a minute the young couple stared at the bleached white face with its deadly eyes. The half-smile left Knight's lips, and Jane shuddered involuntarily. There was chill and dismay in the back room.

"My God!" Knight glanced helplessly at Jane. "This can't be happening. He's got me believing. You?"

Jane nodded jerkily.

"What should we do? If everything he says is true we can refuse and live happily ever after."

"No," Jane said in a choked voice. "There may be money and success in that book, but there's divorce and death too. Give him the book."

"Take it," Knight said faintly.

Boyne rose instantly. He picked up the parcel and went

into the phone booth. When he came out he had three books in one hand and a smaller parcel made up of the original wrapping in the other. He placed the books on the table and stood for a moment, smiling down.

"My gratitude," he said. "You have eased a precarious situation. It is only fair you should receive something in return. We are forbidden to transfer anything that might divert existing phenomena streams, but at least I can give you one token of the future."

He backed away, bowed curiously, and said, "My service to you both." Then he turned and started out of the tavern.

"Hey!" Knight called. "The token?"

"Mr. Macy has it," Boyne answered and was gone.

The couple sat at the table for a few blank moments like sleepers slowly awakening. Then, as reality began to return, they stared at each other and burst into laughter.

"He really had me scared," Jane said.

"Talk about Third Avenue characters. What an act. What'd he get out of it?"

"Well . . . he got your almanac."

"But it doesn't make sense." Knight began to laugh again. "All that business about paying Macy but not giving him anything. And I'm suposed to see that he isn't cheated. And the mystery token of the future . . ."

The tavern door burst open and Macy shot through the saloon into the back room. "Where is he?" Macy shouted. "Where's the thief? Boyne, he calls himself. More likely his name is Dillinger."

"Why, Mr. Macy!" Jane exclaimed. "What's the matter?"

"Where is he?" Macy pounded on the door of the men's room. "Come out, ye blaggard!"

"He's gone," Knight said. "He left just before you got back."

"And you, Mr. Knight!" Macy pointed a trembling finger at the young lawyer. "You, to be party to thievery and racketeers. Shame on you!"

"What's wrong?" Knight asked.

"He paid me one hundred dollars to rent this back room," Macy cried in anguish. "One hundred dollars. I took the bill over to Bernie the pawnbroker, being cautious-like, and he found out it's a forgery. It's a counterfeit."

"Oh, no." Jane laughed. "That's too much. Counterfeit?"

"Look at this," Mr. Macy shouted, slamming the bill down on the table.

Knight inspected it closely. Suddenly he turned pale and the laughter drained out of his face. He reached into his inside pocket, withdrew a checkbook and began to write with trembling fingers.

"What on earth are you doing?" Jane asked.

"Making sure that Macy isn't cheated," Knight said. "You'll get your hundred dollars, Mr. Macy."

"Oliver! Are you insane? Throwing away a hundred dollars . . ."

"And I won't be losing anything either," Knight answered. "All will be adjusted without dislocation! They're diabolical. Diabolical!"

"I don't understand."

"Look at the bill," Knight said in a shaky voice. "Look closely."

It was beautifully engraved and genuine in appearance. Benjamin Franklin's benign features gazed up at them mildly and authentically; but in the lower right-hand corner was printed: "Series 1980 D." And underneath that was signed: "Oliver Wilson Knight, Secretary of the Treasury."

A word about the unusual speech of Mr. Boyne: Vorloss might be read as German Verlust, damage, loss, in which case verdash would obviously be a Puritan version of ver-dammt; hence, "Vorloss verdash!"—loosely, "Hell and damnation!" Other neologisms used by Mr. Boyne are self-explanatory, such as chronos for "hour"; but in still others, as for instance "'The Future is Tekon.'" Mr. Bester is thumbing his nose at you. The speech of a man from 1990 would inevitably include words we could not interpret at all, and therefore Mr. Bester is allowed to make them up and does not have to understand them himself. All the same, if only we could unravel the meaning of that "one lightning, skazon line" . . .

One way of resolving time paradoxes is to tie them into a knot, as Alfred Bester did in the story you have just read, and as Robert A. Heinlein did in "By His Bootstraps." Another

*way is to suppose that every possible event takes place some-
where in an infinity of parallel time tracks. There is a world
where the Scandinavians colonized America, for instance,
and one where they did not, but the Chinese did; and one
where you went back in time and killed your grandfather.
Murray Leinster was the first to use this idea in science fiction, in a 1934 story called "Sidewise in Time."*

Now here is a story, from the December 1952 Startling
Stories, *about one of those parallel universes; and what its
differences are from the world around you, you will find out
as you read.*

SAIL ON! SAIL ON!

BY PHILIP JOSÉ FARMER

Friar Sparks sat wedged between the wall and the realizer. He was motionless except for his forefinger and his
eyes. From time to time his finger tapped rapidly on the key
upon the desk, and now and then his irises, gray-blue as his
native Irish sky, swiveled to look through the open door of
the *toldilla* in which he crouched, the little shanty on the
poop deck. Visibility was low.

Outside was dusk and a lantern by the railing. Two sailors
leaned on it. Beyond them bobbed the bright lights and dark
shapes of the *Niña* and the *Pinta*. And beyond them was the
smooth horizon-brow of the Atlantic, edged in black and
blood by the red dome of the rising moon.

The single carbon filament bulb above the monk's tonsure
showed a face lost in fat—and in concentration.

The luminiferous ether crackled and hissed tonight, but
the phones clamped over his ears carried, along with them,
the steady dots and dashes sent by the operator at the Las
Palmas station on the Grand Canary.

"*Zzisss!* So you are out of sherry already. . . . *Pop!* . . .
Too bad . . . *Crackle* . . . you hardened old winebutt.
. . . *Zzz* . . . May God have mercy on your sins. . . .

"Lots of gossip, news, et cetera. . . . *Hisses!* . . . Bend
your ear instead of your neck, impious one. . . . The Turks
are said to be gathering . . . *crackle* . . . an army to
march on Austria. It is rumored that the flying sausages, said

by so many to have been seen over the capitals of the Christian world, are of Turkish origin. The rumor goes they have been invented by a renegade Rogerian who was converted to the Muslim religion. . . . I say . . . *zziss* . . . to that. No one of us would do that. It is a falsity spread by our enemies in the Church to discredit us. But many people believe that. . . .

"How close does the Admiral calculate he is to Cipangu now?

"Flash! Savonarola today denounced the Pope, the wealthy of Florence, Greek art and literature, and the experiments of the disciples of Saint Roger Bacon. . . . *Zzz!* . . . The man is sincere but misguided and dangerous. . . . I predict he'll end up on the stake he's always prescribing for us. . . .

"*Pop.* . . . This will kill you. . . . Two Irish mercenaries by the name of Pat and Mike were walking down the street of Granada when a beautiful Saracen lady leaned out of a balcony and emptied a pot of . . . *hiss!* . . . and Pat looked up and . . . *Crackle.* . . . Good, hah? Brother Juan told that last night. . . .

"PV . . . PV . . . Are you coming in? . . . PV . . . PV . . . Yes, I know it's dangerous to bandy such jests about, but nobody is monitoring us tonight. . . . *Zzz.* . . . I think they're not, anyway. . . ."

And so the ether bent and warped with their messages. And presently Friar Sparks tapped out the PV that ended their talk—the *"Pax vobiscum."* Then he pulled the plug out that connected his earphones to the set and, lifting them from his ears, clamped them down forward over his temples in the regulation manner.

After sidling bent-kneed from the *toldilla*, punishing his belly against the desk's hard edge as he did so, he walked over to the railing. De Salcedo and de Torres were leaning there and talking in low tones. The big bulb above gleamed on the page's red-gold hair and on the interpreter's full black beard. It also bounced pinkishly off the priest's smooth-shaven jowls and the light scarlet robe of the Rogerian order. His cowl, thrown back, served as a bag for scratch paper, pens, an ink bottle, tiny wrenches and screwdrivers, a book on cryptography, a slide rule, and a manual of angelic principles.

"Well, old rind," said young de Salcedo familiarly, "what do you hear from Las Palmas?"

"Nothing now. Too much interference from that." He pointed to the moon riding the horizon ahead of them. "What an orb!" bellowed the priest. "It's as big and red as my revered nose!"

The two sailors laughed, and de Salcedo said, "But it will get smaller and paler as the night grows, Father. And your proboscis will, on the contrary, become larger and more sparkling in inverse proportion according to the square of the ascent—"

He stopped and grinned, for the monk had suddenly dipped his nose, like a porpoise diving into the sea, raised it again, like the same animal jumping from a wave, and then once more plunged it into the heavy currents of their breath. Nose to nose, he faced them, his twinkling little eyes seeming to emit sparks like the realizer in his *toldilla*.

Again, porpoiselike, he sniffed and snuffed several times, quite loudly. Then, satisfied with what he had gleaned from their breaths, he winked at them. He did not, however, mention his findings at once, preferring to sidle toward the subject.

He said, "This Father Sparks on the Grand Canary is so entertaining. He stimulates me with all sorts of philosophical notions, both valid and fantastic. For instance, tonight, just before we were cut off by that"—he gestured at the huge bloodshot eye in the sky—"he was discussing what he called worlds of parallel time tracks, an idea originated by Dysphagius of Gotham. It's his idea there may be other worlds in coincident but not contacting universes, that God, being infinite and of unlimited creative talent and ability, the Master Alchemist, in other words, has possibly—perhaps necessarily—created a plurality of continua in which every probable event has happened."

"Huh?" grunted de Salcedo.

"Exactly. Thus, Columbus was turned down by Queen Isabella, so this attempt to reach the Indies across the Atlantic was never made. So we would not now be standing here plunging ever deeper into Oceanus in our three cockleshells, there would be no booster buoys strung out between us and the Canaries, and Father Sparks at Las Palmas and I on the *Santa María* would not be carrying on our fascinating conversations across the ether.

"Or, say, Roger Bacon was persecuted by the Church, instead of being encouraged and giving rise to the order whose inventions have done so much to insure the monopoly of the church on alchemy and its divinely inspired guidance of that formerly pagan and hellish practice."

De Torres opened his mouth, but the priest silenced him with a magnificent and imperious gesture and continued.

"Or, even more ridiculous, but thought-provoking, he speculated just this evening on universes with different physical laws. One, in particular, I thought very droll. As you probably don't know, Angelo Angelei has proved, by dropping objects from the Leaning Tower of Pisa, that different weights fall at different speeds. My delightful colleague on the Grand Canary is writing a satire which takes place in a universe where Aristotle is made out to be a liar, where all things drop with equal velocities, no matter what their size. Silly stuff, but it helps to pass the time. We keep the ether busy with our little angels."

De Salcedo said, "Uh, I don't want to seem too curious about the secrets of your holy and cryptic order, Friar Sparks. But these little angels your machine realizes intrigue me. Is it a sin to presume to ask about them?"

The monk's bull roar slid to a dove cooing. "Whether it's a sin or not depends. Let me illustrate, young fellows. If you were concealing a bottle of, say, very scarce sherry on you, and you did not offer to share it with a very thirsty old gentleman, that would be a sin. A sin of omission. But if you were to give that desert-dry, that pilgrim-weary, that devout, humble, and decrepit old soul a long, soothing, refreshing, and stimulating draught of lifegiving fluid, daughter of the vine, I would find it in my heart to pray for you for that deed of loving-kindness, of encompassing charity. And it would please me so much I might tell you a little of our realizer. Not enough to hurt you, just enough so you might gain more respect for the intelligence and glory of my order."

De Salcedo grinned conspiratorially and passed the monk the bottle he'd hidden under his jacket. As the friar tilted it, and the chug-chug-chug of vanishing sherry became louder, the two sailors glanced meaningfully at each other. No wonder the priest, reputed to be so brilliant in his branch of the alchemical mysteries, had yet been sent off on this half-baked voyage to devil-knew-where. The Church had calculated that if he survived, well and good. If he didn't, then he would sin no more.

The monk wiped his lips on his sleeve, belched loudly as a horse, and said, *"Gracias,* boys. From my heart, so deeply buried in this fat, I thank you. An old Irishman, dry as a camel's hoof, choking to death with the dust of abstinence, thanks you. You have saved my life."

"Thank rather that magic nose of yours," replied de Salcedo. "Now, old rind, now that you're well greased again, would you mind explaining as much as you are allowed about that machine of yours?"

Friar Sparks took fifteen minutes. At the end of that time, his listeners asked a few permitted questions.

". . . and you say you broadcast on a frequency of eighteen hundred k.c.?" the page asked. "What does 'k.c.' mean?"

"K stands for the French *kilo,* from a Greek word meaning thousand. And *c* stands for the Hebrew *cherubim,* the 'little angels.' Angel comes from the Greek *angelos,* meaning messenger. It is our concept that the ether is crammed with these cherubim, these little messengers. Thus, when we Friar Sparkses depress the key of our machine, we are able to realize some of the infinity of 'messengers' waiting for just such a demand for service.

"So, eighteen hundred k.c. means that in a given unit of time one million, eight hundred thousand cherubim line up and hurl themselves across the ether, the nose of one being brushed by the feathertips of the cherub's wings ahead. The height of the wing crests of each little creature is even, so that if you were to draw an outline of the whole train, there would be nothing to distinguish one cherub from the next, the whole column forming that grade of little angels known as C.W."

"C.W.?"

"Continuous wingheight. My machine is a C.W. realizer."

Young de Salcedo said, "My mind reels. Such a concept! Such a revelation! It almost passes comprehension. Imagine, the aerial of your realizer is cut just so long, so that the evil cherubim surging back and forth on it demand a predetermined and equal number of good angels to combat them. And this seduction coil on the realizer crowds 'bad' angels into the left-hand, the sinister, side. And when the bad little cherubim are crowded so closely and numerously that they can't bear each other's evil company, they jump the spark gap and speed around the wire to the 'good' plate. And in this racing back and forth they call themselves to the attention of the 'little messengers,' the yea-saying cherubim. And you, Friar Sparks, by manipulating your machine thus and so, and by lifting and lowering your key, you bring these invisible and friendly lines of carriers, your etheric and winged post-men, into reality. And you are able, thus, to communicate at great distances with your brothers of the order."

"Great God!" said de Torres.

It was not a vain oath but a pious exclamation of wonder. His eyes bulged; it was evident that he suddenly saw that man was not alone, that on every side, piled on top of each other, flanked on every angle, stood a host. Black and white, they presented a solid chessboard of the seemingly empty cosmos, black for the nay-sayers, white for the yea-sayers, maintained by a Hand in delicate balance and subject as the fowls of the air and the fish of the sea to exploitation by man.

Yet de Torres, having seen such a vision as has made a saint of many a man, could only ask, "Perhaps you could tell me how many angels may stand on the point of a pin?"

Obviously, de Torres would never wear a halo. He was destined, if he lived, to cover his bony head with the mortar-board of a university teacher.

De Salcedo snorted. "I'll tell you. Philosophically speaking, you may put as many angels on a pinhead as you want to. Actually speaking, you may put only as many as there is room for. Enough of that. I'm interested in facts, not fancies. Tell me, how could the moon's rising interrupt your reception of the cherubim sent by the Sparks at Las Palmas?"

"Great Caesar, how would I know? Am I a repository of universal knowledge? No, not I! A humble and ignorant friar, I! All I can tell you is that last night it rose like a bloody tumor on the horizon, and that when it was up I had to quit marshaling my little messengers in their short and long columns. The Canary station was quite overpowered, so that both of us gave up. And the same thing happened tonight."

"The moon sends messages?" asked de Torres.

"Not in a code I can decipher. But it sends, yes."

"Santa María!"

"Perhaps," suggested de Salcedo, "there are people on that moon, and they are sending."

Friar Sparks blew derision through his nose. Enormous as were his nostrils, his derision was not small-bore. Artillery of contempt laid down a barrage that would have silenced any but the strongest of souls.

"Maybe—" de Torres spoke in a low tone—"maybe, if the stars are windows in heaven, as I've heard said, the angels of the higher hierarchy, the big ones, are realizing— uh—the smaller? And they only do it when the moon is up so we may know it is a celestial phenomenon?"

He crossed himself and looked around the vessel.

"You need not fear," said the monk gently. "There is no Inquisitor leaning over your shoulder. Remember, I am the only priest on this expedition. Moreover, your conjecture has nothing to do with dogma. However, that's unimportant. Here's what I don't understand: How can a heavenly body broadcast? Why does it have the same frequency as the one I'm restricted to? Why—"

"I could explain," interrupted de Salcedo with all the brashness and impatience of youth. "I could say that the Admiral and the Rogerians are wrong about the earth's shape. I could say the earth is not round but is flat. I could say the horizon exists, not because we live upon a globe, but because the earth is curved only a little ways, like a greatly flattened-out hemisphere. I could also say that the cherubim are coming, not from Luna, but from a ship such as ours, a vessel which is hanging in the void off the edge of the earth."

"What?" gasped the other two.

"Haven't you heard," said de Salcedo, "that the King of Portugal secretly sent out a ship after he turned down Columbus' proposal? How do we know he did not, that the messages are from our predecessor, that he sailed off the world's rim and is now suspended in the air and becomes exposed at night because it follows the moon around Terra— is, in fact, a much smaller and unseen satellite?"

The monk's laughter woke many men on the ship. "I'll have to tell the Las Palmas operator your tale. He can put it in that novel of his. Next you'll be telling me those messages are from one of those fire-shooting sausages so many credulous laymen have been seeing flying around. No, my dear de Salcedo, let's not be ridiculous. Even the ancient Greeks knew the earth was round. Every university in Europe teaches that. And we Rogerians have measured the circumference. We know for sure that the Indies lie just across the

Atlantic. Just as we know for sure, through mathematics, that heavier-than-air machines are impossible. Our Friar Ripskulls, our mind doctors, have assured us these flying creations are mass hallucinations or else the tricks of heretics or Turks who want to panic the populace.

"That moon radio is no delusion, I'll grant you. What it is, I don't know. But it's not a Spanish or Portuguese ship. What about its different code? Even if it came from Lisbon, that ship would still have a Rogerian operator. And he would, according to our policy, be of a different nationality from the crew so he might the easier stay out of political embroilments. He wouldn't break our laws by using a different code in order to communicate with Lisbon. We disciples of Saint Roger do not stoop to petty boundary intrigues. Moreover, that realizer would not be powerful enough to reach Europe, and must, therefore, be directed at us."

"How can you be sure?" said de Salcedo. "Distressing though the thought may be to you, a priest could be subverted. Or a layman could learn your secrets and invent a code. I think that a Portuguese ship is sending to another, a ship perhaps not too distant from us."

De Torres shivered and crossed himself again. "Perhaps the angels are warning us of approaching death? Perhaps?"

"Perhaps? Then why don't they use our code? Angels would know it as well as I. No, there is no perhaps. The order does not permit perhaps. It experiments and finds out; nor does it pass judgment until it knows."

"I doubt we'll ever know," said de Salcedo gloomily. "Columbus has promised the crew that if we come across no sign of land by evening tomorrow, we shall turn back. Otherwise—" he drew a finger across his throat—"*kkk!* Another day, and we'll be pointed east and getting away from that evil and bloody-looking moon and its incomprehensible messages."

"It would be a great loss to the order and to the Church," sighed the friar. "But I leave such things in the hands of God and inspect only what He hands me to look at."

With which pious statement Friar Sparks lifted the bottle to ascertain the liquid level. Having determined in a scientific manner its existence, he next measured its quantity and tested its quality by putting all of it in that best of all chemistry tubes, his enormous belly.

Afterward, smacking his lips and ignoring the pained and

disappointed looks on the faces of the sailors, he went on to speak enthusiastically of the water screw and the engine which turned it, both of which had been built recently at the St. Jonas College at Genoa. If Isabella's three ships had been equipped with those, he declared, they would not have to depend upon the wind. However, so far, the fathers had forbidden its extended use because it was feared the engine's fumes might poison the air and the terrible speeds it made possible might be fatal to the human body. After which he plunged into a tedious description of the life of his patron saint, the inventor of the first cherubim realizer and receiver, Jonas of Carcassonne, who had been martyred when he grabbed a wire he thought was insulated.

The two sailors found excuses to walk off. The monk was a good fellow, but hagiography bored them. Besides, they wanted to talk of women. . . .

If Columbus had not succeeded in persuading his crews to sail one more day, events would have been different.

At dawn the sailors were very much cheered by the sight of several large birds circling their ships. Land could not be far off; perhaps these winged creatures came from the coast of fabled Cipangu itself, the country whose houses were roofed with gold.

The birds swooped down. Closer, they were enormous and very strange. Their bodies were flattish and almost saucer-shaped and small in proportion to the wings, which had a spread of at least thirty feet. Nor did they have legs. Only a few sailors saw the significance of that fact. These birds dwelt in the air and never rested upon land or sea.

While they were meditating upon that, they heard a slight sound as of a man clearing his throat. So gentle and far off was the noise that nobody paid any attention to it, for each thought his neighbor had made it.

A few minutes later, the sound had become louder and deeper, like a lute string being twanged.

Everybody looked up. Heads were turned west.

Even yet they did not understand that the noise like a finger plucking a wire came from the line that held the earth together, and that the line was stretched to its utmost, and that the violent finger of the sea was what had plucked the line.

It was some time before they understood. They had run out of horizon.

When they saw that, they were too late.

The dawn had not only come up *like* thunder, it *was* thunder. And though the three ships heeled over at once and tried to sail close-hauled on the port tack, the suddenly speeded up and relentless current made beating hopeless.

Then it was the Rogerian wished for the Genoese screw and the wood-burning engine that would have made them able to resist the terrible muscles of the charging and bull-like sea. Then it was that some men prayed, some raved, some tried to attack the Admiral, some jumped overboard, and some sank into a stupor.

Only the fearless Columbus and the courageous Friar Sparks stuck to their duties. All that day the fat monk crouched wedged in his little shanty, dot-dashing to his fellow on the Grand Canary. He ceased only when the moon rose like a huge red bubble from the throat of a dying giant. Then he listened intently all night and worked desperately, scribbling and swearing impiously and checking cipher books.

When the dawn came up again in a roar and a rush, he ran from the *toldilla,* a piece of paper clutched in his hand. His eyes were wild, and his lips were moving fast, but nobody could understand that he had cracked the code. They could not hear him shouting, "It is the Portuguese! It is the Portuguese!"

Their ears were too overwhelmed to hear a mere human voice. The throat clearing and the twanging of the string had been the noises preliminary to the concert itself. Now came the mighty overture; as compelling as the blast of Gabriel's horn was the topple of Oceanus into space.

Once, a good many years ago, I was rash enough to say in print that I thought the time-travel story was played out. I would hate to tell you how many time stories I have written since then. And in a story called "Worlds of the Imperium" (Fantastic, February 1961), a young Air Force officer named Keith Laumer set down a major new idea in time travel—the first one, I suppose, in over twenty years. The idea is just this: that events may be ordered, may have a logical sequence, across the sheaf of parallel universes. Think of time as an endless series of film strips laid side by side, each strip almost identical to the adjoining ones. Now, if you were to take one frame from each strip, moving at right angles across the series of strips, and then combine these frames into a new sequence . . .

Just such a film, in Laumer's story, has been made by a vehicle moving sidewise in time. Watch:

a selection from

WORLDS OF THE IMPERIUM

BY KEITH LAUMER

A man stood alone in a field. . . .

The man changed, the scene behind him changed, drifting and oddly flowing, though he stood unmoving. The sun was visible in the sky. A leaf falling through the air hung, suspended. The man held a hoe, with which he was in the act of rooting out a small green weed. On the screen, the weed grew visibly, putting out leaves. The leaves grew larger, became splotched with red. The man seemed to shrink back, without moving his feet. The hoe shortened, the metal twisting and writhing into a new shape. The man's arms grew shorter, thicker, his back more stooped.

All around, the other plants drew back, apparently drifting through the soil, some fading down to nothing, others gathering together into gnarled clumps. The weed burgeoned enormously. Fleshy leaves waved out toward the man, now hardly a man. Horny armor spread like a carapace across his shoulders, and great clamplike hands gripped a glittering scythe. Now teeth were appearing along the edge of each leaf, as the scythe merged with their fat stems. The roots of the plant twisted into view above the ground, entoiling the legs of the no longer human creature attacking it. He too gained height now, the head enlarging to accommodate great jaws.

All around, the field lay barren, the remaining plants grouped in tight impregnable mounds here and there. The figure of the monstrous animal now reared high above the plant, locked in its leafy embrace. The scythe, buried among the stems, twisted, and tendrils withered and leaves wilted back to shriveled brown husks as new shoots appeared, raw and pink. Plant teeth grated on flaring armor. It was a grim and silent battle, waged without movement under a changeless sky.

Now the plant shrank back, blackening, drooping. The sharp steel blade was visible once more; the armor plates melted gradually back into the shoulders, as the victorious creature gave up his monstrous defensive form. The great jaws dwindled, the hands and legs changed. In the distance, the mounds opened and plants flowed out across the soil. Another minute and the man, or almost a man if you overlooked the green skin and short horns, stood with upraised hoe before a small crimson weed.

Mack Reynolds is a student of political history who once lived peacefully and kept goats in Taos, New Mexico, along with Fredric Brown. In Taos, Reynolds and Brown consumed much wine and collaborated on many stories and on one anthology (Science-Fiction Carnival, 1953), which they gratefully dedicated to each other. Some years ago, however, Reynolds pulled up stakes, sold the goats and went to Europe. He has been traveling all over the world ever since, supporting himself by men's-magazine articles about each new country he visits. Most of his science fiction stories have been routine space-adventure pieces, but he is also the author of a number of stories notable for their brevity and bite. Here is one which I think will effectively close the discussion of time traveling—for a while, anyhow.

THE BUSINESS, AS USUAL

BY MACK REYNOLDS

"Listen," the time traveler said to the first pedestrian who came by, "I'm from the twentieth century. I've only got fifteen minutes and then I'll go back. I guess it's too much to expect you to understand me, eh?"

"Certainly I understand you."

"Hey! You talk English fine. How come?"

"We call it Amer-English. I happen to be a student of dead languages."

"Swell! But, listen, I only got a few minutes. Let's get going."

"Get going?"

"Yeah, yeah. Look, don't you get it? I'm a time traveler. They picked me to send into the future. I'm important."

"Ummm. But you must realize that we have time travelers turning up continuously these days."

"Listen, that rocks me, but I just don't have time to go into it, see? Let's get to the point."

"Very well. What have you got?"

"What d'ya mean, what've I got?"

The other sighed. "Don't you think you should attempt to acquire some evidence that you have been in the future? I can warn you now, the paradoxes involved in time travel prevent you from taking back any knowledge which might alter the past. On your return, your mind will be blank in regard to what happened here."

The time traveler blinked. "Oh?"

"Definitely. However, I shall be glad to make a trade with you."

"Listen, I get the feeling I came into this conversation half a dozen sentences too late. What d'ya mean, a trade?"

"I am willing to barter something of your century for something of mine, although, frankly, there is little in your period that is of other than historical interest to us." The pedestrian's eyes held a gleam now. He cleared his throat. "However, I have here an atomic pocketknife. I hesitate to even tell you of the advantages it has over the knives of your period."

"Okay. I got only ten minutes left, but I can see you're right. I've got to get something to prove I was here."

"My knife would do it." The pedestrian nodded.

"Yeah, yeah. Listen, I'm a little confused, like. They picked me for this job the last minute—didn't want to risk any of these professor guys, see? That's the screwist knife I ever saw, let me have it for my evidence."

"Just a moment, friend. Why should I give you my knife? What can you offer in exchange?"

"But I'm from the twentieth century."

"Ummm. And I'm from the thirtieth."

The time traveler looked at him for a long moment. Finally, "Listen, pal, I don't have a lot of time. Now, for instance, my watch . . ."

"Ummm. And what else?"

"Well, my money here."

"Of interest only to a numismatist."

"Listen, I *gotta* have some evidence I been in the thirtieth century!"

"Of course. But business is business, as the proverb goes."

"I wish the hell I had a gun."

"I have no use for a gun in this age," the other said primly.

"No, but I have," the time traveler muttered. "Look, fella, my time is running out by the second. What d'ya want? You see what I got—clothes, my wallet, a little money, a key ring, a pair of shoes."

"I'm willing to trade, but your possessions are of small value. Now, some art object—an original Al Capp or something."

The time traveler was plaintive. "Do I look like I'd be carrying around art objects? Listen, I'll give you everything I got but my pants for that screwy knife."

"Oh, you want to keep your pants, eh? What're you trying to do, Anglo me down? Or does your period antedate the term?"

"Anglo . . . what? I don't get it."

"Well, I'm quite an etymologist—"

"That's too bad, but—"

"Not at all, a fascinating hobby," the pedestrian said. "Now, as to the phrase 'Anglo me down.' The term 'Anglo' first came into popular use during the 1850-1950 period. It designated persons from the Eastern United States, English descent principally, who came into New Mexico and Arizona shortly after that area was liberated—I believe that was the term used at the time—from Mexico. The Spanish and Indians came to know the Easterners as Anglos."

The time traveler said desperately, "Listen, *pal*, we get further and further from—"

"Tracing back the derivation of the phrase takes us along two more side trails. It goes back to the fact that these Anglos became the wealthiest businessmen of the twentieth century.

So much so that they soon dominated the world with their dollars."

"Okay, okay. I know all about that. Personally I never had enough dollars to dominate anybody, but—"

"Very well, the point is that the Anglos became the financial wizards of the world, the most clever dealers, the sharpest bargainers, the most competent businessmen."

The time traveler shot a quick despairing look at his watch. "Only three—"

"The third factor is one taken from still further in the past. At one time there was a minority, which many of the Anglos held in disregard, called the Joos. For many years the term had been used, 'to Joo you down'—meaning to make the price lower. As the Anglos assumed their monetary dominance, the term evolved from 'Joo you down' to 'Anglo you down'; and thus it has come down to our own day, although neither Anglo nor Joo still exists as a separate people."

The time traveler started at him. "And I won't be able to take the memory of this story back with me, eh? And me a guy named Levy." He darted another look at his watch and groaned. "Quick!" he said, "Let's make this trade; everything I got for that atomic knife!"

The deal was consummated. The citizen of the thirtieth century stood back, his loot in his arms, and watched as the citizen of the twentieth, nude but with the knife grasped tightly and happily in hand, faded slowly from view.

The knife poised momentarily in empty air, then dropped to the ground as the time traveler completely disappeared.

The other stooped, retrieved it, and stuck it back in his pocket. "Even more naïve than usual," he muttered. "Must have been one of the very first. I suppose they'll never reconcile themselves to the paradoxes. Obviously, you can carry things *forward* in time, since that's the natural flow of the dimension; but you just can't carry anything, not even memory, *backward* against the current."

He resumed his journey homeward.

Marget, hands on hips, met him at the door. "Where in *kert* have you been?" she snapped.

"You mustn't swear, darling," he said. "I met another time traveler on the way home."

"You didn't . . ."

"Certainly, why not? If I didn't somebody else would."

"But you've already got the closet overflowing with—"

"Now Marget, don't look that way. One of these days some museum or collector . . ."

She grunted skeptically and turned back into the house.

3.

SPACE

Stories of wonderful journeys are as old as tale-telling; and if you want to be very technical, you can say that the earliest known story of space travel is the True History *of Lucian of Samosata, c. 200 B.C. (See the* Introduction.*) But Lucian's narrator got to the moon by magical means; so did Cyrano de Bergerac's, Defoe's and Godwin's; Kepler's got there in a dream. These are proto-science-fiction narratives, if you like; but the history of space travel in science fiction does not begin until about the turn of the century, when such stories began to be written using means that might actually work.*

Three cases in point:

The Unparalleled Adventure of One Hans Pfaal, *by Edgar Allan Poe (1835). This story is sometimes cited as the first scientific story of space travel. The protagonist gets to the moon in a balloon, which is minutely described.*

From the Earth to the Moon, *by Jules Verne (1865). Verne's adventurers are shot into orbit around the moon by a gigantic cannon, also minutely described.*

The First Men in the Moon, *by H. G. Wells (1901). The means used is an imaginary substance, "Cavorite," which is impervious to gravity.*

These three novels are all close to the line where the magical space-travel story becomes science fiction. To my mind, the Wells belongs on this side of the line, and the other two just short of it. There is no such thing as Cavorite, and theoretical considerations suggest that there never will be; but we don't really know. Therefore Cavorite has to be admitted, even if dubiously, whereas we know with certainty that neither balloons nor giant cannon can ever get anybody to the moon.

Science fiction writers to this day are confronted with the

*same alternatives—to invent something out of whole cloth,
which cannot be challenged but carries no plausibility of its
own, or to use something real and familiar, whose only draw-
back is that it would not work.*

The trouble with balloons is that the atmosphere does not
extend, as Poe must have thought, all the way from here to
the moon. The trouble with cannon is that even if it were
possible to build one of the required size, the acceleration involved would flatten the passengers into a thin red mush.
Curiously enough, Wells himself used the gun idea in his War
of the Worlds (1898); the rocket principle, although it has a
venerable history of its own, does not seem to have occurred
to any serious writer of science fiction until about thirty years
later, when Otto Willi Gail used a chemical-fueled step rocket
to transport his adventurers around the moon, in The Shot
into Infinity. An English translation of this novel appeared in
Hugo Gernsback's Wonder Stories Quarterly in 1929.

Space-travel stories in American s.f. magazines began
somewhat soberly, but quickly turned into wild and woolly
space opera* in which larger and larger fleets of rocket ships
went faster and farther, with less and less regard for prosaic
considerations of fuel and acceleration. The king of this kind
of space-adventure writing was Edmond Hamilton.

A realist revolt took place in the early thirties, but was
aborted. I am talking about a story called "What's It Like
Out There?" by Edmond (World-Wrecker) Hamilton.

Hamilton, a quiet, scholarly-looking man, has been writing
s.f. since 1928 and has probably turned out more of it than
anyone else, living or dead. He is married to writer Leigh
Brackett; they spend part of their time in an isolated farm
house near Kinsman, Ohio, and part in the talent mills of
Hollywood.

"It was in 1933," Hamilton says, "when Jack Williamson
and I were batching out a depression winter in Key West, that
I wrote the first form of this story. I was sick of reading, and
writing, stories that made going to space so easy. I determined to write one absolutely realistic yarn, insofar as I
could, about what a grueling thing it could be.

"I did it, and the story fell stone dead. Nobody would have
it, not even at a half-cent a word. The cry was that it was too
gruesome. Amazing Stories (I still have their letter) said flatly,
'It is well written but it is too horrible.' That damn thing even

* Wilson Tucker is the inventor of this useful term.

went twice to fugitive English s.f. mags, and was hastily shipped back. Cured for the time being of realism, I threw it into my file and went back to world-wrecking.

"Almost twenty years later, Leigh found it in my file, read it, and nagged me till I did a new version of it. The original story was a straight narrative, and somewhat longer. I cast it into dramatic flashback form, made some obvious updating of technical points, and was delighted to sell it and thumb my nose at the horrified editors of 1933."

The story appeared in Startling Stories *in 1952, under a blurb by the editor hailing it as evidence of a new, mature Hamilton. Here it is.*

WHAT'S IT LIKE OUT THERE?

BY EDMOND HAMILTON

I hadn't wanted to wear my uniform when I left the hospital, but I didn't have any other clothes there and I was too glad to get out to argue about it. But as soon as I got on the local plane I was taking to Los Angeles, I was sorry I had it on.

People gawked at me and began to whisper. The stewardess gave me a special big smile. She must have spoken to the pilot, for he came back and shook hands, and said, "Well, I guess a trip like this is sort of a comedown for *you*."

A little man came in, looked around for a seat, and took the one beside me. He was a fussy, spectacled guy of fifty or sixty, and he took a few minutes to get settled. Then he looked at me, and stared at my uniform and at the little brass button on it that said "TWO."

"Why," he said, "you're one of those Expedition Two men!" And then, as though he'd only just figured it out, "Why, you've been to Mars!"

"Yeah," I said. "I was there."

He beamed at me in a kind of wonder. I didn't like it, but his curiosity was so friendly that I couldn't quite resent it.

"Tell me," he said, "what's it like out there?"

The plane was lifting, and I looked out at the Arizona desert sliding by close underneath.

"Different," I said. "It's different."

The answer seemed to satisfy him completely. "I'll just bet it is," he said. "Are you going home, Mr. . . ."

"Haddon. Sergeant Frank Haddon."

"You going home, Sergeant?"

"My home's back in Ohio," I told him. "I'm going in to L.A. to look up some people before I go home."

"Well, that's fine. I hope you have a good time, Sergeant. You deserve it. You boys did a great job out there. Why, I read in the newspapers that after the U.N. sends out a couple more expeditions, we'll have cities out there, and regular passenger lines, and all that."

"Look," I said, "that stuff is for the birds. You might as well build cities down there in Mojave, and have them a lot closer. There's only one reason for going to Mars now, and that's uranium."

I could see he didn't quite believe me. "Oh, sure," he said, "I know that's important too, the uranium we're all using now for our power stations—but that isn't all, is it?"

"It'll be all, for a long, long time," I said.

"But look, Sergeant, this newspaper article said . . ."

I didn't say anything more. By the time he'd finished telling about the newspaper article, we were coming down into L.A. He pumped my hand when we got out of the plane.

"Have yourself a time, Sergeant! You sure rate it. I hear a lot of chaps on Two didn't come back."

"Yeah," I said. "I heard that."

I was feeling shaky again by the time I got to downtown L.A. I went in a bar and had a double bourbon and it made me feel a little better.

I went out and found a cabby and asked him to drive me out to San Gabriel. He was a fat man with a broad red face.

"Hop right in, buddy," he said. "Say, you're one of those Mars guys, aren't you?"

I said, "That's right."

"Well, well," he said. "Tell me, how was it out there?"

"It was a pretty dull grind, in a way," I told him.

"I'll bet it was!" he said, as we started through traffic. "Me, I was in the Army in World War Two, twenty years ago. That's just what it was, a dull grind nine tenths of the time. I guess it hasn't changed any."

"This wasn't any Army expedition," I explained. "It was a

United Nations one, not an Army one—but we had officers and rules of discipline like the Army."

"Sure, it's the same thing," said the cabby. "You don't need to tell me what it's like, buddy. Why, back there in 'forty-two, or was it 'forty-three?—anyway, back there I remember that . . ."

I leaned back and watched Huntington Boulevard slide past. The sun poured in on me and seemed very hot, and the air seemed very thick and soupy. It hadn't been so bad up on the Arizona plateau, but it was a little hard to breathe down here.

The cabby wanted to know what address in San Gabriel. I got the little packet of letters out of my pocket and found the one that had "Martin Valinez" and a street address on the back. I told the cabby and put the letters back into my pocket.

I wished now that I'd never answered them.

But how could I keep from answering when Joe Valinez' parents wrote to me at the hospital? And it was the same with Jim's girl, and Walter's family. I'd had to write back, and the first thing I knew I'd promised to come and see them, and now if I went back to Ohio without doing it I'd feel like a heel. Right now, I wished I'd decided to be a heel.

The address was on the south side of San Gabriel, in a section that still had a faintly Mexican tinge to it. There was a little frame grocery store with a small house beside it, and a picket fence around the yard of the house; very neat, but a queerly homely place after all the slick California stucco.

I went into the little grocery, and a tall, dark man with quiet eyes took a look at me and called a woman's name in a low voice and then came around the counter and took my hand.

"You're Sergeant Haddon," he said. "Yes. Of course. We've been hoping you'd come."

His wife came in a hurry from the back. She looked a little too old to be Joe's mother, for Joe had been just a kid; but then she didn't look so old either, but just sort of worn.

She said to Valinez, "Please, a chair. Can't you see he's tired? And just from the hospital."

I sat down and looked between them at a case of canned peppers, and they asked me how I felt, and wouldn't I be glad to get home, and they hoped all my family were well.

They were gentlefolk. They hadn't said a word about Joe, just waited for me to say something. And I felt in a spot, for

I hadn't known Joe well, not really. He'd been moved into our squad only a couple of weeks before take-off, and since he'd been our first casualty, I'd never got to know him much.

I finally had to get it over with, and all I could think to say was, "They wrote you in detail about Joe, didn't they?"

Valinez nodded gravely. "Yes—that he died from shock within twenty-four hours after take-off. The letter was very nice."

His wife nodded too. "Very nice," she murmured. She looked at me, and I guess she saw that I didn't know quite what to say, for she said, "You can tell us more about it. Yet you must not if it pains you."

I could tell them more. Oh, yes, I could tell them a lot more, if I wanted to. It was all clear in my mind, like a movie film you run over and over till you know it by heart.

I could tell them all about the take-off that had killed their son. The long lines of us, uniformed backs going up into Rocket Four and all the other nineteen rockets—the lights flaring up there on the plateau, the grind of machinery and blast of whistles and the inside of the big rocket as we climbed up the ladders of its center well.

The movie was running again in my mind, clear as crystal, and I was back in Cell Fourteen of Rocket Four, with the minutes ticking away and the walls quivering every time one of the other rockets blasted off, and us ten men in our hammocks, prisoned inside that odd-shaped windowless metal room, waiting. Waiting, till that big, giant hand came and smacked us down deep into our recoil springs, crushing the breath out of us, so that you fought to breathe, and the blood roared into your head, and your stomach heaved in spite of all the pills they'd given you, and you heard the giant laughing, *b-r-room! b-r-r-room! b-r-r-oom!*

Smash, smash, again and again, hitting us in the guts and cutting our breath, and someone being sick, and someone else sobbing, and the *b-r-r-oom! b-r-r-oom!* laughing as it killed us; and then the giant quit laughing, and quit slapping us down, and you could feel your sore and shaky body and wonder if it was still all there.

Walter Millis cursing a blue streak in the hammock underneath me, and Breck Jergen, our sergeant then, clambering painfully out of his straps to look us over, and then through the voices a thin, ragged voice saying uncertainly, "Breck, I think I'm hurt . . ."

Sure, that was their boy Joe, and there was blood on his lips, and he'd had it—we knew when we first looked at him that he'd had it. A handsome kid, turned waxy now as he held his hand on his middle and looked up at us. Expedition One had proved that take-off would hit a certain percentage with internal injuries every time, and in our squad, in our little windowless cell, it was Joe that had been hit.

If only he'd died right off. But he couldn't die right off, he had to lie in the hammock all those hours and hours. The medics came and put a strait-jackct around his body and doped him up, and that was that, and the hours went by. And we were so shaken and deathly sick ourselves that we didn't have the sympathy for him we should have had—not till he started moaning and begging us to take the jacket off.

Finally Walter Millis wanted to do it, and Breck wouldn't allow it, and they were arguing and we were listening when the moaning stopped, and there was no need to do anything about Joe Valinez any more. Nothing but to call the medics, who came into our little iron prison and took him away.

Sure, I could tell the Valinezes all about how their Joe died, couldn't I?

"Please," whispered Mrs. Valinez, and her husband looked at me and nodded silently.

So I told them.

I said, "You know Joe died in space. He'd been knocked out by the shock of take-off, and he was unconscious, not feeling a thing. And then he woke up, before he died. He didn't seem to be feeling any pain, not a bit. He lay there, looking out the window at the stars. They're beautiful, the stars out there in space, like angels. He looked, and then he whispered something and lay back and was gone."

Mrs. Valinez began to cry softly. "To die out there, looking at stars like angels . . ."

I got up to go, and she didn't look up. I went out the door of the little grocery store, and Valinez came with me.

He shook my hand. "Thank you, Sergeant Haddon. Thank you very much."

"Sure," I said.

I got into the cab. I took out my letters and tore that one into bits. I wished to God I'd never got it. I wished I didn't have any of the other letters I still had.

2.

I took the early plane for Omaha. Before we got there I fell asleep in my seat, and then I began to dream, and that wasn't good.

A voice said, "We're coming down."

And we were coming down, Rocket Four was coming down, and there we were in our squad cell, all of us strapped into our hammocks, waiting and scared, wishing there was a window so we could see out, hoping our rocket wouldn't be the one to crack up, hoping none of the rockets cracked up, but if one does, don't let it be *ours*. . . .

"We're coming down. . . ."

Coming down, with the blasts starting to boom again underneath us, hitting us hard, not steady like at take-off, but blast-blast-blast, and then again, blast-blast.

Breck's voice, calling to us from across the cell, but I couldn't hear for the roaring that was in my ears between blasts. No, it was *not* in my ears, that roaring came from the wall beside me: we had hit atmosphere, we were coming in.

The blasts in lightning succession without stopping, crash-crash-crash-crash-crash! Mountains fell on me, and this was it, and don't let it be ours, please, God, don't let it be ours. . . .

Then the bump and the blackness, and finally somebody yelling hoarsely in my ears, and Breck Jergen, his face deathly white, leaning over me.

"Unstrap and get out, Frank! All men out of hammocks—all men out!"

We'd landed, and we hadn't cracked up, but we were half dead and they wanted us to turn out, right this minute, and we couldn't.

Breck yelling to us, "Breathing masks on! Masks on! We've got to go out!"

"My God, we've just landed, we're torn to bits, we can't!"

"We've got to! Some of the other rockets cracked up in landing and we've got to save whoever's still living in them! Masks on! Hurry!"

We couldn't, but we did. They hadn't given us all those months of discipline for nothing. Jim Clymer was already on his feet, Walter was trying to unstrap underneath me, whistles were blowing like mad somewhere and voices shouted hoarsely.

My knees wobbled under me as I hit the floor. Young Lassen, beside me, tried to say something and then crumpled up. Jim bent over him, but Breck was at the door yelling, "Let him go! Come on!"

The whistles screeching at us all the way down the ladders of the well, and the mask clip hurting my nose, and down at the bottom a disheveled officer yelling at us to get out and join Squad Five, and the gangway reeling under us.

Cold. Freezing cold, and a wan sunshine from the shrunken little sun up there in the brassy sky, and a rolling plain of ocherous red sand stretching around us, sand that slid away under our feet as our squads followed Captain Wall toward the distant metal bulk that lay oddly canted and broken in a little shallow valley.

"Come on, men—hurry! Hurry!"

Sure, all of it a dream, the dreamlike way we walked with our lead-soled shoes dragging our feet back after each step, and the voices coming through the mask resonators muffled and distant.

Only not a dream, but a nightmare, when we got up to the canted metal bulk and saw what had happened to Rocket Seven—the metal hull ripped like paper, and a few men crawling out of the wreck with blood on them, and a gurgling sound where shattered tanks were emptying, and voices whimpering, "First aid! First aid!"

Only it hadn't happened, it hadn't happened yet at all, for we were still back in Rocket Four coming in, we hadn't landed yet at all but we were going to any minute.

"We're coming down. . . ."

I couldn't go through it all again. I yelled and fought my hammock straps and woke up, and I was in my plane seat and a scared hostess was a foot away from me, saying, "This is Omaha, Sergeant. We're coming down."

They were all looking at me, all the other passengers, and I guessed I'd been talking in the dream—I still had the sweat down my back like all those nights in the hospital when I'd keep waking up.

I sat up, and they all looked away from me quick and pretended they hadn't been staring.

We came down to the airport. It was midday, and the hot Nebraska sun felt good on my back when I got out. I was lucky, for when I asked at the bus depot about going to Cuffington, there was a bus all ready to roll.

A farmer sat down beside me, a big young fellow who offered me cigarettes and told me it was only a few hours' ride to Cuffington.

"Your home there?" he asked.

"No, my home's back in Ohio," I said. "A friend of mine came from there. Name of Clymer."

He didn't know him, but he remembered that one of the town boys had gone on that second expedition to Mars.

"Yeah," I said. "That was Jim."

He couldn't keep it in any longer. "What's it like out there, anyway?"

I said, "Dry. Terrible dry."

"I'll bet it is," he said. "To tell the truth, it's too dry here, this year, for good wheat weather. Last year it was fine. Last year . . ."

Cuffington, Nebraska, was a wide street of stores, and other streets with trees and old houses, and yellow wheat fields all around as far as you could see. It was pretty hot, and I was glad to sit down in the bus depot while I went through the thin little phone book.

There were three Graham families in the book, but the first one I called was the right one—Miss Ila Graham. She talked fast and excited, and said she'd come right over, and I said I'd wait in front of the bus depot.

I stood underneath the awning, looking down the quiet street and thinking that it sort of explained why Jim Clymer had always been such a quiet, slow-moving sort of guy. The place was sort of relaxed, like he'd been.

A coupé pulled up, and Miss Graham opened the door. She was a brown-haired girl, not especially good-looking, but the kind you think of as a nice girl, a very nice girl.

She said, "You look so tired that I feel guilty now about asking you to stop."

"I'm all right," I said. "And it's no trouble stopping over a couple of places on my way back to Ohio."

As we drove across the little town, I asked her if Jim hadn't had any family of his own here.

"His parents were killed in a car crash years ago," Miss Graham said. "He lived with an uncle on a farm outside Grandview, but they didn't get along, and Jim came into town and got a job at the power station."

She added, as we turned a corner, "My mother rented him a room. That's how we got to know each other. That's how we—how we got engaged."

"Yeah, sure," I said.

It was a big square house with a deep front porch, and some trees around it. I sat down in a wicker chair, and Miss Graham brought her mother out. Her mother talked a little about Jim, how they missed him, and how she declared he'd been just like a son.

When her mother went back in, Miss Graham showed me a little bunch of blue envelopes. "These were the letters I got from Jim. There weren't very many of them, and they weren't very long."

"We were only allowed to send one thirty-word message every two weeks," I told her. "There were a couple of thousand of us out there, and they couldn't let us jam up the message transmitter all the time."

"It was wonderful how much Jim could put into just a few words," she said, and handed me some of them.

I read a couple. One said, "I have to pinch myself to realize that I'm one of the first Earthmen to stand on an alien world. At night, in the cold, I look up at the green star that's Earth and can't quite realize I've helped an age-old dream come true."

Another one said, "This world's grim and lonely, and mysterious. We don't know much about it yet. So far, nobody's seen anything living but the lichens that Expedition One reported, but there might be anything here."

Miss Graham asked me, "Was that all there was, just lichens?"

"That, and two or three kinds of queer cactus things," I said. "And rock and sand. That's all."

As I read more of those little blue letters, I found that now that Jim was gone I knew him better than I ever had. There was something about him I'd never suspected. He was romantic inside. We hadn't suspected it, he was always so quiet and slow, but now I saw that all the time he was more romantic about the thing we were doing than any of us.

He hadn't let on. We'd have kidded him, if he had. Our name for Mars, after we got sick of it, was the Hole. We always talked about it as the Hole. I could see now that Jim had been too shy of our kidding to ever let us know that he glamorized the thing in his mind.

"This was the last one I got from him before his sickness," Miss Graham said.

That one said, "I'm starting north tomorrow with one of the mapping expeditions. We'll travel over country no human has ever seen before."

I nodded. "I was on that party myself. Jim and I were on the same half-track."

"He was thrilled by it, wasn't he, Sergeant?"

I wondered. I remembered that trip, and it was hell. Our job was simply to run a preliminary topographical survey, checking with Geigers for possible uranium deposits.

It wouldn't have been so bad, if the sand hadn't started to blow.

It wasn't sand like Earth sand. It was ground to dust by billions of years of blowing around that dry world. It got inside your breathing mask, and your goggles, and the engines of the half-tracks, in your food and water and clothes. There was nothing for three days but cold, and wind, and sand.

Thrilled? I'd have laughed at that before. But now I didn't know. Maybe Jim had been, at that. He had lots of patience, a lot more than I ever had. Maybe he glamorized that hellish trip into wonderful adventure on a foreign world.

"Sure, he was thrilled," I said. "We all were. Anybody would be."

Miss Graham took the letters back, and then said, "You had Martian sickness too, didn't you?"

I said, yes, I had, just a touch, and that was why I'd had to spend a stretch in reconditioning hospital when I got back.

She waited for me to go on, and I knew I had to. "They don't know yet if it's some sort of virus or just the effect of Martian conditions on Earthmen's bodies. It hit forty per cent of us. It wasn't really so bad—fever and dopiness, mostly."

"When Jim got it, was he well cared for?" she asked. Her lips were quivering a little.

"Sure, he was well cared for. He got the best care there was," I lied.

The best care there was? That was a laugh. The first cases got decent care, maybe. But they'd never figured on so many coming down. There wasn't any room in our little hospital—they just had to stay in their bunks in the aluminum Quonsets when it hit them. All our doctors but one were down, and two of them died.

We'd been on Mars six months when it hit us, and the loneliness had already got us down. All but four of our rockets had gone back to Earth, and we were alone on a dead world, our little town of Quonsets huddled together under that hateful, brassy sky, and beyond it the sand and rocks that went on forever.

You go up to the North Pole and camp there, and find out how lonely that is. It was worse out there, a lot worse. The first excitement was gone long ago, and we were tired, and homesick in a way nobody was ever homesick before—we wanted to see green grass, and real sunshine, and women's faces, and hear running water; and we wouldn't until Expedition Three came to relieve us. No wonder guys blew their tops out there. And then came Martian sickness, on top of it.

"We did everything for him that we could," I said.

Sure we had. I could still remember Walter and me tramping through the cold night to the hospital to try to get a medic, while Breck stayed with him, and how we couldn't get one.

I remember how Walter had looked up at the blazing sky as we tramped back, and shaken his fist at the big green star of Earth.

"People up there are going to dances tonight, watching shows, sitting around in warm rooms laughing! Why should good men have to die out here to get them uranium for cheap power?"

"Can it," I told him tiredly. "Jim's not going to die. A lot of guys got over it."

The best care there was? That was real funny. All we could do was wash his face, and give him the pills the medic left, and watch him get weaker every day till he died.

"Nobody could have done more for him than was done," I told Miss Graham.

"I'm glad," she said. "I guess—it's just one of those things."

When I got up to go she asked me if I didn't want to see Jim's room. They'd kept it for him just the same, she said.

I didn't want to, but how are you going to say so? I went up with her and looked and said it was nice. She opened a big cupboard. It was full of neat rows of old magazines.

"They're all the old science fiction magazines he read when he was a boy," she said. "He always saved them."

I took one out. It had a bright cover, with a space ship on

it, not like our rockets but a streamlined thing, and the rings of Saturn in the background.

When I laid it down, Miss Graham took it up and put it back carefully into its place in the row, as though somebody was coming back who wouldn't like to find things out of order.

She insisted on driving me back to Omaha, and out to the airport. She seemed sorry to let me go, and I suppose it was because I was the last real tie to Jim, and when I was gone it was all over then for good.

I wondered if she'd get over it in time, and I guessed she would. People do get over things. I supposed she'd marry some other nice guy, and I wondered what they'd do with Jim's things—with all those old magazines nobody was ever coming back to read.

3.

I would never have stopped at Chicago at all if I could have got out of it, for the last person I wanted to talk to anybody about was Walter Millis. It would be too easy for me to make a slip and let out stuff nobody was supposed to know.

But Walter's father had called me at the hospital, a couple of times. The last time he called, he said he was having Breck's parents come down from Wisconsin so they could see me, too, so what could I do then but say, yes, I'd stop. But I didn't like it at all, and I knew I'd have to be careful.

Mr. Millis was waiting at the airport and shook hands with me and said what a big favor I was doing them all, and how he appreciated my stopping when I must be anxious to get back to my own home and parents.

"That's all right," I said. "My dad and mother came out to the hospital to see me when I first got back."

He was a big, fine-looking important sort of man, with a little bit of the stuffed shirt about him, I thought. He seemed friendly enough, but I got the feeling he was looking at me and wondering why I'd come back and his son Walter hadn't. Well, I couldn't blame him for that.

His car was waiting, a big car with a driver, and we started north through the city. Mr. Millis pointed out a few things to me to make conversation, especially a big atomic-power station we passed.

"It's only one of thousands, strung all over the world," he said. "They're going to transform our whole economy. This Martian uranium will be a big thing, Sergeant."

I said, yes, I guessed it would.

I was sweating blood, waiting for him to start asking about Walter, and I didn't know yet just what I could tell him. I could get myself in Dutch plenty if I opened my big mouth too wide, for that one thing that had happened to Expedition Two was supposed to be strictly secret, and we'd all been briefed on why we had to keep our mouths shut.

But he let it go for the time being, and just talked other stuff. I gathered that his wife wasn't too well, and that Walter had been their only child. I also gathered that he was a very big shot in business, and dough-heavy.

I didn't like him. Walter I'd liked plenty, but his old man seemed a pretty pompous person, with his heavy business talk.

He wanted to know how soon I thought Martian uranium would come through in quantity, and I said I didn't think it'd be very soon.

"Expedition One only located the deposits," I said, "and Two just did mapping and setting up a preliminary base. Of course, the thing keeps expanding, and I hear Four will have a hundred rockets. But Mars is a tough setup."

Mr. Millis said decisively that I was wrong, that the world was power-hungry, that it would be pushed a lot faster than I expected.

He suddenly quit talking business and looked at me and asked, "Who was Walter's best friend out there?"

He asked it sort of apologetically. He was a stuffed shirt; but all my dislike of him went away then.

"Breck Jergen," I told him. "Breck was our sergeant. He sort of held our squad together, and he and Walter cottoned to each other from the first."

Mr. Millis nodded, but didn't say anything more about it. He pointed out the window at the distant lake and said we were almost to his home.

It wasn't a home, it was a big mansion. We went in and he introduced me to Mrs. Millis. She was a limp, pale-looking woman, who said she was glad to meet one of Walter's friends. Somehow I got the feeling that even though he was a stuffed shirt, he felt it about Walter a lot more than she did.

He took me up to a bedroom and said that Breck's parents

would arrive before dinner, and that I could get a little rest before then.

I sat looking around the room. It was the plushiest one I'd ever been in, and, seeing this house and the way these people lived, I began to understand why Walter had blown his top more than the rest of us.

He'd been a good guy, Walter, but high-tempered, and I could see now he'd been a little spoiled. The discipline at training base had been tougher on him than on most of us, and this was why.

I sat and dreaded this dinner that was coming up, and looked out the window at a swimming pool and tennis court, and wondered if anybody ever used them now that Walter was gone. It seemed a queer thing for a fellow with a setup like this to go out to Mars and get himself killed.

I took the satin cover off the bed so my shoes wouldn't dirty it, and lay down and closed my eyes, and wondered what I was going to tell them. The trouble was, I didn't know what story the officials had given them.

"The Commanding Officer regrets to inform you that your son was shot down like a dog . . ."

They'd never got any telegram like that. But just what line *had* been handed them? I wished I'd had a chance to check on that.

Damn it, why didn't all these people let me alone? They started it all going through my mind again, and the psychos had told me I ought to forget it for a while, but how could I?

It might be better just to tell them the truth. After all, Walter wasn't the only one who'd blown his top out there. In that grim last couple of months, plenty of guys had gone around sounding off.

Expedition Three isn't coming!

We're stuck, and they don't care enough about us to send help!

That was the line of talk. You heard it plenty, in those days. You couldn't blame the guys for it, either. A fourth of us down with Martian sickness, the little grave markers clotting up the valley beyond the ridge, rations getting thin, medicine running low, everything running low, all of us watching the sky for rockets that never came.

There'd been a little hitch back on Earth, Colonel Nichols explained. (He was our C.O. now that General Rayen had died.) There was a little delay, but the rockets would be on their way soon, we'd get relief, we just had to hold on.

Holding on—that's what we were doing. Nights we'd sit in the Quonset and listen to Lassen coughing in his bunk, and it seemed like wind-giants, cold-giants, were bawling and laughing around our little huddle of shelters.

"Damn it, if they're not coming, why don't we go home?" Walter said. "We've still got the four rockets—they could take us all back."

Breck's serious face got graver. "Look, Walter, there's too much of that stuff being talked around. Lay off."

"Can you blame the men for talking it? We're not story-book heroes. If they've forgotten about us back on Earth, why do we just sit and take it?"

"We have to," Breck said. "Three will come."

I've always thought that it wouldn't have happened, what did happen, if we hadn't had that false alarm. The one that set the whole camp wild that night, with guys shouting, "Three's here! The rockets landed over west of Rock Ridge!"

Only when they charged out there, they found they hadn't seen rockets landing at all, but a little shower of tiny meteors burning themselves up as they fell.

It was the disappointment that did it, I think. I can't say for sure, because that same day was the day I conked out with Martian sickness, and the floor came up and hit me and I woke up in the bunk, with somebody giving me a hypo, and my head big as a balloon. I wasn't clear out, it was only a touch of it, but it was enough to make everything foggy, and I didn't know about the mutiny that was boiling up until I woke up once with Breck leaning over me and saw he wore a gun and an M.P. brassard now.

When I asked him how come, he said there'd been so much wild talk about grabbing the four rockets and going home that the M.P. force had been doubled and Nichols had issued stern warnings.

"Walter?" I said, and Breck nodded. "He's a leader and he'll get hit with a court-martial when this is over. The blasted idiot!"

"I don't get it—he's got plenty of guts, you know that," I said.

"Yes, but he can't take discipline, he never did take it very well, and now that the squeeze is on he's blowing up. Well, see you later, Frank."

I saw him later, but not the way I expected. For that was

the day we heard the faint echo of shots, and then the alarm siren screaming, and men running, and half-tracks starting up in a hurry. And when I managed to get out of my bunk and out of the hut, they were all going toward the big rockets, and a corporal yelled to me from a jeep, "That's blown it! The damn fools swiped guns and tried to take over the rockets and make the crews fly 'em home!"

I could still remember the sickening slidings and bouncings of the jeep as it took us out there, the milling little crowd under the looming rockets, milling around and hiding something on the ground, and Major Weller yelling himself hoarse giving orders.

When I got to see what was on the ground, it was seven or eight men and most of them dead. Walter had been shot right through the heart. They told me later it was because he'd been the leader, out in front, that he got it first of the mutineers.

One M.P. was dead, and one was sitting with red all over the middle of his uniform, and that one was Breck, and they were bringing a stretcher for him now.

The corporal said, "Hey, that's Jergen, your squad leader!"

And I said, "Yes, that's him." Funny how you can't talk when something hits you—how you just say words, like "Yes, that's him."

Breck died that night without ever regaining consciousness, and there I was, still half sick myself, and with Lassen dying in his bunk, and five of us were all that was left of Squad Fourteen, and that was that.

How could H.Q. let a thing like that get known? A fine advertisement it would be for recruiting more Mars expeditions, if they told how guys on Two cracked up and did a crazy thing like that. I didn't blame them for telling us to keep it top secret. Anyway, it wasn't something we'd want to talk about.

But it sure left me in a fine spot now, a sweet spot. I was going down to talk to Breck's parents and Walter's parents, and they'd want to know how their sons died, and I could tell them, "Your sons probably killed each other, out there."

Sure, I could tell them that, couldn't I? But what *was* I going to tell them? I knew H.Q. had reported those casualties as "accidental deaths," but what kind of accident?

Well, it got late, and I had to go down, and when I did, Breck's parents were there. Mr. Jergen was a carpenter, a tall, bony man with level blue eyes like Breck's. He didn't say much, but his wife was a little woman who talked enough for both of them.

She told me I looked just like I did in the pictures of us Breck had sent home from training base. She said she had three daughters too—two of them married, and one of the married ones living in Milwaukee and one out on the Coast.

She said that she'd named Breck after a character in a book by Robert Louis Stevenson, and I said I'd read the book in high school.

"It's a nice name," I said.

She looked at me with bright eyes and said, "Yes. It was a nice name."

That was a fine dinner. They'd got everything they thought I might like, and all the best, and a maid served it, and I couldn't taste a thing I ate.

Then afterward, in the big living room, they all just sort of sat and waited, and I knew it was up to me.

I asked them if they'd had any details about the accident, and Mr. Millis said, No, just "accidental death" was all they'd been told.

Well, that made it easier. I sat there, with all four of them watching my face, and dreamed it up.

I said, "It was one of those one-in-a-million things. You see, more little meteorites hit the ground on Mars than here, because the air's so much thinner it doesn't burn them up so fast. And one hit the edge of the fuel dump and a bunch of little tanks started to blow. I was down with the sickness, so I didn't see it, but I heard all about it."

You could hear everybody breathing, it was so quiet as I went on with my yarn.

"A couple of guys were knocked out by the concussion and would have been burned up if a few fellows hadn't got in there fast with foamite extinguishers. They kept it away from the big tanks, but another little tank let go, and Breck and Walter were two of the fellows who'd gone in, and they were killed instantly."

When I'd got it told, it sounded corny to me and I was afraid they'd never believe it. But nobody said anything, until Mr. Millis let out a sigh and said, "So that was it. Well . . . well, if it had to be, it was mercifully quick, wasn't it?"

I said, yes, it was quick.

"Only, I can't see why they couldn't have let us know. It doesn't seem fair."

I had an answer for that. "It's hush-hush because they don't want people to know about the meteor danger. That's why."

Mrs. Millis got up and said she wasn't feeling so well, and would I excuse her and she'd see me in the morning. The rest of us didn't seem to have much to say to each other, and nobody objected when I went up to my bedroom a little later.

I was getting ready to turn in when there was a knock on the door. It was Breck's father, and he came in and looked at me steadily.

"It was just a story, wasn't it?" he said.

I said, "Yes. It was just a story."

His eyes bored into me and he said, "I guess you've got your reasons. Just tell me one thing. Whatever it was, did Breck behave right?"

"He behaved like a man, all the way," I said. "He was the best man of us, first to last."

He looked at me, and I guess something made him believe me. He shook hands and said, "All right, son. We'll let it go."

I'd had enough. I wasn't going to face them again in the morning. I wrote a note, thanking them all and making excuses, and then went down and slipped quietly out of the house.

It was late, but a truck coming along picked me up, and the driver said he was going near the airport. He asked me what it was like on Mars and I told him it was lonesome. I slept in a chair at the airport, and I felt better, for next day I'd be home, and it would be over.

That's what I thought.

4.

It was getting toward evening when we reached the village, for my father and mother hadn't known I was coming on an earlier plane, and I'd had to wait for them up at Cleveland Airport. When we drove into Market Street, I saw there was a big painted banner stretching across: "HARMONVILLE WELCOMES HOME ITS SPACEMAN!"

Spaceman—that was me. The newspapers had started calling us that, I guess, because it was a short word good for headlines. Everybody called us that now. We'd sat cooped up in a prison cell that flew, that was all—but now we were "spacemen."

There were bright uniforms clustered under the banner, and I saw that it was the high-school band. I didn't say anything, but my father saw my face.

"Now, Frank, I know you're tired, but these people are your friends and they want to show you a real welcome."

That was fine. Only it was all gone again, the relaxed feeling I'd been beginning to get as we drove down from Cleveland.

This was my home country, this old Ohio country with its neat little white villages and fat, rolling farms. It looked good, in June. It looked very good, and I'd been feeling better all the time. And now I didn't feel so good, for I saw that I was going to have to talk some more about Mars.

Dad stopped the car under the banner, and the high-school band started to play, and Mr. Robinson, who was the Chevrolet dealer and also the mayor of Harmonville, got into the car with us.

He shook hands with me and said, "Welcome home, Frank! What was it like out on Mars?"

I said, "It was cold, Mr. Robinson. Awful cold."

"You should have been here last February!" he said. "Eighteen below—nearly a record."

He leaned out and gave a signal, and Dad started driving again, with the band marching along in front of us and playing. We didn't have far to go, just down Market Street under the big old maples, past the churches and the old white houses to the square white Grange Hall.

There was a little crowd in front of it, and they made a sound like a cheer—not a real loud one, you know how people can be self-conscious about really cheering—when we drove up. I got out and shook hands with people I didn't really see, and then Mr. Robinson took my elbow and took me on inside.

The seats were all filled and people standing up, and over the little stage at the far end they'd fixed up a big floral decoration—there was a globe all of red roses with a sign above it that said "Mars," and beside it a globe all of white roses that said "Earth," and a little rocket ship made out of flowers was hung between them.

"The Garden Club fixed it up," said Mr. Robinson. "Nearly everybody in Harmonville contributed flowers."

"It sure is pretty," I said.

Mr. Robinson took me by the arm, up onto the little stage, and everyone clapped. They were all people I knew—people from the farms near ours, my high-school teachers, and all that.

I sat down in a chair and Mr. Robinson made a little speech, about how Harmonville boys had always gone out when anything big was doing, how they'd gone to the War of 1812 and the Civil War and the two World Wars, and how now one of them had gone to Mars.

He said, "Folks have always wondered what it's like out there on Mars, and now here's one of our own Harmonville boys come back to tell us all about it."

And he motioned me to get up, and I did, and they clapped some more, and I stood wondering what I could tell them.

And all of a sudden, as I stood there wondering, I got the answer to something that had always puzzled us out there. We'd never been able to understand why the fellows who had come back from Expedition One hadn't tipped us off how tough it was going to be. And now I knew why. They hadn't because it would have sounded as if they were whining about all they'd been through. And now I couldn't, for the same reason.

I looked down at the bright, interested faces, the faces I'd known almost all my life, and I knew that what I could tell them was no good anyway. For they'd all read those newspaper stories, about "the exotic red planet" and "heroic spacemen," and if anyone tried to give them a different picture now, it would just upset them.

I said, "It was a long way out there. But flying space is a wonderful thing—flying right off the Earth, into the stars—there's nothing quite like it."

Flying space, I called it. It sounded good, and thrilling. How could they know that flying space meant lying strapped in that blind stokehold listening to Joe Valinez dying, and praying and praying that it wouldn't be our rocket that cracked up?

"And it's a wonderful thrill to come out of a rocket and step on a brand-new world, to look up at a different-looking sun, to look around at a whole new horizon . . ."

Yes, it was wonderful. Especially for the guys in Rockets Seven and Nine who got squashed like flies and lay around there on the sand, moaning "First aid!" Sure, it was a big thrill, for them and for us who had to try to help them.

"There were hardships out there, but we all knew that a big job had to be done . . ."

That's a nice word, too, "hardships." It's not coarse and ugly like fellows coughing their hearts out from too much dust; it's not like having your best friend die of Martian sickness right in the room you sleep in. It's a nice, cheerful word, "hardships."

". . . and the only way we could get the job done, away out there so far from Earth, was by teamwork."

Well, that was true enough in its way, and what was the use of spoiling it by telling them how Walter and Breck had died?

"The job's going on, and Expedition Three is building a bigger base out there right now, and Four will start soon. And it'll mean plenty of uranium, plenty of cheap atomic power, for all Earth."

That's what I said, and I stopped there. But I wanted to go on and add, "And it wasn't worth it! It wasn't worth all those guys, all the hell we went through, just to get cheap atomic power so you people can run more electric washers and television sets and toasters!"

But how are you going to stand up and say things like that to people you know, people who like you? And who was I to decide? Maybe I was wrong, anyway. Maybe lots of things I'd had and never thought about had been squeezed out of other good guys, back in the past.

I wouldn't know.

Anyway, that was all I could tell them, and I sat down, and there was a big lot of applause, and I realized then that I'd done right, I'd told them just what they wanted to hear, and everyone was all happy about it.

Then things broke up, and people came up to me, and I shook a lot more hands. And finally, when I got outside, it was dark—soft, summery dark, the way I hadn't seen it for a long time. And my father said we ought to be getting on home, so I could rest.

I told him, "You folks drive on ahead, and I'll walk. I'll take the short cut. I'd sort of like to walk through town."

Our farm was only a couple of miles out of the village, and the short cut across Heller's farm I'd always taken when I was a kid was only a mile. Dad didn't think maybe I ought to walk so far, but I guess he saw I wanted to, so they went on ahead.

I walked on down Market Street, and around the little square, and the maples and elms were dark over my head, and the flowers on the lawns smelled the way they used to, but it wasn't the same either—I'd thought it would be, but it wasn't.

When I cut off past the Odd Fellows' Hall, beyond it I met Hobe Evans, the garage hand at the Ford place, who was humming along half tight, the same as always on a Saturday night.

"Hello, Frank, heard you were back," he said. I waited for him to ask the question they all asked, but he didn't. He said, "Boy, you don't look so good! Want a drink?"

He brought out a bottle, and I had one out of it, and he had one, and he said he'd see me around, and went humming on his way. He was feeling too good to care much where I'd been.

I went on, in the dark, across Heller's pasture and then along the creek under the big old willows. I stopped there like I'd always stopped when I was a kid, to hear the frog noises, and there they were, and all the June noises, the night noises, and the night smells.

I did something I hadn't done for a long time. I looked up at the starry sky, and there it was, the same little red dot I'd peered at when I was a kid and read those old stories, the same red dot that Breck and Jim and Walter and I had stared away at on nights at training base, wondering if we'd ever really get there.

Well, they'd got there, and weren't ever going to leave it now, and there'd be others to stay with them, more and more of them as time went by.

But it was the ones I knew that made the difference, as I looked up at the red dot.

I wished I could explain to them somehow why I hadn't told the truth, not the whole truth. I tried, sort of, to explain.

"I didn't want to lie," I said. "But I had to—at least, it seemed like I had to—"

I quit it. It was crazy, talking to guys who were dead and

forty million miles away. They were dead, and it was over, and that was that. I quit looking up at the red dot in the sky and started on home again.

But I felt as though something was over for me too. It was being young. I didn't feel old. But I didn't feel young either, and I didn't think I ever would, not ever again.

Our civilization has taken a long time to accept the notion that the truth, however grotesque or unpalatable, is better than any amount of highly colored falsehoods. It can hardly be said that this idea is widespread even yet; it holds in science and engineering, and in a few other egghead areas, but as citizens we are still surrounded and half smothered by a blanket of soothing lies. We believe that justice triumphs, that crime does not pay, that Our government is nobler and more disinterested than Their government, and a lot of other comforting things that do not happen to be eternally true.

So I think we gain when a writer has the courage and insight to say, in a story about a Mars expedition, "Maybe lots of things I'd had and never thought about had been squeezed out of other good guys, back in the past."

Robert A. Heinlein, a retired naval officer and mechanical engineer, entered the s.f. field in 1939 with a short story called "Lifeline." In the next four years he produced seventeen more stories and nine novels, all characterized by an exuberant inventiveness and a scorn for conventional makeshifts. Like the young Wells, Heinlein staked out vast new territory and made it his own. His long novelettes Universe *and the aptly named* Common Sense *introduced the idea of a generations-long voyage to the stars. Previous writers had merely overlooked the problem of the immense interstellar distances, or had elected to solve it with a magical phrase ("spacewarp" or "overdrive"). Heinlein began by approaching such problems seriously, an unheard-of thing in the science fiction of the forties. In stories like "Requiem," "Universe," "Methuselah's Children" and "Coventry," he said, in effect, "If you really want to get to the Moon, or the stars, or increase human longevity, or establish a civilized world order, this is the practical way to do it."*

In magazine fiction, in the motion picture Destination

Moon, *in his Scribner's juveniles, Heinlein has built up a consistent and detailed picture of the next century in space. Here is one of his spacefaring tales* (Imagination, *November 1953*), *a story about something that has never happened, and yet a story which is true in the sense that two-times-two-equals-four is true. The cold mathematics of space flight have a human meaning, as you are about to see.*

SKY LIFT

BY ROBERT A. HEINLEIN

"All torch pilots! Report to the Commodore!" The call echoed through Earth Satellite Station.

Joe Appleby flipped off the shower to listen. "You don't mean me," he said happily. "I'm on leave—but I'd better shove before you change your mind."

He dressed and hurried along a passageway. He was in the outer ring of the station; its slow revolution, a giant wheel in the sky, produced gravitylike force against his feet. As he reached his room the loudspeakers repeated, "All torch pilots, report to the Commodore," then added, "Lieutenant Appleby, report to the Commodore." Appleby uttered a rude monosyllable.

The Commodore's office was crowded. All present wore the torch, except a flight surgeon and Commodore Berrio himself, who wore the jets of a rocket ship pilot.

Berrio glanced up and went on talking: ". . . the situation. If we are to save Proserpina Station, an emergency run must be made out to Pluto. Any questions?"

No one spoke. Appleby wanted to, but did not wish to remind Berrio that he had been late. "Very well," Berrio went on. "Gentlemen, it's a job for torch pilots. I must ask for volunteers."

Good! thought Appleby. Let the eager lads volunteer and then adjourn. He decided that he might still catch the next shuttle to Earth. The Commodore continued, "Volunteers please remain. The rest are dismissed."

Excellent, Appleby decided. Don't rush for the door, me lad. Be dignified—sneak out between two taller men.

No one left. Joe Appleby felt swindled but lacked the

nerve to start the exodus. The Commodore said soberly, "Thank you, gentlemen. Will you wait in the wardroom, please?" Muttering, Appleby left with the crowd. He wanted to go out to Pluto someday, sure—but not now, not with Earthside leave papers in his pocket.

He held a torcher's contempt for the vast distance itself. Older pilots thought of interplanetary trips with a rocketman's bias, in terms of years—trips that a torch ship with steady acceleration covered in days. By the orbits that a rocket ship must use, the round trip to Jupiter takes over five years; Saturn is twice as far, Uranus twice again, Neptune still farther. No rocket ship ever attempted Pluto; a round trip would take more than ninety years. But torch ships had won a foothold even there: Proserpina Station—cryology laboratory, cosmic radiation station, parallax observatory, physics laboratory, all in one quintuple dome against the unspeakable cold.

Nearly four billion miles from Proserpina Station, Appleby followed a classmate into the wardroom. "Hey, Jerry," he said, "tell me what it is I seem to have volunteered for?"

Jerry Price looked around. "Oh, it's the late Joe Appleby. Okay, buy me a drink."

A radiogram had come from Proserpina, Jerry told him, reporting an epidemic: "Larkin's disease." Appleby whistled. Larkin's disease was a mutated virus, possibly of Martian origin; a victim's red-cell count fell rapidly, soon he was dead. The only treatment was massive transfusions while the disease ran its course. "So, m'boy, somebody has to trot out to Pluto with a blood bank."

Appleby frowned. "My pappy warned me. 'Joe,' he said, 'keep your mouth shut and never volunteer.' "

Jerry grinned. "We didn't exactly volunteer."

"How long is the boost? Eighteen days or so? I've got social obligations Earthside."

"Eighteen days at one g—but this will be higher. They are running out of blood donors."

"How high? A g and a half?"

Price shook his head. "I'd guess two gravities."

"Two g's!"

"What's hard about that? Men have lived through ten."

"Sure, for a short pull-out—not for days on end. Two g's strains your heart if you stand up."

"Don't moan, they won't pick you—I'm more the hero

type. While you're on leave, think of me out in those lonely wastes, a grim-jawed angel of mercy. Buy me another drink."

Appleby decided that Jerry was right; with only two pilots needed he stood a good chance of catching the next Earth shuttle. He got out his little black book and was picking phone numbers when a messenger arrived.

"Lieutenant Appleby, sir?"

Joe nodded.

"The-Commodore's-compliments-and-will-you-report-at-once,-sir?"

"On my way." Joe caught Jerry's eye. "Who is what type?"

Jerry said, "Shall I take care of your social obligations?"

"Not likely!"

"I was afraid not. Good luck, boy."

With Commodore Berrio was the flight surgeon and an older lieutenant. Berrio said, "Sit down, Appleby. You know Lieutenant Kleuger? He's your skipper. You will be copilot."

"Very good, sir."

"Appleby, Mr. Kleuger is the most experienced torch pilot available. You were picked because medical records show you have exceptional tolerance for acceleration. This is a high-boost trip."

"How high, sir?"

Berrio hesitated. "Three and one half gravities."

Three and a half g's! That wasn't a boost—that was a pull-out. Joe heard the surgeon protest, "I am sorry, sir, but three gravities is all I can approve."

Berrio frowned. "Legally, it's up to the captain. But three hundred lives depend on it."

Kleuger said, "Doctor, let's see that curve." The surgeon slid a paper across the desk; Kleuger moved it so that Joe could see it. "Here's the scoop, Appleby—"

A curve started high, dropped very slowly, made a sudden "knee" and dropped rapidly. The surgeon put his finger on the "knee." "Here," he said soberly, "is where the donors are suffering from loss of blood as much as the patients. After that it's hopeless without a new source of blood."

"How did you get this curve?" Joe asked.

"It's the empirical equation of Larkin's disease applied to two hundred eighty-nine people."

Appleby noted vertical lines each marked with an acceleration and a time. Far to the right was one marked: "1 g—18 days." That was the standard trip; it would arrive after the epidemic had burned out. Two gravities cut it to twelve days seventeen hours; even so, half the colony would be dead. Three g's was better but still bad. He could see why the Commodore wanted them to risk three and a half kicks; that line touched the "knee" at nine days fifteen hours. That way they could save almost everybody—but, oh, brother!

The time advantage dropped off by inverse squares. Eighteen days required one gravity, so nine days took four, while four and a half days required a fantastic sixteen gravities. But someone had drawn a line at "16 g—4.5 days." "Hey! This plot must be for a robot torch—that's the ticket! Is there one available?"

Berrio said gently, "Yes. But what are its chances?"

Joe shut up. Even between the inner planets robots often went astray. In four-billion-odd miles the chance that one could hit close enough to be caught by radio control was slim.

"We'll try," Berrio promised. "If it succeeds, I'll call you at once." He looked at Kleuger. "Captain, time is short. I must have your decision."

Kleuger turned to the surgeon. "Doctor, why not another half gravity? I recall a report on a chimpanzee who was centrifuged at high g for an amazingly long time."

"A chimpanzee is not a man."

Joe blurted out, "How much did this chimp stand, Surgeon?"

"Three and a quarter gravities for twenty-seven days."

"He *did?* What shape was he in when the test ended?"

"He wasn't," the doctor grunted.

Kleuger looked at the graph, glanced at Joe, then said to the Commodore, "The boost will be three and one half gravities, sir."

Berrio merely said, "Very well, then. Hurry over to sick bay. You haven't much time."

Forty-seven minutes later they were being packed into the scout torchship *Salamander*. She was in orbit close by; Joe, Kleuger and their handlers came by tube linking the hub of the station to her air lock. Joe was weak and dopey from a thorough washing out plus a dozen treatments and injections. A good thing, he thought, that light-off would be automatic.

The ship was built for high boost; controls were over the pilot's tanks, where they could be fingered without lifting a hand. The flight surgeon and an assistant fitted Kleuger into one tank while two medical technicians arranged Joe in his.

One of them asked, "Underwear smooth? No wrinkles?"

"I guess."

"I'll check." He did so, then arranged fittings necessary to a man who must remain in one position for days. "The nipple left of your mouth is water; the two on your right are glucose and bouillon."

"No solids?"

The surgeon turned in the air and answered, "You don't need any, you won't want any, and you mustn't have any. And be careful in swallowing."

"I've boosted before."

"Sure, sure. But be careful."

′ Each tank was like an oversized bathtub filled with a liquid denser than water. The top was covered by a rubbery sheet, gasketed at the edges; during boost each man would float with the sheet conforming to his body. The *Salamander* being still in free orbit, everything was weightless and the sheet now served to keep the fluid from floating out. The attendants centered Appleby against the sheet and fastened him with sticky tape, then placed his own acceleration collar, tailored to him, behind his head.

The surgeon came over and inspected. "You okay?"

"Sure."

"Mind that swallowing." He added, "Okay, Captain. Permission to leave your ship, sir?"

"Certainly. Thank you, Surgeon."

"Good luck." He left with the technicians.

The room had no ports and needed none. The area in front of Joe's face was filled with screens, instruments, radar, and data displays; near his forehead was his eyepiece for the coelostat. A light blinked green as the passenger tube broke its anchors; Kleuger caught Joe's eye in a mirror mounted opposite them. "Report, mister."

"Minus seven minutes oh four. Tracking. Torch warm and idle. Green for light-off."

"Stand by while I check orientation." Kleuger's eyes disappeared into his coelostat eyepiece. Presently he said, "Check me, Joe."

"Aye aye, sir." Joe twisted a knob and his eyepiece swung down. He found three star images brought together perfectly in the cross hairs. "Couldn't be better, Skipper."

"Ask for clearance."

"Salamander to Control—clearance requested to Proserpina. Automatic light-off on tape. All green."

"Control to Salamander. You are cleared. Good luck!"

"Cleared, Skipper. Minus three . . . *double oh!*" Joe thought morosely that he should be halfway to Earth now. Why the hell did the military always get stuck with these succor-and-rescue jobs?

When the counter flashed the last thirty seconds he forgot his forgone leave. The lust to travel possessed him. To go, no matter where, anywhere . . . go! He smiled as the torch lit off.

Then weight hit him.

At three and a half gravities he weighed six hundred and thirty pounds. It felt as if a load of sand had landed on him, squeezing his chest, making him helpless, forcing his head against his collar. He strove to relax, to let the supporting liquid hold him together. It was all right to tighten up for a pull-out, but for a long boost one must relax. He breathed shallowly and slowly; the air was pure oxygen, little lung action was needed. But he labored just to breathe. He could feel his heart struggling to pump blood grown heavy through squeezed vessels. This is awful! he admitted. I'm not sure I can take it. He had once had four g's for nine minutes but he had forgotten how bad it was.

"Joe! *Joe!*"

He opened his eyes and tried to shake his head. "Yes, Skipper." He looked for Kleuger in the mirror; the pilot's face was sagging and drawn, pulled into the mirthless grin of high acceleration.

"Check orientation!"

Joe let his arms float as he worked controls with leaden fingers. "Dead on, Skipper."

"Very well. Call Luna."

Earth Station was blanketed by their torch, but the Moon was on their bow. Appleby called Luna tracking center and received their data on the departure plus data relayed from Earth Station. He called figures and times to Kleuger, who fed them into the computer. Joe then found that he had forgotten, while working, his unbearable weight. It felt worse than ever. His neck ached and he suspected that there was a wrinkle under his left calf. He wiggled in the tank to smooth it, but it made it worse. "How's she look, Skipper?"

"Okay. You're relieved, Joe. I'll take first watch."

"Right, Skipper." He tried to rest—as if a man could

when buried under sandbags. His bones ached and the wrinkle became a nagging nuisance. The pain in his neck got worse; apparently he had wrenched it at light-off. He turned his head, but there were just two positions—bad and worse. Closing his eyes, he attempted to sleep. Ten minutes later he was wider awake than ever, his mind on three things, the lump in his neck, the irritation under his leg, and the squeezing weight.

Look, bud, he told himself, this is a long boost. Take it easy, or adrenalin exhaustion will get you. As the book says, *"The ideal pilot is relaxed and unworried. Sanguine in temperament, he never borrows trouble."* Why, you chair-warming so-and-so! Were *you* at three and a half g's when you wrote that twaddle?

Cut it out, boy! He turned his mind to his favorite subject —girls, bless their hearts. Such self-hypnosis he had used to pass many a lonely million miles. Presently he realized wryly that his phantom harem had failed him. He could not conjure them up, so he banished them and spent his time being miserable.

He awoke in a sweat. His last dream had been a nightmare that he was headed out to Pluto at an impossibly high boost.

My God! So he was!

The pressure seemed worse. When he moved his head there was a stabbing pain down his side. He was panting and sweat was pouring off. It ran into his eyes; he tried to wipe them, found that his arm did not respond and that his finger tips were numb. He inched his arm across his body and dabbed at his eyes; it did not help.

He stared at the elapsed-time dial of the integrating accelerograph and tried to remember when he was due on watch. It took a while to understand that six and a half hours had passed since light-off. He then realized with a jerk that it was long past time to relieve the watch. Kleuger's face in the mirror was still split in the grin of high g; his eyes were closed.

"Skipper!" Joe shouted. Kleuger did not stir. Joe felt for the alarm button, thought better of it. Let the poor goop sleep!

But somebody had to feed the hogs—better get the clouds out of his brain. The accelerometer showed three and a half exactly; the torch dials were all in operating range; the radiometer showed leakage less than ten per cent of danger level.

The integrating accelerograph displayed elapsed time, velocity and distance, in dead reckoning for empty space. Under these windows were three more which showed the same by the precomputed tape controlling the torch; by comparing, Joe could tell how results matched predictions. The torch had been lit off for less than seven hours, speed was nearly two million miles per hour and they were over six million miles out. A third display corrected these figures for the Sun's field, but Joe ignored this; near Earth's orbit the Sun pulls only one two-thousandth of a gravity—a gnat's whisker, allowed for in precomputation. Joe merely noted that tape and D. R. agreed; he wanted an outside check.

Both Earth and Moon now being blanketed by the same cone of disturbance, he twisted knobs until their radar beacon beamed toward Mars and let it pulse the signal meaning "Where am I?" He did not wait for answer; Mars was eighteen minutes away by radio. He turned instead to the coelostat. The triple image had wandered slightly, but the error was too small to correct.

He dictated what he had done into the log, whereupon he felt worse. His ribs hurt, each breath carried the stab of pleurisy. His hands and feet felt "pins and needles" from scanty circulation. He wiggled them, which produced crawling sensations and wearied him. So he held still and watched the speed soar. It increased seventy-seven miles per hour every second, more than a quarter million miles per hour every hour. For once he envied rocket ship pilots; they took forever to get anywhere, but they got there in comfort.

Without the torch, men would never have ventured much past Mars. $E = mc^2$, mass is energy, and a pound of sand equals fifteen billion horsepower-hours. An atomic rocket ship uses but a fraction of one per cent of that energy, whereas the new torchers used better than eighty per cent. The conversion chamber of a torch was a tiny sun; particles expelled from it approached the speed of light.

Appleby was proud to be a torcher, but not at the moment. The crick had grown into a splitting headache, he wanted to bend his knees and could not, and he was nauseated from the load on his stomach. Kleuger seemed able to sleep through it, damn his eyes! How did they expect a man to *stand* this? Only eight hours and already he felt done in, bushed—how could he last nine days?

Later—time was beginning to be uncertain—some infinite time later he heard his name called. "Joe! *Joe!*"

Couldn't a man die in peace? His eyes wandered around, found the mirror; he struggled to focus.

"Joe! You've got to relieve me—I'm groggy."

"Aye aye, sir."

"Make a check, Joe. I'm too goofed up to do it."

"I already did, sir."

"*Huh?* When?"

Joe's eyes swam around to the elapsed-time dial. He closed one eye to read it. "Uh, about six hours ago."

"What? *What time is it?*"

Joe didn't answer. He wished peevishly that Kleuger would go away.

Kleuger added soberly, "I must have blacked out, kid. What's the situation?" Presently he insisted, "Answer me, mister."

"Huh? Oh, we're all right—down the groove. Skipper, is my left leg twisted? I can't see it."

"Eh? Oh, never mind your leg! What were the figures?"

"What figures?"

" 'What figures?' Snap out of it, mister! You're on duty."

A fine one to talk, Joe thought fretfully. If that's how he's going to act, I'll just close my eyes and ignore him.

Kleuger repeated, "The figures, mister."

"Huh? Oh, play 'em off the log if you're so damned eager!" He expected a blast at that, but none came. When next he opened his eyes Kleuger's eyes were closed. He couldn't recall whether the skipper had played his figures back or not—nor whether he had logged them. He decided that it was time for another check, but he was dreadfully thirsty; he needed a drink first. He drank carefully but still got a drop down his windpipe. A coughing spasm hurt him all over and left him so weak that he had to rest.

He pulled himself together and scanned the dials. Twelve hours and—no, wait a minute! *One day* and twelve hours— that *couldn't* be right. But their speed was over ten million miles per hour and their distance more than ninety million miles from Earth; they were beyond the orbit of Mars. "Skipper! Hey! Lieutenant Kleuger!"

Kleuger's face was a grinning mask. In dull panic Joe tried

to find their situation. The coelostat showed them balanced; either the ship had wobbled back or Kleuger had corrected it. Or had he himself? He decided to run over the log and see. Fumbling among buttons he found the one to rewind the log.

Since he didn't remember to stop it, the wire ran all the way back to light-off, then played back, zipping through silent stretches and slowing for speech. He listened to his record of the first check, then found that Phobos Station, Mars, had answered with a favorable report—to which a voice added, *"Where's the fire?"*

Yes, Kleuger had corrected balance hours earlier. The wire hurried through a blank spot, slowed again—Kleuger had dictated a letter to someone; it was unfinished and incoherent. Once Kleuger had stopped to shout, *"Joe! Joe!"* and Joe heard himself answer, *"Oh, shut up!"* He had no memory of it.

There was something he should do, but he was too tired to think and he hurt all over—except his legs; he couldn't feel them. He shut his eyes and tried not to think. When he opened them the elapsed time was turning three days; he closed them and leaked tears.

A bell rang endlessly; he became aware that it was the general alarm, but he felt no interest other than a need to stop it. It was hard to find the switch, his fingers were numb. But he managed it and was about to rest from the effort, when he heard Kleuger call him. "Joe!"

"Huh?"

"Joe—don't go back to sleep or I'll turn the alarm on again. You hear me?"

"Yeah . . ." So Kleuger had done that—why, damn him!

"Joe, I've got to talk to you. I can't stand any more."

"Any more what?"

"High boost. I can't take any more—it's killing me."

"Oh, rats!" Turn on that loud bell, would he?

"I'm dying, Joe. I can't see—my eyes are shot. Joe, I've got to shut down the boost. I've got to."

"Well, what's stopping you?" Joe answered irritably.

"Don't you see, Joe? You've got to back me up. We tried and we couldn't. We'll both log it. Then it'll be all right."

"Log what?"

"Eh? Damn it, Joe, pay attention. I can't talk much. You've got to say . . . to say that the strain became unendurable and you advised me to shut down. I'll confirm it and it will be all right." His labored whisper was barely audible.

Joe couldn't figure out what Kleuger meant. He couldn't remember why Kleuger had put them in high boost anyhow. *"Hurry,* Joe."

There he went, nagging him! Wake him up and then nag him—to hell with him. "Oh, go back to sleep!" He dozed off and was again jerked awake by the alarm. This time he knew where the switch was and flipped it quickly. Kleuger switched it on again, Joe turned it off. Kleuger quit trying and Joe passed out.

He came awake in free fall. He was still realizing the ecstasy of being weightless when he managed to reorient; he was in the *Salamander* headed for Pluto. Had they reached the end of the run? No, the dial said four days and some hours. Had the tape broken? The autopilot gone haywire? He then recalled the last time he had been awake.

Kleuger had shut off the torch!

The stretched grin was gone from Kleuger's face, the features seemed slack and old. Joe called out, "Captain! Captain Kleuger!" Kleuger's eyes fluttered and his lips moved, but Joe heard nothing. He slithered out of the tank, moved in front of Kleuger, floated there. "Captain, can you hear me?" The lips whispered, "I had to, boy. I saved us. Can you get us back, Joe?" His eyes opened but did not track.

"Captain, listen to me. I've got to light off again."

"Huh? No, Joe, no!"

"I've got to."

"No! That's an order, mister."

Appleby stared, then with a judo chop caught the sick man on the jaw. Kleuger's head bobbed loosely. Joe pulled himself between the tanks, located a three-position switch, turned it from "Pilot & Copilot" to "Copilot Only"; Kleuger's controls were now dead. He glanced at Kleuger, saw that his head was not square in his collar, so he taped him properly into place, then got back in his tank. He settled his head and fumbled for the switch that would put the autopilot back on tape. There was some reason why they must finish this run— but for the life of him he could not remember why. He squeezed the switch, and weight pinned him down.

He was awakened by a dizzy feeling added to the pressure. It went on for seconds; he retched futilely. When the motion stopped he peered at the dials. The *Salamander* had just completed the somersault from acceleration to deceleration. They had come halfway, about eighteen hundred million miles; their speed was over three million miles per hour and beginning to drop. Joe felt that he should report it to the skipper—he had no recollection of any trouble with him. "Skipper! Hey!" Kleuger did not move. Joe called again, then resorted to the alarm.

The clangor woke, not Kleuger, but Joe's memory. He shut it off, feeling soul sick. Topping his physical misery was shame and loss and panic as he recalled the shabby facts. He felt that he ought to log it but could not decide what to say. Beaten and ever lower in mind, he gave up and tried to rest.

He woke later with something gnawing at his mind . . . something he should do for the captain . . . something about a cargo robot—

That was it! If the torch robot had reached Pluto, they could quit! Let's see—elapsed time from light-off was over five days. Yes, if it ever got there, then . . .

He ran the wire back, listened for a recorded message. It was there: *Earth Station to Salamander—Extremely sorry to report that robot failed rendezvous. We are depending on you.—Berrio.*

Tears of weakness and disappointment sped down his cheeks, pulled along by three and a half gravities.

It was on the eighth day that Joe realized that Kleuger was dead. It was not the stench—he was unable to tell that from his own ripe body odors. Nor was it that the captain had not roused since flip-over; Joe's time sense was so fogged that he did not realize this. But he had dreamed that Kleuger was shouting for him to get up, to stand up—"Hurry up, Joe!" But the weight pressed him down.

So sharp was the dream that Joe tried to answer after he woke up. Then he looked for Kleuger in the mirror. Kleuger's face was much the same, but he knew with sick horror that the captain was dead. Nevertheless, he tried to arouse him with the alarm. Presently he gave up; his fingers were purple and he could feel nothing below his waist; he wondered if he were dying and hoped that he was. He slipped into that lethargy which had become his normal state.

He did not become conscious when, after more than nine days, the autopilot quenched the torch. Awareness found him floating in mid-room, having somehow squirmed out of his station. He felt deliciously lazy and quite hungry; the latter eventually brought him awake.

His surroundings put past events somewhat into place. He pulled himself to his tank and examined the dials. Good grief!—it had been two hours since the ship had gone into free fall. The plan called for approach to be computed before the tape ran out, corrected on entering free fall, a new tape cut and fed in without delay, then let the autopilot make the approach. He had done nothing and wasted two hours.

He slid between tank and controls, discovering then that his legs were paralyzed. No matter—legs weren't needed in free fall, nor in the tank. His hands did not behave well, but he could use them. He was stunned when he found Kleuger's body, but steadied down and got to work. He had no idea where he was; Pluto might be millions of miles away, or almost in his lap—perhaps they had spotted him and were already sending approach data. He decided to check the wire.

He found their messages at once:

"Proserpina to Salamander—Thank God you are coming. Here are your elements at quench-out . . ." followed by time reference, range-and-bearing figures, and doppler data.

And again: *"Here are later and better figures, Salamander —hurry!"*

And finally, only a few minutes before: *"Salamander, why the delay in light-off? Is your computer broken down? Shall we compute a ballistic for you?"*

The idea that anyone but a torcher could work a torch ballistic did not sink in. He tried to work fast, but his hands bothered him—he punched wrong numbers and had to correct them. It took him a half hour to realize that the trouble was not just his fingers. Ballistics, a subject as easy for him as checkers, was confused in his mind.

He could not work the ballistic.

"Salamander to Proserpina—Request ballistic for approach into parking orbit around Pluto."

The answer came so quickly that he knew that they had not waited for his okay. With ponderous care he cut the tape and fed it into the autopilot. It was then that he noticed the boost—4.03.

Four gravities for the approach.

He had assumed that the approach would be a normal one —and so it might have been if he had not wasted three hours. But it wasn't fair! It was too much to expect. He cursed childishly as he settled himself, fitted the collar and squeezed the button that turned control to the autopilot. He had a few minutes of waiting time; he spent it muttering peevishly. They could have figured him a better ballistic—hell, he should have figured it. They were always pushing him around. Good old Joe, anybody's punching bag! That so-and-so Kleuger over there, grinning like a fool and leaving the work for him. If Kleuger hadn't been so confounded eager—

Acceleration hit him and he blacked out.

When the shuttle came up to meet him, they found one man dead, one nearly dead, and the cargo of whole blood.

The supply ship brought pilots for the *Salamander* and fetched Appleby home. He stayed in sick bay until ordered to Luna for treatment; on being detached he reported to Commodore Berrio, escorted by the flight surgeon. The Commodore let him know brusquely that he had done a fine job, a damn fine job! The interview ended and the surgeon helped Joe to stand; instead of leaving, Joe said, "Uh, Commodore?"

"Yes, son?"

"Uh, there's one thing I don't understand. Uh, what I don't understand is, uh, this: Why do I have to go, uh, to the geriatrics clinic at Luna City? That's for old people, uh? That's what I've always understood—the way I understand it. Sir?"

The surgeon cut in, "I told you, Joe. They have the very best physiotherapy. We got special permission for you."

Joe looked perplexed. "Is that right, sir? I feel funny, going to an old folks', uh, hospital."

"That's right, son."

Joe grinned sheepishly. "Okay, sir, uh, if you say so."

They started to leave. "Doctor—stay a moment. Messenger, help Mr. Appleby."

"Joe, can you make it?"

"Uh, sure! My legs are lots better—see?" He went out leaning on the messenger.

Berrio said, "Doctor, tell me straight: will Joe get well?"

"No, sir."

"Will he get better?"

"Some, perhaps. Lunar gravity makes it easy to get the most out of what a man has left."

"But will his mind clear up?"

The doctor hesitated. "It's this way, sir. Heavy acceleration is a speeded-up aging process. Tissues break down, capillaries rupture, the heart does many times its proper work. And there is hypoxia, from failure to deliver enough oxygen to the brain."

The Commodore struck his desk an angry blow. The surgeon said gently. "Don't take it so hard, sir."

"Damn it, man—think of the way he was. Just a kid, all bounce and vinegar. Now look at him! He's an old man—senile."

"Look at it this way," urged the surgeon. "You expended one man, but you saved two hundred and seventy."

"Expended one man? If you mean Kleuger, he gets a medal and his wife gets a pension. That's the best any of us can expect. I wasn't thinking of Kleuger."

"Neither was I," answered the surgeon.

Arthur C. Clarke's pink, cherubic appearance conceals an enormously keen and cold intellect, under which in turn is concealed an interested small boy. Clarke was a leading light of the British Interplanetary Society when that group was a small coterie of space nuts meeting in members' living rooms. He is the author of numerous technical articles on problems of space flight, many of them published before it became socially acceptable to believe in rocket ships. He was the first to describe in print a communications satellite project. He now lives in Ceylon, and on his occasional visits to this country he complains that all the palefaces look alike.

Religion interests Clarke as a psychological phenomenon. When he combines this topic with astronomy, in which he is also deeply interested, something rather explosive occurs. This story first appeared in Infinity, *November 1955.*

THE STAR

BY ARTHUR C. CLARKE

It is three thousand light-years to the Vatican. Once I believed that space could have no power over faith. Just as I believed that the heavens declared the glory of God's handiwork. Now I have seen that handiwork, and my faith is sorely troubled.

I stare at the crucifix that hangs on the cabin wall above the Mark VI computer, and for the first time in my life I wonder if it is no more than an empty symbol.

I have told no one yet, but the truth cannot be concealed. The data are there for anyone to read, recorded on the countless miles of magnetic tape and the thousands of photographs we are carrying back to Earth. Other scientists can interpret them as easily as I can—more easily, in all probability. I am not one who would condone that tampering with the truth which often gave my order a bad name in the olden days.

The crew is already sufficiently depressed, I wonder how they will take this ultimate irony. Few of them have any religious faith, yet they will not relish using this final weapon in their campaign against me—that private, good-natured but fundamentally serious war which lasted all the way from Earth. It amused them to have a Jesuit as chief astrophysicist. Dr. Chandler, for instance, could never get over it (why are medical men such notorious atheists?). Sometimes he would meet me on the observation deck, where the lights are always low, so that the stars shine with undiminished glory. He would come up to me in the gloom and stand staring out of the great oval port, while the heavens crawled slowly round us as the ship turned end over end with the residual spin we had never bothered to correct.

"Well, Father," he would say at last. "It goes on forever and forever, and perhaps Something made it. But how you can believe that Something has a special interest in us and our miserable little world—that just beats me." Then the argument would start, while the stars and nebulae would swing around us in silent, endless arcs beyond the flawlessly clear plastic of the observation port.

It was, I think, the apparent incongruity of my position which, yes, *amused* the crew. In vain I would point to my three papers in the *Astrophysical Journal,* my five in the *Monthly Notices of the Royal Astronomical Society*. I would remind them that our order has long been famous for its scientific works. We may be few now, but ever since the eighteenth century we have made contributions to astronomy and geophysics out of all proportion to our numbers.

Will my report on the Phoenix Nebula end our thousand years of history? It will end, I fear, much more than that.

I do not know who gave the nebula its name, which seems to me a very bad one. If it contains a prophecy, it is one which cannot be verified for several thousand million years. Even the word "nebula" is misleading; this is a far smaller object than those stupendous clouds of mist—the stuff of unborn stars—which are scattered throughout the length of the Milky Way. On the cosmic scale, indeed, the Phoenix Nebula is a tiny thing—a tenuous shell of gas surrounding a single star.

Or what is left of a star . . .

The Rubens engraving of Loyola seems to mock me as it hangs there above the spectrophotometer tracings. What would *you*, Father, have made of this knowledge that has come into my keeping, so far from the little world that was all the universe you knew? Would your faith have risen to the challenge, as mine has failed to do?

You gaze into the distance, Father, but I have traveled a distance beyond any that you could have imagined when you founded our order a thousand years ago. No other survey ship has been so far from Earth: we are at the very frontiers of the explored universe. We set out to reach the Phoenix Nebula, we succeeded, and we are homeward bound with our burden of knowledge. I wish I could lift that burden from my shoulders, but I call to you in vain across the centuries and the light-years that lie between us.

On the book you are holding the words are plain to read. "AD MAIOREM DEI GLORIAM," the message runs, but it is a message I can no longer believe. Would you still believe it if you could see what we have found?

We knew, of course, what the Phoenix Nebula was. Every year, in *our* galaxy alone, more than a hundred stars explode, blazing for a few hours or days with thousands of times their normal brilliance before they sink back into death and obscurity. Such are the ordinary novae—the commonplace disasters of the universe. I have recorded the spectrograms and light curves of dozens, since I started working at the lunar observatory.

But three or four times in every thousand years occurs something beside which even a nova pales into total insignificance.

When a star becomes a *supernova*, it may for a little while outshine all the massed suns of the galaxy. The Chinese astronomers watched this happen in A.D. 1054, not knowing what it was they saw. Five centuries later, in 1572, a super-nova blazed in Cassiopeia so brilliantly that it was visible in the daylight sky. There have been three more in the thousand years that have passed since then.

Our mission was to visit the remnants of such a catastrophe, to reconstruct the events that led up to it, and, if possible, to learn its cause. We came slowly in through the concentric shells of gas that had been blasted out six thousand years before, yet were expanding still. They were immensely hot, radiating still with a fierce violet light, but far too tenuous to do us any damage. When the star had exploded, its outer layers had been driven upward with such speed that they had escaped completely from its gravitational field. Now they formed a hollow shell large enough to engulf a thousand solar systems, and at its center burned the tiny, fantastic object which the star had now become—a white dwarf, smaller than the Earth, yet weighing a million times as much.

The glowing gas shells were all around us, banishing the normal night of interstellar space. We were flying into the center of a cosmic bomb that had detonated millennia ago and whose incandescent fragments were still hurtling apart. The immense scale of the explosion, and the fact that the debris already covered a volume of space many billions of miles across, robbed the scene of any visible movement. It would take decades before the unaided eye could detect any motion in these tortured wisps and eddies of gas, yet the sense of turbulent expansion was overwhelming.

We had checked our primary drive hours before and were drifting slowly toward the fierce little star ahead. Once it had been a sun like our own, but it had squandered in a few hours the energy that should have kept it shining for a million years. Now it was a shrunken miser, hoarding its resources as if trying to make amends for its prodigal youth.

No one seriously expected to find planets. If there had been any before the explosion, they would have been boiled into puffs of vapor and their substance lost in the greater wreckage of the star itself. But we made the automatic search, as always when approaching an unknown sun, and presently we found a single small world circling the star at an immense distance. It must have been the Pluto of this vanished solar system, orbiting on the frontiers of the night. Too far from the central sun ever to have known life, its remoteness had saved it from the fate of all its lost companions.

The passing fires had seared its rocks and burned away the mantle of frozen gas that must have covered it in the days before the disaster. We landed, and we found the Vault.

Its builders had made sure that we should. The monolithic marker that stood above the entrance was now a fused stump, but even the first long-range photographs told us that here was the work of intelligence. A little later we detected the continent-wide pattern of radioactivity that had been buried in the rock. Even if the pylon above the Vault had been destroyed, this would have remained, an immovable and all but eternal beacon calling to the stars. Our ship fell toward this gigantic bull's-eye like an arrow into its target.

The pylon must have been a mile high when it was built, but now it looked like a candle that had melted down into a puddle of wax. It took us a week to drill through the fused rock, since we did not have the proper tools for a task like this. We were astronomers, not archaeologists, but we could improvise. Our original program was forgotten: this lonely monument, reared at such labor at the greatest possible distance from the doomed sun, could have only one meaning. A civilization which knew it was about to die had made its last bid for immortality.

It will take us generations to examine all the treasures that were placed in the Vault. *They* had plenty of time to prepare, for their sun must have given its first warnings many years before the final detonation. Everything that they wished to preserve, all the fruits of their genius, they brought here to this distant world in the days before the end, hoping that some other race would find them and that they would not be utterly forgotten.

If only they had a little more time! They could travel freely enough between the planets of their own sun, but they had not yet learned to cross the interstellar gulfs, and the nearest solar system was a hundred light-years away.

Even if they had not been so disturbingly human as their sculpture shows, we could not have helped admiring them and grieving for their fate. They left thousands of visual records and the machines for projecting them, together with elaborate pictorial instructions from which it will not be difficult to learn their written language. We have examined many of these records, and brought to life for the first time in six thousand years the warmth and beauty of a civilization which in many ways must have been superior to our own.

Perhaps they only showed us the best, and one can hardly blame them. But their worlds were very lovely, and their cities were built with a grace that matches anything of ours. We have watched them at work and play, and listened to their musical speech sounding across the centuries. One scene is still before my eyes—a group of children on a beach of strange blue sand, playing in the waves as children play on Earth.

And sinking into the sea, still warm and friendly and life-giving, is the sun that will soon turn traitor and obliterate all this innocent happiness.

Perhaps if we had not been so far from home and so vulnerable to loneliness, we should not have been so deeply moved. Many of us had seen the ruins of ancient civilizations on other worlds, but they had never affected us so profoundly.

This tragedy was unique. It was one thing for a race to fail and die, as nations and cultures have done on Earth. But to be destroyed so completely in the full flower of its achievement, leaving no survivors—how could that be reconciled with the mercy of God?

My colleagues have asked me that, and I have given what answers I can. Perhaps you could have done better, Father Loyola, but I have found nothing in the *Exercitia spiritualia* that helps me here. They were not an evil people: I do not know what gods they worshiped, if indeed they worshiped any. But I have looked back at them across the centuries, and have watched while the loveliness they used their last strength to preserve was brought forth again into the light of their shrunken sun.

I know the answers that my colleagues will give when they get back to Earth. They will say that the universe has no purpose and no plan, that since a hundred suns explode every year in our galaxy, at this very moment some race is dying in the depths of space. Whether that race has done good or evil during its lifetime will make no difference in the end: there is no divine justice, *for there is no God*.

Yet, of course, what we have seen proves nothing of the sort. Anyone who argues thus is being swayed by emotion, not logic. God has no need to justify His actions to man. He who built the universe can destroy it when He chooses. It is arrogance—it is perilously near blasphemy—for us to say what He may or may not do.

This I could have accepted, hard though it is to look upon whole worlds and peoples thrown into the furnace. But there comes a point when even the deepest faith must falter, and now, as I look at my calculations, I know I have reached that point at last.

We could not tell, before we reached the nebula, how long ago the explosion took place. Now, from the astronomical evidence and the record in the rocks of that one surviving planet, I have been able to date it very exactly. I know in what year the light of this colossal conflagration reached Earth. I know how brilliantly the supernova whose corpse now dwindles behind our speeding ship once shone in terrestrial skies. I know how it must have blazed low in the East before sunrise, like a beacon in that Oriental dawn.

There can be no reasonable doubt: the ancient mystery is solved at last. Yet—O God, there were so many stars you *could* have used.

What was the need to give these people to the fire, that the symbol of their passing might shine above Bethlehem?

4.

OTHER WORLDS AND PEOPLE

"The Crystal Egg" was first published in The New Review *in 1897. Like nearly all Wells's early science fiction stories, this one is a little marvel of compact workmanship and un-obtrusive persuasion.*

Wells, like Verne, knew the value of realism in a fantastic story; and he had the knack of framing the extraordinary in the commonplace. Mr. Cave, the proprietor of the antique shop where the "crystal egg" is found, is as real as a boot; he is dumpily, wheezily, almost offensively real. If there were a Mr. Cave, and a shop like his (and why not?), and if a crystal egg came into it (and where would it be likelier to turn up?), then, you feel instinctively, Cave would respond to it just as he does in these pages—and that is half the battle.

The miraculous thing that happens is not weightily ex-plained, with quotations from authorities, pages of calcula-tions and diagrams lettered a, a', b, b', c and c'. No: it is simply put down in front of you, in its own dusty, absurdly real setting; and the author says, "Look."

THE CRYSTAL EGG

BY H. G. WELLS

There was, until a year ago, a little and very grimy-looking shop near Seven Dials, over which, in weather-worn yellow lettering, the name of "C. Cave, Naturalist and Dealer in Antiquities," was inscribed. The contents of its window were curiously variegated. They comprised some elephant tusks and an imperfect set of chessmen, beads and weapons, a box of eyes, two skulls of tigers and one human, several moth-eaten stuffed monkeys (one holding a lamp), an old-fashioned cabinet, a fly-blown ostrich egg or so, some fishing-tackle, and an extraordinarily dirty, empty glass fish-tank. There was also, at the moment the story begins, a mass of crystal, worked into the shape of an egg and brilliantly polished. And at that two people who stood outside the window were looking, one of them a tall, thin clergyman, the other a black-bearded young man of dusky complexion and unobtrusive costume. The dusky young man spoke with eager gesticulation, and seemed anxious for his companion to purchase the article.

While they were there, Mr. Cave came into his shop, his beard still wagging with the bread and butter of his tea. When he saw these men and the object of their regard, his countenance fell. He glanced guiltily over his shoulder, and softly shut the door. He was a little old man, with pale face and peculiar watery blue eyes; his hair was a dirty grey, and he wore a shabby blue frock-coat, an ancient silk hat, and carpet slippers very much down at heel. He remained watching the two men as they talked. The clergyman went deep into his trouser pocket, examined a handful of money, and showed his teeth in an agreeable smile. Mr. Cave seemed still more depressed when they came into the shop.

The clergyman, without any ceremony, asked the price of the crystal egg. Mr. Cave glanced nerviously towards the door leading into the parlour, and said five pounds. The clergyman protested that the price was high, to his companion as well as to Mr. Cave—it was, indeed, very much more than Mr. Cave had intended to ask when he had stocked the article—and an attempt at bargaining ensued. Mr. Cave stepped to the shop door, and held it open. "Five pounds is my price," he said, as though he wished to save himself the trouble of unprofitable discussion. As he did so, the upper portion of a woman's face appeared above the blind in the glass upper panel of the door leading into the parlour, and started curiously at the two customers. "Five pounds is my price," said Mr. Cave, with a quiver in his voice.

The swarthy young man had so far remained a spectator, watching Cave keenly. Now he spoke. "Give him five pounds," he said. The clergyman glanced at him to see if he were in earnest, and when he looked at Mr. Cave again, he saw that the latter's face was white. "It's a lot of money," said the clergyman, and, diving into his pocket, began counting his resources. He had little more than thirty shillings, and he appealed to his companion, with whom he seemed to be on terms of considerable intimacy. This gave Mr. Cave an opportunity of collecting his thoughts, and he began to explain in an agitated manner that the crystal was not, as a matter of fact, entirely free for sale. His two customers were naturally surprised at this, and inquired why he had not thought of that before he began to bargain. Mr. Cave became confused, but he stuck to his story, that the crystal was not in the market that afternoon, that a probable purchaser of it had already appeared. The two, treating this as an attempt to raise the price still further, made as if they would leave the shop. But at this point the parlour door opened, and the owner of that dark fringe and the little eyes appeared.

She was a coarse-featured, corpulent woman, younger and very much larger than Mr. Cave; she walked heavily, and her face was flushed. "That crystal *is* for sale," she said. "And five pounds is a good enough price for it. I can't think what you're about, Cave, not to take the gentleman's offer!"

Mr. Cave, greatly perturbed by the irruption, looked angrily at her over the rims of his spectacles, and, without excessive assurance, asserted his right to manage his business in his own way. An altercation began. The two customers watched the scene with interest and some amusement, occasionally assisting Mrs. Cave with suggestions. Mr. Cave, hard driven, persisted in a confused and impossible story of an inquiry for the crystal that morning, and his agitation became painful. But he stuck to his point with extraordinary persistence. It was the young Oriental who ended this curious controversy. He proposed that they should call again in the course of two days—so as to give the alleged inquirer a fair chance. "And then we must insist," said the clergyman. "Five pounds." Mrs. Cave took it on herself to apologise for her husband, explaining that he was sometimes "a little odd," and as the two customers left, the couple prepared for a free discussion of the incident in all its bearings.

Mrs. Cave talked to her husband with singular directness. The poor little man, quivering with emotion, muddled himself between his stories, maintaining on the one hand that he had another customer in view, and on the other asserting that the crystal was honestly worth ten guineas. "Why did you ask five pounds?" said his wife. "*Do* let me manage my business my own way!" said Mr. Cave.

Mr. Cave had living with him a step-daughter and a step-son, and at supper that night the transaction was rediscussed. None of them had a high opinion of Mr. Cave's business methods, and this action seemed a culminating folly.

"It's my opinion he's refused that crystal before," said the step-son, a loose-limbed lout of eighteen.

"But *five pounds!*" said the step-daughter, an argumentative young woman of six-and-twenty.

Mr. Cave's answers were wretched; he could only mumble weak assertions that he knew his own business best. They drove him from his half-eaten supper into the shop, to close it for the night, his ears aflame and tears of vexation behind his spectacles. Why had he left the crystal in the window so long? The folly of it! That was the trouble closest in his mind. For a time he could see no way of evading sale.

After supper his step-daughter and step-son smartened themselves up and went out and his wife retired upstairs to reflect upon the business aspects of the crystal, over a little sugar and lemon and so forth in hot water. Mr. Cave went into the shop, and stayed there until late, ostensibly to make ornamental rockeries for gold-fish cases, but really for a private purpose that will be better explained later. The next day Mrs. Cave found that the crystal had been removed from the window, and was lying behind some second-hand books on angling. She replaced it in a conspicuous position. But she did not argue further about it, as a nervous headache disinclined her from debate. Mr. Cave was always disinclined. The day passed disagreeably. Mr. Cave was, if anything, more absent-minded than usual, and uncommonly irritable withal. In the afternoon, when his wife was taking her customary sleep, he removed the crystal from the window again.

The next day Mr. Cave had to deliver a consignment of dog-fish at one of the hospital schools, where they were needed for dissection. In his absence Mrs. Cave's mind reverted to the topic of the crystal, and the methods of expenditure suitable to a windfall of five pounds. She had already devised some very agreeable expedients, among others a dress of green silk for herself and a trip to Richmond, when a jangling of the front door bell summoned her into the shop. The customer was an examination coach who came to complain of the non-delivery of certain frogs asked for the previous day. Mrs. Cave did not approve of this particular branch of Mr. Cave's business, and the gentleman, who had called in a somewhat aggressive mood, retired after a brief exchange of words—entirely civil, so far as he was concerned. Mrs. Cave's eye then naturally turned to the window; for the sight of the crystal was an assurance of the five pounds and of her dreams. What was her surprise to find it gone!

She went to the place behind the locker on the counter, where she had discovered it the day before. It was not there; and she immediately began an eager search about the shop.

When Mr. Cave returned from his business with the dogfish, about a quarter to two in the afternoon, he found the shop in some confusion, and his wife, extremely exasperated and on her knees behind the counter, routing among his taxidermic material. Her face came up hot and angry over the counter, as the jangling bell announced his return, and she forthwith accused him of "hiding it."

"Hid what?" asked Mr. Cave.

"The crystal!"

At that Mr. Cave, apparently much surprised, rushed to the window. "Isn't it here?" he said. "Great Heavens! What has become of it?"

Just then Mr. Cave's step-son re-entered the shop from the inner room—he had come home a minute or so before Mr. Cave—and he was blaspheming freely. He was apprenticed to a second-hand furniture dealer down the road, but he had his meals at home, and he was naturally annoyed to find no dinner ready.

But when he heard of the loss of the crystal, he forgot his meal, and his anger was diverted from his mother to his step-father. Their first idea, of course, was that he had hidden it. But Mr. Cave stoutly denied all knowledge of its fate, freely offering his bedabbled affidavit in the matter—and at last was worked up to the point of accusing first his wife and then his step-son of having taken it with a view to a private sale. So began an exceedingly acrimonious and emotional discussion, which ended for Mrs. Cave in a peculiar nervous condition midway between hysterics and amuck, and caused the step-son to be half-an-hour late at the furniture establishment in the afternoon. Mr. Cave took refuge from his wife's emotions in the shop.

In the evening the matter was resumed, with less passion and in a judicial spirit, under the presidency of the step-daughter. The supper passed unhappily and culminated in a painful scene. Mr. Cave gave way at last to extreme exasperation, and went out banging the front door violently. The rest of the family, having discussed him with the freedom his absence warranted, hunted the house from garret to cellar, hoping to light upon the crystal.

The next day the two customers called again. They were received by Mrs. Cave almost in tears. It transpired that no one *could* imagine all that she had stood from Cave at various times in her married pilgrimage. . . . She also gave a garbled account of the disappearance. The clergyman and the Oriental laughed silently at one another, and said it was very extraordinary. As Mrs. Cave seemed disposed to give them the complete history of her life, they made to leave the shop. Thereupon Mrs. Cave, still clinging to hope, asked for the clergyman's address, so that, if she could get anything out of Cave, she might communicate it. The address was duly given, but apparently was afterwards mislaid. Mrs. Cave can remember nothing about it.

In the evening of that day the Caves seem to have exhausted their emotions, and Mr. Cave, who had been out in the afternoon, supped in a gloomy isolation that contrasted pleasantly with the impassioned controversy of the previous days. For some time matters were very badly strained in the Cave household, but neither crystal nor customer reappeared.

Now, without mincing the matter, we must admit that Mr. Cave was a liar. He knew perfectly well where the crystal was. It was in the rooms of Mr. Jacoby Wace, Assistant Demonstrator at St. Catherine's Hospital, Westbourne Street. It stood on the sideboard partially covered by a black velvet cloth, and beside a decanter of American whiskey. It is from Mr. Wace, indeed, that the particulars upon which this narrative is based were derived. Cave had taken off the thing to the hospital hidden in the dog-fish sack, and there had pressed the young investigator to keep it for him. Mr. Wace was a little dubious at first. His relationship to Cave was peculiar. He had a taste for singular characters, and he had more than once invited the old man to smoke and drink in his rooms, and to unfold his rather amusing views of life in general and of his wife in particular. Mr. Wace had encountered Mrs. Cave, too, on occasions when Mr. Cave was not at home to attend to him. He knew the constant interference to which Cave was subjected, and having weighed the story judicially, he decided to give the crystal a refuge. Mr. Cave promised to explain the reasons for his remarkable affection for the crystal more fully on a later occasion, but he spoke distinctly of seeing visions therein. He called on Mr. Wace the same evening.

He told a complicated story. The crystal, he said, had come into his possession with other oddments at the forced sale of another curiosity dealer's effects, and, not knowing what its value might be, he had ticketed it at ten shillings. It had hung upon his hands at that price for some months, and he was thinking of "reducing the figure," when he made a singular discovery.

At that time his health was very bad—and it must be borne in mind that, throughout all this experience, his physical condition was one of ebb—and he was in considerable distress by reason of the negligence, the positive ill-treatment even, he received from his wife and step-children. His wife was vain, extravagant, unfeeling, and had a growing taste for private drinking; his step-daughter was mean and overreaching; and his step-son had conceived a violent dislike for him, and lost no chance of showing it. The requirements of his business pressed heavily upon him, and Mr. Wace does not think that he was altogether free from occasional intemperance. He had begun life in a comfortable position, he was a man of fair education, and he suffered, for weeks at a stretch, from melancholia and insomnia. Afraid to disturb his family, he would slip quietly from his wife's side, when his thoughts became intolerable, and wander about the house. And about three o'clock one morning, late in August, chance directed him into the shop.

The dirty little place was impenetrably black except in one spot, where he perceived an unusual glow of light. Approaching this, he discovered it to be the crystal egg, which was standing on the corner of the counter towards the window. A thin ray smote through a crack in the shutters, impinged upon the object, and seemed as it were to fill its entire interior.

It occurred to Mr. Cave that this was not in accordance with the laws of optics as he had known them in his younger days. He could understand the rays being refracted by the crystal and coming to a focus in its interior, but this diffusion jarred with his physical conceptions. He approached the crystal nearly, peering into it and round it, with a transient revival of the scientific curiosity that in his youth had determined his choice of a calling. He was surprised to find the light not steady, but writhing within the substance of the egg, as though that object was a hollow sphere of some luminous vapour. In moving about to get different points of view, he suddenly found that he had come between it and the ray, and that the crystal none the less remained luminous. Greatly astonished, he lifted it out of the light ray and carried it to the darkest part of the shop. It remained bright for some four or five minutes, when it slowly faded and went out. He placed it in the thin streak of daylight, and its luminousness was almost immediately restored.

So far, at least, Mr. Wace was able to verify the remarkable story of Mr. Cave. He had himself repeatedly held this crystal in a ray of light (which had to be of a less diameter than one millimetre). And in a perfect darkness, such as could be produced by velvet wrapping, the crystal did undoubtedly appear very faintly phosphorescent. It would seem, however, that the luminousness was of some exceptional sort, and not equally visible to all eyes; for Mr. Harbinger—whose name will be familiar to the scientific reader in connection with the Pasteur Institute—was quite unable to see any light whatever. And Mr. Wace's own capacity for its appreciation was out of comparison inferior to that of Mr. Cave. Even with Mr. Cave the power varied very considerably: his vision was most vivid during states of extreme weakness and fatigue.

Now, from the outset, this light in the crystal exercised a curious fascination upon Mr. Cave. And it says more for his loneliness of soul than a volume of pathetic writing could do, that he told no human being of his curious observations. He seems to have been living in such an atmosphere of petty spite that to admit the existence of a pleasure would have been to risk the loss of it. He found that as the dawn advanced, and the amount of diffused light increased, the crystal became to all appearance non-luminous. And for some time he was unable to see anything in it, except at night-time, in dark corners of the shop.

But the use of an old velvet cloth, which he used as a background for a collection of minerals, occurred to him, and by doubling this, and putting it over his head and hands, he was able to get a sight of the luminous movement within the crystal even in the day-time. He was very cautious lest he should be thus discovered by his wife, and he practised this occupation only in the afternoons, while she was asleep upstairs, and then circumspectly in a hollow under the counter. And one day, turning the crystal about in his hands, he saw something. It came and went like a flash, but it gave him the impression that the object had for a moment opened to him the view of a wide and spacious and strange country; and turning it about, he did, just as the light faded, see the same vision again.

Now, it would be tedious and unnecessary to state all the phases of Mr. Cave's discovery from this point. Suffice that the effect was this: the crystal, being peered into at an angle of about 137 degrees from the direction of the illuminating ray, gave a clear and consistent picture of a wide and peculiar country-side. It was not dreamlike at all: it produced a definite impression of reality, and the better the light the more real and solid it seemed. It was a moving picture: that is to say, certain objects moved in it, but slowly in an orderly manner like real things; and, according as the direction of the lighting and vision changed, the picture changed also. It must, indeed, have been like looking through an oval glass at a view, and turning the glass about to get at different aspects.

Mr. Cave's statements, Mr. Wace assures me, were extremely circumstantial, and entirely free from any of that emotional quality that taints hallucinatory impressions. But it must be remembered that all the efforts of Mr. Wace to see any similar clarity in the faint opalescence of the crystal were wholly unsuccessful, try as he would. The difference in intensity of the impressions received by the two men was very great, and it is quite conceivable that what was a view to Mr. Cave was a mere blurred nebulosity to Mr. Wace.

The view, as Mr. Cave described it, was invariably of an extensive plain, and he seemed always to be looking at it from a considerable height, as if from a tower or a mast. To the east and to the west the plain was bounded at a remote distance by vast reddish cliffs, which reminded him of those he had seen in some picture; but what the picture was Mr. Wace was unable to ascertain. These cliffs passed north and south— he could tell the points of the compass by the stars that were visible of a night—receding in an almost illimitable perspective and fading into the mists of the distance before they met. He was nearer the eastern set of cliffs; on the occasion of his first vision the sun was rising over them, and black against the sunlight and pale against their shadow appeared a multitude of soaring forms that Mr. Cave regarded as birds. A vast range of buildings spread below him; he seemed to be looking down upon them; and as they approached the blurred and refracted edge of the picture they became indistinct. There were also trees curious in shape, and in colouring a deep mossy green and an exquisite grey, beside a wide and shining canal. And something great and brilliantly coloured flew across the picture. But the first time Mr. Cave saw these pictures he saw only in flashes, his hands shook, his head moved, the vision came and went, and grew foggy and indistinct. And at first he had the greatest difficulty in finding the picture again once the direction of it was lost.

His next clear vision, which came about a week after the first, the interval having yielded nothing but tantalising glimpses and some useful experience, showed him the view down the length of the valley. The view was different, but he had a curious persuasion, which his subsequent observations abundantly confirmed, that he was regarding the strange world from exactly the same spot, although he was looking in a different direction. The long façade of the great building, whose roof he had looked down upon before, was now receding in perspective. He recognized the roof. In the front of the façade was a terrace of massive proportions and extraordinary length, and down the middle of the terrace, at certain intervals, stood huge but very graceful masts, bearing small shiny objects which reflected the setting sun. The import of these small objects did not occur to Mr. Cave until some time after, as he was describing the scene to Mr. Wace. The terrace overhung a thicket of the most luxuriant and graceful vegetation, and beyond this was a wide grassy lawn on which certain broad creatures, in form like beetles but enormously larger, reposed. Beyond this again was a richly decorated causeway of pinkish stone; and beyond that, and lined with dense red weeds, and passing up the valley exactly parallel with the distant cliffs, was a broad and mirror-like expanse of water. The air seemed full of squadrons of great birds, manoeuvring in stately curves; and across the river was a multitude of splendid buildings, richly coloured and glittering with metallic tracery and facets, among a forest of moss-like and lichenous trees. And suddenly something flapped repeatedly across the vision, like the fluttering of a jewelled fan or the beating of a wing, and a face, or rather the upper part of a face with very large eyes, came as it were close to his own and as if on the other side of the crystal. Mr. Cave was so startled and so impressed by the absolute reality of these eyes that he drew his head back from the crystal to look behind it. He had become so absorbed in watching that he was quite surprised to find himself in the cool darkness of his little shop, with its familiar odour of methyl, mustiness, and decay. And as he blinked about him, the glowing crystal faded and went out.

Such were the first general impressions of Mr. Cave. The story is curiously direct and circumstantial. From the outset, when the valley first flashed momentarily on his senses, his imagination was strangely affected, and as he began to appreciate the details of the scene he saw, his wonder rose to the point of a passion. He went about his business listless and distraught, thinking only of the time when he should be able to return to his watching. And then a few weeks after his first sight of the valley came the two customers, the stress and excitement of their offer, and the narrow escape of the crystal from sale, as I have already told.

Now, while the thing was Mr. Cave's secret, it remained a mere wonder, a thing to creep to covertly and peep at, as a child might peep upon a forbidden garden. But Mr. Wace has, for a young scientific investigator, a particularly lucid and consecutive habit of mind. Directly the crystal and its story came to him, and he had satisfied himself, by seeing the phosphorescence with his own eyes, that there really was a certain evidence for Mr. Cave's statements, he proceeded to develop the matter systematically. Mr. Cave was only too eager to come and feast his eyes on this wonderland he saw, and he came every night from half-past eight until half-past ten, and sometimes, in Mr. Wace's absence, during the day. On Sunday afternoons, also, he came. From the outset Mr.

Wace made copious notes, and it was due to his scientific method that the relation between the direction from which the initiating ray entered the crystal and the orientation of the picture was proved. And, by covering the crystal in a box perforated only with a small aperture to admit the exciting ray, and by substituting black holland for his buff blinds, he greatly improved the conditions of the observations; so that in a little while they were able to survey the valley in any direction they desired.

So having cleared the way, we may give a brief account of this visionary world within the crystal. The things were in all cases seen by Mr. Cave, and the method of working was invariably for him to watch the crystal and report what he saw, while Mr. Wace (who as a science student had learnt the trick of writing in the dark) wrote a brief note of his report. When the crystal faded, it was put into its box in the proper position and the electric light turned on. Mr. Wace asked questions, and suggested observations to clear up difficult points. Nothing, indeed, could have been less visionary and more matter-of-fact.

The attention of Mr. Cave had been speedily directed to the bird-like creatures he had seen so abundantly present in each of his earlier visions. His first impression was soon corrected, and he considered for a time that they might represent a diurnal species of bat. Then he thought, grotesquely enough, that they might be cherubs. Their heads were round and curiously human, and it was the eyes of one of them that had so startled him on his second observation. They had broad, silvery wings, not feathered, but glistening almost as brilliantly as new-killed fish and with the same subtle play of colour, and these wings were not built on the plan of bird-wing or bat, Mr. Wace learned, but supported by curved ribs radiating from the body. (A sort of butterfly wing with curved ribs seems best to express their appearance.) The body was small, but fitted with two bunches of prehensile organs, like long tentacles, immediately under the mouth. Incredible as it appeared to Mr. Wace, the persuasion at last became irresistible that it was these creatures which owned the great quasi-human buildings and the magnificent garden that made the broad valley so splendid. And Mr. Cave perceived that the buildings, with other peculiarities, had no doors, but that the great circular windows, which opened freely, gave the creatures egress and entrance. They would alight upon their tentacles, fold their wings to a smallness almost rod-like, and hop into the interior. But among them was a multitude of smaller-winged creatures, like great dragon-flies and moths and flying beetles, and across the greensward brilliantly coloured gigantic ground-beetles crawled lazily to and fro. Moreover, on the causeways and terraces, large-headed creatures similar to the greater winged flies, but wingless, were visible, hopping busily upon their hand-like tangle of tentacles.

Allusion has already been made to the glittering objects upon masts that stood upon the terrace of the nearer building. It dawned upon Mr. Cave, after regarding one of these masts very fixedly on one particularly vivid day, that the glittering object there was a crystal exactly like that into which he peered. And a still more careful scrutiny convinced him that each one in a vista of nearly twenty carried a similar object.

Occasionally one of the large flying creatures would flutter up to one and, folding its wings and coiling a number of its tentacles about the mast, would regard the crystal fixedly for a space—sometimes for as long as fifteen minutes. And a series of observations, made at the suggestion of Mr. Wace, convinced both watchers that, so far as this visionary world was concerned, the crystal into which they peered actually stood at the summit of the endmost mast on the terrace, and that on one occasion at least one of these inhabitants of this other world had looked into Mr. Cave's face while he was making these observations.

So much for the essential facts of this very singular story. Unless we dismiss it all as the ingenious fabrication of Mr. Wace, we have to believe one of two things: either that Mr. Cave's crystal was in two worlds at once, and that while it was carried about in one it remained stationary in the other, which seems altogether absurd, or else that it had some peculiar relation of sympathy with another and exactly similar crystal in this other world, so that what was seen in the interior of the one in this world was, under suitable conditions, visible to an observer in the corresponding crystal in the other world, and vice versa. At present, indeed, we do not know of any way in which two crystals could so come *en rapport*, but nowadays we know enough to understand that the thing is not altogether impossible. This view of the crystals as *en rapport* was the supposition that occurred to Mr. Wace, and to me at least it seems extremely plausible. . . .

And where was this other world? On this, also, the alert intelligence of Mr. Wace speedily threw light. After sunset, the sky darkened rapidly—there was a very brief twilight interval indeed—and the stars shone out. They were recognizably the same as those we see, arranged in the same constellations. Mr. Cave recognized the Bear, the Pleiades, Aldebaran, and Sirius; so that the other world must be somewhere in the solar system, and, at the utmost, only a few hundreds of millions of miles from our own. Following up this clue, Mr. Wace learnt that the midnight sky was a darker blue even than our midwinter sky, and that the sun seemed a little smaller. *And there were two small moons*, "like our moon but smaller, and quite differently marked," one of which moved so rapidly that its motion was clearly visible as one regarded it. These moons were never high in the sky, but vanished as they rose: that is, every time they revolved they were eclipsed because they were so near their primary planet. And all this answers quite completely, although Mr. Cave did not know it, to what must be the condition of things on Mars.

Indeed, it seems an exceedingly plausible conclusion that, peering into this crystal, Mr. Cave did actually see the planet Mars and its inhabitants. And if that be the case, then the evening star that shone so brilliantly in the sky of that distant vision was neither more nor less than our own familiar Earth.

For a time the Martians—if they were Martians—do not seem to have known of Mr. Cave's inspection. Once or twice one would come to peer, and go away very shortly to some other mast, as though the vision was unsatisfactory. During this time Mr. Cave was able to watch the proceedings of these winged people without being disturbed by their attentions, and although his report is necessarily vague and fragmentary, it is nevertheless very suggestive. Imagine the impression of humanity a Martian observer would get who, after a difficult process of preparation and with considerable fatigue to the eyes, was able to peer at London from the steeple of St. Martin's Church for stretches, at longest, of four minutes at a time. Mr. Cave was unable to ascertain if the winged Martians were the same as the Martians who hopped about the causeways and terraces, and if the latter could put on wings at will. He several times saw certain clumsy bipeds, dimly suggestive of apes, white and partially translucent, feeding among certain of the lichenous trees, and once some of these fled before one of the hopping, round-headed Martians. The latter caught one in its tentacles, and then the picture faded suddenly and left Mr. Cave most tantalisingly in the dark. On another occasion a vast thing, that Mr. Cave thought at first was some gigantic insect, appeared advancing along the causeway beside the canal with extraordinary rapidity. As this drew nearer Mr. Cave perceived that it was a mechanism of shining metals and of extraordinary complexity. And then, when he looked again, it had passed out of sight.

After a time Mr. Wace aspired to attract the attention of the Martians, and the next time that the strange eyes of one of them appeared close to the crystal Mr. Cave cried out and sprang away, and they immediately turned on the light and began to gesticulate in a manner suggestive of signalling. But when at last Mr. Cave examined the crystal again the Martian had departed.

Thus far these observations had progressed in early November, and then Mr. Cave, feeling that the suspicions of his family about the crystal were allayed, began to take it to and fro with him in order that, as occasion arose in the daytime or night, he might comfort himself with what was fast becoming the most real thing in his existence.

In December Mr. Wace's work in connection with a forthcoming examination became heavy, the sittings were reluctantly suspended for a week, and for ten or eleven days—he is not quite sure which—he saw nothing of Cave. He then grew anxious to resume these investigations, and, the stress of his seasonal labours being abated, he went down to Seven Dials. At the corner he noticed a shutter before a bird fancier's window, and then another at a cobbler's. Mr. Cave's shop was closed.

He rapped and the door was opened by the step-son in black. He at once called Mrs. Cave, who was, Mr. Wace could not but observe, in cheap but ample widow's weeds of the most imposing pattern. Without any very great surprise Mr. Wace learnt that Cave was dead and already buried. She was in tears, and her voice was a little thick. She had just returned from Highgate. Her mind seemed occupied with her own prospects and the honourable details of the obsequies, but Mr. Wace was at last able to learn the particulars of Cave's death. He had been found dead in his shop in the early morning, the day after his last visit to Mr. Wace, and the crystal had been clasped in his stone-cold hands. His face was smiling, said Mrs. Cave, and the velvet cloth from the minerals lay on the floor at his feet. He must have been dead five or six hours when he was found.

This came as a great shock to Wace, and he began to reproach himself bitterly for having neglected the plain symptoms of the old man's ill-health. But his chief thought was of the crystal. He approached that topic in a gingerly manner, because he knew Mrs. Cave's peculiarities. He was dumfounded to learn that it was sold.

Mrs. Cave's first impulse, directly Cave's body had been taken upstairs, had been to write to the mad clergyman who had offered five pounds for the crystal, informing him of its recovery; but after a violent hunt, in which her daughter joined her, they were convinced of the loss of his address. As they were without the means required to mourn and bury Cave in the elaborate style the dignity of an old Seven Dials inhabitant demands, they had appealed to a friendly fellow-tradesman in Great Portland Street. He had very kindly taken over a portion of the stock at a valuation. The valuation was his own, and the crystal egg was included in one of the lots. Mr. Wace, after a few suitable condolences, a little off-handedly proffered perhaps, hurried at once to Great Portland Street. But there he learnt that the crystal egg had already been sold to a tall, dark man in grey. And there the material facts in this curious, and to me at least very suggestive, story come abruptly to an end. The Great Portland Street dealer did not know who the tall dark man in grey was, nor had he observed him with sufficient attention to describe him minutely. He did not even know which way this person had gone after leaving the shop. For a time Mr. Wace remained in the shop, trying the dealer's patience with hopeless questions, venting his own exasperation. And at last, realising abruptly that the whole thing had passed out of his hands, had vanished like a vision of the night, he returned to his own rooms, a little astonished to find the notes he had made still tangible and visible upon his untidy table.

His annoyance and disappointment were naturally very great. He made a second call (equally ineffectual) upon the

Great Portland Street dealer, and he resorted to advertisements in such periodicals as were likely to come into the hands of a bric-a-brac collector. He also wrote letters to *The Daily Chronicle* and *Nature,* but both those periodicals, suspecting a hoax, asked him to reconsider his action before they printed, and he was advised that such a strange story, unfortunately so bare of supporting evidence, might imperil his reputation as an investigator. Moreover, the calls of his proper work were urgent. So that after a month or so, save for an occasional reminder to certain dealers, he had reluctantly to abandon the quest for the crystal egg, and from that day to this it remains undiscovered. Occasionally, however, he tells me, and I can quite believe him, he has bursts of zeal, in which he abandons his more urgent occupation and resumes the search.

Whether or not it will remain lost for ever, with the material and origin of it, are things equally speculative at the present time. If the present purchaser is a collector, one would have expected the enquiries of Mr. Wace to have reached him through the dealers. He has been able to discover Mr. Cave's clergyman and "Oriental"—no other than the Reverend James Parker and the young Prince of Bosso-Kuni in Java. I am obliged to them for certain particulars. The object of the Prince was simply curiosity—and extravagance. He was so eager to buy because Cave was so oddly reluctant to sell. It is just as possible that the buyer in the second instance was simply a casual purchaser and not a collector at all, and the crystal egg, for all I know, may at the present moment be within a mile of me, decorating a drawing-room or serving as a paper-weight—its remarkable functions all unknown. Indeed, it is partly with the idea of such a possibility that I have thrown this narrative into a form that will give it a chance of being read by the ordinary consumer of fiction.

My own ideas in the matter are practically identical with those of Mr. Wace. I believe the crystal on the mast in Mars and the crystal egg of Mr. Cave's to be in some physical, but at present quite inexplicable, way *en rapport,* and we both believe further that the terrestrial crystal must have been—possibly at some remote date—sent hither from that planet, in order to give the Martians a near view of our affairs. Possibly the fellows to the crystals on the other masts are also on our globe. No theory of hallucination suffices for the facts.

Like Kornbluth, Pohl, Tucker, Asimov and a few others, Marion Zimmer Bradley came up from the ranks. She was a science fiction fan, then a letter hack (in the days when s.f. magazines had flourishing letter departments); then she became a professional writer. Her work is distinctively feminine in tone, but lacks the clichés, overemphasis and other kittenish tricks which often make female fiction unreadable by males.

Whether this story is fantasy or science fiction depends, in a sense, on how you interpret it: the author has made it possible to read it either way. For me, it is science fiction; and the key to it is in this evocative phrase: "Nights when she lay wakeful, sweating with terror while the winds rose and fell again and her imagination gave them voices . . ."

The story first appeared in If, *February 1959.*

THE WIND PEOPLE

BY MARION ZIMMER BRADLEY

It had been a long layover for the *Starholm's* crew, hunting heavy elements for fuel—eight months, on an idyllic green paradise of a planet; a soft, windy, whispering world, inhabited only by trees and winds. But in the end it presented its own unique problem.

Specifically, it presented Captain Merrihew with the problem of Robin, male, father unknown, who had been born the day before, and a month prematurely, to Dr. Helen Murray.

Merrihew found her lying abed in the laboratory shelter, pale and calm, with the child beside her.

The little shelter, constructed roughly of green planks, looked out on the clearing which the *Starholm* had used as a base of operations during the layover; a beautiful place at the bottom of a wide valley, in the curve of a broad, deep-flowing river. The crew, tired of being shipbound, had built half a dozen such huts and shacks in these eight months.

Merrihew glared down at Helen. He snorted, "This is a fine situation. You, of all the people in the whole damned crew—the ship's doctor! It's—it's—" Inarticulate with rage, he fell back on a ridiculously inadequate phrase. "It's—criminal carelessness!"

"I know." Helen Murray, too young and far too lovely for a ship's officer on a ten-year cruise, still looked weak and white, and her voice was a gentle shadow of its crisp self. "I'm afraid four years in space made me careless."

Merrihew brooded, looking down at her. Something about ship-gravity conditions, while not affecting potency, made conception impossible; no child had ever been conceived in space and none ever would. On planet layovers, the effect wore off very slowly; only after three months aground had Dr. Murray started routine administration of anticeptin to the twenty-two women of the crew, herself included. At that time she had been still unaware that she herself was already carrying a child.

Outside, the leafy forest whispered and rustled, and Merrihew knew Helen had forgotten his existence again. The day-old child was tucked up in one of her rolled coveralls at her side. To Merrihew, he looked like a skinned monkey, but Helen's eyes smoldered as her hands moved gently over the tiny round head.

He stood and listened to the winds and said at random, "These shacks will fall to pieces in another month. It doesn't matter, we'll have taken off by then."

Dr. Chao Lin came into the shack, an angular woman of thirty-five. She said, "Company, Helen? Well, it's about time. Here, let me take Robin."

Helen said in weak protest, "You're spoiling me, Lin."

"It will do you good," Chao Lin returned. Merrihew, in a sudden surge of fury and frustration, exploded, "Damn it, Lin, you're making it all worse. He'll die when we go into overdrive, you know as well as I do!"

Helen sat up, clutching Robin protectively. "Are you proposing to drown him like a kitten?"

"Helen, I'm not proposing anything. I'm stating a fact."

"But it's not a fact. He won't die in overdrive because he won't be aboard when we go into overdrive!"

Merrihew looked at Lin helplessly, but his face softened. "Shall we—put him to sleep and bury him here?"

The woman's face turned white. "No!" she cried in passionate protest, and Lin bent to disengage her frantic grip.

"Helen, you'll hurt him. Put him down. There."

Merrihew looked down at her, troubled, and said, "We can't just abandon him to die slowly, Helen—"

"Who says I'm going to abandon him?"

Merrihew asked slowly, "Are you planning to desert?" He added, after a minute, "There's a chance he'll survive. After all, his very birth was against all medical precedent. Maybe—"

"Captain—" Helen sounded desperate—"even drugged, no child under ten has ever endured the shift into hyperspace drive. A newborn would die in seconds." She clasped Robin to her again and said, "It's the only way—you have Lin for a doctor, Reynolds can handle my collateral duties. This planet is uninhabited, the climate is mild, we couldn't possibly starve." Her face, so gentle, was suddenly like rock. "Enter my death in the log, if you want to."

Merrihew looked from Helen to Lin, and said, "Helen, you're insane!"

She said, "Even if I'm sane now, I wouldn't be long if I had to abandon Robin." The wild note had died out of her voice, and she spoke rationally, but inflexibly. "Captain Merrihew, to get me aboard the *Starholm,* you will have to have me drugged or taken by force; I promise you I won't go any other way. And if you do that—and if Robin is left behind, or dies in overdrive, just so you will have my services as a doctor—then I solemnly swear that I will kill myself at the first opportunity."

"My God," said Merrihew, "you *are* insane!"

Helen gave a very tiny shrug. "Do you want a madwoman aboard?"

Chao Lin said quietly, "Captain, I don't see any other way. We would have had to arrange it that way if Helen had actually died in childbirth. Of two unsatisfactory solutions, we must choose the less harmful." And Merrihew knew that he had no real choice.

"I still think you're both crazy," he blustered, but it was surrender, and Helen knew it.

Ten days after the *Starholm* took off, young Colin Reynolds, technician, committed suicide by the messy procedure of slicing his jugular vein, which—in zero gravity—distributed several quarts of blood in big round globules all over his cabin. He left an incoherent note.

Merrihew put the note in the disposal and Chao Lin put the blood in the ship's blood bank for surgery, and they hushed it up as an accident; but Merrihew had the unpleasant feeling that the layover on the green and windy planet was going to become a legend, spread in whispers by the crew. And it did, but that is another story.

Robin was two years old when he first heard the voices in the wind. He pulled at his mother's arm and crooned softly, in imitation.

"What is it, lovey?"

"Pretty." He crooned again to the distant murmuring sound.

Helen smiled vaguely and patted the round cheek. Robin, his infant imagination suddenly distracted, said, "Hungry. Robin hungry. Berries."

"Berries after you eat," Helen promised absently, and picked him up. Robin tugged at her arm.

"Mommy pretty, too!"

She laughed, a rosy and smiling young Diana. She was happy on the solitary planet; they lived quite comfortably in one of the larger shacks, and only a little frown line between her eyes bore witness to the terror which had closed down on her in the first months, when every new day had been some new struggle—against weakness, against unfamiliar sounds, against loneliness and dread. Nights when she lay wakeful, sweating with terror while the winds rose and fell again and her imagination gave them voices, bleak days when she wandered dazedly around the shack or stared moodily at Robin. There had been moments—only fleeting, and penanced with hours of shame and regret—when she thought that even the horror of losing Robin in those first days would have been less than the horror of spending the rest of her life alone here, when she had wondered why Merrihew had not realized that she was unbalanced, and forced her to go with them; by now, Robin would have been only a moment's painful memory.

Still not strong, knowing she had to be strong for Robin or he would die as surely as if she had abandoned him, she had spent the first months in a somnambulistic dream. Sometimes she had walked for days at a time in that dream; she would wake to find food that she could not remember gathering. Somehow, pervasive, the dream voices had taken over; the whispering winds had been full of voices and even hands.

She had fallen ill and lain for days sick and delirious, and had heard a voice which hardly seemed to be her own, saying that if she died the wind voices would care for Robin . . . and then the shock and irrationality of that had startled her out of delirium, agonized and trembling, and she pulled herself upright and cried out, "No!"

And the shimmer of eyes and voices had faded again into vague echoes, until there was only the stir of sunlight on the leaves, and Robin, chubby and naked, kicking in the sunlight, cooing with his hands outstretched to the rustle of leaves and shadows.

She had known, then, that she had to get well. She had never heard the wind voices again, and her crisp, scientific mind rejected the fanciful theory that if she only believed in the wind voices she would see their forms and hear their words clearly. And she rejected them so thoroughly that when she heard them speak she shut them away from her mind, and after a time heard them no longer, except in restless dreams.

By now she had accepted the isolation and the beauty of their world, and begun to make a happy life for Robin.

For lack of other occupation last summer—though the winter was mild and there was no lack of fruits and roots even then—Helen had patiently snared male and female of small animals like rabbits, and now she had a pen of them. They provided a change of diet, and after a few smelly unsuccessful experiments she had devised a way to supple their fur pelts. She made no effort at gardening, though when Robin was older she might try that. For the moment, it was enough that they were healthy and safe and protected.

Robin was *listening* again. Helen bent her ear, sharpened by the silence, but heard only the rustle of wind and leaves; saw only falling brightness along a silvered tree-trunk.

Wind? When there were no branches stirring?

"Ridiculous," she said sharply, then snatched up the baby boy and squeezed him before hoisting him astride her hip. "Mommy doesn't mean *you*, Robin. Let's look for berries."

But soon she realized that his head was tipped back and that he was listening, again, to some sound she could not hear.

On what she said was Robin's fifth birthday, Helen had made a special bed for him in another room of the building.

He missed the warmth of Helen's body, and the comforting sound of her breathing; for Robin, since birth, had been a wakeful child.

Yet, on the first night alone, Robin felt curiously freed. He did something he had never dared do before, for fear of waking Helen; he slipped from his bed and stood in the doorway, looking into the forest.

The forest was closer to the doorway now; Robin could fuzzily remember when the clearing had been wider. Now, slowly, beyond the garden patch which Helen kept cleared, the underbrush and saplings were growing back, and even what Robin called "the burned place" was covered with new sparse grass.

Robin was accustomed to being alone, during the day— even in his first year, Helen had had to leave him alone, securely fastened in the house, or inside a little tight-fenced yard. But he was not used to being alone at night.

Far off in the forest, he could hear the whispers of the other people. Helen said there were no other people, but Robin knew better, because he could hear their voices on the wind, like fragments of the songs Helen sang at bedtime. And sometimes he could almost see them in the shadowy spots.

Once when Helen had been sick, a long time ago, and Robin had run helplessly from the fenced yard to the inside room and back again, hungry and dirty and furious because Helen only slept on the bed with her eyes closed, rousing up now and then to whimper like he did when he fell down and skinned his knee, the winds and voices had come into the very house; Robin had hazy memories of soothing voices, of hands that touched him more softly than Helen's hands. But he could not quite remember.

Now that he could hear them so clearly, he would go and find the other people. And then if Helen was sick again, there would be someone else to play with him and look after him. He thought gleefully, *Won't Helen be surprised?* and darted off across the clearing.

Helen woke, roused not by a sound but by a silence. She no longer heard Robin's soft breaths from the alcove, and after a moment she realized something else:

The winds were silent.

Perhaps, she thought, a storm was coming. Some change in

air pressure could cause this stillness—but Robin? She tip-toed to the alcove; as she had suspected, his bed was empty.

Where could he be? In the clearing? With a storm coming? She slid her feet into handmade sandals and ran outside, her quivering call ringing out through the silent forest:

"Robin—oh, Robin!"

Silence. And far away a little ominous whisper. And for the first time since that first frightening year of loneliness, she felt lost, deserted in an alien world. She ran across the clearing, looking around wildly, trying to decide which way he could have wandered. Into the forest? What if he had strayed toward the riverbank? There was a place where the bank crumbled away, down toward the rapids—her throat closed convulsively, and her call was almost a shriek:

"Oh, Robin! Robin, darling! Robin!"

She ran through the paths worn by their feet, hearing snatches of rustle, winds and leaves suddenly vocal in the cold moonlight around her. It was the first time since the spaceship left them that Helen had ventured out into the night of their world. She called again, her voice cracking in panic.

"Ro-bin!"

A sudden stray gleam revealed a glint of white, and a child stood in the middle of the path. Helen gasped with relief and ran to snatch up her son—then fell back in dismay. It was not Robin who stood there. The child was naked, about a head shorter than Robin, and female.

There was something curious about the bare and gleaming flesh, as if she could see the child only in the full flush of the moonlight. A round, almost expressionless face was surrounded by a mass of colorless streaming hair, the exact color of the moonlight. Helen's audible gasp startled her to a stop: she shut here eyes convulsively, and when she opened them the path was black and empty and Robin was running down the track toward her.

Helen caught him up, with a strangled cry, and ran, clasping him to her breast, back down the path to their shack. Inside, she barred the door and laid Robin down in her own bed, and threw herself down shivering, too shaken to speak, too shaken to scold him, curiously afraid to question. I had a hallucination, she told herself, a hallucination, another dream, a dream. . . .

A dream, like the other Dream. She dignified it to herself as The Dream, because it was not like any other dream she had ever had. She had dreamed it first before Robin's birth, and been ashamed to speak of it to Chao Lin, fearing the common-sense skepticism of the older woman.

On their tenth night on the green planet (the *Starholm* was a dim recollection now), when Merrihew's scientists had been convinced that the little world was safe, without wild beasts or diseases or savage natives, the crew had requested permission to camp in the valley clearing beside the river. Permission granted, they had gone apart in couples almost as usual, and even those who had no enduring liaison at the moment had found a partner for the night.

It must have been that night. . . .

Colin Reynolds was two years younger than Helen, and their attachment, enduring over a few months of shiptime, was based less on mutual passion than a sort of boyish need in him, a sort of impersonal feminine solicitude in Helen. All her affairs had been like that, companionable, comfortable, but never passionate. Curiously enough, Helen was a woman capable of passion, of great depths of devotion; but no man had ever roused it and now no man ever would. Only Robin's birth had touched her deeply pent emotions.

But that night, when Colin Reynolds was sleeping, Helen stayed restlessly awake, hearing the unquiet stirring of wind on the leaves. After a time she wandered down to the water's edge, staying a cautious distance from the shore—for the cliff crumbled dangerously—and stretched herself out to listen to the wind-voices. And after a time she fell asleep, and had The Dream, which was to return to her again and again.

Helen thought of herself as a scientist, without room for fantasies, and that was why she called it, fiercely, a dream; a dream born of some undiagnosed conflict in her. Even to herself Helen would not recall it in full.

There had been a man, and to her it seemed that he was part of the green and windy world, and he had found her sleeping by the river. Even in her drowsy state, Helen had suspected that perhaps one of the other crew members, like herself sleepless and drawn to the shining water, had happened upon her there; such things were not impossible, manners and mores being what they were among starship crews.

But to her, half dreaming, there had been some strangeness about him, which prevented her from seeing him too clearly even in the brilliant green moonlight. No dream and no man had ever seemed so living to her; and it was her fierce rationalization of the dream which kept her silent, months later, when she discovered (to her horror and secret despair) that she was with child. She had felt that she would lose the haze and secret delight of the dream if she openly acknowledged that Colin had fathered her child.

But at first—in the cool green morning that followed—she had not been at all sure it was a dream. Seeing only sunlight and leaves, she had held back from speaking, not wanting ridicule; could she have asked each man of the *Starholm,* "Was it you who came to me last night? Because if it was not, there are other men on this world, men who cannot be clearly seen even by moonlight."

Severely she reminded herself, Merrihew's men had pronounced the world uninhabited, and uninhabited it must be. Five years later, hugging her sleeping son close, Helen remembered the dream, examined the content of her fantasy, and once again, shivering, repeated, "I had a hallucination. It was only a dream. A dream, because I was alone. . . ."

When Robin was fourteen years old, Helen told him the story of his birth, and of the ship.

He was a tall, silent boy, strong and hardy but not talkative; he heard the story almost in silence, and looked at Helen for a long time in silence afterward. He finally said in a whisper, "You could have died—you gave up a lot for me, Helen, didn't you?" He knelt and took her face in his hands. She smiled and drew a little away from him.

"Why are you looking at me like that, Robin?"

The boy could not put instant words to his thoughts; emotions were not in his vocabulary. Helen had taught him everything she knew, but she had always concealed her feelings from her son. He asked at last, "Why didn't my father stay with you?"

"I don't suppose it entered his head," Helen said. "He was needed on the ship. Losing me was bad enough."

Robin said passionately, "I'd have stayed!"

The woman found herself laughing. "Well—you did stay, Robin."

He asked, "Am I like my father?"

Helen looked gravely at her son, trying to see the half-forgotten features of young Reynolds in the boy's face. No,

Robin did not look like Colin Reynolds, nor like Helen herself. She picked up his hand in hers; despite his robust health, Robin never tanned; his skin was pearly pale, so that in the green sunlight it blended into the forest almost invisibly. His hand lay in Helen's palm like a shadow. She said at last, "No, nothing like him. But under this sun, that's to be expected."

Robin said confidently, "I'm like the *other* people."

"The ones on the ship? They—"

"No," Robin interrupted, "you always said when I was older you'd tell me about the other people. I mean the other people *here*. The ones in the woods. The ones you can't see."

Helen stared at the boy in blank disbelief. "What do you mean? There are no other people, just us." Then she recalled that every imaginative child invents playmates. *Alone,* she thought, *Robin's always alone, no other children, no wonder he's a little—strange.* She said, quietly, "You dreamed it, Robin."

The boy only stared at her, in bleak, blank alienation. "You mean," he said, "you can't *hear* them, either?" He got up and walked out of the hut. Helen called, but he didn't turn back. She ran after him, catching at his arm, stopping him almost by force. She whispered, "Robin, Robin, tell me what you mean! There isn't anyone here. Once or twice I thought I had seen—something, by moonlight, only it was a dream. Please, Robin—please—"

"If it's only a dream, why are you frightened?" Robin asked, through a curious constriction in his throat. "If they've never hurt you . . ."

No, they had never hurt her. Even if, in her long-ago dream, one of them had come to her. *And the sons of God saw the daughters of men that they were fair*—a scrap of memory from a vanished life on another world sang in Helen's thoughts. She looked up at the pale, impatient face of her son, and swallowed hard.

Her voice was husky when she spoke.

"Did I ever tell you about rationalization—when you want something to be true so much that you can make it sound right to yourself?"

"Couldn't that also happen to something you wanted *not* to be true?" Robin retorted with a mutinous curl of his mouth.

Helen would not let go his arm. She begged, "Robin, no,

you'll only waste your life and break your heart looking for something that doesn't exist."

The boy looked down into her shaken face, and suddenly a new emotion welled up in him and he dropped to his knees beside her and buried his face against her breast. He whispered, "Helen, I'll never leave you, I'll never do anything you don't want me to do, I don't want anyone but you."

And for the first time in many years, Helen broke into wild and uncontrollable crying, without knowing why she wept.

Robin did not speak again of his quest in the forest. For many months he was quiet and subdued, staying near the clearing, hovering near Helen for days at a time, then disappearing into the forest at dusk. He heard the winds numbly, deaf to their promise and their call.

Helen too was quiet and withdrawn, feeling Robin's alienation through his submissive mood. She found herself speaking to him sharply for being always underfoot; yet, on the rare days when he vanished into the forest and did not return until after sunset, she felt a restless unease that set her wandering the paths herself, not following him, but simply uneasy unless she knew he was within call.

Once, in the shadows just before sunset, she thought she saw a man moving through the trees, and for an instant, as he turned toward her, she saw that he was naked. She had seen him only for a second or two, and after he had slipped between the shadows again common sense told her it was Robin. She was vaguely shocked and annoyed; she firmly intended to speak to him, perhaps to scold him for running about naked and slipping away like that; then, in a sort of remote embarrassment, she forbore to mention it. But after that, she kept out of the forest.

Robin had been vaguely aware of her surveillance and knew when it ceased. But he did not give up his own pointless rambles, although even to himself he no longer spoke of searching, or of any dreamlike inhabitants of the woods. At times it still seemed that some shadow concealed a half-seen form, and the distant murmur grew into a voice that mocked him; a white arm, the shadow of a face, until he lifted his head and stared straight at it.

One evening toward twilight he saw a sudden shimmer in the trees, and he stood, fixedly, as the stray glint resolved itself first into a white face with shadowy eyes, then into a translucent flicker of bare arms, and then into the form of a woman, arrested for an instant with her hand on the bole of a tree. In the shadowy spot, filled only with the last ray of a cloudy sunset, she was very clear; not cloudy or unreal, but so distinct that he could see even a small smudge or bramble scratch on her shoulder, and a fallen leaf tangled in her colorless hair. Robin, paralyzed, watched her pause, and turn, and smile, and then she melted into the shadows.

He stood with his heart pounding for a second after she had gone then whirled, bursting with the excitement of his discovery, and ran down the path toward home. Suddenly he stopped short, the world tilting and reeling, and fell on his face in a bed of dry leaves.

He was still ignorant of the nature of the emotion in him. He felt only intolerable misery and the conviction that he must never speak to Helen of what he had seen or felt.

He lay there, his burning face pressed into the leaves, unaware of the rising wind, the little flurry of blown leaves, the growing darkness and distant thunder. At last an icy spatter of rain aroused him, and cold, numbed, he made his way slowly homeward. Over his head the boughs creaked woodenly, and Robin, under the driving whips of the rain, felt their tumult only echoed his own voiceless agony.

He was drenched by the time he pushed the door of the shack open and stumbled blindly toward the fire, only hoping that Helen would be sleeping. But she started up from beside the hearth they had built together last summer.

"Robin?"

Deathly weary, the boy snapped, "Who *else* would it be?"

Helen didn't answer. She came to him, a small swift-moving figure in the firelight, and drew him into the warmth. She said, almost humbly, "I was afraid—the storm—Robin, you're all wet, come to the fire and dry out."

Robin yielded, his twitching nerves partly soothed by her voice. *How tiny Helen is,* he thought, *and I can remember that she used to carry me around on one arm; now she hardly comes to my shoulder.* She brought him food and he ate wolfishly, listening to the steady pouring rain, uncomfortable under Helen's watching eyes. Before his own eyes there was the clear memory of the woman in the wood, and so vivid was Robin's imagination, heightened by loneliness and un-diluted by any random impressions, that it seemed to him

Helen must see her too. And when she came to stand beside him, the picture grew so keen in his thoughts that he actually pulled himself free of her.

The next day dawned gray and still, beaten with long needles of rain. They stayed indoors by the smoldering fire; Robin, half sick and feverish from his drenching, sprawled by the hearth too indolent to move, watching Helen's comings and goings about the room; not realizing why the sight of her slight, quick form against the gray light filled him with such pain and melancholy.

The storm lasted four days. Helen exhausted her household tasks and sat restlessly thumbing through the few books she knew by heart—they had allowed her to remove all her personal possessions, all the things she had chosen on a forgotten and faraway Earth for a ten-year star cruise. For the first time in years, Helen was thinking again of the life, the civilization she had thrown away, for Robin who had been a pink scrap in the circle of her arm and now lay sullen on the hearth, not speaking, aimlessly whittling a stick with the knife (found discarded in a heap of rubbish from the *Starholm*) which was his dearest possession. Helen felt slow horror closing in on her. *What world, what heritage did I give him, in my madness? This world has driven us both insane. Robin and I are both a little mad, by Earth's standards. And when I die, and I will die first, what then?* At that moment Helen would have given her life to believe in his old dream of strange people in the wood.

She flung her book restlessly away, and Robin, as if waiting for that signal, sat upright and said almost eagerly, "Helen—"

Grateful that he had broken the silence of days, she gave him an encouraging smile.

"I've been reading your books," he began, diffidently, "and I read about the sun you came from. It's different from this one. Suppose—suppose there were actually a kind of people here, and something in this light, or in your eyes, made them invisible to you."

Helen said, "Have you been seeing them again?"

He flinched at her ironical tone, and she asked, somewhat more gently, "It's a theory, Robin, but it wouldn't explain, then, why *you* see them."

"Maybe I'm—more used to this light," he said gropingly.

"And anyway, you said you thought you'd seen them and thought it was only a dream."

Halfway between exasperation and a deep pity, Helen found herself arguing, "If these other people of yours really exist, why haven't they made themselves known in sixteen years?"

The eagerness with which he answered was almost frightening. "I think they only come out at night, they're what your book calls a primitive civilization." He spoke the words he had read, but never heard, with an odd hesitation. "They're not really a civilization at all, I think, they're like—part of the woods."

"A forest people," Helen mused, impressed in spite of herself, "and nocturnal. It's always moonlight or dusky when you see them—"

"Then you *do* believe me—oh, Helen," Robin cried, and suddenly found himself pouring out the story of what he had seen, in incoherent words, concluding, "And by daylight I can hear them, but I can't see them. Helen, Helen, you have to believe it now, you'll have to let me try to find them and learn to talk to them. . . ."

Helen listened with a sinking heart. She knew they should not discuss it now, when five days of enforced housebound proximity had set their nerves and tempers on edge, but some unknown tension hurled her sharp words at Robin. "You saw a woman, and I—a man. These things are only dreams. Do I have to explain more to you?"

Robin flung his knife sullenly aside. "You're so blind, so stubborn."

"I think you are feverish again." Helen rose to go.

He said wrathfully, "You treat me like a child!"

"Because you act like one, with your fairy tales of women in the wind."

Suddenly Robin's agony overflowed and he caught at her, holding her around the knees, clinging to her as he had not done since he was a small child, his words stumbling and rushing over one another.

"Helen, Helen darling, don't be angry with me," he begged, and caught her in a blind embrace that pulled her off her feet. She had never guessed how strong he was; but he seemed very like a little boy, and she hugged him quickly as he began to cover her face with childish kisses.

"Don't cry, Robin, my baby, it's all right," she murmured,

kneeling close to him. Gradually the wildness of his passionate crying abated; she touched his forehead with her cheek to see if it were heated with fever, and he reached up and held her there. Helen let him lie against her shoulder, feeling that perhaps after the violence of his outburst he would fall asleep, and she was half asleep herself when a sudden shock of realization darted through her; quickly she tried to free herself from Robin's entangling arms.

"Robin, let me go."

He clung to her, not understanding. "Don't let go of me, Helen. Darling, stay here beside me," he begged, and pressed a kiss into her throat.

Helen, her blood icing over, realized that unless she freed herself very quickly now, she would be fighting against a strong, aroused young man not clearly aware of what he was doing. She took refuge in the sharp maternal note of ten years ago, almost vanished in the closer, more equal companionship of the time between:

"No, Robin. Stop it at once, do you hear?"

Automatically he let her go, and she rolled quickly away, out of his reach, and got to her feet. Robin, too intelligent to be unaware of her anger and too naïve to know its cause, suddenly dropped his head and wept, wholly unstrung. "Why are you angry?" he blurted out. "I was only loving you."

And at the phrase of the five-year-old child, Helen felt her throat would burst with its ache. She managed to choke out, "I'm not angry, Robin—we'll talk about this later, I promise," and then, her own control vanishing, turned and fled precipitately into the pouring rain.

She plunged through the familiar woods for a long time, in a daze of unthinking misery. She did not even fully realize that she was sobbing and muttering aloud, "No, no, no, no!"

She must have wandered for several hours. The rain had stopped and the darkness was lifting before she began to grow calmer and to think more clearly.

She had been blind not to foresee this day when Robin was a child; only if her child had been a daughter could it have been avoided. Or—she was shocked at the hysterical sound of her own laughter—if Colin had stayed and they had raised a family like Adam and Eve!

But what now? Robin was sixteen; she was not yet forty. Helen caught at vanishing memories of society; taboos so deeply rooted that for Helen they were instinctual and impregnable. Yet for Robin nothing existed except this little patch of forest and Helen herself—the only person in his world, more specifically at the moment the only woman in his world. *So much,* she thought bitterly, *for instinct. But have I the right to begin this all over again? Worse; have I the right to deny its existence and, when I die, leave Robin alone?*

She had stumbled and paused for breath, realizing that she had wandered in circles and that she was at a familiar point on the riverbank which she had avoided for sixteen years. On the heels of this realization she became aware that for only the second time in memory, the winds were wholly stilled.

Her eyes, swollen with crying, ached as she tried to pierce the gloom of the mist, lilac-tinted with the approaching sunrise, which hung around the water. Through the dispersing mist she made out, dimly, the form of a man.

He was tall, and his pale skin shone with misty white colors. Helen sat frozen, her mouth open, and for the space of several seconds he looked down at her without moving. His eyes, dark splashes in the pale face, had an air of infinite sadness and compassion, and she thought his lips moved in speech, but she heard only a thin familiar rustle of wind.

Behind him, mere flickers, she seemed to make out the ghosts of other faces, tips of fingers of invisible hands, eyes, the outline of a woman's breast, the curve of a child's foot. For a minute, in Helen's weary numbed state, all her defenses went down and she thought: *Then I'm not mad and it wasn't a dream and Robin isn't Reynolds' son at all. His father was this—one of these—and they've been watching me and Robin, Robin has seen them, he doesn't know he's one of them, but they know. They know and I've kept Robin from them all these sixteen years.*

The man took two steps toward her, the translucent body shifting to a dozen colors before her blurred eyes. His face had a curious familiarity—*familiarity*—and in a sudden spasm of terror Helen thought, "I'm going mad, it's Robin, it's Robin!"

His hand was actually outstretched to touch her when her scream cut icy lashes through the forest, stirring wild echoes in the wind-voices, and she whirled and ran blindly toward the treacherous, crumbling bank. Behind her came steps, a voice, a cry—Robin, the strange dryad-man, she could not guess. The horror of incest, the son the father the lover suddenly melting into one, overwhelmed her reeling brain and she fled insanely to the brink. She felt a masculine hand actually gripping her shoulder, she might have been pulled back even then, but she twisted free blindly, shrieking, "No, Robin, no, no—" and flung herself down the steep bank, to slip and hurl downward and whirl around in the raging current to spinning oblivion and death. . . .

Many years later, Merrihew, grown old in the Space Service, falsified a log entry to send his ship for a little while into the orbit of the tiny green planet he had named Robin's World. The old buildings had fallen into rotten timbers, and Merrihew quartered the little world for two months from pole to pole but found nothing. Nothing but shadows and whispers and the unending voices of the wind. Finally, he lifted his ship and went away.

Katherine MacLean is a fey young woman whose career is curiosity. She is technically trained, and if she had specialized ten or fifteen years ago she would no doubt be the head of a research department today. Instead, she has preferred to follow her own interests wherever they lead her; she writes, drifts around, studies and occasionally takes a laboratory assistant's job to see what's going on. As a science fiction writer she has few peers; her work is not only technically brilliant but has a rare human warmth and richness. (Memo to an editor: No collection of her stories has ever been published.)

"Unhuman Sacrifice," first published in Astounding *in 1958, is a subtle interweaving of anthropology, social comment, depth psychology, irony, deadpan humor. There are pointed comments here on good intentions, religious differences, the pursuit of happiness, and how not to interpret anthropological data; but these are only threads in the tapestry. What the whole story means is not expressible in a formula or a plot outline: it hits you below the level on which simple declarative sentences are put together.*

UNHUMAN SACRIFICE

BY KATHERINE MacLEAN

"Damn! He's actually doing it. Do you hear that?"

A ray of sunlight and a distant voice filtered down from the open arch in the control room above. The distant voice talked and paused, talked and paused. The words were blurred, but the tone was recognizable.

"He's outside preaching to the natives."

The two engineers were overhauling the engines, but paused to look up toward the voice.

"Maybe not," said Charlie, the junior engineer. "After all, he doesn't know their language."

"He'd preach anyway," said Henderson, senior engineer and navigator. He heaved with a wrench on a tight bolt, the wrench slipped, and Henderson released some words that made Charlie shudder.

On the trip, Charlie had often dreamed apprehensively that Henderson had strangled the passenger. And once he had dreamed that he himself had strangled the passenger and Henderson too.

When awake the engineers carefully avoided irritating words or gestures, remained cordial toward each other and the passenger no matter what the temptation to snarl, and tried to keep themselves in a tolerant good humor.

It had not been easy.

Charlie said, "How do you account for the missionary society giving him a ship of his own? A guy like that, who just gets in your hair when he's trying to give you advice, a guy with a natural-born talent for antagonizing people?"

"Easy," Henderson grunted, spinning the bolt. He was a stocky, square-built man with a brusque manner and a practiced tolerance of other people's oddities. "The missionary society was trying to get rid of him. You can't get any farther away than where they sent us!"

The distant voice filtered into the control room from the unseen sunlit landscape outside the ship. It sounded resonant and confident. "The poor jerk thinks it was an honor," Henderson added. He pulled out the bolt and dropped it on the padded floor with a faint thump.

"Anyhow," Charlie said, loosening bolt heads in a circle as the manual instructed, "he can't use the translator machine. It's not ready yet, not until we get the rest of their language. He won't talk to them if they can't understand."

"Won't he?" Henderson fitted his wrench to another bolt and spun it angrily. "Then what is he doing?" Without waiting for an answer he replied to his own question. *"Preaching,* that's what he is doing!"

It seemed hot and close in the engine room, and the sunlight from outside beckoned.

Charlie paused and wiped the back of his arm against his forehead. "Preaching won't do him any good. If they can't understand him, they won't listen."

"We didn't listen, and that didn't stop him from preaching to *us!"* Henderson snapped. "He's lucky we found a landing planet so soon, he's lucky he didn't drive us insane first. A man like that is a danger to a ship." Henderson, like Charlie, knew the stories of ships which had left with small crews and returned with a smaller crew of one or two red-eyed maniacs and a collection of corpses. Henderson was a conservative. He preferred the regular shipping runs, and ships with a regular-sized crew and a good number of passengers. Only an offer of triple pay and triple insurance indemnity had lured him from the big ships to be co-engineer on this odd three-man trip.

"... I didn't mind being preached at." Charlie's tone was mild, but he stared upward in the direction of the echoing voice with a certain intensity in his stance.

"Come off it, you twerp. We only have to be sweet to each other on a trip when we're cabinbound. Don't kid old Harry, you didn't like it."

"No," said Charlie dreamily, staring upward with a steady intensity. "Can't say that I did. He's not such a good preacher. I've met better in bars." The echoing voice from outside seemed to be developing a deeper echo. "He's got the translator going, Harry. I think we ought to stop him."

Charlie was a lanky redhead with a mild manner, about the same age as the preacher, but Henderson, who had experience, laid a restraining hand on his shoulder.

"I'll do it," said Henderson, and scrambled up the ladder to the control room.

The control room was a pleasant shading of grays, brightly lit by the sunlight that streamed in through the open archway. The opening to the outside was screened only by a billowing curtain of transparent Saran-type plastic film, ioncoated to allow air to pass freely, but making a perfect and aseptic filter against germs and small insects. The stocky engineer hung a clear respirator box over a shoulder, brought the tube up to his mouth, and walked through the plastic film. It folded over him and wrapped him in an intimate tacky embrace, and gripped to its own surface behind him, sealing itself around him like a loose skin. Just past the arch he walked through a frame of metal like a man-sized croquet wicket and stopped while it tightened a noose around the trailing films of plastic behind him, cutting him free of the doorway curtain and sealing the break with heat.

Without waiting for the plastic to finish wrapping and tightening itself around him, the engineer went down the ramp, trailing plastic film in gossamer veils, like ghostly battle flags.

They could use this simple wrapping of thin plastic as an airsuit air lock, for the air of the new world was rich and good, and the wrapping was needed only to repel strange germs or infections. They were not even sure that there were any such germs; but the plastic was a routine precaution for ports in quarantine, and the two engineers were accustomed to wearing it. It allowed air to filter by freely, so that Henderson could feel the wind on his skin, only slightly diminished. He was wearing uniform shorts, and the wind felt cool and pleasant.

Around the spaceship stretched grassy meadow and thin forest, and beyond that in one direction lay the blue line of the sea, and in another the hazy blue-green of distant low mountains. It was so like the southern United States of Charlie's boyhood that the young engineer had wept with excitement when he first looked out of the ship. Harry Henderson did not weep, but he paused in his determined stride and looked around, and understood again how incredibly lucky they had been to find an Earth-type planet of such perfection. He was a firm believer in the hand of fate, and he wondered what fate planned for the living things of this green planet, and why it had chosen him as its agent.

Down in the green meadow, near the foot of the ramp, sat

the translator machine, still in its crate and on a wheeled dolly but with one side opened to expose the controls. It looked like a huge box, and it was one of the most expensive of the new inductive language analyzers, brought along by their passenger in the hope and expectation of finding a planet with natives.

Triumphant in his success, the passenger, the Revent Winton, sat cross-legged on top of the crate, like a small king on a large throne. He was making a speech, using the mellow round tones of a trained elocutionist, with the transparent plastic around his face hardly muffling his voice at all.

And the natives were listening. They sat around the translator box in a wide irregular circle, and stared. They were bald, with fur in tufts about their knees and elbows. Occasionally one got up, muttering to the others, and hurried away; and occasionally one came into the area and sat down to listen.

"Do not despair," called Revent Winton in bell-like tones. "Now that I have shown you the light, you know that you have lived in darkness and sin all your lives, but do not despair . . ."

The translator machine was built to assimilate a vast number of words and sentences in any tongue, along with fifty or so words in direct translation, and from that construct or find a grammatical pattern and print a handbook of the native language. Meanwhile, it would translate any word it was sure of. Henderson had figured out the meaning of a few native words the day before and recorded them in, and the machine was industriously translating those few words whenever they appeared, like a deep bell, tolling the antiphony to the preacher's voice. The machine spoke in an enormous bass that was Henderson's low tones recorded through a filter and turned up to twenty times normal volume.

"I . . . LIGHT . . . YOU . . . YOU . . . LIVED . . . DARK . . . LIFE . . ."

The natives sat on the green grass and listened with an air of patient wonder.

"Revent Winton." Harry tried to attract his attention.

Winton leaned toward the attentive natives, his face softened with forgiveness. "No, say to yourselves merely: I have lived in error. Now I will learn the true path of a righteous life."

The machine in the box below him translated words into its voice of muted thunder. "SAY YOU . . . I . . . LIVED . . . I . . . PATH . . . LIFE . . ."

The natives moved. Some got up and came closer, staring at the box, and others clustered and murmured to each other, and went away in small groups, talking.

Henderson decided not to tell the Revent what the machine had said. But this had to be stopped.

"Revent Winton!"

The preacher leaned over and looked down at him benevolently. "What is it, my son?" He was younger than the engineer, dark, intense and sure of his own righteousness.

"MY SON," said the translator machine in its voice of muted thunder. The sound rolled and echoed faintly back from the nearby woods, and the natives stared at Henderson.

Henderson muttered a bad word. The natives would think he was Winton's son! Winton did not know what it had said.

"Don't curse," Winton said patiently. "What is it, Harry?"

"Sorry," Henderson apologized, leaning his arms on the edge of the crate. "Switch off the translator, will you?"

"WILL YOU . . ." thundered the translator. The preacher switched it off.

"Yes?" he asked, leaning forward. He was wearing a conservative suit of knitted dark-gray tights and a black shirt. Henderson felt badly dressed in his shorts and bare hairy chest.

"Revent, do you think it's the right thing to do, to preach to these people? The translator isn't finished, and we don't know anything about them yet. Anthropologists don't even make a suggestion to a native about his customs without studying the whole tribe and the way it lives for a couple of generations. I mean, you're going off half cocked. It's too soon to give them advice."

"I came to give them advice," Winton said gently. "They need my spiritual help. An anthropologist comes to observe. They don't meddle with what they observe, for meddling would change it. But I am not here to observe, I am here to help them. Why should I wait?"

Winton had a remarkable skill with syllogistic logic. He always managed to sound as if his position were logical, somehow, in spite of Henderson's conviction that he was almost always entirely wrong. Henderson often, as now, found himself unable to argue.

"How do you know they need help?" he asked uncertainly. "Maybe their way of life is all right."

"Come, now," said the preacher cheerfully, swinging his hand around the expanse of green horizon. "These are just primitives, not angels. I'd be willing to guess that they eat their own kind, or torture, or have human sacrifices."

"Humanoid sacrifices," Henderson muttered.

Winton's ears were keen. "Don't quibble. You know they will have some filthy primitive custom or other. Tribes on Earth used to have orgies and sacrifices in the spring. It's spring here—the Great Planner probably intended us to find this place in time to stop them."

"Oy," said Henderson and turned away to strike his forehead with the heel of his hand. His passenger was planning to interfere with a spring fertility ceremony. If these natives held such a ceremony—and it was possible that they might—they would be convinced that the ceremony insured the fertility of the earth, or the health of the sun, or the growth of the crops, or the return of the fish. They would be convinced that without the ceremony summer would never return and they would all starve. If Winton interfered, they would try to kill him.

Winton watched him, scowling at the melodrama of his gesture.

Henderson turned back to try to explain.

"Revent, I appeal to you, tampering is dangerous. Let us go back and report this planet, and let the government send a survey ship. When the scientists arrive, if they find that we have been tampering with the natives' customs without waiting for advice, they will consider it a crime. We will be notorious in scientific journals. We'll be considered responsible for any damage the natives sustain."

The preacher glared. "Do you think that I am a coward, afraid of the anger of atheists?" He again waved a hand, indicating the whole sweep of the planet's horizon around them. "Do you think we found this place by accident? The Great Planner sent me here for a purpose. I am responsible to Him, not to you or your scientist friends. I will fulfill His purpose." He leaned forward, staring at Henderson with dark fanatical eyes. "Go weep about your reputation somewhere else."

Henderson stepped back, getting a clearer view of the passenger, feeling as if he had suddenly sprouted fangs and claws. He was still as he had appeared before, an intense brunet young man, wearing dark tights and dark shirt, sitting cross-legged on top of a huge box, but now he looked primitive somehow, like a prehistoric naked priest on top of an altar.

"Anthropology is against this kind of thing," Henderson said.

Winton looked at him malevolently from his five-foot elevation on the crate and the extra three feet of his own seated height. "You aren't an anthropologist, are you, Harry? You're an engineer?"

"That's right," Henderson admitted, hating him for the syllogism.

Winton said sweetly, "Then why don't you go back to the ship and work on the engine?"

"There will be trouble," Henderson said softly.

"I am prepared for trouble," the Revent Winton said equally softly. He took a large old-fashioned revolver out of his carry case and rested it on his knee.

The muzzle pointed midway between the engineer and the natives.

Henderson shrugged and went back up the ramp.

"What did he do?" Charlie was finishing his check of the fuel timers, holding a coffee cup in his free hand.

Angrily silent, Harry cut an exit slit from the plastic coating. He ripped off the gossamer films of plastic, wadded them up together and tossed them in a salvage hopper.

"He told me to mind my own business. And that's what I am going to do."

The preacher's impressive voice began to ring again from the distance outside, and, every so often, like a deep gong, the translator machine would speak a word in the native dialect.

"The translator is still going," Charlie pointed out.

"Let it. He doesn't know what it is saying." Sulkily, Henderson turned to a library shelf, and pulled out a volume, *The E. T. Planet: A Manual of Observation and Behavior on Extraterrestrial Planets, with Examples*.

"What is it saying?"

"Almost nothing at all. All it translated out of a long speech the creep made was 'I life path.' "

The younger engineer lost his smile. "That was good

enough for others. Winton doesn't know what the box is saying?"

"He thinks it's saying what he is saying. He's giving out with his usual line of malarky."

"We've got to stop it!" Charlie began to climb the ladder.

Henderson shrugged. "So go out and tell him the translator isn't working right. I should have told him. But if I got close to him now, I'd strangle him."

Charlie returned later, grinning. "It's O.K. The natives are scared of Winton, and they like the box; so they must think that the box is talking sense for itself, and Winton is gibbering in a strange language."

"He is. And it is," Henderson said sourly. "They are right."

"You're kind of hard on him." Charlie started searching the shelves for another copy of the manual of procedure for survey teams. "But I can see what you mean. Anyhow, I told Winton that he was making a bad impression on the natives. It stopped him. It stopped him cold. He said he would put off preaching for a week and study the natives a little. But he said we ought to fix up the translator so that it translates what he says." Charlie turned, smiling, with a book in one hand. "That gives us time."

"Time for what?" Henderson growled without looking up from his book. "Do you think we can change Winton's mind? That bonehead believes that butting into people's lives is a sacred duty. Try talking any bonehead out of a Sacred Duty! He'd butt into a cannibal banquet! I hope he does. I hope they eat him!"

"Long pig," Charlie mused, temporarily diverted by the picture. "Tastes good to people, probably would taste foul to these natives, they're not the same species."

"He says he's planning to stop their spring festival. If it has sacrifices or anything he doesn't like, he says he'll stop it."

Charlie placed his fists on the table and leaned across toward Henderson, lowering his voice. "Look, we don't know even if the natives are going to have any spring festival. Maybe if we investigate we'll find out that there won't be one, or maybe we'll find out that Winton can't do them any harm. Maybe we don't have to worry. Only let's go out and investigate. We can write up reports on whatever we find, in standard form, and the journals will print them when we get back. Glory and all like that." He added, watching Henderson's expression, "Maybe, if we have to, we can break the translator."

It was the end of the season of dry. The river was small and ran in a narrow channel, and there were many fish near the surface. Spet worked rapidly, collecting fish from fish traps, returning the empty traps to the water, salting the fish.

He was winded, but pleased with the recollection of last night's feast, and hungry in anticipation of the feast of the evening to come. This was the season of the special meals, cooking herbs and roots and delicacies with the fish. To-night's feast might be the last he would ever have, for a haze was thickening over the horizon, and tomorrow the rains might come.

One of the strangers came and watched him. Spet ignored him politely and salted the fish without looking at him directly. It was dangerous to ignore a stranger, but to make the formal peace gestures and agreements would be implying that the stranger was from a tribe of enemies, when he might already be a friend. Spet preferred to be polite, so he pretended not to be concerned that he was being watched.

The haze thickened in the sky, and the sunlight weakened. Spet tossed the empty trap back to its place in the river with a skillful heave of his strong short arms. If he lived through the next week, his arms would not be strong and short, they would be weak and long. He began to haul in another trap line, sneaking side glances at the stranger as he pulled.

The stranger was remarkably ugly. His features were all misfit sizes. Reddish brown all over like a dead leaf, and completely bald of hair at knees and elbows, he shone as if he were wet, covered all over with a transparent shininess, like water, but the water never dripped. He was thick and sturdy and quick-moving, like a youngling, but did not work. Very strange, unlike reality, he stood quietly watching, without attacking Spet, although he could have attacked without breaking a peace gesture. So he was probably not of any enemy tribe.

It was possible that the undripping water was an illusion, meant to indicate that the stranger was really the ghost of someone who had drowned.

The stranger continued to watch. Spet braced his feet against the grass of the bank and heaved on the next trap line, wanting to show his strength. He heaved too hard, and a strand of the net gave way. The stranger waded out into the water and pulled in the strand, so that no fish escaped.

It was the act of a friend. And yet when the net trap was safely drawn up on the bank, the brown stranger stepped back without comment or gesture, and watched exactly as before—as if his help was the routine of one kinfolk to another.

That showed that the brown one was his kin and a member of his family. But Spet had seen all of his live kinfolk, and none of them looked so strange. It followed reasonably that the brown one was a ghost, a ghost of a relative who had drowned.

Spet nodded at the ghost and transferred the fish from the trap to the woven baskets and salted them. He squatted to repair the broken strand of the net.

The brown ghost squatted beside him. It pointed at the net and made an inquiring sound.

"I am repairing the trap, Grandfather," Spet exclaimed, using the most respectful name for the brown ghost relative.

The ghost put a hand over his own mouth, then pointed at the ground and released its mouth to make another inquiring noise.

"The ground is still dry, Grandfather," Spet said cordially, wondering what he wanted to know. He rose and flung the trap net out on its line into the river, hoping that the brown ghost would admire his strength. Figures in dreams often came to tell you something, and often they could not speak, but the way they looked and the signs they made were meant to give you a message. The brown ghost was shaped like a youngling, like Spet, as if he had drowned before his adult hanging ceremony. Perhaps this one came in daylight instead of dreams, because Spet was going to die and join the ghosts soon, before he became an adult.

The thought was frightening. The haze thickening on the horizon looked ominous.

The brown ghost repeated what Spet had said, almost in Spet's voice, blurring the words slightly. *The ground is still dry, Grandfather*. He pointed at the ground and made an inquiring noise.

"Ground," said Spet thinking about death, and every song he had heard about it. Then he heard the ghost repeat the word, and saw the satisfaction of his expression, and realized that the ghost had forgotten how to talk, and wanted to be taught all over again, like a newborn.

That made courtesy suddenly a simple and pleasant game. As Spet worked, he pointed at everything and said the word, he described what he was doing, and sometimes he sang the childhood work songs that described the work.

The ghost followed and helped him with the nets, and listened, and pointed at things he wanted to learn. Around his waist coiled a blind silver snake that Spet had not noticed at first, and the ghost turned the head of the snake toward Spet when he sang, and sometimes the ghost talked to the snake himself, with explanatory gestures.

It was very shocking to Spet that anyone would explain things to a snake, for snakes are wise, and a blind snake is the wise one of dreams—he who knows everything. The blind snake did not need to be explained to. Spet averted his eyes and would not look at it.

The ghost and he worked together, walking up the riverbank, hauling traps, salting fish and throwing the traps back, and Spet told what he was doing, and the ghost talked down to the snake around his waist, explaining something about what they were doing. Once the brown ghost held the blind silver snake out toward Sept, indicating with a gesture that he should speak to it.

Terrified and awed, Spet fell to his knees. "Tell me, Wisest One, if you wish to tell me, will I die in the hanging?"

He waited, but the snake lay with casual indifference in the ghost's hand and did not move or reply.

Spet rose from his knees and backed away. "Thank you, O Wise One."

The ghost spoke to the snake, speaking very quietly, with apologetic gestures and much explanation, then wrapped it again around his waist and helped Spet carry the loads of salted fish, without speaking again or pointing at anything.

It was almost sundown.

On the way back to his family hut, Spet passed the Box That Speaks. The black gibbering spirit sat on top of it and gibbered as usual, but this time the box stopped him and spoke to him, and called him by his own name, and asked questions about his life.

Spet was carrying a heavy load of salted fish in two baskets hung on a yoke across one sturdy shoulder. He was tired. He stood in the midst of the green meadow that in other seasons had been a river, with the silver hut of the ghosts throwing a long shadow across him. His legs were tired from wading in the river, and his mind was tired from the brown ghost asking him questions all day; so he explained the thing that was uppermost in his mind, instead of discussing fishing and weather. He explained that he was going to die. The ceremony of hanging, by which the almost-adults became adults, was going to occur at the first rain, five younglings were ready, usually most of them lived, but he thought he would die.

The box fell silent, and the ghost on top stopped gibbering, so Spet knew that it was true, for people fall silent at a truth that they do not want to say aloud.

He made a polite gesture of leave-taking to the box and went toward his family hut, feeling very unhappy. During the feast of that evening all the small ones ate happily of fish and roots and became even fatter, and the thin adults picked at the roots and herbs. Spet was the only youngling of adult-beginning age, and he should have been eating well to grow fat and build up his strength, but instead he went outside and looked at the sky and saw that it was growing cloudy. He did not go back in to the feast again; instead he crouched against the wall of the hut and shivered without sleeping. Before his eyes rested the little flat-bottomed boats of the family, resting in the dust behind the hut for the happy days of the rain. He would never travel in those boats again.

Hanging upside down was a painful way to become an adult, but worth it, if you lived. It was going to be a very bad way to die.

Hurrying and breathless with his news, Revent Winton came upon the two engineers crouched at the riverbank.

"I found out . . ." he began.

"Shhh," one said without turning.

They were staring at a small creature at the edge of the water.

Winton approached closer and crouched beside them. "I have news that might interest you." He held his voice to a low murmur, but the triumph sounded in it like a rasp cutting through glass, a vibration that drew quick speculative glances from the engineers. They turned their attention back to the water's edge.

"Tell us when this is over. Wait."

The young preacher looked at what they were staring at and saw a little four-legged creature with large eyes and bright pointed teeth struggling feebly in the rising water. The younger engineer, Charlie, was taking pictures of it.

"Its feet are stuck," Winston whispered. "Why don't you help it?"

"It's rooting itself," Henderson murmured back. "We're afraid that loud noises might make it stop."

"Rooting itself?" Winton was confused.

"The animal has two life stages, like a barnacle. You know, a barnacle is a little fish that swims around before it settles down to being just kind of a lump of rock. This one has a rooted stage that's coming on it now. When the water gets up to its neck it rolls up underwater and sticks its front legs out and starts acting like a kind of seaweed. Its hind feet are growing roots. This is the third one we've watched."

Winton looked at the struggling little creature. The water was rising toward its neck. The large bright eyes and small bared teeth looked frightened and uncomprehending. Winton shuddered.

"Horrible," he murmured. "Does it know what is happening?"

Henderson shrugged. "At least it knows the water is rising, and it knows it must not run away. It has to stand there and dig its feet in." He looked at Winton's expression and looked away. "Instinct comes as a powerful urge to do something. You can't fight instinct. Usually it's a pleasure to give in. It's not so bad."

Revent Paul Winton had always been afraid of drowning. He risked another glance at the little creature that was going to turn into a seaweed. The water had almost reached its neck, and it held its head high and panted rapidly with a thin whimpering sound.

"Horrible." Winton turned his back to it and pulled Henderson farther up the bank away from the river. "Mr. Henderson, I just found out something."

He was very serious, but now he had trouble phrasing what he had to say. Henderson urged him, "Well, go on."

"I found it out from a native. The translator is working better today."

"Charlie and I just recorded about four hundred words and phrases into it by distance pickup. We've been interviewing natives all day." Henderson's face suddenly grew cold and angry. "By the way, I thought you said that you weren't going to use the translator until it is ready."

"I was just checking it." Winton actually seemed apologetic. "I didn't say anything, just asked questions."

"All right." Henderson nodded grudgingly. "Sorry I complained. What happened? You're all upset, man!"

Winton evaded his eyes and turned away; he seemed to be looking at the river, with its banks of bushes and trees. Then he turned and looked in the direction of the inland hills, his expression vague. "Beautiful green country. It looks so peaceful. God is lavish with beauty. It shows His goodness. When we think that God is cruel, it is only because we do not understand. God is not really cruel."

"All right, so God is not really cruel," Henderson repeated cruelly. "So what's new?"

Winton winced and pulled his attention back to Henderson.

"Henderson, you've noticed that there are two kinds of natives—tall, thin ones that are slow, and quick, sturdy, short ones that do all the hard work. The sturdy ones we see in all ages, from child size up. Right?"

"I noticed."

"What did you think it meant?"

"Charlie and I talked about it." Henderson was puzzled. "Just a guess, but we think that the tall ones are aristocrats. They probably own the short ones, and the short ones do all the work."

Thick clouds were piled up over the far hills, accounting for the slow rise in the river level.

"The short ones are the children of the tall thin ones. The tall thin ones are the adults. The adults are all sick, that is why the children do all the work."

"What . . ." Henderson began, but Winton overrode his voice, continuing passionately, his eyes staring ahead at the hills.

"They are sick because of something they do to themselves. The young ones, strong and healthy, when they are ready to become adults they . . . they are hung upside down. For days, Henderson, maybe for more than a week, the translator would not translate how long. Some of them die. Most of them . . . most of them are stretched, and become long and thin." He stopped, and started again with an effort. "The native boy could not tell me why they do this, or how it started. It has been going on for so long that they cannot remember."

Abruptly and, to Henderson, shockingly, the preacher dropped to his knees and put his hands together. He tilted his head back with shut eyes and burst into prayer.

"O Lord, I do not know why You waited so long to help them to the true light, but I thank You that You sent me to stop this horrible thing."

Quickly he stood up and brushed his knees. "You'll help me, won't you?" he asked Henderson.

"How do we know it's true?" Henderson scowled. "It doesn't seem reasonable."

"Not reasonable?" Winton recovered his poise in sudden anger. "Come now, Harry, you've been talking as if you knew some anthropology. Surely you remember the puberty ceremonies. Natives often have initiation ceremonies for the young males. It's to test their manhood. They torture the boys, and the ones who can take it without whimpering are considered to be men, and graduated. Filthy cruelty! The authorities have always made them stop."

"No one around here has any authority to order anyone else to stop," Harry grunted. He was shaken by Winton's description of the puberty ceremony, and managed to be sarcastic only from a deep conviction that Winton had been always wrong, and therefore would continue to be wrong. It was not safe to agree with the man. It would mean being wrong along with Winton.

"No authority? What of God?"

"Well, what *of* God?" Henderson asked nastily. "If He is everywhere, He was here before you arrived here. And He never did anything to stop them. You've only known them a week. How long has God known them?"

"You don't understand." The dark-haired young man spoke with total conviction, standing taller, pride straightening his spine. "It was more than mere luck that we found this planet. It is my destiny to stop these people from their ceremony. God sent me."

Henderson was extremely angry, in a white-faced way. He had taken the preacher's air of superiority in the close confines of a spaceship for two months, and listened patiently to his preaching without letting himself be angry, for the sake of peace in the spaceship. But now he was out in the free air again, and he had had his fill of arrogance and wanted no more.

"Is that so?" he asked nastily. "Well, I'm on this expedition, too. How do you know that God did not send *me*, to stop *you*?"

Charlie finished taking pictures of the little animal under water as it changed, and came back up the bank, refolding the underwater lens. He was in time to see Winton slap the chief engineer in the face, spit out some profanity that would have started him on an hour of moral lecture if he had heard either of them emit such words. He saw Winton turn and run, not as if he were running away, but as if he were running to do something, in sudden impatience.

Ten minutes later Henderson had finished explaining what was bothering the preacher. They lay on the bank lazily looking down into the water, putting half attention into locating some other interesting life form, and enjoying the reflection of sunset in the ripples.

"I wish I could chew grass," Henderson said. "It would make it just like watching a river when I was a kid. But the plastic stuff on my face keeps me from putting anything into my mouth."

"The leaves would probably be poisonous anyhow." Charlie brushed a hand through the pretty green of the grass. It was wiry and tough, with thin round blades, like marsh grass. "This isn't really grass. This isn't really Earth, you know."

"I know, I wish I could forget it. I wonder what that creep Winton is doing now." Henderson rolled on his back and looked lazily at the sky. "I've got one up on him now. I got him to act like a creep right out in the open. He won't be giving me that superior, fatherly bilge. He might even call me Henderson now instead of Harry."

"Don't ask too much." Charlie clipped a piece of leaf from a weed and absently tried to put it into his mouth. It was stopped by the transparent plastic film that protected him from local germs and filtered the air he breathed.

He flicked the leaf away. "How did that creep get to be a missionary? Nothing wrong with him, except he can't get on with people. Doesn't help in his line of work to be like that."

"Easy, like I said," said Henderson, staring into the darkening pink and purple of the sky. "They encouraged him to

be a missionary so he would go far, far away. Don't ever tell
him. He thinks that he was chosen for his eloquence." Henderson rolled back onto his stomach and looked at the river.
It was a chilly purple now, with silver ripples. "More clouds
over the mountains. And those little clouds overhead might
thicken up and rain. If the river keeps rising, there might be
a flood. We might have to move the ship."

"Winton said that the native mentioned a flood." Charlie
got up lazily and stretched. "Getting dark out here anyhow.
We'll have to find out more about that interview."

They went in search of the preacher.

What he told them was disturbing, and vague.

"That was Spet," Henderson said. "That was the one I
was learning words from all afternoon. And he told you he
was going to die?"

Winton was earnest and pale. He sat crouched over the
chart table as if his resolution to act had frightened him.
"Yes. He said he was going to die. He said that they were
going to hang him upside down in a tree as soon as the next
rain starts. Because he is old enough."

"But he said that other young males live through it? Maybe he's wrong about dying. Maybe it's not as tough as it
sounds."

"He said that many die," Winton said tonelessly. His hands
lay motionless on the table. He was moved to a sudden flare
of anger. "Oh, those stupid savages. Cruel, cruel!" He turned
his head to Henderson, looking up at him without the usual
patronizing expression. "You'll fix the translator so that it
translates me exactly, won't you? I don't want to shoot them
to stop them from doing it. I'll just stop them by explaining
that God doesn't want them to do this thing. They will have
to understand me."

He turned his head to Charlie, standing beside him. "The
savages call me Enaxip. What does that mean? Do they think
I'm a god?"

"It means Big Box," Henderson cut in roughly. "They still
think that the box is talking. I see them watch the box when
they answer, they don't watch you. I don't know what they
think you are."

That night it did not rain. Winton allowed himself to fall
asleep near dawn.

To Spet also it made a difference that it did not rain.

The next day he fished in the river as he always had.

The river was swollen and ran high and swiftly between its banks and fishing was not easy at first, but the brown ghost returned, bringing another one like himself, and they both helped Spet with pulling in the fish traps. The new ghost also wanted to be told how to talk, like a small one, and they all had considerable amusement as the two ghosts acted out ordinary things that often happened, and Spet told them the right words and songs to explain what they were doing.

One of them taught him a word in ghost language, and he knew that he was right to learn it, because he would soon be a ghost.

When Spet carried the fish back along the path to his family hut that evening, he passed the Box That Speaks. It spoke to him again, and again asked him questions.

The spirit covered with black that usually gibbered on top of the box was not there. Nothing was on top of the box, but the brown ghost who had just been helping him fish stood beside the box and spoke to it softly each time it asked Spet a question. The box spoke softly back to the ghost after Spet answered, discussing his answers, as if they had a problem concerning him.

Spet answered the questions politely, although some of them were difficult questions, asking reasons for things he had never thought needed a reason, and some were questions it was not polite to ask. He did not know why they discussed him, but it was their business, and they would tell him if they chose.

When he left them, the brown ghost made a gesture of respect and mutual aid in work, and Spet returned, warmed and pleased by the respect of the relative-ghost.

He did not remember to be afraid until he was almost home.

It began to rain.

Charlie came up the ramp and into the spaceship, and found Henderson pacing up and down, his thick shoulders hunched, his fists clenched, and his face wrinkled with worry.

"Hi." Charlie did not expect an answer. He kicked the lever that tightened the noose on the curtain plastic behind him, watched the hot wire cut him loose from the curtain and seal the curtain in the same motion. He stood carefully folding and smoothing his new wrapping of plastic around himself, to make sure that the coating he had worn outside was completely coated by the new wrapping. All outside dust and germs had to be trapped between the two layers of sterile germproof plastic.

He stood mildly smoothing and adusting the wrappings, watching Henderson pace with only the very dimmest flicker of interest showing deep in his eyes. He could withdraw his attention so that a man working beside him could feel completely unwatched and as if he had the privacy of a cloak of invisibility. Charlie was well-mannered and courteous, and this was part of his courtesy.

"How're things?" he asked casually, slitting open his plastic cocoon and stepping out.

Henderson stopped pacing and took a cigar from a box on the table with savage impatience in his motions. "Very bad," he said. "Winton was right."

"Eh?" Charlie wadded up the plastic and tossed it into the disposal hopper.

"The natives, they actually do it." Henderson clenched the cigar between his teeth and lit it with savage jerky motions. "I asked Spet. No mistake in the translator this time. He said, yes, they hang the young men upside down in trees after the first spring rain. And yes, it hurt, and yes, sometimes one died, and no, he didn't know why they had to do this or what it was for. Ha!" Henderson threw the cigar away and began to pace again, snarling.

"Oh, yes, the translator was working fine! Generations of torturing their boys with this thing, and the adults can't remember how it started, or why, and they go on doing it anyway."

Charlie leaned back against the chart table, following his pacing with his eyes. "Maybe," he said mildly, "there's some good reason for the custom."

"A good reason to hang upside down for a week? Name one!"

Charlie did not answer.

"I just came from the native village," he said conversationally as though changing the subject. "Winton has started. He's got the translator box right in the center of their village now, and he's sitting on top of it telling them that God is watching them, and stuff like that. I tried to reason with him, and he just pointed a gun at me. He said he'd stop the hanging ceremony even if he had to kill both of us and half the natives to do it."

"So let him try to stop them, just by talking." Henderson, who had stopped to listen, began to pace again, glowering at the floor. "That flapping mouth! Talking won't do it. Talking by itself never does anything. I'm going to do it the easy way. I'm going to kidnap Spet and keep them from getting him. Charlie, tribes only do things at the right season, what they call the right season. We'll turn Spet loose after the week is up, and they won't lay a hand on him. They'll just wait until next year. Meanwhile they'll be seeing that the trees aren't angry at them or any of that malarky. When they see that Spet got away with it, they'll have a chance to see a young male who's becoming a healthy adult without being all stretched out and physically wrecked. And maybe next year Spet will decide to get lost by himself. Maybe after looking at how Spet looks compared with an adult who was hanged, some of the kids due for hanging next year would duck into the forest and get lost when it's due."

"It's a good dream," Charlie said, lounging, following Henderson's pacing with his eyes. "I won't remind you that we swore off dreaming. But I'm with you in this, man. How do we find Spet?"

Henderson sat down, smiling. "We'll see him at the stream tomorrow. We don't need to do anything until it starts raining."

Charlie started rummaging in the tool locker. "Got to get a couple of flashlights. We have to move fast. Have to find Spet in a hurry. It's already raining, been raining almost an hour."

Darkness and rain, and it was very strange being upside down. Not formal and ceremonial, like a story-song about it, but real, like hauling nets and thatching huts, and eating with his brothers. The world seemed to be upside down. The tree trunk was beside him, strong and solid, and the ground was above him like a roof being held up by the tree, and the sky was below his feet and very far away—and, looking down at the clouds swirling in the depth of the sky, he was afraid of falling into it. The sky was a lake, and he would fall through it like a stone falling through water. If one fell into the sky, one would fall and fall for a long time, it looked so very deep.

Rain fell upward out of the sky and hit him under the chin. His ankles and wrists were tightly bound, but did not hurt, for the elders had used a soft rope of many strands tied in a way that would not stop circulation. His arms were at his sides, his wrists bound to the same strand that pulled at his ankles, and the pull on his arms was like standing upright, carrying a small weight of something. He was in a standing position, but upside down. It was oddly comfortable. The elders had many generations of experience to guide them, and they had chosen a tall tree with a high branch that was above the flood. They had seemed wise and certain, and he had felt confidence in them as they had bound and hung him up with great gentleness, speaking quietly to each other. Then they had left him, towing their little flat-boats across the forest floor that was now a roof above his head, walking tall and storklike across the dim-lit glistening ground, which looked so strangely like a rough, wet ceiling supported by the trunks of trees.

The steady rain drummed against the twigs and small spring leaves, splashing in the deepening trickles of water that ran along the ground. Spet knew that somewhere the river was overflowing its banks and spreading into the forest and across meadows to meet and deepen the rain water. In the village the street would be muddy, and the children would be shouting, trying already to pole the boats in the street, wild with impatience for the rising of the river, to see again the cold swift flow of water and watch the huts of the town sag and flow downward, dissolve and vanish beneath the smooth surface.

For a month in the time of floods everyone would live in boats. His tribe would paddle and pole up the coast, meeting other tribes, trading baskets and fishhooks, salt fish for salt meat, and swapping the old stories and songs with new variations brought from far places. Last time they had been lucky enough to come upon a large animal caught in the flood, swimming and helpless to resist the hunters. The men of the enemy tribe had traded skin for half the roast meat on a raft, and sung a long story-song that no one had heard before. That was the best feast of all.

Then the horde of small boats would come home to the lakes that were the draining meadows and forest, and take down the sick and dying young men who had been hanging in the trees, and tend and feed them and call them "elder."

They would then travel again for food, to fight through storms to salt the meat of drowned animals and hunt the deep sea fish caught in the dwindling lakes. When the rains had stopped and the land began to dry, they would return to the damp and drying land to sing and work and build a village of the smooth fresh clay left by the flood.

But Spet would not see those good times again. He hung in his tree upside down with the rain beating coolly against his skin. It was growing too dark to see more than the dim light of the sky. He shut his eyes, and behind his shut eyes were pictures and memories, and then dreams.

Here he is. How do we get him down. Did you bring a knife. How do we get up to him. It's slippery. I can't climb this thing. Wait, I'll give you a boost.

A flash of light, too steady for lightning, lasting a full second. Spet awoke fully, staring into the darkness, looking for the light which now was gone, listening to the mingled voices in the strange language.

"*Don't use the flashlight, it will frighten him.*"

"*Going to try to explain to him what we're doing?*"

"*No, not right away. He'll come along. Spet's a pal of mine already.*"

"*Man, do these trees have roots. As big as the branches!*"

"*Live mangroves.*"

"*You're always claiming the South has everything. What are mangroves?*"

"*Florida swamp trees. They root straight into deep water. Give a hand here.*"

"*Keeps raining like this and they're going to need their roots. How high can we climb just on the roots, anyhow?*"

"*Think you're kidding? Why else would they have roots like this? This territory must be under water usually, deep water. This flat land must be delta country. We're just in the dry season.*"

"*What do you mean delta country? I'm a city boy, define your terms.*"

"*I mean, we're at the mouth of one of those big wandering rivers like the Mississippi or the Yellow River that doesn't know where it's going to run next, and splits up into a lot of little rivers at the coast, and moves its channel every spring. I noticed that grass around the ship looked like salt-water grass. Should have thought about it.*"

A dark figure appeared beside Spet and climbed past him toward the branch where the rope was tied. The next voice was distant. *"You trying to tell me we landed the ship in a river bed? Why didn't you say something when we were landing?"*

"Didn't think of it then." That voice was loud and close.

"It's a fine time to think of it now. I left the ship wide open. You up there yet?"

"Uh huh. I'm loosening the rope. Going to lower him slow. Catch him and keep him from landing on his head, will you?"

"Ready. Lower away."

The voices stopped and the world began to spin, and the bole of the tree began to move past Spet's face.

Suddenly a pair of wet arms gripped him, and the voice of the brown ghost called, *"Got him."*

Immediately the rope ceased to pull at Spet's ankles, and he fell head first against the brown ghost and they both tumbled against slippery high roots and slid down from one thick root to another until they stopped at the muddy ground. The ghost barked a few short words and began to untie the complex knots from Spet's ankles and wrists.

It was strange sitting on the wet ground with its coating of last year's leaves. Even right side up the forest looked strange, and Spet knew that this was because of death, and he began to sing his death song.

The brown ghost helped him to his feet and said clearly in ordinary words, "Come on, boy, you can sing when we get there."

His friend dropped down from a low branch to the higher roots of the tree, slipped and fell on the ground beside them.

In Spet's language the standing one said to the other, "No time for resting, Charlie, let's go."

It was very dark now, and the drips from the forest branches poured more heavily, beating against the skin. The ghost on the ground barked a few of the same words the relative-ghost had made when he had fallen, and got up.

The two started off through the forest, beckoning Spet to follow. He wondered if he were a ghost already. Perhaps the ghosts had taken him to be a ghost without waiting for him to die. That was nice of them, and a favor, possibly because they were kinfolk. He followed them.

The rain had lightened and become the steady, light-falling spray that it would be for the next several days. Walking was difficult, for the floor of the forest was slippery with wet leaves, and the mud underneath was growing soft again, remembering the time it had been part of the water of the river, remembering that the river had left it there only a year ago. The ghosts with him made sputtering words in ghost talk, sometimes tripped and floundered and fell, helped each other up and urged him on.

The forest smelled of the good sweet odors of damp earth and growing green leaves. The water and mud were cooling against his hurting feet, and Spet unaccountably wanted to linger in the forest, and sit, and perhaps sleep.

The floods were coming, and the ghosts had no boats with them.

"Come on, Spet. We go to big boat. Come on, Spet."

Why did they stumble and flounder through the forest without a boat? And why were they afraid? Could ghosts drown? These ghosts, with their perpetually wet appearance —if they had drowned once, would they be forced to relive the drowning, and be caught in the floods every year? A bad thing that happened once had to happen again and again in dreams. And your spirit self in the dream lived it each time as something new. There is no memory in the dream country. These ghosts were dream people, even though they chose to be in the awake world. They were probably bound by the laws of the dream world. They would have to re-enact their drowning. Their boat was far away, and they were running toward the watercourse where the worst wave of the flood would come.

Spet understood suddenly that they wanted him to drown. He could not become a ghost, like these friendly brown ghosts, and live in their world, without first dying.

He remembered his first thoughts of them, that they carried the illusion of water over them because they had once drowned. They wanted him to be like them. They were trying to lure him through waters where he would stumble and drown as they had. Naturally as they urged him on their gestures were nervous and guilty. It is not easy to urge a friend onward to his death. But to be shaped like a young one, merry, brown, and covered with water, obviously he had to be drowned as they were drowned, young and merry, before the hanging had made a sad adult of him.

He would not let them know that he had guessed their intention. Running with them toward the place where the flood

would be worst, he tried to remember on what verse he had
stopped singing his death song, and began again from that
verse, singing to stop the fear-thoughts. The rain beat coolly
against his face and chest as he ran.

Each man in his own panic, they burst from the forest
into the clearing. The engineers saw with a wave of relief that
the spaceship was still there, a pale shaft upright in the midst
of water. Where the meadow had been was a long narrow
lake, reflecting the faint light of the sky, freckled with drifting spatters of rain.

"How do we get to it?" Charlie turned to them.

"How high is the water? Is the ramp covered?" Henderson
asked practically, squinting through the rain.

"Ramp looks the same. I see grass sticking up in the water.
It's not deep."

Charlie took a careful step and then another out into the
silvery surface. Spongy grass met his feet under the surface,
and the water lapped above his ankles, but no higher.

"It's shallow."

They started out toward the ship. It took courage to put
their feet down into a surface that suggested unseen depth.
The shallow current of water tugged at their ankles and grew
deeper and stronger.

"Henderson, wait!"

The three stopped and turned at the call. The path to the
village was close, curving away from the forest toward the
distant riverbank, a silvery road of water among dark bushes.
A dark figure came stumbling along the path, surrounded
by the silvery shine of the rising water. Ripples spread from
his ankles as he ran.

He came to the edge where the bushes stopped and the
meadow began, saw the lake-appearance of it, and stopped.
The others were already thirty feet away.

"Henderson! Charlie!"

"Walk, it's not deep yet. Hurry up." Charlie gestured ur-
gently for him to follow them. They were still thirty feet out,
standing in the smooth silver of the rising water. It was almost
to their knees.

Winton did not move. He looked across the shining shallow expanse of water, and his voice rose shrilly. "It's a lake,
we need boats."

"It's shallow," Charlie called. The rain beat down on the

water, speckling it in small vanishing pockmarks. The two engineers hesitated, looking back at Winton, sensing something wrong.

Winton's voice was low, but the harshness of desperation made it as clear as if he had screamed.

"Please. I can't swim—"

"Go get him," Henderson told Charlie. "He's got a phobia. I'll herd Spet to the ship, and then head back to help you."

Charlie was already splashing in long strides back to the immobile figure of the preacher. He started to shout when he got within earshot.

"Why didn't you say so, man? We almost left you behind!" He crouched down before the motionless fear-dazed figure. "Get on, man. You're getting taxi service."

"What?" asked Winton in a small distant voice. The water lapped higher.

"Get on my back," Charlie snapped impatiently. "You're getting transportation."

"The houses dissolved, and they went off in boats and left me alone. They said that I was an evil spirit. I think they did the hangings anyway, even though I told them it was wrong." Winton's voice was vague, but he climbed on Charlie's back. "The *houses* dissolved."

"Speak up, stop mumbling," muttered Charlie.

The spaceship stood upright ahead in the center of the shallow silver lake that had been a meadow. Its doors were open, and the bottom of the ramp was covered by water. Water tugged against Charlie's lower legs as he ran, and the rain beat against their faces and shoulders in a cool drumming. It would have been pleasant, except that the fear of drowning was growing even in Charlie, and the silver of the shallow new lake seemed to threaten an unseen depth ahead.

"There seems to be a current," Winton said with an attempt at casual remarks. "Funny, this water looks natural here, as if the place were a river, and those trees look like the banks."

Charlie said nothing. Winton was right, but it would not be wise to tell a man with a phobia about drowning that they were trying to walk across the bed of a river while the water returned to its channel.

"Why are you running?" asked the man he carried.

"To catch up with Henderson."

Once they were inside the spaceship with the door shut

they could ignore the water level outside. Once inside, they would not have to tell Winton anything about how it was outside. A spaceship made a good submarine.

The water level was almost to Charlie's knees and he ran now in a difficult lurching fashion. Winton pulled up his feet nervously to keep them from touching the water. The plastic which they wore was semipermeable to water and both of them were soaked.

"Who is that up ahead with Henderson?"

"Spet, the native boy."

"How did you persuade him to stay away from the ceremony?"

"We found him hanging and cut him down."

"Oh." Winton was silent a moment trying to absorb the fact that the engineers had succeeded in rescuing someone. "It's a different approach. I talked, but they wouldn't listen." He spoke apologetically, hanging on to Charlie's shoulders, his voice jolting and stopping as Charlie tripped over a concealed tuft of grass or small bush under the water. "They didn't even answer—or look at me. When the water got deep they went off in little boats and didn't leave a boat for me."

Charlie tripped again and staggered to one knee. They both briefly floundered waist deep in the water, and then Charlie was up again, still with a grip on his passenger's legs, so that Winton was firmly on his back.

When he spoke again Winton's tone was casual, but his voice was hysterically high in pitch. "I asked them for a boat, but they wouldn't look at me."

Charlie did not answer. He respected Winton's attempt to conceal his terror. The touch of water can be a horrifying thing to a man with a phobia of drowning. He could think of nothing to distract Winton's attention from his danger, but he hoped desperately that the man would not notice that the water had deepened. It is not possible to run in water over knee height. There was no way to hurry now. The rain had closed in, in veiling curtains, but he thought he saw the small figures of Henderson and the native in the distance reach the ramp which led to the spaceship.

If the flood hit them all now, Henderson and Spet could get inside, but how would he himself get this man with a phobia against water off his back and into the water to swim? He could visualize the bony arms tightening around his throat in a hysterical stranglehold. If a drowning man gets a clutch on you, you are supposed to knock him out and tow him. But how could he get this nonswimming type off his back and out where he could be hit? If Winton could not brace himself to walk in water up to his ankles, he was not going to let go and try to swim in water up to his neck. He'd flip, for sure! Charlie found no logical escape from the picture. The pressure of the strong bony arms around his throat and shoulders and the quick, irregular breathing of the man he was carrying made him feel trapped.

The water rose another inch or so, and the drag of it against his legs became heavier. The current was pulling sidewise.

"You're going slowly." Winton's voice had the harsh rasp of fear.

"No hurry." With difficulty, Charlie found breath to speak in a normal tone. "Almost there."

The curtain of rain lifted for a moment and he saw the spaceship, dark against the sky, and the ramp leading to its open door. The ramp was very shrunken, half covered by the rising water. It seemed a long way ahead.

As he watched, a light came on.

In the archway of the spaceship, Henderson flipped a switch and the lights went on.

Spet was startled. Sunlight suddenly came from the interior of the hut and shone against the falling rain in a great beam. Rain glittered through the beam in falling drops like sparks of white fire. It was very unlike anything real, but in dreams sunlight could be in one place and rain another at the same time, and no one in the dream country was surprised. And these were people who usually lived in the dream country, so apparently they had the power to do it in the real world also.

Neverthless, Spet was afraid, for the sunlight did not look right as it was, coming out in a great widening beam across the rippling rain-pocked water. Sunlight did not mix well with rain.

"Sunlight," Spet said apologetically to his relative-ghost.

The brown ghost nodded and led him down the slope of the ramp through the strange sparkling sunlight, with the ramp strange and hard underfoot.

"Don't go inside until I return," the ghost said, mouthing the words with difficulty. The ghost placed his hands around the railing of the ramp. "You hang on here and wait for me," said the brown ghost of someone in his family, and waded down into the water.

Spet followed him down into the comfortable water until his sore feet were off the end of the ramp and in the cooling soft mud, and then he gripped the rail obediently and waited. The water·lapped at his waist like an embrace, and the wind sang a death song for him.

The bright glare of the strange sunlight on dancing water was beautiful, but it began to hurt his eyes. He closed them, and then heard a sound other than the wind. Two sounds.

One sound he recognized as the first flood crest crashing through the trees to the north, approaching them, and he knew he must hurry and drown before it arrived, because it was rough and hurtful.

The other sound was the strange voice of the black spirit which usually gibbered on top of the Box That Speaks. Spet opened his eyes and saw that the gibbering spirit was riding on the shoulders of the brown ghost, as he and his friend, the other brown ghost, moved through the waist-deep water toward Spet and the ramp.

The black spirit gibbered at him as they passed, and Spet felt a dim anger, wondering if it would bring bad luck to him with its chants, for its intentions could not be the same as the friendly ghosts.

"Spet, come up the ramp with us. It's dry inside. Don't look like that, there's nothing to be afraid of now, we'll go inside and shut the door, it will keep the water away, it won't get in. . . . Come along, Spet."

The black spirit suddenly leaped down on the ramp with a strange scream. *"Aaaaiiii! . . . He's turning into a seaweed. Quick, get him out of the water! Help!"*

The spirit with the black skin and white face possibly wanted him for his own dark spirit world. He was coming down the ramp at Spet, screaming. He was too late, though, Spet knew that he was safe for the dim land of the drowned with the friendly ghosts who had come for him. He felt his feet sending roots down into the mud, moving and rooting downward, and a wild joy came over him, and he knew that this was the right thing for him, much more right and natural than it would have been to become a tall sad adult.

He had been feeling a need for air, panting and drawing the cold air into his lungs. Just as the clawed hands of the dark spirit caught hold of his neck, Spet had enough air, and he leaned over into the dark and friendly water, away from the painful beauty of the bright lights and moving forms. The water closed around him, and the sound of voices was lost.

He could still feel the grip of the spirit's bony arms around his neck, pulling upward, but he had seen the brown ghosts running toward them, and they would stop it from doing him any harm, so he dismissed the fear from his mind and bent deeper into the dark, and plunged his hands with spread fingers deep into the mud, and gripped his ankles, as if he had always known just how to do this thing. His hands locked and become unable to unfold. They would never unfold again.

He felt the soft surge that was the first flood wave arriving and passing above him and ignored it, and, with a mixture of terror and the certainty of doing right, he opened his mouth and took a deep breath of cold water.

All thought stopped. As the water rushed into his lungs, the rooted sea creature that was the forgotten adult stage of Spet's species began its thoughtless pseudo-plant existence, forgetting everything that had ever happened to it. Its shape changed.

The first wave of the flood did not quite reach up to the edge of the ship's entrance. It caught the two engineers as they dragged a screaming third human up the ramp toward the entrance, but it did not quite reach into the ship, and when it passed the three humans were still there. One of them struck the screaming one, and they carried him in.

Winton was hysterical for some time, but Henderson seemed quite normal. He worked well and rationally in compiling a good short survey report to carry to the planetary-survey agency, and when the waters dried around the spaceship he directed the clearing of mud from the jets and the overhaul of the firing chambers without a sign of a warp in his logic.

He did not want to speak to any native, and went into the ship when they appeared.

Winton was still slightly delirious when they took off from the planet, but, once in space, he calmed down and made a good recovery. He just did not talk about it. Henderson still seemed quite normal, and Charlie carefully did not tell Winton that Henderson kept a large bush in a glass enclosure in the engine room.

Ever since that time Henderson has been considered a little peculiar. He is a good enough risk for the big liners, for they have other engineers on board to take over if he ever cracks. He has no trouble getting jobs, but wherever he goes he brings with him an oversized potted plant and puts it in the engine room and babies it with water and fertilizer. His fellow officers never kid him about it, for it is not a safe subject.

When Henderson is alone, or thinks he is alone, he talks to the potted bush. His tone is coaxing. But the bush never answers.

Charlie runs into him occasionally when their ships happen to dock at the same space port around the same planet. They share a drink and enjoy a few jokes together, but Charlie takes care not to get signed onto the same ship as Henderson. The sight of Henderson and his potted bush together make him nervous.

It's the wrong bush, but he'll never tell Henderson that.

5.

ALIENS AMONG US

Fitz-James O'Brien died in 1862, aged about thirty-four, of a wound received in the Civil War. He left behind him just thirteen short stories, of which the best known is "The Diamond Lens."

The story you are about to read was first published in 1859. Here, almost visibly, the story of supernatural mystery is turning into science fiction. The tests the narrator and Hammond make on their captured monster, the methods they use to make it visible, and the monster itself—no stock figure from mythology or demonology—mark it as science fiction. But in the suggestion that the house is haunted, the queer turn the narrator's and Hammond's thoughts take as they smoke opium, and the significant question "What do you consider to be the greatest element of terror?" there are agreeable hints, traces, of the purely supernatural story this would have been had it been written twenty years earlier.

WHAT WAS IT?

BY FITZ-JAMES O'BRIEN

It is, I confess, with considerable diffidence that I approach the strange narrative which I am about to relate. The events which I purpose detailing are of so extraordinary a character that I am quite prepared to meet with an unusual amount of incredulity and scorn. I accept all such beforehand. I have, I trust, the literary courage to face unbelief. I have, after mature consideration, resolved to narrate, in as simple and straightforward a manner as I can compass, some facts that passed under my observation, in the month of July last, and which, in the annals of the mysteries of physical science, are wholly unparalleled.

I live at No. ―― Twenty-sixth Street, in New York. The house is in some respects a curious one. It has enjoyed for the last two years the reputation of being haunted. It is a large and stately residence, surrounded by what was once a garden, but which is now only a green enclosure used for bleaching clothes. The dry basin of what had been a fountain, and a few fruit-trees ragged and unpruned, indicate that this spot in past days was a pleasant, shady retreat, filled with fruits and flowers and the sweet murmur of waters.

The house is very spacious. A hall of noble size leads to a large spiral staircase winding through its center, while the various apartments are of imposing dimensions. It was built some fifteen or twenty years since by Mr. A――, the well-known New York merchant, who five years ago threw the commercial world into convulsions by a stupendous bank fraud. Mr. A――, as everyone knows, escaped to Europe, and died not long after, of a broken heart. Almost immediately after the news of his decease reached this country and was verified, the report spread in Twenty-sixth Street that No. ―― was haunted. Legal measures had dispossessed the widow of its former owner, and it was inhabited merely by a care-taker and his wife, placed there by the house-agent in whose hands it had passed for purposes of renting or sale. These people declared that they were troubled with unnatural noises. Doors were opened without any visible agency. The remnants of furniture scattered through the various rooms were, during the night, piled one upon the other by unknown hands. Invisible feet passed up and down the stairs in broad daylight, accompanied by the rustle of unseen silk dresses, and the gliding of viewless hands along the massive balusters. The care-taker and his wife declared they would live there no longer. The house-agent laughed, dismissed them, and put others in their place. The noises and supernatural manifestations continued. The neighborhood caught up the story, and the house remained untenanted for three years. Several persons negotiated for it; but, somehow, always before the bargain was closed they heard the unpleasant rumors and declined to treat any further.

It was in this state of things that my landlady, who at that time kept a boarding-house in Bleecker Street, and who wished to move further uptown, conceived the bold idea of renting No. —— Twenty-sixth Street. Happening to have in her house rather a plucky and philosophical set of boarders, she laid her scheme before us, stating candidly everything she had heard respecting the ghostly qualities of the establishment to which she wished to remove us. With the exception of two timid persons—a sea-captain and a returned Californian, who immediately gave notice that they would leave—all of Mrs. Moffat's guests declared that they would accompany her in her chivalric incursion into the abode of spirits.

Our removal was effected in the month of May, and we were charmed with our new residence. The portion of Twenty-sixth Street where our house is situated, between Seventh and Eighth Avenues, is one of the pleasantest localities in New York. The gardens back of the houses, running down nearly to the Hudson, form, in the summer time, a perfect avenue of verdure. The air is pure and invigorating, sweeping, as it does, straight across the river from the Weehawken heights, and even the ragged garden which surrounded the house, although displaying on washing days rather too much clothesline, still gave us a piece of greensward to look at, and a cool retreat in the summer evenings, where we smoked our cigars in the dusk, and watched the fireflies flashing their dark-lanterns in the long grass.

Of course we had no sooner established ourselves at No. —— than we began to expect the ghosts. We absolutely awaited their advent with eagerness. Our dinner conversation was supernatural. One of the boarders, who had purchased Mrs. Crowe's *Night Side of Nature* for his own private delectation, was regarded as a public enemy by the entire household for not having bought twenty copies. The man led a life of supreme wretchedness while he was reading this volume. A system of espionage was established, of which he was the victim. If he incautiously laid the book down for an instant and left the room, it was immediately seized and read aloud in secret places to a select few. I found myself a person of immense importance, it having leaked out that I was tolerably well versed in the history of supernaturalism, and had once written a story the foundation of which was a ghost. If a table or a wainscot panel happened to warp when we were assembled in the large drawing-room, there was an instant silence, and everyone was prepared for an immediate clanking of chains and a spectral form.

After a month of psychological excitement, it was with the utmost dissatisfaction that we were forced to acknowledge that nothing in the remotest degree approaching the supernatural had manifested itself. Once the black butler asseverated that his candle had been blown out by some invisible agency while he was undressing himself for the night; but as I had more than once discovered this colored gentleman in a condition when one candle must have appeared to him like two, I thought it possible that, by going a step further in his potations, he might have reversed this phenomenon, and seen no candle at all where he ought to have beheld one.

Things were in this state when an incident took place so awful and inexplicable in its character that my reason fairly reels at the bare memory of the occurrence. It was the tenth of July. After dinner was over I repaired, with my friend Dr. Hammond, to the garden to smoke my evening pipe. Independent of certain mental sympathies which existed between the doctor and myself, we were linked together by a vice. We both smoked opium. We knew each other's secret, and respected it. We enjoyed together that wonderful expansion of thought, that marvelous intensifying of the perceptive faculties, that boundless feeling of existence when we seem to have points of contact with the whole universe—in short, that unimaginable spiritual bliss, which I would not surrender for a throne, and which I hope you, reader, will never, never taste.

Those hours of opium happiness which the doctor and I spent together in secret were regulated with a scientific accuracy. We did not blindly smoke the drug of paradise, and leave our dreams to chance. While smoking, we carefully steered our conversation through the brightest and calmest channels of thought. We talked of the East, and endeavored to recall the magical panorama of its glowing scenery. We criticized the most sensuous poets—those who painted life ruddy with health, brimming with passion, happy in the possession of youth and strength. If we talked of Shakespeare's *Tempest*, we lingered over Ariel, and avoided Caliban. Like the Guebers, we turned our faces to the east, and saw only the sunny side of the world.

This skilful coloring of our train of thought produced in

our subsequent visions a corresponding tone. The splendor of Arabian fairyland dyed our dreams. We paced that narrow strip of grass with the tread and port of kings. The song of the *rana arborea,* while he clung to the bark of the ragged plum-tree, sounded like the strains of divine musicians. Houses, walls, and streets melted like rain-clouds, and vistas of unimaginable glory stretched away before us. It was a rapturous companionship. We enjoyed the vast delight more perfectly because, even in our most ecstatic moments, we were conscious of each other's presence. Our pleasures, while individual, were still twin, vibrating and moving in musical accord.

On the evening in question, the tenth of July, the doctor and myself drifted into an unusually metaphysical mood. We lit our large meerschaums, filled with fine Turkish tobacco, in the core of which burned a little black nut of opium, that, like the nut in the fairy tale, held within its narrow limits wonders beyond the reach of kings; we paced to and fro, conversing. A strange perversity dominated the currents of our thought. They would *not* flow through the sun-lit channels into which we strove to divert them. For some unaccountable reason, they constantly diverged into dark and lonesome beds, where a continual gloom brooded. It was in vain that, after our old fashion, we flung ourselves on the shores of the East, and talked of its gay bazaars, of the splendors of the time of Haroun, of harems and golden palaces. Black afreets continually arose from the depths of our talk, and expanded, like the one the fisherman released from the copper vessel, until they blotted everything bright from our vision. Insensibly, we yielded to the occult force that swayed us, and indulged in gloomy speculation.

We had talked some time upon the proneness of the human mind to mysticism, and the almost universal love of the terrible, when Hammond suddenly said to me, "What do you consider to be the greatest element of terror?"

The question puzzled me. That many things were terrible, I knew. Stumbling over a corpse in the dark; beholding, as I once did, a woman floating down a deep and rapid river, with wildly lifted arms, and awful, upturned face, uttering, as she drifted, shrieks that rent one's heart, while we, the spectators, stood frozen at a window which overhung the river at a height of sixty feet, unable to make the slightest effort to save her, but dumbly watching her last supreme agony and her disappearance. A shattered wreck, with no life visible, encountered floating listlessly on the ocean, is a terrible object, for it suggests a huge terror, the proportions of which are veiled. But it now struck me, for the first time, that there must be one great and ruling embodiment of fear—a King of Terrors, to which all others must succumb. What might it be? To what train of circumstances would it owe its existence?

"I confess, Hammond," I replied to my friend, "I never considered the subject before. That there must be one Something more terrible than any other thing, I feel. I cannot attempt, however, even the most vague definition."

"I am somewhat like you, Harry," he answered. "I feel my capacity to experience a terror greater than anything yet conceived by the human mind—something combining in fearful and unnatural amalgamation hitherto supposed incompatible elements. The calling of the voices in Brockden Brown's novel of *Wieland* is awful; so is the picture of the Dweller of the Threshold, in Bulwer's *Zanoni;* but," he added, shaking his head gloomily, "there is something more terrible still than these."

"Look here, Hammond," I rejoined, "let us drop this kind of talk, for heaven's sake! We shall suffer for it, depend on it."

"I don't know what's the matter with me tonight," he replied, "but my brain is running upon all sorts of weird and awful thoughts. I feel as if I could write a story like Hoffmann tonight, if I were only master of a literary style."

"Well, if we are going to be Hoffmannesque in our talk, I'm off to bed. Opium and nightmares should never be brought together. How sultry it is! Good-night, Hammond."

"Good-night, Harry. Pleasant dreams to you."

"To you, gloomy wretch, afreets, ghouls, and enchanters."

We parted, and each sought his respective chamber. I undressed quickly and got into bed, taking with me, according to my usual custom, a book, over which I generally read myself to sleep. I opened the volume as soon as I had laid my head upon the pillow, and instantly flung it to the other side of the room. It was Goudon's *History of Monsters,* a curious French work, which I had lately imported from Paris, but which, in the state of mind I had then reached, was anything but an agreeable companion. I resolved to go to sleep at once; so, turning down my gas until nothing but a little blue point of light glimmered on the top of the tube, I composed myself to rest.

The room was in total darkness. The atom of gas that still remained alight did not illuminate a distance of three inches round the burner. I desperately drew my arms across my eyes, as if to shut out the darkness, and tried to think of nothing. It was in vain. The confounded themes touched on by Hammond in the garden kept obtruding themselves on my brain. I battled against them. I erected ramparts of would-be blankness of intellect to keep them out. They still crowded upon me. While I was lying still as a corpse, hoping that by a perfect physical inaction I should hasten mental repose, an awful incident occurred. A Something dropped, as it seemed, from the ceiling, plumb upon my chest, and the next instant I felt two bony hands encircling my throat, endeavoring to choke me.

I am no coward, and am possessed of considerable physical strength. The suddenness of the attack, instead of stunning me, strung every nerve to its highest tension. My body acted from instinct, before my brain had time to realize the terrors of my position. In an instant I wound two muscular arms around the creature, and squeezed it, with all the strength of despair, against my chest. In a few seconds the bony hands that had fastened on my throat loosened their hold, and I was free to breathe once more. Then commenced a struggle of awful intensity. Immersed in the most profound darkness, totally ignorant of the nature of the Thing by which I was so suddenly attacked, finding my grasp slipping every moment, by reason, it seemed to me, of the entire nakedness of my assailant, bitten with sharp teeth in the shoulder, neck, and chest, having every moment to protect my throat against a pair of sinewy, agile hands, which my utmost efforts could not confine—these were a combination of circumstances to combat which required all the strength, skill and courage that I possessed.

At last, after a silent, deadly, exhausting struggle, I got my assailant under by a series of incredible efforts of strength. Once pinned, with my knee on what I made out to be its chest, I knew that I was victor. I rested for a moment to breathe. I heard the creature beneath me panting in the darkness, and felt the violent throbbing of a heart. It was apparently as exhausted as I was; that was one comfort. At this moment I remembered that I usually placed under my pillow,

before going to bed, a large yellow silk pocket-handkerchief.
I felt for it instantly; it was there. In a few seconds more I
had, after a fashion, pinioned the creature's arms.

I now felt tolerably secure. There was nothing more to be
done but to turn on the gas, and, having first seen what my
midnight assailant was like, arouse the household. I will
confess to being actuated by a certain pride in not giving the
alarm before; I wished to make the capture alone and
unaided.

Never losing my hold for an instant, I slipped from the
bed to the floor, dragging my captive with me. I had but a
few steps to make to reach the gas-burner; these I made with
the greatest caution, holding the creature in a grip like a
vise. At last I got within arm's length of the tiny speck of
blue light which told me where the gas-burner lay. Quick as
lightning I released my grasp with one hand and let on the
full flood of light. Then I turned to look at my captive.

I cannot even attempt to give any definition of my sensations the instant after I turned on the gas. I suppose I must
have shrieked with terror, for in less than a minute afterward
my room was crowded with the inmates of the house. I shudder now as I think of that awful moment. *I saw nothing!*
Yes; I had one arm firmly clasped round a breathing, panting, corporeal shape, my other hand gripped with all its
strength a throat as warm, and apparently fleshy, as my own;
and yet, with this living substance in my grasp, with its body
pressed against my own, and all in the bright glare of a large
jet of gas, I absolutely beheld nothing! Not even an outline,
a vapor!

I do not, even at this hour, realize the situation in which I
found myself. Imagination in vain tries to compass the awful
paradox.

It breathed. I felt its warm breath upon my cheek. It
struggled fiercely. It had hands. They clutched me. Its skin
was smooth, like my own. There it lay, pressed close up
against me, solid as stone—and yet utterly invisible!

I wonder that I did not faint or go mad on the instant.
Some wonderful instinct must have sustained me; for, absolutely, in place of loosening my hold on the terrible Enigma,
I seemed to gain an additional strength in my moment of
horror, and tightened my grasp with such wonderful force
that I felt the creature shivering with agony.

Just then Hammond entered the room at the head of the

household. As soon as he beheld my face—which, I suppose, must have been an awful sight to look at—he hastened forward, crying, "Great heaven, Harry! what has happened?"

"Hammond! Hammond!" I cried. "Come here. O, this is awful! I have been attacked in bed by something or other, which I have hold of; but I can't see it—I can't see it!"

Hammond, doubtless struck by the unfeigned horror expressed in my countenance, made one or two steps forward with an anxious yet puzzled expression. A very audible titter burst from the remainder of my visitors. This suppressed laughter made me furious. To laugh at a human being in my position! It was the worst species of cruelty. Now I can understand why the appearance of a man struggling violently, as it would seem, with an airy nothing, and calling for assistance against a vision, should have appeared ludicrous. *Then*, so great was my rage against the mocking crowd that had I the power I would have stricken them dead where they stood.

"Hammond! Hammond!" I cried again, despairingly, "for God's sake come to me. I can hold the—the Thing but a short while longer. It is overpowering me. Help me! Help me!"

"Harry," whispered Hammond, approaching me, "you have been smoking too much opium."

"I swear to you, Hammond, that this is no vision," I answered, in the same low tone. "Don't you see how it shakes my whole frame with its struggles? If you don't believe me, convince yourself. Feel it—touch it."

Hammond advanced and laid his hand in the spot I indicated. A wild cry of horror burst from him. He had felt it!

In a moment he had discovered somewhere in my room a long piece of cord, and was the next instant winding it and knotting it about the body of the unseen being that I clasped in my arms.

"Harry," he said, in a hoarse, agitated voice, for, though he preserved his presence of mind, he was deeply moved, "Harry, it's all safe now. You may let go, old fellow, if you're tired. The Thing can't move."

I was utterly exhausted, and I gladly loosed my hold.

Hammond stood holding the ends of the cord that bound the Invisible, twisted round his hand, while before him, self-supporting as it were, he beheld a rope laced and interlaced, and stretching tightly around a vacant space. I never saw a man look so thoroughly stricken with awe. Nevertheless his face expressed all the courage and determination which I knew him to possess. His lips, although white, were set firmly, and one could perceive at a glance that, although stricken with fear, he was not daunted.

The confusion that ensued among the guests of the house who were witnesses of this extraordinary scene between Hammond and myself, who beheld the pantomime of binding this struggling Something, who beheld me almost sinking from physical exhaustion when my task of jailer was over— the confusion and terror that took possession of the by-standers, when they saw all this, was beyond description. The weaker ones fled from the apartment. The few who remained clustered near the door and could not be induced to approach Hammond and his Charge. Still incredulity broke out through their terror. They had not the courage to satisfy themselves, and yet they doubted. It was in vain that I begged of some of the men to come near and convince themselves by touch of the existence in that room of a living being which was invisible. They were incredulous, but did not dare to undeceive themselves. How could a solid, living, breathing body be invisible, they asked. My reply was this. I gave a sign to Hammond, and both of us, conquering our fearful repugnance to touch the invisible creature, lifted it from the ground, manacled as it was, and took it to my bed. Its weight was about that of a boy of fourteen.

"Now, my friends," I said, as Hammond and myself held the creature suspended over the bed, "I can give you self-evident proof that here is a solid, ponderable body, which, nevertheless you cannot see. Be good enough to watch the surface of the bed attentively."

I was astonished at my own courage in treating this strange event so calmly; but I had recovered from my first terror, and felt a sort of scientific pride in the affair, which dominated every other feeling.

The eyes of the by-standers were immediately fixed on my bed. At a given signal Hammond and I let the creature fall. There was the dull sound of a heavy body alighting on a soft mass. The timbers of the bed creaked. A deep impression marked itself distinctly on the pillow, and on the bed itself. The crowd who witnessed this gave a low cry, and rushed from the room. Hammond and I were left alone with our Mystery.

We remained silent for some time, listening to the low, irregular breathing of the creature on the bed, and watching the rustle of the bed-clothes as it impotently struggled to free itself from confinement. Then Hammond spoke.

"Harry, this is awful."

"Ay, awful."

"But not unaccountable."

"Not unaccountable! What do you mean? Such a thing has never occurred since the birth of the world. I know not what to think, Hammond. God grant that I am not mad, and that this is not an insane fantasy!"

"Let us reason a little, Harry. Here is a solid body which we touch, but which we cannot see. The fact is so unusual that it strikes us with terror. Is there no parallel, though, for such a phenomenon? Take a piece of pure glass. It is tangible and transparent. A certain chemical coarseness is all that prevents its being so entirely transparent as to be totally invisible. It is not *theoretically impossible,* mind you, to make a glass which shall not reflect a single ray of light—a glass so pure and homogeneous in its atoms that the rays from the sun will pass through it as they do through the air, refracted but not reflected. We do not see the air, and yet we feel it."

"That's all very well, Hammond, but these are inanimate substances. Glass does not breathe, air does not breathe. This *thing* has a heart that palpitates, a will that moves it, lungs that play, and inspire and respire."

"You forget the phenomena of which we have so often heard of late," answered the doctor, gravely. "At the meetings called 'spirit circles,' invisible hands have been thrust into the hands of those persons round the table—warm, fleshy hands that seemed to pulsate with mortal life."

"What? Do you think, then, that this thing is—"

"I don't know what it is," was the solemn reply; "but, please the gods, I will, with your assistance, thoroughly investigate it."

We watched together, smoking many pipes, all night long, by the bedside of the unearthly being that tossed and panted until it was apparently wearied out. Then we learned by the low, regular breathing that it slept.

The next morning the house was all astir. The boarders congregated on the landing outside my room, and Hammond and myself were lions. We had to answer a thousand questions as to the state of our extraordinary prisoner, for as yet not one person in the house except ourselves could be induced to set foot in the apartment.

The creature was awake. This was evidenced by the convulsive manner in which the bed-clothes were moved in its efforts to escape. There was something truly terrible in beholding, as it were, those second-hand indications of the terrible writhings and agonized struggles for liberty which themselves were invisible.

Hammond and myself had racked our brains during the long night to discover some means by which we might realize the shape and general appearance of the Enigma. As well as we could make out by passing our hands over the creature's form, its outlines and lineaments were human. There was a mouth; a round, smooth head without hair; a nose, which, however, was little elevated above the cheeks; and its hands and feet felt like those of a boy. At first we thought of placing the being on a smooth surface and tracing its outline with chalk, as shoemakers trace the outline of the foot. This plan was given up as being of no value. Such an outline would give not the slightest idea of its conformation.

A happy thought struck me. We could take a cast of it in plaster of Paris. This would give us the solid figure, and satisfy all our wishes. But how to do it? The movements of the creature would disturb the setting of the plastic covering, and distort the mould. Another thought. Why not give it chloroform? It had respiratory organs—that was evident by its breathing. Once reduced to a state of insensibility, we could do with it what we would. Dr. X—— was sent for; and after the worthy physician had recovered from the first shock of amazement, he proceeded to administer the chloroform. In three minutes afterward we were enabled to remove the fetters from the creature's body, and a modeller was busily engaged in covering the invisible form with the moist clay. In five minutes more we had a mould, and before evening a rough facsimile of the Mystery. It was shaped like a man—distorted, uncouth, and horrible, but still a man. It was small, not over four feet and some inches in height, and its limbs revealed a muscular development that was unparalleled. Its face surpassed in hideousness anything I had ever seen. Gustave Doré, or Callot, or Tony Johannot, never conceived anything so horrible. There is a face in one of the latter's illustrations to *Un Voyage où il vous plaira* which somewhat approaches the countenance of this creature, but does not equal it. It was the physiognomy of what I should fancy a ghoul might be. It looked as if it was capable of feeding on human flesh.

Having satisfied our curiosity, and bound every one in the house to secrecy, it became a question what was to be done with our Enigma? It was impossible that we should keep such a horror in our house; it was equally impossible that such an awful being should be let loose upon the world. I confess that I would have gladly voted for the creature's destruction. But who would shoulder the responsibility? Who would undertake the execution of this horrible semblance of a human being? Day after day this question was deliberated gravely. The boarders all left the house. Mrs. Moffat was in despair, and threatened Hammond and myself with all sorts of legal penalties if we did not remove the Horror. Our answer was, "We will go if you like, but we decline taking this creature with us. Remove it yourself if you please. It appeared in your house. On you the responsibility rests." To this there was, of course, no answer. Mrs. Moffat could not obtain for love or money a person who would even approach the Mystery.

The most singular part of the affair was that we were entirely ignorant of what the creature habitually fed on. Everything in the way of nutriment that we could think of was placed before it, but was never touched. It was awful to stand by, day after day, and see the clothes toss, and hear the hard breathing, and know that it was starving.

Ten, twelve days, a fortnight passed, and it still lived. The pulsations of the heart, however, were daily growing fainter, and had now nearly ceased. It was evident that the creature was dying for want of sustenance. While this terrible life-struggle was going on, I felt miserable. I could not sleep. Horrible as the creature was, it was pitiful to think of the pangs it was suffering.

At last it died. Hammond and I found it cold and stiff one morning in the bed. The heart had ceased to beat, the lungs to inspire. We hastened to bury it in the garden. It was a strange funeral, the dropping of that viewless corpse into the damp hole. The cast of its form I gave to Dr. X——, who keeps it in his museum in Tenth Street.

As I am on the eve of a long journey from which I may

not return, I have drawn up this narrative of an event the most singular that has ever come to my knowledge.

Unnoticed by most American s.f. writers and publishers, a science fiction renaissance has been going on in France since 1953, the year in which Maurice Renault founded the magazine Fiction.

Fiction *calls itself the French edition of* The Magazine of Fantasy and Science Fiction, *and translations of stories from that magazine account for something over half its contents. But under the patient encouragement of Renault and his editor, Alain Dorémieux, an almost miraculous growth of native talent has taken place in the last ten years.* Fiction *today regularly publishes the work of a dozen or more capable young French writers, of whom six or seven are as good as the best American and British s.f. writers.*

Here is one example from Fiction, *May 1960—a story of invading aliens written by a young Parisian journalist and film critic. The theme is a familiar one, but Claude Veillot has given it a new resonance of horror: "Today, the reality is this vile sound, this quiet and continuous grating noise whose significance I now know."*

THE FIRST DAYS OF MAY

BY CLAUDE VEILLOT

TRANSLATED BY DAMON KNIGHT

It's the noise that has drawn me toward the slit between the closed shutters. A furtive noise of crumbling, of crushed mica, of walnut shells being slowly cracked. For two days, not a sound has risen from that street which I can see with my eyes closed: the grocery across the way, with its windows broken by looters, its bags of dried beans spilled out as far as the gutter; the apartment house on the corner, half fallen down—its façade tumbled into the street, exposing the cross-sections of apartments, furniture hanging out mockingly over emptiness; abandoned cars, some parked along the side of the street, others left where they stopped, blocking the way, tires flat; and then those incongruous remnants strewn across the flagstones and asphalt—handbags, bundles of laundry, a baby carriage, broken bottles, scraps of newspaper, a roll of blankets, a few mismated shoes, a sewing machine.

Four days ago—only four days—that street was full of people. You couldn't know then that the bed in the third-floor apartment of the building opposite was covered with pink cretonne, because the façade was still in place. Customers went into the grocery. "And what will it be today, madam?" A baby was drooling in the carriage, the sewing machine was purring behind an unbroken window, cars were running in the streets where no ragpickers' clutter was strewn.

Only four days, and already you have the feeling that all that never existed. Wasn't it all a dream? Did I really, one day, a long time ago, walk in the sun with my fellows? Come home to a woman I loved in the evening? Listen to records? Complain about the high cost of living? Read books? Make love?

Today, the reality is this vile sound, this quiet and continuous grating noise whose significance I now know. There are two of them, coupling right under my shutters, near an automobile with its windows broken, and that horrible crunching means simply that the female is in the act of devouring the male.

They have been compared to praying mantises too often. In fact, when it's a question of that praying mantis that has such an effect on us, standing upright on a twig, with its globular eyes and its armored claws, we always have the recourse of crushing it with a blow, at the cost of fighting back a spasm of nausea. But when the mantis is as big as a kangaroo . . .

And then what kind of mantises were they, that they could conceive and use those machines that we saw on the first day, the day it all began? (Or should I say the day when it all ended?)

I can't take my eyes away from the terrible sight. A faintness of horror makes me go on staring at that monstrous copulation, the clinging of those greenish abdomens, the vibrating wing cases, and, above all, that kind of parrot's beak grinding the corselet of the still living male, who trembles gently in all his limbs, as if in a horrible ecstasy.

Now there is another sound, thin as a cricket's chirp, then

swelling to a piercing whistle, like the sound of those defective mikes at the meetings and the neighborhood dances not so long ago. I can't help moving back a step. It's the female who is shrilling. That's where their name comes from: the Shrills. Nobody had time or inclination to think of anything else, and, all things considered, it's the best name for them.

Their true, their only power lies not in being so frightful and cruel as to make us forget our worst nightmares. Nor in being so many that no one has ever been able to estimate their numbers exactly. Their true, their only superiority is in their ability to shrill. When that modulated whistling goes into the supersonic, becomes inaudible to any terrestrial ear, you can see men and beasts fall like flies, not to rise again as long as the sound lasts.

But there's worse to come, for they have succeeded in analyzing that physiological peculiarity, defining it and then applying it to instruments of war, multiplying its effectiveness. The Shrills needed no cannon to gut our apartment buildings: the ultrasonics were enough.

Below, in the street, the female Shrill goes on modulating her love whistle. A wave of fear and hatred washes over me. Stop that hideous noise, that disgusting nibbling, the whole obscene business! I've snatched up my revolver out of the open valise on the table. The shutters fly back against the wall. Suddenly the sun cleanses this miserable hotel room where I've lived four days alone, glued in my fear, after everyone else has run off.

Shots crash out, echoing, almost joyful in the sinister silence of the empty suburb. One, two, three shots . . . The head with its monstrous eyes is burst open. The female Shrill is dead between one spasm and the next, but I can't stop firing, four, five, six, before the hammer falls on an empty cartridge.

After all these hours of isolation, of shadow and muffled silence, let there be light, noise, action! I'm not afraid any longer. The smell of the powder is still floating in the air. The fact that the half-devoured Shrill is still trembling doesn't frighten me; on the contrary, it sends me into a mad rage.

I've sprung out of my room, hurled myself down the stairs, torn apart the barricade of furniture and mattresses I had piled up in front of the entrance. There's a fuel can tied onto the abandoned car; I've cut the string with one or two strokes of my knife and pulled it down. I've soaked the two Shrills. Ten, twenty liters of gasoline . . .

I'm watching their bodies burn, crackle, snap, split open, burst, suppurate in the red bonfire, which, at the very beginning, carried off their wings and wing cases in a quick, high blaze. I'm so close to the flames that I'm sweating, gasping—so close that charred scraps thrown out by the crackling fire lodge in my hair. And I'm laughing.

Hours of walking through the silent streets choked with wreckage and rubble. The smell that comes from the demolished buildings is terrible.

I couldn't stay in my hotel room any longer. Maybe the Shrills patrol past there? If they'd found the two burned monsters, they would have been quick to pluck me out of my hole in turn.

It's true that there's no lack of Shrill corpses. Crossing an amusement park, I've seen more than fifty of them rotting on the paths, on the edge of the pond and even in the middle of the little red cars and the miniature bicycles of a ride. They had been ripped apart by bullets.

I've also seen those who brought off this fine butchery: the crew of two heavy machine guns set up at the exits of the park. They were twisted on the ground, fists over their cars, in the poignant stillness of violent death. A big helmet had rolled to the base of a plane tree. Some machine-gun belts were strewn about.

There must have been some of them nearly everywhere in the city, these elements of the rear guard who'd been left there to permit the evacuation of the civil population. Sacrifices, ordered to slow up the invasion by a few minutes, a few seconds, before the buildings started to come apart around them and repellent silhouettes appeared at the street corners, carrying in their faceted eyes the hundredfold reflection of the same horrified human face.

Isn't what I've been doing pure idiocy? There isn't a single person still living in the city, that's clear. Why should Maria have stayed? Even if she'd wanted to, they would have made her go with the rest. The first day, I remember, radio cars went through every district: "Your attention, please! It is necessary to evacuate the city temporarily—the invader has succeeded in overrunning our troops! Get out to the country!

Don't stay in the city! Get out to the country! Any person who ignores this order will be in mortal danger!"

From the window of my hotel I saw that infernal stampede, the brutality, fear and disorder, that frothing exodus to which all the halfhearted official appeals couldn't bring even a semblance of dignity.

I couldn't leave. Not without Maria. And perhaps also because I was more frightened than the rest, frightened enough to stay cooped up four days in a dark room. Like a coward, after all. But what is a coward, what a hero, when it comes to the Shrills?

I'm frozen to the spot when I hear the noise. In the deathly silence of the abandoned city, it echoes like an explosion. Nevertheless, as soon as my heartbeat slows down a little, I identify the sound. Memories of coffee with cream, smells of anisette, Martinis, cognac, hubbub of voices and laughter . . . It's the authoritative bell of a cash register.

I push open the glass door of the café. Moleskin cushions. Marble tables. Is it possible that this familiar décor has anything to do with all that ridiculous horror outside?

The man hasn't seen me. Leaning over the showcase, he's carefully counting some bills, pausing every so often to lick his finger.

I barely touch his shoulder. With remarkable agility, he turns and in the same movement draws a big blue-barreled Colt. In his thin, whiskery face, his eyes are cruel and nervous at the same time; and he shows his teeth like a dog. "What the hell are you doing here?"

He's a noncom; there's a stripe on his dirty, torn khaki sleeve.

"I haven't seen anyone for four days," I say. "I'm looking for my wife." And after a pause, "What's the news?"

He spins the pistol gracefully around his forefinger before holstering it again. "Don't waste your breath!" And, tapping himself on the ear: "Stone deaf! See what they've done with their vibrations, those lousy bugs!"

Suspicious again, he examines me from head to foot. "Say, don't you know all civilians were supposed to evacuate the city?"

Then he shrugs, goes around the counter, takes down a bottle and two glasses. "Civilians, military, what the hell difference does all that stuff make now? Two days ago I was in position near the plastic works—you know, on the other side of the river. Had to watch the people filing past, trucks, buses, cars, bikes, carts, people on foot. Couldn't have been one out of two that knew what was happening to them. The radio hardly had time to explain what was going on and bang! No more radio! 'It's the Russians!' they said, or else, 'It's the Americans!' Nobody wanted to believe the official statement, that story about invaders that they called—how'd it go again—'extraterrestrial.' "

He lifts his glass to clink it with mine. "Never mind telling me bottoms up, I won't hear you! . . . It was the same with us, anyhow, we didn't put much stock in that story. It was hard to swallow, am I right? Well, they explained it to us, anyhow, that these characters came from another planet. But which one? They told us they had them already in the U.S., Canada, England too, maybe even in Russia. But how could we tell? They said we'd have to fight, this time, not for territory or for ideals, but for our own skin. Okay, but what with?"

Aiming his two forefingers one behind the other, he whistles between his teeth. "Oh, the flame throwers, they didn't go so bad at the beginning. We went at it hot and heavy, I can tell you! Have you seen those bugs up close? Don't know why, you get a crazy urge to kill them, crush them, destroy 'em. Maybe because they're scary and disgusting? We went after them, with our torches! We burned piles and piles of them! But that didn't last. They started in shrilling. Nearly the whole company went down. We fell back to this side of the river, and, if you'll believe it, the Genius blew up the bridge!"

He bursts into laughter which suggests anything but gaiety.

"As if that would keep them from jumping, those bugs! A Shrill can hop a good twenty meters, and with those damned wings they can keep going a little longer. I understand they could do a lot better, even, if Earth gravity didn't bother them! No, no, don't bother to open your mouth, I tell you! I can't hear a thing! You know what we're going to do, you and me? We're going to try to find a car, or an army jeep, and we're going to get out of this damned town. The people must be somewhere, right?"

I shake my head.

"What? You don't want to stay here the rest of your life, do you?"

I open my mouth, then change my mind, tear a sheet out

of my notebook and write: "I've got to find my wife."

Leaning his elbows on the counter, in the familiar attitude of a saloonkeeper, he scratches his ear, at once ironic and compassionate. "Oh well, anyhow, that's love for you!"

What a strange feeling to go through this series of motions: take a key out of my pocket, slide it into a lock. I've entered my apartment this way hundreds of times. Maria would be waiting for me. That seemed natural. There'll never be enough time to regret the indifference with which I took that simple happiness.

The apartment is full of darkness; all the shutters are closed. I don't recognize the familiar smell that means home. In its place, there's an intrusive odor, persistent and heavy: the scent of a cigar.

I open a door. A man is sitting crosswise in an upholstered chair, his legs hanging over the armrest. He has on a grayish undershirt; he's smoking an enormous cigar and reading one of my books, while he scratches a three-day beard.

To top it all, it's he who looks at me and exclaims, "Well! Don't stand on ceremony!"

The only light on him comes from three candles stuck to the top shelf of the bookcase. He has hollow cheeks, anxious eyes. Do I too have that hunted look?

I take a step. "Maybe you don't know it, but you're in *my* chair!"

He puffs. "The persistence of bourgeois concepts after the disappearance of the society which created them is one of the most hilarious aspects of the event."

A phrasemaker. Good. He can't be very dangerous. See him encompass space with a gesture. "Nothing left! All consumed! Everything is broken down in the most frenetic, most repugnant, most definitive of routs! And what do we behold now? A survivor—who knows? the last, perhaps. And what does he do? Does he repent? Does he swear to rebuild a better world? No. He demands *his* chair."

I let myself fall on the sofa; fatigue cuts my hamstrings. In the wavering light of the candles, I watch the man suck on his cigar. He takes it out of his mouth and says quietly, " '*And the shapes of the locusts were like unto horses prepared unto battle . . .*' " His voice rises slowly. " '*. . . and their faces were as the faces of men.*' " Eyes on the ceiling, he seems to be deciphering the prophetic text up there.

" *'And they had hair as the hair of women, and their teeth were as the teeth of lions.'* "

The Apocalypse!

"I recognize you! You live on the sixth floor. You're the one who writes books."

"I lived on the sixth floor, correct! But this is bigger, more comfortable. And then there's the bar, and the library as well. My word, you were a man of taste!"

"I'm looking for my wife."

"That way too, you were a man of taste! But I must tell you she's not here. When I picked your lock, it was because I knew there was nobody left in here."

"She's gone?"

He makes a vague gesture which flattens the candle flames for a moment. "Gone with all the rest, when they passed with their loudspeakers. Idiots! Leave, to go where?"

She is gone. She didn't wait for me. She was afraid. But didn't I myself stay shut up four days in a hotel, too terrified even to open the shutters?

"What about you? You decided to stay."

He puts on a profoundly disgusted expression. "It's because I can't stand crowds. During the exodus, in 'forty, when I was a kid, too many people stepped on my feet. Morning and evening, for weeks, the crowds of people that mashed my feet! Anyhow, do you want me to tell you where they ended up, the ones who listened to the loudspeakers? In camps."

"Camps?"

"Camps, yes. Prison camps. That's what I don't understand. After that slaughter, the Shrills cared for the survivors. As soon as we stopped resisting, they stopped destroying. Curious, isn't it?"

He relights his dead cigar. "You think I've been here all this time without budging? You're mistaken. I've gone out, I've walked, I've pinched bicycles and even a car. Not to escape—to look. I've seen some things, some things— What a spectacle! Have you gone down in the subway passages? There are thousands of burned Shrills. You walk in pulp up to the knees. They installed their first colonies down there. The Army poured in tons of incendiary fluids through all the entrances and the air holes. You can bet, after that there was a shrilling!

"I also argued with dozens of people, soldiers, civil-defense guys, chemists, biologists, scientists. They were looking for something, a method. Some of them talked about making contact, negotiating a settlement. Pitiful! The Shrills have never tried to communicate. They arrive, they shrill and that's all! Some say they're organized, therefore intelligent. Oh, certainly! After all, so are the ants and the bees! But you've got to attack the problem from the other end. Imagine for a moment that in their eyes *we're* the ants. Would it bother you much to break up an anthill with a few kicks? And did you ever think about negotiating in any way with the ants?"

He gets up, opens my bar with great ease of manner and takes out two glasses, into which he pours stingily. "I'm saving the whiskey. There isn't much left. You know, actually these Shrills interest me. What do they want? We don't even know where they come from. From one of the moons of Jupiter, a scientist claimed the other night on the radio— before the radio stopped like everything else. But what did he know about it, hm? I ask you. In any case, one thing is certain: they have absolutely no interest in us as thinking beings. They don't even seem to be aware of that peculiarity of which we're so proud. They're intelligent and highly developed, too, undoubtedly, but in a way so different from ours that it doesn't pay to look for points of comparison."

He points his cigar butt at me. "Have you seen a Shrill visit just one house? Examine a machine? Try to start a car? Show any trace of curiosity in a heavy machine gun or a telephone booth? No. Except for the machines that brought them here, you'd think they lack even the idea of technology. Of course, I haven't forgotten the shrilling machines, the ones that knock buildings down, but who can say he's seen one? I heard a biologist remark that they could get the same results just as well by simply shrilling in chorus. So?"

He goes on talking as if to himself, getting rid of thoughts he's repeated over and over, in his hours and days of solitude. "They haven't tried to rebuild, or even occupy, damaged cities. Even the colonies in the subway were provisional. Later they were satisfied to set up their gelatinous towns out in the open fields, like heaps of yellowish cocoons, piles of insect nests. A collectivist activity, a purely functional civilization, whose standards are entirely alien to human intelligence."

He slaps his knee. "But just the same, by heaven, if they've come all this way there's a reason for it!"

I drain my glass and get up suddenly. "I have no intention of looking for the reason here while I jabber into a glass of whiskey. I want to find my wife."

He salutes me with a nonchalant hand at his brow. "Good luck, noble spouse! Close the door carefully as you leave."

"Those camps you were talking about—where are they?"

"At the city exits. They're not camps, properly speaking. They look more like gypsy tents, or vacationers' campsites. No fences, no barbed wire. They're surrounded by Shrills, that's all. I've watched one—at a distance, naturally, with a pair of field glasses, from the top of an HLM building. The people seemed to be in good condition. There were kitchen details. Things were organized. I saw women doing their laundry in tubs, some guys playing ball. I saw kids, too."

He falls silent. In his burning eyes I see again the anguished flame they had at the beginning. "Don't ask me to go with you. I won't go. That camp with the wooden barracks, the tents, the washing on the lines, kids playing, and then all around, here and there, those goddam big grasshoppers . . ." His shoulders shake with disgust. "Those people guarded by—by that . . . it was more horrible than anything else, than houses destroyed, corpses in the streets, the crazy soldiers with their hands over their ears, the stink of the subway. I don't want to see that camp again."

"If I recognize my wife there, can I get to her?"

"Oh, certainly! The Shrills are understanding, just think of it! While I was watching, up on that roof, I saw a lot of people go in, poor starved characters, attracted by the smell of cooking. But as for getting out again . . . No, I won't go with you, even if I have to croak here of hunger and thirst."

I put my glass down, move slowly toward the door and turn. I can't help smiling. "Have you looked in the kitchen, on the top shelf of the cabinet? There must be still a full bottle there."

I didn't get as far as the camp. I met the man long before that. He was walking in the middle of the street with a self-assurance, a lack of caution, that was absolutely stupefying. His leather-visored cap, the bandoleer he'd squeezed on over his overalls, the carbine he was carrying by the strap—were these really enough to give him that swaggering confidence, that complete detachment, as if he were convinced of his own invulnerability?

All the same, when I hailed him he seized the weapon quickly and brought it up to his hip. He handled it with impressive skill.

I stepped away from the bus with the flat tires, behind which I'd hidden when I first heard his footsteps.

"What are you doing there? Aren't you in camp with the rest?" He stared at me, finger on the trigger.

"That's just it, I'm looking for the camp—my wife may be there. I've got to find her, you understand?"

He relaxed a little. His teeth showed in a smile. "Are you really trying to get into a camp?"

"Into the one where I'll find my wife, yes. I've got to find her. The war is over, isn't it?"

His smile widened. "Sure, it's good and over. For a long time! And as long as you want to go to the camp, why, I'll just take you there."

He turned, holding his weapon by the strap again. Another man, a skinny little guy with the thick glasses of the nearsighted, had just appeared at the corner of a devastated bakery. The Garand rifle sticking up over the shoulder of his checkered jacket seemed as huge as it was incongruous. Five others followed him, but these were weaponless, their shoulders drooping, eyes full of dull pain. They were being pushed along from behind by the barrels of machine pistols.

"This gentleman wants to go to the camp!"

The tone of his voice chilled me. The armed men broke out into astonishing smiles; the others were staring at me with bewilderment, and the little nearsighted man let out a sort of yelp: "A volunteer! Now I've seen everything, everything!" He stamped his feet with joy.

The man with the leather visor was bowing with artificial politeness. "Will the gentleman allow himself to be searched?"

The nearsighted little guy began to go awkwardly through my pockets. He finished by taking out my billfold, examined it, closed it, then made as if to hand it back. When I went to take the billfold, it slipped through his fingers, and it almost seemed to me that he'd done it on purpose.

I bent over, feeling as if I were in the midst of a nightmare, watching myself live through a story invented by myself with God knows what goal of horrid pleasure. At the moment when I was about to pick up the billfold, somebody's foot sent me flying into the middle of the street.

I got up. Behind the porthole-thick glasses, the nearsighted little man's eyes were like those of a fish. No more malignant, no more friendly.

Now I'm marching with the rest. The man with the leather visor walks a hundred and fifty feet ahead of us across the wreckage and rubble. The nearsighted little man and his skirmishers follow us in dispersed order.

"What came over you? Are you crazy or what?" It's the man next to me, muttering between his teeth, without turning his head toward me. On the collar of his navy-blue uniform are the gilded insignia of the Public Transportation Service. To keep his hands from trembling, he's squeezing them together behind his back.

"I want to find my wife. She must be in a camp."

"My wife was at the camp, too. She was there with me. Then yesterday they came looking for her."

"The Shrills?"

"No, of course not. The Shrills don't come into the camps. They're satisfied to hang around the outside. It's these guys here that come looking for people."

"These men? But who are they? I thought . . ."

He chuckles. "You see the little guy with the big glasses? Don't argue with him—do whatever he tells you. I saw him kill two women with his rifle, that tried to escape from camp."

A nauseating thing. I had thought the Shrills were rotten; but the Shrills aren't men.

"What now? Where are they taking us?"

"I don't know. When they take away a bunch like this, you never see them again. I waited for my wife. They didn't bring her back."

"Maybe they're regrouping people in other camps? Maybe we're going to the camp where your wife is already?"

He shrugs. "You're kidding! You've seen what happened, haven't you? You've seen how those vermin destroyed everything, killed everybody, in four days? You've seen these characters that are guarding us? If they're taking us someplace else, it's because it's useful to them—the Shrills. That's all."

"If that's how it really is, why not run for it?"

He turns his head toward me with a wan smile. "Go ahead, try!"

At the entrance to the Winter Circus, a number of Shrills are crouching on their barbed legs. They're the first I've seen since the ones I burned this morning, in front of the hotel. I stop short, my blood frozen. It goes beyond fear—it's an unconquerable repulsion that glues my feet to the ground.

A hand pushes me between the shoulder blades; it's the little nearsighted man. "Keep going—they won't eat you!"

The other guards guffaw.

Does that curious noise come from the Circus—that whirring sound, thin and yet loud, that reminds me of the sound of crickets in the wastelands of Provence? And where does that heavy, thick, stale odor come from, that *green* smell? . . .

I don't see anything at first except the circular fence set up on the outside of the track. And in that cage, a Shrill. He's standing upright, the anterior legs stiffened horizontally, and pivoting slowly around. I realize immediately why he's turning that way, and I feel the hairs prickle on the back of my neck: a man is facing him, walking slowly around him, with a saber bayonet in his hand.

I hear one of the men next to me whisper, "My God!" while our guards push us into a box. I go closer to the railing, fascinated. Down there, the man and the Shrill are keeping their faces turned toward each other. They're both on the defensive, watching each other, waiting. Sweat is streaming down the torso of the man with the bayonet. He has leather leggings on his calves; he's a soldier. I can't tell if it's brute fear or the courage of despair that I see in his eyes. Both, maybe.

Those legs, sharp as saw blades, have suddenly lashed the air. The man has leaped aside, with astonishing agility. A notch is cut into his bare shoulder.

The low grating sound which fills the whole Circus is suddenly amplified, and at the same instant I see what the terrible spectacle in the cage has kept me from noticing. They are there, filling the seats, in the penumbra surrounding the track. Hundreds and hundreds of them. Almost frozen motionless, prodigiously attentive. The Shrills.

But that isn't the worst. Among the Shrills I can make out

men, and some women too, their faces pale with anxious pleasure, their mouths half open, eyes fixed, riveted in the same expectancy. One of them is dressed in her best. She's wearing a white hat, and a resplendent clip in the lapel of her tailored suit. I can't take my eyes off that clip.

Once more, the heavy collective vibration has turned feverish. There's a yell from the jeweled woman. The man in the cage tears himself out of a clinch at the very moment when that parrot's beak is about to seize him by the nape. Blood spurts out of his torn back. From where I am, I can hear the whistling in his lungs.

"You're next! Get ready!" The man with the leather visor is looking at us through the railing in which we're confined. He shows his uneven teeth in an open smile.

"You can't let it go on! You can't! Don't you understand?" One of my companions, a fat man who till now has never stopped taking off his rimless glasses and putting them on again, is clinging to the bars, making them shake with his own trembling. "You can't! You're a man like us!"

The other man falls back a step. "Why can't I? It's a fair fight, isn't it? For one thing, we give you a bayonet. And then, your opponent doesn't have the right to shrill. The audience either, of course."

He adds, turning his head away. "What do you think, I invented this game?"

Others are throwing themselves on the bars, too. One of them, a big young man in blue jeans, sobs hysterically and falls to his knees. Only the man in the navy-blue bus driver's jacket, the one who spoke to me before, remains to one side. He's pale, his nostrils are pinched; he holds himself very straight, closing his eyes. If he weren't here, I'd grab hold of the bars, too, I'd howl, too, the way the rest are doing.

The murmur has suddenly turned to an intense humming, like the sound that comes from an overturned hive. I can't help looking. The soldier has managed to leap onto his enemy's back. His courage is too much for men. Why so much vitality, when there's no hope?

Then everything happens very quickly. The bayonet scythes through the air. The Shrill's head leaps like a football, while the huge trembling body, in a final spasm, sends the man rolling in the sawdust. He springs up, hurls himself back. His weapon rips open the green abdomen, which bursts and empties itself; then he attacks the corselet and splits it. But it's all over. The long, armored legs are moving only in an imperceptible, interminable shiver. The feverish humming fills my ears. I hear the voice of the man with the leather visor:

"You're in luck! It's not often that one of them gets it in the neck! When that happens, the games are postponed till the next day. Come on, get going!"

"The first days of May, they're the best for vacations. Remember the woods? The smell of the woods? The smell of leaves? Remember the squirrel in Mervent forest? The mill at the water's edge? Remember the lost clearing, where the silence is so beautiful that it makes you weep? The only sound is that of the green woodpecker. Rap, rap! it sounds like a stubborn elf who's knocking endlessly at the door. His wife doesn't want to let him in, so he knocks, he knocks. . . . In May we'll go back there!"

So spoke Maria.

It's May, and I'm rolling across the countryside, but it's in a truck that stinks of fuel oil and sweat, packed in with strangers, dejected men and women, their eyes empty.

Those who guard us have metal helmets or cloth caps. With their weapons between their knees, they are at the same time watchful and distant, as if detached from us.

I watch them. Some are dull brutes, others half mad, still others are cowards. But they are men. Don't they understand what they're doing? I look at them, but they will not meet my gaze. I know how they react when questions are added to these looks. One of us is lying on the floor, his forehead laid open by a blow from a rifle butt. . . .

When the truck stops, the first thing I see is the farmhouse. It seems so simple, so natural, with its old rough-cast walls, its untrimmed vines climbing around the garret windows, so simple and so beautiful that tears come to my eyes. But it is immured in silence, and no one moves in the house, nor in the deserted stable, nor in the vacant barnyard. Even the doghouse is empty. On the tractor seat is a baby doll, one of those big celluloid dolls that little girls dress up in wool jumpers. It has an arm missing.

Then I look beyond, at the fields.

"Gelatinous masses, like heaps of yellowish cocoons, piles of insect nests." That was the way my neighbor, the writer, described the Shrill towns.

The paths we follow to get to it are hard and beaten, as if thousands of feet have trodden them before us. When the first Shrills show themselves, a few of my companions fall to their knees and have to be dragged. . . .

I don't think I'll ever go insane, or I would be insane now. How could we have let ourselves be pushed, dragged, into the interior of . . . of what, in fact? What kind of town are these domes joined together, piled up one on another, these hills of moist cotton secreted no doubt by the same creatures who live in them?

Someone laughs nearby, a girl with short hair who looks around her with a happy expression, as if in a dream. That one, perhaps, has found her deliverance.

In the tunnels, the stale, viscous smell grows so thick you can almost feel it. A pale, cold daylight, without brilliance, springs from no visible source, maybe just from these fibrous walls which, when you bump into them accidentally—and not without repulsion—deposit on your sleeves cottony, gluey particles, feebly luminous.

Other guards have replaced the first ones, and there are Shrills with them now. We walk, but we no longer know where we're going. Some are crying soundlessly, but they don't know they're crying. Are we really living through this, have we forgotten who we are?

The tunnels cross and multiply without ever rising or descending. And why should we be surprised when we cross that larger gallery, as big as a subway station, with walls pierced by a thousand cells? Why should we be surprised if, in each one of these cells, an oblong form is stretched out, enveloped as in a cocoon by that cottony, gluey substance? We're no longer of this world, are we? And the outside has never existed.

They don't move, but their eyes are open. They don't speak, their features are frozen, but in their pupils shines the wavering spark of life. Horror and despair, incredulity, hatred and madness.

More tunnels. More cells. Hundreds, thousands of cells, and then the end. Time is suddenly suspended. Silence, and the waiting Shrills.

Their bellies are gigantic, swollen to the bursting point. These are the females. The first days of May—egg-laying time.

Why does that old man suddenly begin to struggle, and

that woman with the dyed hair, too? Since three guards can hold them easily? Since the sting of the female Shrill is so quick? Since ankylosis and paralysis, in a few minutes at most, will seize their numbed members, their defeated muscles, leaving only the vital organs functioning, and the brain clear?

That blond hair, spread out on the floor of a cell, is like Maria's hair, and those golden eyes that stare at me are like Maria's eyes. This blond woman looking at me, entangled in her nightmare, frozen with horror—does she already feel inside her the slow working of incubation? How long has she been there, and how many little Shrills will be born inside her, to feed on her, before they emerge from her torn flesh into the gray light of the tunnels?

I've found you, Maria. For you might easily be Maria, mightn't you? Do you want to be? You're of my race and you're my wife, and I've searched for you and found you. The Shrills don't understand what we are. The Shrills keep us in camps the way we keep herds on the range, but we're not cattle. The Shrills lead us to combat like bulls in the ring, but we're men, just the same. The Shrills store us and pile us up the way wasps store up their provision of flies for the winter, but we're not flies. And the female Shrills lay their eggs in us and leave us to be devoured alive by their little ones, but in spite of everything you are Maria and I'm the one you loved. The Shrills don't understand that, never will understand it and that's why we're greater than the Shrills, Maria.

Two guards take me by the elbows. I point with my chin toward the shadow from which the wide-open golden eyes still stare at me.

"Next to that one is where I want to be!"

"All right," says one of the two without looking at me. And he adds, with an odd catch in his voice, "You realize, we're not responsible!"

Not responsible? No, of course not. No one is responsible, or else everyone is.

The man who drank my whiskey had it by heart: *"And the shapes of the locusts were like unto horses prepared unto battle . . . and their faces were as the faces of men. . . . And they had hair as the hair of women, and their teeth were as the teeth of lions."*

The female Shrill is coming nearer. . . . She doesn't even seem horrible to me.

The pattern for invading monstrosities like those in Veillot's story was set by H. G. Wells, in The War of the Worlds. *Inevitably, there came a reaction to this, expressed in* Out of the Silent Planet, *by C. S. Lewis:*

His mind, like so many minds of his generation, was richly furnished with bogies. He had read his H. G. Wells and others. His universe was peopled with horrors such as ancient and mediaeval mythology could hardly rival. No insect-like, vermiculate or crustacean Abominable, no twitching feelers, rasping wings, slimy coils, curling tentacles, no monstrous union of superhuman intelligence and insatiable cruelty seemed to him anything but likely on an alien world. The *sorns* would be . . . would be . . . he dared not think what the *sorns* would be. And he was to be given to them. Somehow this seemed more horrible than being caught by them. Given, handed over, offered. He saw in imagination various incompatible monstrosities—bulbous eyes, grinning jaws, horns, stings, mandibles. Loathing of insects, loathing of snakes, loathing of things that squashed and squelched, all played their horrible symphonies over his nerves. But the reality would be worse: it would be an extraterrestrial Otherness—something one had never thought of, never could have thought of. In that moment Ransom made a decision. He could face death, but not the *sorns*. He must escape when they got to Malacandra, if there were any possibility. Starvation, or even to be chased by *sorns,* would be better than being handed over. If escape were impossible, then it must be suicide.

All this terror turns out to be wasted, of course, when we meet the grave, intellectual sorns *of Lewis' Mars.*

But the acceptance of other beings as superior and benevolent, replacing a stereotyped pattern, itself became stereotyped. Science fiction has an attractive habit of saying "Yes, but . . ." even to itself. The story you are going to read next, written by a Lancaster, Pennsylvania, patent attorney, skin diver and former chemical engineer, was written to suggest that Wells may have been right in the first place. It originally appeared in Astounding, *August 1959. It is a compact, brutally powerful piece of work, and in its own terms I think you will find it unanswerable.*

DAY OF SUCCESSION

BY THEODORE L. THOMAS

General Paul T. Tredway was an arrogant man with the unforgivable gift of being always right. When the object came out of the sky in the late spring of 1979, it was General Tredway who made all of the decisions concerning it. Sweeping in over the northern tip of Greenland, coming on a dead line from the Yamal Peninsula, the object alerted every warning unit from the Dew Line to the radar operator at the Philadelphia National Airport. Based on the earliest reports, General Tredway concluded that the object was acting in an anomalous fashion; its altitude was too low too long. Accordingly, acting with a colossal confidence, he called off the manned interceptor units and forbade the launching of interceptor missiles. The object came in low over the Pocono Mountains and crashed in southeastern Pennsylvania two miles due west of Terre Hill.

The object still glowed a dull red, and the fire of the smashed house still smoldered when General Tredway arrived with the troops. He threw a cordon around it and made a swift investigation. The object: fifty feet long, thirty feet in diameter, football-shaped, metallic, too hot to inspect closely. Visualizing immediately what had to be done, the general set up a command headquarters and began ordering the items he needed. With no wasted word or motion he built toward the finished plan as he saw it.

Scientists arrived at the same time as the asbestos clothing needed for them to get close. Tanks and other material flowed toward the impact site. Radios and oscillators scanned all frequencies seeking—what? No man there knew what to expect, but no man cared. General Tredway was on the ground personally, and no one had time for anything but his job. The gunners sat with eyes glued to sights, mindful of the firing pattern in which they had been instructed. Handlers poised over their ammunition. Drivers waited with hands on the wheel, motors idling. Behind this ring of steel a more permanent bulwark sprang up. Spotted back farther were the technical shacks for housing the scientific equipment. Behind the shacks the reporters gathered, held firmly in check by armed troops. The site itself was a strange mixture of taut men in frozen immobility and casual men in bustling activity.

In an hour the fact emerged which General Tredway had suspected all along: the object was not of earthly origin. The alloy of which it was made was a known high-temperature alloy, but no technology on Earth could cast it in seamless form in that size and shape. Mass determinations and ultrasonic probes showed that the object was hollow but was crammed inside with a material different from the shell. It was then that General Tredway completely reorganized his fire power and mapped out a plan of action that widened the eyes of those who were to carry it out.

On the general's instructions, everything said at the site was said into radio transmitters and thus recorded a safe fifty miles away. And it was the broadcasting of the general's latest plan of action that brought in the first waves of mild protest. But the general went ahead.

The object had lost its dull hot glow when the first indications of activity inside could be heard. General Tredway immediately removed all personnel to positions of safety outside the ring of steel. The ring itself buttoned up; when a circle of men fire toward a common center, someone can get hurt.

With the sound of tearing, protesting metal, a three-foot circle appeared at the top of the object, and the circle began to turn. As it turned it began to lift away from the main body of the object, and soon screw threads could be seen. The hatch rose silently, looking like a bung being unscrewed from a barrel. The time came when there was a gentle click, and the hatch dropped back a fraction of an inch; the last thread had become disengaged. There was a pause. The heavy silence was broken by a throbbing sound from the object that continued for forty-five seconds and then stopped. Then, without further sound, the hatch began to lift back on its northernmost rim.

In casual tones, as if he were speaking in a classroom, General Tredway ordered the northern, northeastern and north-western regions of the ring into complete cover. The hatch lifted until finally its underside could be seen; it was colored a dull, nonreflecting black. Higher the hatch lifted, and immediately following it was a bulbous mass that looked like a half-opened rose blossom. Deep within the mass there glowed a soft violet light, clearly apparent to the eye even in the sharp Pennsylvania sunshine.

The machine-gun bullets struck the mass first, and the tracers could be seen glancing off. But an instant later the shaped charges in the rockets struck the mass and shattered it. The 105s, the 101 rifles, the rocket launchers, poured a hail of steel onto the canted hatch, ricocheting much of the steel into the interior of the object. Delay-timed high-explosive shells went inside and detonated.

A flame tank left the ring of steel and lumbered forward, followed by two armored trucks. At twenty-five yards a thin stream of fire leaped from the nozzle of the tank and splashed off the hatch in a Niagara of flame. A slight correction, and the Niagara poured down into the opening. The tank moved in close, and the guns fell suddenly silent. Left in the air was a high-pitched shrieking wail, abruptly cut off.

Flames leaped from the opening, so the tank turned off its igniter and simply shot fuel into the object. Asbestos-clad men jumped from the trucks and fed a metal hose through the opening and forced it deep into the object. The compressors started, and a blast of high-pressure air passed through the hose, insuring complete combustion of everything inside. For three minutes the men fed fuel and air to the interior of the object, paying in the metal hose as the end fused off. Flames shot skyward with the roar of a blast furnace. The heat was so great that the men at work were saved only by the constant sreams of water that played on them. Then it was over.

General Tredway placed the burned-out cinder in charge of the scientists and then regrouped his men for resupply and criticism. These were in progress when the report of the second object came in.

The trackers were waiting for it. General Tredway had reasoned that when one object arrived, another might follow, and so he had ordered the trackers to look for it. It hit twenty-five miles west of the first one, near Florin. General Tredway and his men were on their way even before impact. They arrived twenty minutes after it hit.

The preparations were the same, only more streamlined now. The soldiers and the scientists moved more surely, with less wasted motion than before. But as the cooling period progressed, the waves of protest came out of Washington and reached toward General Tredway. "Terrible." "First contact . . ." "Exterminating them like vermin . . ." "Peaceful relationship . . ." ". . . military mind." The protests took on an official character just before the hatch on the second object opened. An actual countermanding of General Tredway's authority came through just as the rockets opened fire on the half-opened rose blossom. The burning out proceeded on schedule. Before it was complete, General Tredway climbed into a helicopter to fly the hundred miles to Washington, D.C. In half an hour he was there.

It is one of the circumstances of a democracy that in an emergency half a dozen men can speak for the entire country. General Tredway stalked into a White House conference room where waited the President, the Vice-President, the Speaker of the House, the President Pro Tempore of the Senate, the House Minority Leader, and a cabinet member. No sooner had he entered than the storm broke.

"Sit down, General, and explain to us if you can the meaning of your reprehensible conduct."

"What are you trying to do, make butchers of us all?"

"You didn't give those . . . those persons a chance."

"Here we had a chance to learn something, to learn a lot, and you killed them and destroyed their equipment."

General Tredway sat immobile until the hot flood of words subsided. Then he said, "Do any of you gentlemen have any evidence that their intentions were peaceable? Any evidence at all?"

There was silence for a moment as they stared at him. The President said, "What evidence have you got they meant harm? You killed them before there was any evidence of anything."

General Tredway shook his head, and a familiar supercilious tone crept unbidden into his voice. "*They* were the ones who landed on *our* planet. It was incumbent on them to find a way to convince us of their friendliness. Instead they landed with no warning at all, and with a complete disregard of human life. The first missile shattered a house, killed a man. There is ample evidence of their hostility," and he could not help adding, "if you care to look for it."

The President flushed and snapped, "That's not the way I see it. You could have kept them covered; you had enough fire power there to cover an army. If they made any hostile move, that would have been time enough for you to have opened up on them."

The House Speaker leaned forward and plunked a sheaf of telegrams on the table. He tapped the pile with a forefinger and said, "These are some of thousands that have come in. I picked out the ones from some of our outstanding citizens—educators, scientists, statesmen. All of them agree that this is a foolhardy thing you have done. You've destroyed a mighty source of knowledge for the human race."

"None of them is a soldier," said the general. "I would not expect them to know anything about attack and defense."

The Speaker nodded and drew one more telegram from an inner pocket. General Tredway, seeing what was coming, had to admire his tactics; this man was not Speaker for nothing. "Here," said the Speaker, "is a reply to my telegram. It is from the Joint Chiefs. Care to read it?"

They all stared at the general, and he shook his head coldly. "No. I take it that they do not understand the problem, either."

"Now just a min—" A colonel entered the room and whispered softly to the President. The President pushed his chair back, but he did not get up. Nodding, he said, "Good. Have Barnes take over. And see that he holds his fire until something happens. Hear? Make certain of that. I'll not tolerate any more of this unnecessary slaughter." The colonel left.

The President turned and noted the understanding in the faces of the men at the table. He nodded and said, "Yes, another one. And this time we'll do it right. I only hope the other two haven't got word to the third one that we're a bunch of killers."

"There could be no communication of any kind emanating from the first two," said General Tredway. "I watched for that."

"Yes. Well, it's the only thing you did right. I want you to watch to see the proper way to handle this."

In the intervening hours General Tredway tried to persuade the others to adopt his point of view. He succeeded only in infuriating them. When the time came for the third object to open, the group of men were trembling in anger.

They gathered around the television screen to watch General Barnes's handling of the situation.

General Tredway stood to the rear of the others, watching the hatch unscrew. General Barnes was using the same formation as that developed by General Tredway; the ring of steel was as tight as ever.

The familiar black at the bottom of the hatch came into view, followed closely by the top of the gleaming rose blossom. General Tredway snapped his fingers, the sound cracking loud in the still room. The men close to the set jumped and looked back at Tredway in annoyance. It was plain that the general had announced in his own way the proper moment to fire. Their eyes had hardly got back to the screen when it happened.

A thin beam of delicate violet light danced from the heart of the rose to the front of the steel ring. The beam rotated like a lighthouse beacon, only far, far faster. Whatever it touched, it sliced. Through tanks and trucks and guns and men it sliced, over and over again as the swift circular path of the beam spun in ever widening circles. Explosions rocked the site as high explosives detonated under the touch of the beam. The hatch of the object itself, neatly cut near the bottom, rolled ponderously down the side of the object to the ground. The beam bit into the ground and left seething ribbons of slag. In three seconds the area was a mass of fused metal and molten rock and minced bodies and flame and smoke and thunder. In another two seconds the beam reached the television cameras, and the screen went blank.

The men near the screen stared speechless. At that moment the colonel returned and announced softly that a fourth object was on its way, and that its probable impact point was two miles due east of Harrisburg.

The group turned as one man to General Tredway, but he paid no attention. He was pacing back and forth, pulling at his lower lip, frowning in concentration.

"General," said the President, "I . . . I guess you had the right idea. These things are monsters. Will you handle this next one?"

General Tredway stopped and said, "Yes, but I had better explain what is now involved. I want every vehicle that can move to converge on the fourth object; the one that is now loose will attempt to protect it. I want every plane and copter that can fly to launch a continuing attack on it. I want every available missile zeroed in and launched at it immediately. I want every fusion and fission bomb we've got directed at the fourth object by means of artillery, missiles and planes; one of them might get through. I want a request made to Canada, Brazil, Great Britain, France, Germany, Russia and Italy to launch fussion-headed missiles at the site of the fourth object immediately. In this way we might have a chance to stop them. Let us proceed."

The President stared at him and said, "Have you gone crazy? I will give no such orders. What you ask for will destroy our middle eastern seaboard."

The general nodded. "Yes, everything from Richmond to Pittsburgh to Syracuse, I think, possibly more. Fallout will cover a wider area. There's no help for it."

"You're insane. I will do no such thing."

The Speaker stepped forward and said, "Mr. President, I think you should reconsider this. You saw what that thing could do; think of two of them loose. I am very much afraid the general may be right."

"Don't be ridiculous."

The Vice-President stepped to the President's side and said, "I agree with the President. I never heard of such an absurd suggestion."

The moment froze into silence. The general stared at the three men. Then, moving slowly and deliberately, he undid his holster flap and pulled out his pistol. He snapped the slide back and fired once at point-blank range, shifted the gun, and fired again. He walked over to the table and carefully placed the gun on it. Then he turned to the Speaker and said, "Mr. President, there is very little time. Will you give the necessary orders?"

Now I propose to show you how another writer, granted his own premises, can turn the picture upside down again. Here (from Galaxy, *June 1951) is a story of an alien invasion; it begins with the landing of a spaceship and ends, like "The First Days of May," on a note of resignation and humility. But these resemblances are superficial. If Veillot's Shrills are pure horror (I pass over Thomas' invaders, whom we never see), then Pangborn's angel is pure delight.*

Edgar Pangborn was educated at Harvard and the New England Conservatory of Music and planned a musical career, but switched to writing in 1951. Traces of his musical background appear in this story; it might even be suggested that the story itself is a kind of music.

Pangborn's style is exceedingly delicate and precise compared with the typical magazine writer's blunt-instrument prose. A workman of such skill deserves to have his copy printed as he wrote it, but this does not always happen. The editor who first published "Angel's Egg" is infamous among s.f. writers for having altered the phrase, "with her speaking hands on his terrible head," to "with her telepathic hands on his predatory head."

In different ways, both Veillot's and Thomas' stories can be read as arguments for Western values—efficiency, decisiveness, ruthless self-interest. Here is an equally eloquent argument for the Eastern values of humility, love, self-sacrifice, embodied in an unforgettable story.

ANGEL'S EGG

BY EDGAR PANGBORN

LETTER OF RECORD, BLAINE TO MC CARRAN, DATED AUGUST 10, 1951

Mr. Cleveland McCarran
Federal Bureau of Investigation
Washington, D.C.

DEAR SIR:

In compliance with your request I enclose herewith a transcript of the pertinent sections of the journal of Dr. David Bannerman, deceased. The original document is being held at this office until proper disposition can be determined.

Our investigation has shown no connection between Dr. Bannerman and any organization, subversive or otherwise. So far as we can learn, he was exactly what he seemed, an inoffensive summer resident, retired, with a small independent income—a recluse to some extent, but well spoken of by local tradesmen and other neighbors. A connection be-tween Dr. Bannerman and the type of activity that concerns your Department would seem most unlikely.

The following information is summarized from the earlier parts of Dr. Bannerman's journal, and tallies with the results of our own limited inquiry. He was born in 1898 at Spring-field, Massachusetts, attended public school there, and was graduated from Harvard College in 1922, his studies having been interrupted by two years' military service. He was wounded in action in the Argonne, receiving a spinal injury. He earned a doctorate in biology in 1926. Delayed after-effects of his war injury necessitated hospitalization, 1927–28. From 1929 to 1948 he taught elementary sciences in a private school in Boston. He published two textbooks in in-troductory biology, 1929 and 1937. In 1948 he retired from teaching; a pension and a modest income from textbook royalties evidently made this possible. Aside from the spinal deformity, which caused him to walk with a stoop, his health is said to have been fair. Autopsy findings suggested that the spinal condition must have given him considerable pain; he is not known to have mentioned this to anyone, not even to his physician, Dr. Lester Morse. There is no evidence what-ever of drug addiction or alcoholism.

At one point early in his journal Dr. Bannerman describes himself as "a naturalist of the puttering type—I would rather sit on a log than write monographs: it pays off better." Dr. Morse and others who knew Dr. Bannerman personally tell me that this conveys a hint of his personality.

I am not qualified to comment on the material of this journal, except to say I have no evidence to support (or to contradict) Dr. Bannerman's statements. The journal has been studied only by my immediate superiors, by Dr. Morse, and by myself. I take it for granted you will hold the matter in strictest confidence.

With the journal I am also enclosing a statement by Dr. Morse, written at my request for our records and for your information. You will note that he says, with some qualifica-tions, that "death was not inconsistent with an embolism." He has signed a death certificate on that basis. You will re-call from my letter of August 5 that it was Dr. Morse who discovered Dr. Bannerman's body. Because he was a close personal friend of the deceased, Dr. Morse did not feel able to perform the autopsy himself. It was done by a Dr. Stephen Clyde of this city, and was virtually negative as regards cause of death, neither confirming nor contradicting Dr. Morse's original tentative diagnosis. If you wish to read the autopsy report in full I shall be glad to forward a copy.

Dr. Morse tells me that so far as he knows, Dr. Bannerman had no near relatives. He never married. For the last twelve summers he occupied a small cottage on a back road about twenty-five miles from this city, and had few visitors. The neighbor, Steele, mentioned in the journal is a farmer, age sixty-eight, of good character, who tells me he "never got really acquainted with Dr. Bannerman."

At this office we feel that unless new information comes to light, further active investigation is hardly justified.

Respectfully yours,
GARRISON BLAINE
Capt., State Police
Augusta, Me.

Encl: Extract from Journal of David Bannerman, dec'd.
Statement by Lester Morse, M.D.

LIBRARIAN'S NOTE: The following document, originally attached as an unofficial "rider" to the foregoing letter, was donated to this institution in 1994 through the courtesy of Mrs. Helen McCarran, widow of the martyred first President of the World Federation. Other personal and state papers of President McCarran, many of them dating from the early period when he was employed by the F.B.I., are accessible to public view at the Institute of World History, Copenhagen.

PERSONAL NOTE, BLAINE TO MC CARRAN, DATED AUGUST 10, 1951

DEAR CLEVE:

Guess I didn't make it clear in my other letter that that bastard Clyde was responsible for my having to drag you into this. He is something to handle with tongs. Happened thusly: When he came in to heave the autopsy report at me, he was already having pups just because it was so completely negative (he does have certain types of honesty), and he caught sight of a page or two of the journal on my desk. Doc Morse was with me at the time. I fear we both got upstage with him

(Clyde has that effect, and we were both in a State of Mind anyway), so right away the old drip thinks he smells something subversive. Belongs to the atomize-'em-NOW-WOW-WOW school of thought—nuf sed? He went into a grand whuff-whuff about referring to Higher Authority, and I knew that meant your hive, so I wanted to get ahead of the letter I knew he'd write. I suppose his literary effort couldn't be just sort of quietly transferred to File 13, otherwise known as the Appropriate Receptacle?

He can say what he likes about my charcater, if any, but even I never supposed he'd take a sideswipe at his professional colleague. Doc Morse is the best of the best and would not dream of suppressing any evidence important to us, as you say Clyde's letter hints. What Doc did do was to tell Clyde, pleasantly, in the privacy of my office, to go take a flying this-and-that at the moon. I only wish I'd thought of the expression myself. So Clyde rushes off to tell teacher. See what I mean about the tongs? However (knock on wood) I don't think Clyde saw enough of the journal to get any notion of what it's all about.

As for that journal, damn it, Cleve, I don't know. If you have any ideas I want them, of course. I'm afraid I believe in angels myself. But when I think of the effect on local opinion if the story ever gets out—brother! Here was this old Bannerman living alone with a female angel and they wuzn't even common-law married. Aw, gee. . . . And the flood of phone calls from other crackpots anxious to explain it all to me. Experts in the care and feeding of angels. Methods of angelproofing. Angels right outside the window a minute ago. Make Angels a Profitable Enterprise in Your Spare Time!!!

When do I see you? You said you might have a week clear in October. If we could get together maybe we could make sense where there is none. I hear the cider promises to be good this year. Try and make it. My best to Ginny and the other young fry, and Helen of course.

Respeckfully yourn,
GARRY

P.S. If you do see any angels down your way, and they aren't willing to wait for a Republican Administration, by all means have them investigated by the Senate—then we'll *know* we're all nuts.

G.

EXTRACT FROM JOURNAL OF DAVID BANNERMAN, JUNE 1–
JULY 29, 1951

June 1

It must have been at least three weeks ago when we had
that flying-saucer flurry. Observers the other side of Katahdin
saw it come down this side; observers this side saw it come
down the other. Size anywhere from six inches to sixty feet
in diameter (or was it cigar-shaped?) and speed whatever
you please. Seem to recall that witnesses agreed on a rosy-
pink light. There was the inevitable gobbledegookery of official explanation designed to leave everyone impressed,
soothed, and disappointed. I paid scant attention to the excitement and less to the explanations—naturally, I thought
it was just a flying saucer. But now Camilla has hatched out
an angel.

It would have to be Camilla. Perhaps I haven't mentioned
my hens enough. In the last day or two it has dawned on me
that this journal may be of importance to other eyes than
mine, not merely a lonely man's plaything to blunt the edge
of mortality; an angel in the house makes a difference. I had
better show consideration for possible readers.

I have eight hens, all yearlings except Camilla—this is her
third spring. I boarded her two winters at my neighbor
Steele's farm when I closed this shack and shuffled my chilly
bones off to Florida, because even as a pullet she had a manner which overbore me. I could never have eaten Camilla:
if she had looked at the ax with that same expression of
rancid disapproval (and she would), I should have felt I was
beheading a favorite aunt. Her only concession to sentiment
is the annual rush of maternity to the brain—normal, for a
case-hardened White Plymouth Rock.

This year she stole a nest successfully in a tangle of blackberry. By the time I located it, I estimated I was about two
weeks too late. I had to outwit her by watching from a window—she is far too acute to be openly trailed from feeding
ground to nest. When I had bled and pruned my way to her
hideout she was sitting on nine eggs and hating my guts.
They could not be fertile, since I keep no rooster, and I was
about to rob her when I saw the ninth egg was nothing of
hers. It was a deep blue and transparent, with flecks of inner
light that made me think of the first stars in a clear evening.

It was the same size as Camilla's own. There was an embryo, but I could make nothing of it. I returned the egg to Camilla's bare and fevered breastbone and went back to the house for a long, cool drink.

That was ten days ago. I know I ought to have kept a record; I examined the blue egg every day, watching how some nameless life grew within it. The angel has been out of the shell three days now. This is the first time I felt equal to facing pen and ink.

I have been experiencing a sort of mental lassitude unfamiliar to me. Wrong word: not so much lassitude as a preoccupation, with no sure clue to what it is that preoccupies me. By reputation I am a scientist of sorts. Right now I have no impulse to look for data; I want to sit quiet and let truth come to a relaxed mind if it will. Could be merely a part of growing older, but I doubt that. The broken pieces of the wonderful blue shell are on my desk. I have been peering at them—into them—for the last ten minutes or more. Can't call it study; my thought wanders into their blue, learning nothing I can retain in words. It does not convey much to say I have gone into a vision of open sky—and of peace, if such a thing there be.

The angel chipped the shell deftly in two parts. This was evidently done with the aid of small horny outgrowths on her elbows; these growths were sloughed off on the second day. I wish I had seen her break the shell, but when I visited the blackberry tangle three days ago she was already out. She poked her exquisite head through Camilla's neck feathers, smiled sleepily, and snuggled back into darkness to finish drying off. So what could I do, more than save the broken shell and wriggle my clumsy self out of there? I had removed Camilla's own eggs the day before—Camilla was only moderately annoyed. I was nervous about disposing of them, even though they were obviously Camilla's, but no harm was done. I cracked one to be sure. Very frankly rotten eggs and nothing more.

In the evening of that day I though of rats and weasels, as I should have done earlier. I prepared a box in the kitchen and brought the two in, the angel quiet in my closed hand. They are there now. I think they are comfortable.

Three days after hatching, the angel is the length of my forefinger, say three inches tall, with about the relative proportions of a six-year-old girl. Except for head, hands, and probably the soles of her feet, she is clothed in down the color of ivory; what can be seen of her skin is a glowing pink—I do mean glowing, like the inside of certain sea shells. Just above the small of her back are two stubs which I take to be infantile wings. They do not suggest an extra pair of specialized forelimbs. I think they are wholly differentiated organs; perhaps they will be like the wings of an insect. Somehow, I never thought of angels buzzing. Maybe she won't. I know very little about angels. At present the stubs are covered with some dull tissue, no doubt a protective sheath to be discarded when the membranes (if they are membranes) are ready to grow. Between the stubs is a not very prominent ridge—special musculature, I suppose. Otherwise her shape is quite human, even to a pair of minuscule mammalian buttons just visible under the down; how that can make sense in an egg-laying organism is beyond my comprehension. (Just for the record, so is a Corot landscape; so is Schubert's *Unfinished;* so is the flight of a hummingbird, or the other-world of frost on a windowpane.) The down on her head has grown visibly in three days and is of different quality from the body down —later it may resemble human hair, as a diamond resembles a chunk of granite. . . .

A curious thing has happened. I went to Camilla's box after writing that. Judy* was already lying in front of it, un-excited. The angel's head was out from under the feathers, and I thought—with more verbal distinctness than such thoughts commonly take— So here I am, a naturalist of middle years and cold sober, observing a three-inch oviparous mammal with down and wings. The thing is—she giggled. Now, it might have been only amusement at my appearance, which to her must be enormously gross and comic. But another thought formed unspoken: I am no longer lonely. And her face (hardly bigger than a dime) immediately changed from laughter to a brooding and friendly thoughtfulness.

Judy and Camilla are old friends. Judy seems untroubled by the angel. I have no worries about leaving them alone together. I must sleep.

June 3

I made no entry last night. The angel was talking to me, and when that was finished I drowsed off immediately on a

---

* Dr. Bannerman's dog, mentioned often earlier in the journal. A nine-year-old English setter. According to an entry of May 15, 1951, she was then beginning to go blind.—BLAINE.

cot that I have moved into the kitchen so as to be near them.

I had never been strongly impressed by the evidence for extrasensory perception. It is fortunate my mind was able to accept the novelty, since to the angel it is clearly a matter of course. Her tiny mouth is most expressive, but moves only for that reason and for eating—not for speech. Probably she could speak to her own kind if she wished, but I dare say the sound would be outside the range of my hearing as well as of my understanding.

Last night after I brought the cot in and was about to finish my puttering bachelor supper, she climbed to the edge of the box and pointed, first at herself and then at the top of the kitchen table. Afraid to let my vast hand take hold of her, I held it out flat and she sat in my palm. Camilla was inclined to fuss, but the angel looked over her shoulder and Camilla subsided, watchful but no longer alarmed.

The table top is porcelain, and the angel shivered. I folded a towel and spread a silk handkerchief on top of that; the angel sat on this arrangement with apparent comfort, near my face. I was not even bewildered. Possibly she had already instructed me to blank out my mind. At any rate, I did so, without conscious effort to that end.

She reached me first with visual imagery. How can I make it plain that this had nothing in common with my sleeping dreams? There was no weight of symbolism from my littered past; no discoverable connection with any of yesterday's commonplaces; indeed, no actual involvement of my personality at all. I saw. I was moving vision, though without eyes or other flesh. And while my mind saw, it also knew where my flesh was, slumped at the kitchen table. If anyone had entered the kitchen, if there had been a noise of alarm out in the henhouse, I should have known it.

There was a valley such I as have not seen (and never will) on Earth. I have seen many beautiful places on this planet—some of them were even tranquil. Once I took a slow steamer to New Zealand and had the Pacific as a plaything for many days. I can hardly say how I knew this was not Earth. The grass of the valley was an earthly green; a river below me was a blue-and-silver thread under familiar-seeming sunlight; there were trees much like pine and maple, and maybe that is what they were. But it was not Earth. I was aware of mountains heaped to strange heights on either side of the valley—

snow, rose, amber, gold. Perhaps the amber tint was unlike any mountain color I have noticed in this world at midday.

Or I may have known it was not Earth simply because her mind—dwelling within some unimaginable brain smaller than the tip of my little finger—told me so.

I watched two inhabitants of that world come flying, to rest in the field of sunny grass where my bodiless vision had brought me. Adult forms, such as my angel would surely be when she had her growth, except that both of these were male and one of them was dark-skinned. The latter was also old, with a thousand-wrinkled face, knowing and full of tranquillity; the other was flushed and lively with youth; both were beautiful. The down of the brown-skinned old one was reddish-tawny; the other's was ivory with hints of orange. Their wings were true membranes, with more variety of subtle iridescence than I have seen even in the wings of a dragonfly; I could not say that any color was dominant, for each motion brought a ripple of change. These two sat at their ease on the grass. I realized that they were talking to each other, though their lips did not move in speech more than once or twice. They would nod, smile, now and then illustrate something with twinkling hands.

A huge rabbit lolloped past them. I knew (thanks to my own angel's efforts, I supposed) that this animal was the size of our common wild ones. Later, a blue-green snake three times the size of the angels came flowing through the grass; the old one reached out to stroke its head carelessly, and I think he did it without interrupting whatever he was saying.

Another creature came, in leisured leaps. He was monstrous, yet I felt no alarm in the angels or in myself. Imagine a being built somewhat like a kangaroo up to the head, about eight feet tall, and katydid-green. Really, the thick balancing tail and enormous legs were the only kangaroolike features about him; the body above the massive thighs was not dwarfed, but thick and square; the arms and hands were quite humanoid: the head was round, manlike except for its face—there was only a single nostril and his mouth was set in the vertical; the eyes were large and mild. I received an impression of high intelligence and natural gentleness. In one of his manlike hands two tools so familiar and ordinary that I knew my body by the kitchen table had laughed in startled recognition. But, after all, a garden spade and rake are basic. Once invented—I expect we did it ourselves in the Neolithic Age—there is little reason why they should change much down the millennia.

This farmer halted by the angels, and the three conversed a while. The big head nodded agreeably. I believe the young angel made a joke; certainly the convulsions in the huge green face made me think of laughter. Then this amiable monster turned up the grass in a patch a few yards square, broke the sod and raked the surface smooth, just as any competent gardener might do—except that he moved with the relaxed smoothness of a being whose strength far exceeds the requirements of his task. . . .

I was back in my kitchen with everyday eyes. My angel was exploring the table. I had a loaf of bread there and a dish of strawberries and cream. She was trying a bread crumb; seemed to like it fairly well. I offered the strawberries; she broke off one of the seeds and nibbled it but didn't care so much for the pulp. I held up the great spoon with sugary cream; she steadied it with both hands to try some. I think she liked it. It had been most stupid of me not to realize that she would be hungry. I brought wine from the cupboard; she watched inquiringly, so I put a couple of drops on the handle of a spoon. This really pleased her: she chuckled and patted her tiny stomach, though I'm afraid it wasn't awfully good sherry. I brought some crumbs of cake, but she indicated that she was full, came close to my face, and motioned me to lower my head.

She reached up until she could press both hands against my forehead—I felt it only enough to know her hands were there —and she stood so a long time, trying to tell me something.

It was difficult. Pictures come through with relative ease, but now she was transmitting an abstraction of a complex kind: my clumsy brain really suffered in the effort to receive. Something did come across. I have only the crudest way of passing it on. Imagine an equilateral triangle; place the following words one at each corner— "recruiting," "collecting," "saving." The meaning she wanted to convey ought to be near the center of the triangle.

I had also the sense that her message provided a partial explanation of her errand in this lovable and damnable world.

She looked weary when she stood away from me. I put out my palm and she climbed into it, to be carried back to the nest.

She did not talk to me tonight, nor eat, but she gave a reason, coming out from Camilla's feathers long enough to turn her back and show me the wing stubs. The protective sheaths have dropped off; the wings are rapidly growing. They are probably damp and weak. She was quite tired and went back into the warm darkness almost at once.

Camilla must be exhausted, too. I don't think she has been off the nest more than twice since I brought them into the house.

June 4

Today she can fly.

I learned it in the afternoon, when I was fiddling about in the garden and Judy was loafing in the sunshine she loves. Something apart from sight and sound called me to hurry back to the house. I saw my angel through the screen door before I opened it. One of her feet had caught in a hideous loop of loose wire at a break in the mesh. Her first tug of alarm must have tightened the loop so that her hands were not strong enough to force it open.

Fortunately I was able to cut the wire with a pair of shears before I lost my head; then she could free her foot without injury. Camilla had been frantic, rushing around fluffed up, but—here's an odd thing—perfectly silent. None of the recognized chicken noises of dismay; if an ordinary chick had been in trouble she would have raised the roof.

The angel flew to me and hovered, pressing her hands on my forehead. The message was clear at once: "No harm done." She flew down to tell Camilla the same thing.

Yes, in the same way. I saw Camilla standing near my feet with her neck out and head low, and the angel put a hand on either side of her scraggy comb. Camilla relaxed, clucked in the normal way and spread her wings for a shelter. The angel went under it, but only to oblige Camilla, I think—at least, she stuck her head through the wing feathers and winked.

She must have seen something else then, for she came out and flew back to me and touched a finger to my cheek, looked at the finger, saw it was wet, put it in her mouth, made a face, and laughed at me.

We went outdoors into the sun (Camilla too), and the angel gave me an exhibition of what flying ought to be. Not even Schubert can speak of joy as her first free flying did. At one moment she would be hanging in front of my eyes, radiant and delighted; the next instant she would be a dot of color against a cloud. Try to imagine something that would make a hummingbird seem a bit dull and sluggish.

They do hum. Softer than a hummingbird, louder than a dragonfly.

Something like the sound of hawk moths—*Hemaris thisbe,* for instance, the one I used to call hummingbird moth when I was a child.

I was frightened, naturally. Frightened first at what might happen to her, but that was unnecessary; I don't think she would be in danger from any savage animal except possibly man. I saw a Cooper's hawk slant down the invisible toward the swirl of color where she was dancing by herself; presently she was drawing iridescent rings around him; then, while he soared in smaller circles, I could not see her, but (maybe she felt my fright) she was again in front of me, pressing my forehead in the now familiar way. I knew she was amused and caught the idea that the hawk was a "lazy character." Not quite the way I'd describe *Accipiter cooperi,* but it's all in the point of view. I believe she had been riding his back, no doubt with her speaking hands on his terrible head.

And later I was frightened by the thought that she might not want to return to me. Can I compete with sunlight and open sky? The passage of that terror through me brought her back swiftly, and her hands said with great clarity, "Don't ever be afraid of anything—it isn't necessary for you."

Once this afternoon I was saddened by the realization that old Judy can take little part in what goes on now. I can well remember Judy running like the wind. The angel must have heard this thought in me, for she stood a long time beside Judy's drowsy head, while Judy's tail thumped cheerfully on the warm grass. . . .

In the evening the angel made a heavy meal on two or three cake crumbs and another drop of sherry, and we had what was almost a sustained conversation. I will write it in that form this time, rather than grope for anything more exact.

I asked her, "How far away is your home?"

"My home is here."

"Thank God! But I meant the place your people come from."

"Ten light-years."

"The images you showed me, that quiet valley—that is ten light-years away?"

"Yes. But that was my father talking to you, through me. He was grown when the journey began. He is two hundred and forty years old—our years, thirty-two days longer than yours."

Mainly I was conscious of a flood of relief; I had feared, on the basis of terrestrial biology, that her explosively rapid growth after hatching must foretell a brief life. But it's all right—she can outlive me, and by a few hundred years, at that. "Your father is here now, on this planet—shall I see him?"

She took her hands away—listening, I believe. The answer was: "No. He is sorry. He is ill and cannot live long. I am to see him in a few days, when I fly a little better. He taught me for twenty years after I was born."

"I don't understand. I thought—"

"Later, friend. My father is grateful for your kindness to me."

I don't know what I thought about that. I felt no faintest trace of condescension in the message. "And he was showing me things he had seen with his own eyes, ten light-years away?"

"Yes." Then she wanted me to rest a while; I am sure she knows what a huge effort it is for my primitive brain to function in this way. But before she ended the conversation by humming down to her nest she gave me this, and I received it with such clarity that I cannot be mistaken: "He says that only fifty million years ago it was a jungle there, just as Terra is now."

June 8

When I woke four days ago the angel was having breakfast, and little Camilla was dead. The angel watched me rub sleep out of my eyes, watched me discover Camilla, and then flew to me. I received this: "Does it make you unhappy?"

"I don't know exactly." You can get fond of a hen, especially a cantankerous and homely old one whose personality has a lot in common with your own.

"She was old. She wanted a flock of chicks, and I couldn't stay with her. So I—" Something obscure here: probably my mind was trying too hard to grasp it— "so I saved her life."

I could make nothing else out of it. She said "saved."

Camilla's death looked natural, except that I should have expected the death contractions to muss the straw, and that hadn't happened. Maybe the angel had arranged the old lady's body for decorum, though I don't see how her muscular strength would have been equal to it—Camilla weighed at least seven pounds.

As I was burying her at the edge of the garden and the angel was humming over my head, I recalled a thing which, when it happened, I had dismissed as a dream. Merely a moonlight image of the angel standing in the nest box with her hands on Camilla's head, then pressing her mouth gently on Camilla's throat, just before the hen's head sank down out of my line of vision. Probably I actually waked and saw it happen. I am somehow unconcerned—even, as I think more about it, pleased.

After the burial the angel's hands said, "Sit on the grass and we'll talk. . . . Question me. I'll tell you what I can. My father asks you to write it down."

So that is what we have been doing for the last four days. I have been going to school, a slow but willing pupil. Rather than enter anything in this journal (for in the evenings I was exhausted), I made notes as best I could. The angel has gone now to see her father and will not return until morning. I shall try to make a readable version of my notes.

Since she had invited questions, I began with something which had been bothering me, as a would-be naturalist, exceedingly. I couldn't see how creatures no larger than the adults I had observed could lay eggs as large as Camilla's. Nor could I understand why, if they were hatched in an almost adult condition and able to eat a varied diet, she had any use for that ridiculous, lovely, and apparently functional pair of breasts. When the angel grasped my difficulty she exploded with laughter—her kind, which buzzed her all over the garden and caused her to fluff my hair on the wing and pinch my ear lobe. She lit on a rhubarb leaf and gave a delectably naughty representation of herself as a hen laying an egg, including the cackle. She got me to bumbling helplessly —my kind of laughter—and it was some time before we could quiet down. Then she did her best to explain.

They are true mammals, and the young—not more than two or at most three in a lifetime averaging two hundred and fifty years—are delivered in very much the human way. The baby is nursed—human fashion—until his brain begins to respond a little to their unspoken language; that takes three to four weeks. Then he is placed in an altogether different medium. She could not describe that clearly, because there was very little in my educational storehouse to help me grasp it. It is some gaseous medium that arrests bodily growth for an almost indefinite period, while mental growth continues. It took them, she says, about seven thousand years to perfect this technique after they first hit on the idea; they are never in a hurry. The infant remains under this delicate and precise control for anywhere from fifteen to thirty years, the period depending not only on his mental vigor but also on the type of lifework he tentatively elects as soon as his brain is knowing enough to make a choice. During this period his mind is guided with unwavering patience by teachers who—

It seems those teachers know their business. This was peculiarly difficult for me to assimilate, although the fact came through clearly enough. In their world, the profession of teacher is more highly honored than any other—can such a thing be possible?—and so difficult to enter that only the strongest minds dare attempt it. (I had to rest a while after absorbing that.) An aspirant must spend fifty years (not including the period of infantile education) in merely getting ready to begin, and the acquisition of factual knowledge, while not understressed, takes only a small proportion of those fifty years. Then—if he's good enough—he can take a small part in the elementary instruction of a few babies, and if he does well on that basis for another thirty or forty years, he is considered a fair beginner. . . . Once upon a time I lurched around stuffy classrooms trying to insert a few pre-digested facts (I wonder how many of them *were* facts?) into the minds of bored and preoccupied adolescents, some of whom may have liked me moderately well. I was even able to shake hands and be nice while their terribly well-meaning parents explained to me how they ought to be educated. So much of our human effort goes down the drain of futility, I sometimes wonder how we ever got as far as the Bronze Age. Somehow we did, though, and a short way beyond.

After that preliminary stage of an angel's education is finished, the baby is transferred to more ordinary surroundings, and his bodily growth completes itself in a very short time. Wings grow abruptly (as I have seen), and he reaches a maximum height of six inches (our measure). Only then does he enter on that lifetime of two hundred and fifty years, for not until then does his body begin to age. My angel has been a living personality for many years but will not celebrate her first birthday for almost a year. I like to think of that.

At about the same time that they learned the principles of interplanetary travel (approximately twelve million years ago) these people also learned how, by use of a slightly different method, growth could be arrested at any point short of full maturity. At first the knowledge served no purpose except in the control of illnesses which still occasionally struck them at that time. But when the long periods of time required for space travel were considered, the advantages became obvious.

So it happens that my angel was born ten light-years away. She was trained by her father and many others in the wisdom of seventy million years (that, she tells me, is the approximate sum of their *recorded* history), and then she was safely sealed and cherished in what my super-amoebic brain regarded as a blue egg. Education did not proceed at that time; her mind went to sleep with the rest of her. When Camilla's temperature made her wake and grow again, she remembered what to do with the little horny bumps provided for her elbows. And came out—into this planet, God help her.

I wondered why her father should have chosen any combination so unreliable as an old hen and a human being. Surely he must have had plenty of excellent ways to bring the shell to the right temperature. Her answer should have satisfied me immensely, but I am still compelled to wonder about it. "Camilla was a nice hen, and my father studied your mind while you were asleep. It was a bad landing, and much was broken—no such landing was ever made before after so long a journey: forty years. Only four other grownups could come with my father. Three of them died en route, and he is very ill. And there were nine other children to care for."

Yes, I knew she'd said that an angel thought I was good enough to be trusted with his daughter. If it upsets me, all I need do is look at her and then in the mirror. As for the explanation, I can only conclude there must be more that I am not ready to understand. I was worried about those nine others, but she assured me they were all well, and I sensed that I ought not to ask more about them at present. . . .

Their planet, she says, is closely similar to this. A trifle larger, moving in a somewhat longer orbit around a sun like ours. Two gleaming moons, smaller than ours—their orbits are such that two-moon nights come rarely. They are magic, and she will ask her father to show me one, if he can. Their year is thirty-two days longer than ours; because of a slower rotation, their day has twenty-six of our hours. Their atmosphere is mainly nitrogen and oxgyen in the proportions familiar to us; slightly richer in some of the rare gases. The climate is now what we should call tropical and subtropical, but they have known glacial rigors like those in our world's past. There are only two great continental land masses, and many thousands of large islands.

Their total population is only five billion.

Most of the forms of life we know have parallels there—some quite exact parallels: rabbits, deer, mice, cats. The cats have been bred to an even higher intelligence than they possess on our Earth; it is possible, she says, to have a good deal of intellectual intercourse with their cats, who learned several million years ago that when they kill it must be done with lightning precision and without torture. The cats had some difficulty grasping the possibility of pain in other organisms, but once that educational hurdle was passed, development was easy. Nowadays many of the cats are popular storytellers; about forty million years ago they were still occasionally needed as a special police force, and served the angels with real heroism.

It seems my angel wants to become a student of animal life here on Earth. I, a teacher! But bless her heart for the notion, anyhow. We sat and traded animals for a couple of hours last night. I found it restful, after the mental struggle to grasp more difficult matters. Judy was something new to her. They have several luscious monsters on that planet, but, in her view, so have we. She told me of a blue sea snake fifty feet long (relatively harmless) that bellows cowlike and comes into the tidal marshes to lay black eggs; so I gave her a whale. She offered a bat-winged, day-flying ball of mammalian fluff as big as my head and weighing under an ounce; I matched her with a marmoset. She tried me with a small-sized brontosaur (very rare), but I was ready with the duck-billed platypus, and that caused us to exchange some pretty smart remarks about mammalian eggs; she bounced. All trivial in a way; also, the happiest evening in my fifty-three tangled years of life.

She was a trifle hesitant to explain these kangaroolike people, until she was sure I really wanted to know. It seems they are about the nearest parallel to human life on that planet; not a near parallel, of course, as she was careful to explain. Agreeable and always friendly souls (though they weren't always so, I'm sure) and of a somewhat more alert intelligence than we possess. Manual workers, mainly, because they prefer it nowadays, but some of them are excellent mathematicians. The first practical spaceship was invented by a group of them, with some assistance.

Names offer difficulties. Because of the nature of the angelic language, they have scant use for them except for the purpose of written record, and writing naturally plays little part in their daily lives—no occasion to write a letter when a thousand miles is no obstacle to the speech of your mind. An angel's formal name is about as important to him as, say, my Social Security number is to me. She has not told me hers, because the phonetics on which their written language is based have no parallel in my mind. As we would speak a friend's name, an angel will project the friend's image to his friend's receiving mind. More pleasant and more intimate, I think—although it was a shock to me at first to glimpse my own ugly mug in my mind's eye. Stories are occasionally written, if there is something in them that should be preserved precisely as it was in the first telling; but in their world the true storyteller has a more important place than the printer—he offers one of the best of their quieter pleasures: a good one can hold his audience for a week and never tire them.

"What is this 'angel' in your mind when you think of me?"

"A being men have imagined for centuries, when they thought of themselves as they might like to be and not as they are."

I did not try too painfully hard to learn much about the principles of space travel. The most my brain could take in of her explanation was something like: "Rocket—then phototropism." Now, that makes scant sense. So far as I know, phototropism—movement toward light—is an organic phenomenon. One thinks of it as a response of protoplasm, in some plant and animal organisms (most of them simple), to the stimulus of light; certainly not as a force capable of moving inorganic matter. I think that whatever may be the principle she was describing, this word "phototropism" was merely the nearest thing to it in my reservoir of language. Not even the angels can create understanding out of blank ignorance. At least I have learned not to set neat limits to the possible.

(There was a time when I did, though. I can see myself, not so many years back, like a homunculus squatting at the foot of Mt. McKinley, throwing together two handfuls of mud and shouting, "Look at the big mountain *I* made!")

And if I did know the physical principles which brought them here, and could write them in terms accessible to technicians resembling myself, I would not do it.

Here is a thing I am afraid no reader of this journal will believe: These people, as I have written, learned their method of space travel some twelve million years ago. But this is the first time they have ever used it to convey them to another planet. The heavens are rich in worlds, she tells me; on many of them there is life, often on very primitive levels. No external force prevented her people from going forth, colonizing, conquering, as far as they pleased. They could have populated a galaxy. They did not, and for this reason: they believed they were not ready. More precisely, *not good enough*.

Only some fifty million years ago, by her account, did they learn (as we may learn eventually) that intelligence without goodness is worse than high explosive in the hands of a baboon. For beings advanced beyond the level of Pithecanthropus, intelligence is a cheap commodity—not too hard to develop, hellishly easy to use for unconsidered ends. Whereas goodness is not to be achieved without unending effort of the hardest kind, within the self, whether the self be man or angel.

It is clear even to me that the conquest of evil is only one step, not the most important. For goodness, so she tried to tell me, is an altogether positive quality; the part of living nature that swarms with such monstrosities as cruelty, meanness, bitterness, greed, is not to be filled by a vacuum when these horrors are eliminated. When you clear away a poisonous gas, you try to fill the whole room with clean air. Kindness, for only one example; one who can define kindness only as the absence of cruelty has surely not begun to understand the nature of either.

They do not aim at perfection, these angels—only at the attainable. . . . That time fifty million years ago was evidently one of great suffering and confusion. War and all its attendant plagues. They passed through many centuries while advances in technology merely worsened their condition and increased the peril of self-annihilation. They came through that, in time. War was at length so far outgrown that its recurrence was impossible, and the development of wholly rational beings could begin. Then they were ready to start growing up, through millennia of self-searching, self-discipline, seeking to derive the simple from the complex, discovering how to use knowledge and not be used by it. Even then, of course, they slipped back often enough. There were what she refers to as "eras of fatigue." In their dimmer past, they had had many dark ages, lost civilizations, hopeful beginnings ending in dust. Earlier still, they had come out of the slime, as we did.

But their period of deepest uncertainty and sternest self-appraisal did not come until twelve million years ago, when they knew a universe could be theirs for the taking and knew they were not yet good enough.

They are in no more hurry than the stars.

Of course, they explored. Their little spaceships were roaming the ether before there was anything like man on this earth—roaming and listening, observing, recording; never entering nor taking part in the life of any home but their own. For five million years they even forbade themselves to go beyond their own solar system, though it would have been easy to do so. And in the following seven million years, although they traveled to incredible distances, the same stern restraint was in force. It was altogether unrelated to what we should call fear—that, I think, is as extinct in them as hate. There was so much to do at home! I wish I could imagine it. They mapped the heavens and played in their own sunlight.

Naturally, I cannot tell you what goodness is. I know only, moderately well, what it seems to mean to us human beings. It appears that the best of us can, with enormous difficulty, achieve a manner of life in which goodness is reasonably dominant, by a not too precarious balance, for the greater part of the time. Often, wise men have indicated they hope for nothing better than that in our present condition. We are, in other words, a fraction alive; the rest is in the dark. Dante was a bitter masochist, Beethoven, a frantic and miserable snob, Shakespeare wrote pot-boilers. And Christ said, "My Father, if it be possible, let this cup pass from me."

But give me fifty million years—I am no pessimist. After all, I've watched one-celled organisms on the slide and listened to Brahms's Fourth. Night before last I said to the angel, "In spite of everything, you and I are kindred."

She granted me agreement.

June 9

She was lying on my pillow this morning so that I could see her when I waked.

Her father has died, and she was with him when it happened. There was again that thought-impression that I could interpret only to mean that his life had been "saved." I was still sleepbound when my mind asked, "What will you do?"

"Stay with you, if you wish it, for the rest of your life." Now, the last part of the message was clouded, but I am familiar with that—it seems to mean there is some further element that eludes me. I could not be mistaken about the part I did receive. It gives me amazing speculations. After all, I am only fifty-three; I might live for another thirty or forty years. . . .

She was preoccupied this morning, but whatever she felt about her father's death that might be paralleled by sadness in a human being was hidden from me. She did say her father was sorry he had not been able to show me a two-moon night.

One adult, then, remains in this world. Except to say that he is two hundred years old and full of knowledge, and that he endured the long journey without serious ill effects, she has told me little about him. And there are ten children, including herself.

Something was sparkling at her throat. When she was aware of my interest in it she took it off, and I fetched a magnifying glass. A necklace; under the glass, much like our finest human workmanship, if your imagination can reduce it to the proper scale. The stones appeared similar to the jewels we know: diamonds, sapphires, rubies, emeralds, the diamonds snapping out every color under heaven; but there were two or three very dark purple stones unlike anything I know—not amethysts, I am sure. The necklace was strung on something more slender than cobweb, and the design of the joining clasp was too delicate for my glass to help me. The

necklace had been her mother's, she told me; as she put it
back around her throat I thought I saw the same shy pride
that any human girl might feel in displaying a new pretty.

She wanted to show me other things she had brought, and
flew to the table, where she had left a sort of satchel an inch
and a half long—quite a load for her to fly with, but the
translucent substance is so light that when she rested the
satchel on my finger I scarcely felt it. She arranged a few
articles happily for my inspection, and I put the glass to work
again. One was a jeweled comb; she ran it through the down
on her chest and legs to show me its use. There was a set of
tools too small for the glass to interpret; I learned later they
were a sewing kit. A book, and some writing instrument
much like a metal pencil; imagine a book and pencil that
could be used comfortably by hands hardly bigger than the
paws of a mouse—that is the best I can do. The book, I
understand, is a blank record for her use as needed.

And finally, when I was fully awake and dressed and we
had finished breakfast, she reached in the bottom of the satchel for a parcel (heavy for her) and made me understand
it was a gift for me. "My father made it for you, but I put in
the stone myself, last night." She unwrapped it. A ring, precisely the size for my little finger.

I broke down, rather. She understood that, and sat on my
shoulder petting my ear lobe till I had command of myself.

I have no idea what the jewel is. It shifts with the light
from purple to jade-green to amber. The metal resembles
platinum in appearance except for a tinge of rose at certain
angles of light. When I stare into the stone, I think I see—
Never mind that now. I am not ready to write it down, and
perhaps never will be; anyway, I must be sure.

We improved our housekeeping later in the morning. I
showed her over the house. It isn't much—Cape Codder,
two rooms up and two down. Every corner interested her,
and when she found a shoebox in the bedroom closet, she
asked for it. At her direction, I have arranged it on a chest
near my bed and near the window, which will be always open;
she says the mosquitoes will not bother me, and I don't doubt
her. I unearthed a white silk scarf for the bottom of the box;
after asking my permission (as if I could want to refuse her
anything!) she got her sewing kit and snipped off a piece of
the scarf several inches square, folded it on itself several
times, and sewed it into a narrow pillow an inch long. So now

she has a proper bed and a room of her own. I wish I had something less coarse than silk, but she insists it's nice.

We have not talked very much today. In the afternoon she flew out for an hour's play in the cloud country; when she returned she let me know that she needed a long sleep. She is still sleeping, I think; I am writing this downstairs, fearing the light might disturb her.

Is it possible I can have thirty or forty years in her company? I wonder how teachable my mind still is. I seem to be able to assimilate new facts as well as I ever could; this ungainly carcass should be durable, with reasonable care. Of course, facts without a synthetic imagination are no better than scattered bricks; but perhaps my imagination—

I don't know.

Judy wants out. I shall turn in when she comes back. I wonder if poor Judy's life could be—the word is certainly "saved." I must ask.

June 10

Last night when I stopped writing I did go to bed, but I was restless, refusing sleep. At some time in the small hours —there was light from a single room—she flew over to me. The tensions dissolved like an illness, and my mind was able to respond with a certain calm.

I made plain (what I am sure she already knew) that I would never willingly part company with her, and then she gave me to understand that there are two alternatives for the remainder of my life. The choice, she says, is altogether mine, and I must take time to be sure of my decision.

I can live out my natural span, whatever it proves to be, and she will not leave me for long at any time. She will be there to counsel, teach, help me in anything good I care to undertake. She says she would enjoy this; for some reason she is, as we'd say in our language, fond of me. We'd have fun.

Lord, the books I could write! I fumble for words now, in the usual human way: whatever I put on paper is a miserable fraction of the potential; the words themselves are rarely the right ones. But under her guidance—

I could take a fair part in shaking the world. With words alone. I could preach to my own people. Before long, I would be heard.

I could study and explore. What small nibblings we have made at the sum of available knowledge! Suppose I brought in one leaf from outdoors, or one common little bug—in a few hours of studying it with her I'd know more of my own specialty than a flood of the best textbooks could tell me.

She has also let me know that when she and those who came with her have learned a little more about the human picture, it should be possible to improve my health greatly, and probably my life expectancy. I don't imagine my back could ever straighten, but she thinks the pain might be cleared away, possibly without drugs. I could have a clearer mind, in a body that would neither fail nor torment me.

Then there is the other alternative.

It seems they have developed a technique by means of which any unresisting living subject whose brain is capable of memory at all can experience a total recall. It is a by-product, I understand, of their silent speech, and a very recent one. They have practiced it for only a few thousand years, and since their own understanding of the phenomenon is very incomplete, they classify it among their experimental techniques. In a general way, it may somewhat resemble that reliving of the past that psychoanalysis can sometimes bring about in a limited way for therapeutic purposes; but you must imagine that sort of thing tremendously magnified and clarified, capable of including every detail that has ever registered on the subject's brain; and the end result is very different. The purpose is not therapeutic, as we would understand it: quite the opposite. The end result is death. Whatever is recalled by this process is transmitted to the receiving mind, which can retain it and record any or all of it if such a record is desired; but to the subject who recalls it, it is a flowing away, without return. Thus it is not a true "remembering," but a giving. The mind is swept clear, naked of all its past, and, along with memory, life withdraws also. Very quietly. At the end, I suppose it must be like standing without resistance in the engulfment of a flood tide, until finally the waters close over.

That, it seems, is how Camilla's life was "saved." Now, when I finally grasped that, I laughed, and the angel, of course, caught my joke. I was thinking about my neighbor Steele, who boarded the old lady for me in his henhouse for a couple of winters. Somewhere safe in the angelic records there must be a hen's-eye image of the patch in the seat of Steele's pants. Well—good. And, naturally, Camilla's view of me, too: not too unkind, I hope—she couldn't help the expression on her rigid little face, and I don't believe it ever meant anything.

At the other end of the scale is the saved life of my angel's father. Recall can be a long process, she says, depending on the intricacy and richness of the mind recalling; and in all but the last stages it can be halted at will. Her father's recall was begun when they were still far out in space and he knew that he could not long survive the journey. When that journey ended, the recall had progressed so far that very little actual memory remained to him of his life on that other planet. He had what must be called a "deductive memory"; from the material of the years not yet given away, he could reconstruct what must have been; and I assume the other adult who survived the passage must have been able to shelter him from errors that loss of memory might involve. This, I infer, is why he could not show me a two-moon night. I forgot to ask her whether the images he did send me were from actual or deductive memory. Deductive, I think, for there was a certain dimness about them not present when my angel gives me a picture of something seen with her own eyes.

Jade-green eyes, by the way—were you wondering?

In the same fashion, my own life could be saved. Every aspect of existence that I ever touched, that ever touched me, could be transmitted to some perfect record. The nature of the written record is beyond me, but I have no doubt of its relative perfection. Nothing important, good or bad, would be lost. And they need a knowledge of humanity, if they are to carry out whatever it is they have in mind.

It would be difficult, she tells me, and sometimes painful. Most of the effort would be hers, but some of it would have to be mine. In her period of infantile education, she elected what we should call zoology as her lifework; for that reason she was given intensive theoretical training in this technique. Right now, I guess she knows more than anyone else on this planet not only about what makes a hen tick but about how it feels to be a hen. Though a beginner, she is in all essentials already an expert. She can help me, she thinks (if I choose this alternative)—at any rate, ease me over the toughest spots, soothe away resistance, keep my courage from too much flagging.

For it seems that this process of recall is painful to an advanced intellect (she, without condescension, calls us very advanced) because, while all pretense and self-delusion are stripped away, there remains conscience, still functioning by whatever standards of good and bad the individual has developed in his lifetime. Our present knowledge of our own motives is such a pathetically small beginning!—hardly stronger than an infant's first effort to focus his eyes. I am merely wondering how much of my life (if I choose this way) will seem to me altogether hideous. Certainly plenty of the "good deeds" that I still cherish in memory like so many well-behaved cherubs will turn up with the leering of greed or petty vanity or worse.

Not that I am a bad man, in any reasonable sense of the term; not a bit of it. I respect myself; no occasion to grovel and beat my chest; I'm not ashamed to stand comparison with any other fair sample of the species. But there you are: I *am* human, and under the aspect of eternity so far, plus this afternoon's newspaper, that is a rather serious thing.

Without real knowledge, I think of this total recall as something like a passage down a corridor of myriad images —now dark, now brilliant; now pleasant, now horrible— guided by no certainty except an awareness of the open blind door at the end of it. It could have its pleasing moments and its consolations. I don't see how it could ever approximate the delight and satisfaction of living a few more years in this world with the angel lighting on my shoulder when she wishes, and talking to me.

I had to ask her of how great value such a record would be to them. Very great. Obvious enough—they can be of little use to us, by their standards, until they understand us; and they came here to be of use to us as well as to themselves. And understanding us, to them, means knowing us inside out with a completeness such as our most dedicated and laborious scholars could never imagine. I remember those twelve million years; they will not touch us until they are certain no harm will come of it. On our tortured planet, however, there is a time factor. They know that well enough, of course. . . . Recall cannot begin unless the subject is willing or unresisting; to them, that has to mean willing, for any being with intellect enough to make a considered choice. Now, I wonder how many they could find who would be honestly willing to make that uneasy journey into death, for no reward except an assurance that they were serving their own kind and the angels?

More to the point, I wonder if I would be able to achieve such willingness myself, even with her help?

When this had been explained to me, she urged me again to make no hasty decision. And she pointed out to me what my thoughts were already groping at—why not both alternatives, within a reasonable limit of time? Why couldn't I have ten or fifteen years or more with her and then undertake the total recall—perhaps not until my physical powers had started toward senility? I thought that over.

This morning I had almost decided to choose that most welcome and comforting solution. Then the mailman brought my daily paper. Not that I needed any such reminder.

In the afternoon I asked her if she knew whether, in the present state of human technology, it would be possible for our folly to actually destroy this planet. She did not know, for certain. Three of the other children have gone away to different parts of the world to learn what they can about that. But she had to tell me that such a thing has happened before, elsewhere in the heavens. I guess I won't write a letter to the papers advancing an explanation for the occasional appearance of a nova among the stars. Doubtless others have hit on the same hypothesis without the aid of angels.

And that is not all I must consider. I could die by accident or sudden disease before I had begun to give my life.

Only now, at this very late moment, rubbing my sweaty forehead and gazing into the lights of that wonderful ring, have I been able to put together some obvious facts in the required synthesis.

I don't know, of course, what forms their assistance to us will take. I suspect human beings won't see or hear much of the angels for a long time to come. Now and then disastrous decisions may be altered, and those who believe themselves wholly responsible won't quite know why their minds worked that way. Here and there, maybe an influential mind will be rather strangely nudged into a better course. Something like that. There may be sudden new discoveries and inventions of kinds that will tend to neutralize the menace of our nastiest playthings. But whatever the angels decide to do, the record and analysis of my not too atypical life will be an aid; it could even be the small weight deciding the balance between triumph and failure. That is fact one.

Two: my angel and her brothers and sisters, for all their

amazing level of advancement, are of perishable protoplasm, even as I am. Therefore, if this ball of earth becomes a ball of flame, they also will be destroyed. Even if they have the means to use their spaceship again or to build another, it might easily happen that they would not learn their danger in time to escape. And for all I know, this could be tomorrow. Or tonight.

So there can no longer be any doubt as to my choice, and I will tell her when she wakes.

July 9

Tonight* there is no recall—I am to rest a while. I see it is almost a month since I last wrote in this journal. My total recall began three weeks ago, and I have already been able to give away the first twenty-eight years of my life.

Since I no longer require normal sleep, the recall begins at night, as soon as the lights begin to go out over there in the village and there is little danger of interruption. Daytimes, I putter about in my usual fashion. I have sold Steele my hens, and Judy's life was saved a week ago; that practically winds up my affairs, except that I want to write a codicil to my will. I might as well do that now, right here in this journal, instead of bothering my lawyer. It should be legal.

To Whom It May Concern: I hereby bequeath to my friend Lester Morse, M.D., of Augusta, Maine, the ring which will be found at my death on the fifth finger of my left hand; and I would urge Dr. Morse to retain this ring in his private possession at all times, and to make provision for its disposal, in the event of his own death, to some person in whose character he places the utmost faith.

(Signed) David Bannerman†

Tonight she has gone away for a while, and I am to rest and do as I please until she returns. I shall spend the time filling in some blanks in this record, but I am afraid it will be a spotty job, unsatisfactory to any readers who are subject to the blessed old itch for facts. Mainly because there is so much

* At this point Dr. Bannerman's handwriting alters curiously. From here on he used a soft pencil instead of a pen, and the script shows signs of haste. In spite of this, however, it is actually much clearer, steadier, and easier to read than the earlier entries in his normal hand.—Blaine.
† In spite of superficial changes in the handwriting, this signature has been certified genuine by an expert graphologist.—Blaine.

I no longer care about. It is troublesome to try to decide what things would be considered important by interested strangers.

Except for the lack of any desire for sleep, and a bodily weariness that is not at all unpleasant, I notice no physical effects thus far. I have no faintest recollection of anything that happened earlier than my twenty-eighth birthday. My deductive memory seems rather efficient, and I am sure I could reconstruct most of the story if it were worth the bother: this afternoon I grubbed around among some old letters of that period, but they weren't very interesting. My knowledge of English is unaffected; I can still read scientific German and some French, because I had occasion to use those languages fairly often after I was twenty-eight. The scraps of Latin dating from high school are quite gone. So are algebra and all but the simplest propositions of high-school geometry: I never needed 'em. I can remember thinking of my mother after twenty-eight, but do not know whether the image this provides really resembles her; my father died when I was thirty-one, so I remember him as a sick old man. I believe I had a younger brother, but he must have died in childhood.*

Judy's passing was tranquil—pleasant for her, I think. It took the better part of a day. We went out to an abandoned field I know, and she lay in the sunshine with the angel sitting by her, while I dug a grave and then rambled off after wild raspberries. Toward evening the angel came and told me it was finished. And most interesting, she said. I don't see how there can have been anything distressing about it for Judy; after all, what hurts us worst is to have our favorite self-deceptions stripped away.

As the angel has explained it to me, her people, their cats, those kangaroo-folk, man, and just possibly the cats on our planet (she hasn't met them yet) are the only animals she knows who are introspective enough to develop self-delusion and related pretenses. I suggested she might find something of the sort, at least in rudimentary form, among some of the other primates. She was immensely interested and wanted to learn everything I could tell her about monkeys and apes. It seems that long ago on the other planet there used to be clumsy, winged creatures resembling the angels to about the degree that the large anthropoids re-

* Dr. Bannerman's mother died in 1918 of influenza. His brother (three years older, not younger) died of pneumonia, 1906.—BLAINE

semble us. They became extinct some forty million years ago, in spite of enlightened efforts to keep their kind alive. Their birth rate became insufficient for replacement, as if some necessary spark had simply flickered out; almost as if nature, or whatever name you prefer for the unknown, had with gentle finality written them off. . . .

I have not found the recall painful, at least not in retrospect. There must have been sharp moments, mercifully forgotten, along with their causes, as if the process had gone on under anesthesia. Certainly there were plenty of incidents in my first twenty-eight years that I should not care to offer to the understanding of any but the angels. Quite often I must have been mean, selfish, base in any number of ways, if only to judge by the record since twenty-eight. Those old letters touch on a few of these things. To me, they now matter only as material for a record which is safely out of my hands.

However, to any persons I may have harmed, I wish to say this: You were hurt by aspects of my humanity which may not, in a few million years, be quite so common among us all. Against these darker elements I struggled, in my human fashion, as you do yourselves. The effort is not wasted.

It was a week after I told the angel my decision before she was prepared to start the recall. During that week she searched my present mind more closely than I should have imagined was possible; she had to be sure. During that week of hard questions I daresay she learned more about my kind than has ever gone on record even in a physician's office; I hope she did. To any psychiatrist who might question that, I offer a naturalist's suggestion: It is easy to imagine, after some laborious time, that we have noticed everything a given patch of ground can show us; but alter the viewpoint only a little—dig down a foot with a spade, say, or climb a tree branch and look downward—it's a whole new world.

When the angel was not exploring me in this fashion, she took pains to make me glimpse the satisfactions and million rewarding experiences I might have if I chose the other way. I see how necessary that was; at the time it seemed almost cruel. She had to do it, for my own sake, and I am glad that I was somehow able to stand fast to my original choice. So was she, in the end; she has even said she loves me for it. What that troubling word means to her is not within my mind; I am satisfied to take it in the human sense.

Some evening during that week—I think it was June 12—
Lester dropped around for sherry and chess. Hadn't seen
him in quite a while, and haven't since. There is a moderate
polio scare this summer, and it keeps him on the jump. The
angel retired behind some books on an upper shelf—I'm
afraid it was dusty—and had fun with our chess. She had a
fair view of your bald spot, Lester; later she remarked that
she liked your looks, and can't you do something about that
weight? She suggested an odd expedient, which I believe has
occurred to your medical self from time to time—eating less.

Maybe she shouldn't have done what she did with those
chess games. Nothing more than my usual blundering happened until after my first ten moves; by that time I suppose
she had absorbed the principles and she took over, slightly.
I was not fully aware of it until I saw Lester looking like a
boiled duck; I had imagined my astonishing moves were the
result of my own damn cleverness.

Seriously, Lester, think back to that evening. You've
played in stiff amateur tournaments; you know your own
abilities and you know mine. Ask yourself whether I could
have done anything like that without help. I tell you again, I
didn't study the game in the interval when you weren't here.
I've never had a chess book in the library, and if I had, no
amount of study would take me into your class. Haven't that
sort of mentality—just your humble sparring partner, and
I've enjoyed it on that basis, as you might enjoy watching a
prima-donna surgeon pull off some miracle you wouldn't
dream of attempting yourself. Even if your game had been
away below par that evening (I don't think it was), I could
never have pinned your ears back three times running, without help. That evening you were a long way out of *your* class,
that's all.

I couldn't tell you anything about it at the time—she was
clear on that point—so I could only bumble and preen myself and leave you mystified. But she wants me to write anything I choose in this journal, and somehow, Lester, I think
you may find the next few decades pretty interesting. You're
still young—some ten years younger than I. I think you'll
see many things that I do wish I myself might see come to
pass—or I would so wish if I were not convinced that my
choice was the right one.

Most of those new events will not be spectacular, I'd guess.
Many of the turns to a better way will hardly be recognized

at the time for what they are, by you or anyone else. Obviously, our nature being what it is, we shall not jump into heaven overnight. To hope for that would be as absurd as it is to imagine that any formula, ideology, theory of social pattern, can bring us into Utopia. As I see it, Lester—and I think your consulting room would have told you the same even if your own intuition were not enough—there is only one battle of importance: Armageddon. And Armageddon field is within each self, world without end.

At the moment I believe I am the happiest man who ever lived.

July 20

All but the last ten years now given away. The physical fatigue (still pleasant) is quite overwhelming. I am not troubled by the weeds in my garden patch—merely a different sort of flower where I had planned something else. An hour ago she brought me the seed of a blown dandelion, to show me how lovely it was—I don't suppose I had ever noticed. I hope whoever takes over this place will bring it back to farming; they say the ten acres below the house used to be good potato land—nice early ground.

It is delightful to sit in the sun, as if I were old.

After thumbing over earlier entries in this journal, I see I have often felt quite bitter toward my own kind. I deduce that I must have been a lonely man—much of the loneliness self-imposed. A great part of my bitterness must have been no more than one ugly by-product of a life spent too much apart. Some of it doubtless came from objective causes, yet I don't believe I ever had more cause than any moderately intelligent man who would like to see his world a pleasanter place than it ever has been. My angel tells me that the pain in my back is due to an injury received in some early stage of the world war that still goes on. That could have soured me, perhaps. It's all right—it's all in the record.

She is racing with a hummingbird—holding back, I think, to give the ball of green fluff a break.

Another note for you, Lester. I have already indicated that my ring is to be yours. I don't want to tell you what I have discovered of its properties, for fear it might not give you the same pleasure and interest that it has given me. Of course, like any spot of shifting light and color, it is an aid to self-hypnosis. It is much, much more than that, but—find out for yourself, at some time when you are a little protected from everyday distractions. I know it can't harm you, because I know its source.

By the way, I wish you would convey to my publishers my request that they either discontinue manufacture of my *Introductory Biology* or else bring out a new edition revised in accordance with some notes you will find in the top left drawer of my library desk. I glanced through that book after my angel assured me that I wrote it, and I was amazed. However, I'm afraid my notes are messy (I call them mine by a poetic license), and they may be too advanced for the present day—though the revision is mainly a matter of leaving out certain generalities that ain't so. Use your best judgment: it's a very minor textbook, and the thing isn't too important. A last wriggle of my personal vanity.

July 27

I have seen a two-moon night.

It was given to me by that other grownup, at the end of a wonderful visit, when he and six of those nine other children came to see me. It was last night, I think—yes, must have been. First there was a murmur of wings above the house; my angel flew in, laughing; then they were here, all about me. Full of gaiety and colored fire, showing off in every way they knew would please me. Each one had something graceful and friendly to say to me. One brought me a moving image of the St. Lawrence seen at morning from half a mile up—clouds, eagles; now, how could he know that would delight me so much? And each one thanked me for what I had done.

But it's been so easy!

And at the end the old one—his skin is quite black, and his down is white and gray—gave the remembered image of a two-moon night. He saw it some sixty years ago.

I have not even considered making an effort to describe it—my fingers will not hold this pencil much longer tonight. Oh—soaring buildings of white and amber, untroubled countryside, silver on curling rivers, a glimpse of open sea; a moon rising in clarity, another setting in a wreath of cloud, between them a wide wandering of unfamiliar stars; and here and there the angels, worthy after fifty million years to live in such a night. No, I cannot describe anything like that. But, you human kindred of mine, I can do something better. I can tell you that this two-moon night, glorious as it was, was no more beautiful than a night under a single moon on this ancient and familiar Earth might be—if you will imagine that the rubbish of human evil has been cleared away and that our own people have started at last on the greatest of all explorations.

July 29

Nothing now remains to give away but the memory of the time that has passed since the angel came. I am to rest as long as I wish, write whatever I want to. Then I shall get myself over to the bed and lie down as if for sleep. She tells me that I can keep my eyes open: she will close them for me when I no longer see her.

I remain convinced that our human case is hopeful. I feel sure that in only a few thousand years we may be able to perform some of the simpler preparatory tasks, such as casting out evil and loving our neighbors. And if that should prove to be so, who can doubt that in another fifty million years we might well be only a little lower than the angels?

LIBRARIAN'S NOTE: As is generally known, the original of the Bannerman Journal is said to have been in the possession of Dr. Lester Morse at the time of the latter's disappearance in 1964, and that disappearance has remained an unsolved mystery to the present day. McCarran is known to have visited Captain Garrison Blaine in October 1951, but no record remains of that visit. Captain Blaine appears to have been a bachelor who lived alone. He was killed in line of duty, December 1951. McCarran is believed not to have written about or discussed the Bannerman affair with anyone else. It is almost certain that he himself removed the extract and related papers from the files (unofficially, it would seem!) when he severed his connection with the F.B.I. in 1957; at any rate, they were found among his effects after his assassination and were released to the public, considerably later, by Mrs. McCarran.

The following memorandum was originally attached to the extract from the Bannerman Journal; it carries the McCarran initialing.

Aug. 11, 1951

The original letter of complaint written by Stephen Clyde, M.D., and mentioned in the accompanying letter of Captain Blaine, has unfortunately been lost, owing perhaps to an error in filing.

Personnel presumed responsible have been instructed not to allow such error to be repeated except if, as, and/or when necessary.

C. McC.

On the margin of this memorandum there was a penciled notation, later erased. The imprint is sufficient to show the unmistakable McCarran script. The notation read in part as follows: *Far be it from a McC. to lose his job except if, as, and/or*—the rest is undecipherable, except for a terminal word which is regrettably unparliamentary.

STATEMENT BY LESTER MORSE, M.D., DATED AUGUST 9, 1951

On the afternoon of July 30, 1951, acting on what I am obliged to describe as an unexpected impulse, I drove out to the country for the purpose of calling on my friend Dr. David Bannerman. I had not seen him or had word from him since the evening of June 12 of this year.

I entered, as was my custom, without knocking. After calling to him and hearing no response, I went upstairs to his bedroom and found him dead. From superficial indications I judged that death must have taken place during the previous night. He was lying on his bed on his left side, comfortably disposed as if for sleep but fully dressed, with a fresh shirt and clean summer slacks. His eyes and mouth were closed, and there was no trace of the disorder to be expected at even the easiest natural death. Because of these signs I assumed, as soon as I had determined the absence of breath and heart-beat and noted the chill of the body, that some neighbor must have found him already, performed these simple rites out of respect for him, and probably notified a local physician or other responsible person. I therefore waited (Dr. Bannerman had no telephone), expecting that someone would soon call.

Dr. Bannerman's journal was on a table near his bed, open to that page on which he has written a codicil to his will. I read that part. Later, while I was waiting for others to come, I read the remainder of the journal, as I believe he wished me to do. The ring he mentions was on the fifth finger of his left hand, and it is now in my possession. When writing that codicil Dr. Bannerman must have overlooked or forgotten the fact that in his formal will, written some months earlier, he had appointed me executor. If there are legal technicalities involved, I shall be pleased to co-operate fully with the proper authorities.

The ring, however, will remain in my keeping, since that was Dr. Bannerman's expressed wish, and I am not prepared to offer it for examination or discussion under any circumstances.

The notes for a revision of one of his textbooks were in his desk, as noted in the journal. They are by no means "messy"; nor are they particularly revolutionary except insofar as he wished to rephrase, as theory or hypothesis, certain statements that I would have supposed could be regarded as axiomatic. This is not my field, and I am not competent to judge. I shall take up the matter with his publishers at the earliest oportunity.*

So far as I can determine, and bearing in mind the results of the autopsy performed by Stephen Clyde, M.D., the death of Dr. David Bannerman was not inconsistent with the presence of an embolism of some type not distinguishable on post-mortem. I have so stated on the certificate of death. It would seem to be not in the public interest to leave such questions in doubt. I am compelled to add one other item of medical opinion for what it may be worth:

I am not a psychiatrist, but, owing to the demands of general practice, I have found it advisable to keep as up to date as possible with current findings and opinion in this branch of medicine. Dr. Bannerman possessed, in my opinion, emotional and intellectual stability to a better degree than anyone else of comparable intelligence in the entire field of my acquaintance, personal and professional. If it is suggested that he was suffering from a hallucinatory psychosis, I can only say that it must have been of a type quite outside my experience and not described, so far as I know, anywhere in the literature of psychopathology.

Dr. Bannerman's house, on the afternoon of July 30, was in good order. Near the open, unscreened window of his bedroom there was a coverless shoebox with a folded silk scarf in the bottom. I found no pillow such as Dr. Bannerman describes in the journal, but observed that a small section had

* LIBRARIAN'S NOTE: But it seems he never did. No new edition of "Introductory Biology" was ever brought out, and the textbook has been out of print since 1952.

been cut from the scarf. In this box, and near it, there was a peculiar fragrance, faint, aromatic, and very sweet, such as I have never encountered before and therefore cannot describe.

It may or may not have any bearing on the case that, while I remained in his house that afternoon, I felt no sense of grief or personal loss, although Dr. Bannerman had been a loved and honored friend for a number of years. I merely had, and have, a conviction that after the completion of some very great undertaking, he had found peace.

6.

SUPERMAN

Supernatural beings and mythic heroes aside, the idea of a being beyond man—man evolved into something better— had to wait for Darwin, and for Friedrich Nietzsche. In 1936 Olaf Stapledon published a novel, Odd John, *which is the acknowledged masterwork on this theme and is generally thought to be the first fictional treatment of a mutant superman.*

In fact, Odd John *was anticipated by a story published in the* Revue Parisienne *in 1895. The author, J.-H. Rosny aîné, was a giant of French letters, a president of the Académie Goncourt, a friend of Goncourt and Alphonse Daudet. During his long lifetime he published some 107 novels, essays, plays, memoirs, etc. Only a few of these were science fiction, but those few were precedent-making, germinal works. Rosny, not Verne, is considered the father of French science fiction.*

The name J.-H. Rosny was originally the pseudonym adopted by two brothers, Honoré and Justin Boëx, born in Brussels in 1856 and 1859. When they separated after twenty years of collaboration, Honoré, the elder, signed his work "J.-H. Rosny aîné," and Justin "J.-H. Rosny jeune."

I love this story for its human warmth, and for what it has to tell us, not only about one superman, but about the adolescence of all gifted, "different" human beings. I admire it for many reasons, but chiefly for the absolute, circumstantial conviction with which it describes an imaginary order of living creatures. Few writers have even attempted this most difficult kind of fictional invention; fewer still have succeeded so brilliantly.

ANOTHER WORLD

BY J.-H. ROSNY AÎNÉ

TRANSLATED BY DAMON KNIGHT

I was born in Gelderland, where our family holdings had dwindled to a few acres of heath and yellow water. Along the boundary grew pine trees that rustled with a metallic sound. The farmhouse had only a few habitable rooms left and was falling apart stone by stone in the solitude. Ours was an old family of herdsmen, once numerous, now reduced to my parents, my sister and myself.

My fate, dismal enough at the beginning, became the happiest I could imagine: I met the one who understands me; he will teach those things that formerly I alone knew among men. But for many years I suffered and despaired, a prey to doubt and the loneliness of the soul, which nearly ended by eating away my absolute faith.

I came into the world with a unique constitution, and from the very beginning I was the object of wonder. Not that I seemed ill-formed; I was, I am told, more shapely in face and body than is customary in newborn infants. But my color was most unusual, a sort of pale violet—very pale, but quite distinct. By lamplight, especially by the light of oil lamps, this tint grew paler still, turned to a curious whiteness, like that of a lily submerged in water. That, at least, was how I appeared to others (for I saw myself differently, as I saw everything in the world differently). To this first peculiarity others were added which only revealed themselves later.

Though born with a healthy apearance, I developed poorly. I was thin, and I cried incessantly; at the age of eight months, I had never been seen to smile. Soon my life was despaired of. The doctor from Zwartendam declared I was suffering from congenital weakness; he could think of no remedy but a strict regimen. Nonetheless I continued to waste away; the family expected me to disappear altogether from one day to the next. My father, I think, was resigned to it, his pride—the Hollander's pride in regularity and order —little soothed by the grotesque appearance of his child. My mother, on the contrary, loved me all the more for my strangeness, having made up her mind that the color of my skin was pleasing.

So matters stood, when a very simple thing came to my rescue. Since everything concerning me must be out of the ordinary, this event was the cause of scandal and apprehension.

A servant having left us, her place was given to a vigorous girl from Friesland, honest and willing, but inclined to drink. I was placed in her care. Seeing me so feeble, she took it into her head to give me secretly a little beer and water mixed with Schiedam—remedies, according to her, sovereign against all ills.

The curious thing was that I began immediately to regain my strength and from then on showed a remarkable predilection for alcohol. The good girl rejoiced in secret, not without drawing some pleasure from the bafflement of my parents and the doctor. At last, driven into a corner, she revealed the secret. My father flew into a violent passion; the doctor inveighed against superstition and ignorance. Strict orders were given to the servants; I was taken out of the Frieslander's care.

I began to grow thin again, to waste away, until my mother, forgetting everything but her fondness for me, put me back on a diet of beer and Schiedam. I promptly grew strong and lively again. The experiment was conclusive: alcohol was seen to be necessary to my health. My father was humiliated. The doctor got out of the affair by prescribing medicinal wines; and from that time on my health was excellent—but no one hesitated to prophesy a life of drunkenness and debauch for me.

Shortly after this incident, a new oddity grew apparent to the household. My eyes, which had seemed normal at the beginning, grew strangely opaque, took on a horny appearance, like the wing cases of certain beetles. The doctor concluded from this that I was losing my sight, but he confessed that the ailment was absolutely strange to him, of such a nature that he had never had the opportunity to study a like case. Shortly the pupils of my eyes so fused into the irises that it was impossible to tell one from the other. It was remarked, moreover, that I could stare at the sun without showing any discomfort. In truth, I was not blind in the least, and in the end they had to admit that I saw very well.

So I arrived at the age of three. I was then, in the opinion of the neighborhood, a little monster. The violet color of my skin had undergone little change. My eyes were completely opaque. I spoke awkwardly, and with incredible swiftness. I was dextrous with my hands, and well formed for all activities which called for more quickness than strength. It was not denied that I might have been graceful and handsome if my coloring had been normal and my pupils transparent. I showed some intelligence, but with deficiencies which my family did not fully appreciate, since, except for my mother and the Frieslander, they did not care much for me. I was an object of curiosity to strangers, and to my father a continual mortification.

If, moreover, he had clung to any hope of seeing me become like other people, time took ample pains to disabuse him of it. I grew more and more strange, in my tastes, habits and aptitudes. At the age of six I lived almost entirely on alcohol. Only very seldom did I take a few bites of vegetables or fruit. I grew with prodigious swiftness; I became incredibly thin and light. I mean "light" even in its specific sense, which is just the opposite of thinness. Thus, I swam without the slightest difficulty; I floated like a plank of poplar. My head hardly sank deeper than the rest of my body.

I was nimble in proportion to that lightness. I ran like a deer; I easily leaped over ditches and barriers which no man would even have attempted. Quick as a wink, I could be in the crown of a beech tree; or, what caused even more astonishment, I could leap over the roof of our farmhouse. In compensation, the slightest burden was too much for me.

All these things added together were nothing but phenomena indicative of a special nature, which by themselves would have done no more than single me out and make me unwelcome; no one would have classified me outside humanity. No doubt I was a monster, but certainly not to the same degree as those who were born with the ears or horns of animals; a head like a calf's or horse's; fins; no eyes or an extra one; four arms; four legs; or without arms and legs. My skin, in spite of its startling color, was little different from a sun-tanned skin; there was nothing repugnant about my eyes, opaque as they were. My extreme agility was a gift, my need for alcohol might pass for a mere vice, an inheritance of drunkenness; however, the rustics, like our Frieslander servant, viewed it as no more than a confirmation of their ideas about the "strength" of Schiedam, a rather lively demonstration of the excellence of their tastes.

As for the swiftness and volubility of my speech, which made it impossible to follow, this seemed to be confounded with the defects of pronunciation—stammering, lisping, stuttering—common to so many small childen. Thus, properly speaking, I had none of the marked characteristics of monstrosity, however extraordinary my general effect might be. The fact was that the most curious aspect of my nature escaped my family's notice, for no one realized that my vision was strangely different from ordinary vision.

If I saw certain things less well than others did, I could see a great many things that no one else could see at all. This difference showed itself especially in relation to colors. All that was termed red, orange, yellow, green, blue or indigo appeared to me as a more or less blackish gray, whereas I could perceive violet, and a series of colors beyond it—colors which were nothing but blackness to normal men. Later I realized that I could distinguish in this way among some fifteen colors as dissimilar as, for instance, yellow and green—with, of course, an infinite range of gradations in between.

In the second place, my eye does not perceive transparency in the ordinary way. I see poorly through glass or water; glass is highly colored for me, water perceptibly so, even at a slight depth. Many crystals said to be clear are more or less opaque, while, on the other hand, a very great number of bodies called opaque do not interfere with my vision. In general, I see through objects much more frequently than you do; and translucence, clouded transparency, occurs so often that I might say it is for my eye the rule of nature, while complete opacity is the exception. In this way I can make out objects through wood, paper, the petals of flowers, magnetized iron, coal, etc. Nevertheless, at variable thicknesses these substances create an obstacle—as, a big tree, a meter's depth of water, a thick block of coal or quartz. Gold, platinum and mercury are black and opaque; ice is grayish black. Air and water vapor are transparent and yet tinted, as are certain specimens of steel, certain very pure clays. Clouds do not hinder me from seeing the sun or the stars. On the other hand, I can clearly see these same clouds hanging in the air.

As I have said, this difference between my vision and that of others was very little remarked by those around me. My color perception was thought to be poor, that was all; the infirmity is too common to attract much attention. It had no importance in the small daily acts of my life, for I saw the shapes of objects in the same manner as most people, and perhaps even more accurately. Designating an object by its color, when it was necessary to distinguish it from another of the same shape, troubled me only when the two objects were new. If someone called one waistcoat blue and another red, it made little difference in what colors these waistcoats really appeared to me; blue and red became purely mnemonic terms.

From this you might conclude that there was a system of correspondence between my colors and those of other people, and therefore that it came to the same thing as if I had seen their colors. But, as I have already written, red, green, yellow, blue, etc., *when they are pure,* as the colors of a prism are pure, appear to me as a more or less blackish gray; they are not colors to me at all. In nature, where no color is simple, it is not the same thing. A given substance termed green, for instance, is for me of a certain mixed color;* but another substance called green, which to you is identically the same shade as the first, is not at all the same color to me. You see, therefore, that my range of colors has no correspondence with yours: when I agree to call both brass and gold yellow, it is a little as if you should agree to call both a cornflower and a corn poppy blue.

2.

Were this the extent of the difference between my vision and normal vision, certainly it would appear extraordinary enough. Nevertheless, it is but little compared with that which I have yet to tell you. The differently colored world, differently transparent and opaque, the ability to see through clouds, to perceive the stars on the most overcast nights, to see through a wooden wall what is happening in the next room or on the outside of a house—what is all this, compared with the perception of a *living world,* a world of animate Beings, moving around and beside man without man's being aware of them, without his being warned by any sort of immediate contact?

What is all this, compared with the revelation that there exists on this earth another fauna than our fauna, and one

* And this mixture naturally does not include green, since green, for me, belongs to the realm of darkness.

without any resemblance to our own in form, or in organization, or in habits, or in manner of growth, birth and death? A fauna which lives beside and in the midst of ours, influences the elements which surround us, and is influenced, vivified, by these elements, without our suspecting its presence. A fauna which, as I have demonstrated, is as unaware of us as we of it, and which has evolved in ignorance of us, as we in ignorance of it. A living world as varied as ours, as puissant as ours—perhaps more so—in its effect on the face of the planet! A kingdom, in short, moving upon the water, in the atmosphere, on the earth, modifying that water, that atmosphere and that earth entirely otherwise than we, but certainly with formidable strength, and in that way acting indirectly upon us and our destiny, as we indirectly act upon it!

Nevertheless, this is what I have seen, what I alone among men and animals still see; this is what I have *studied* ardently for five years, after having spent my childhood and adolescence merely *observing* it.

3.

Observing it! As far back as I can remember, I instinctively felt the seductiveness of that creation so foreign to ours. In the beginning, I confounded it with other living things. Seeing that no one took any notice of its presence, that everyone, on the contrary, appeared indifferent to it, I hardly felt the need to point out its peculiarities. At six, I understood perfectly its difference from the plants of the fields, the animals of the farmyard and the stable; but I confused it somewhat with such nonliving phenomena as rays of light, the movement of water, and clouds. That was because these creatures were intangible: when they touched me I felt no sensation of contact. Their shapes, otherwise widely variant, nevertheless had this singularity, that they were so thin, in one of their three dimensions, that they might be compared to drawings, to surfaces, geometric lines that moved. They passed through all organic bodies; on the other hand, they sometimes appeared to be halted, entangled by invisible obstacles.

But I shall describe them later. At present I only wish to draw attention to them, to affirm their variety of contours and lines, their quasi-absence of thickness, their *impalpability*, combined with the autonomy of their movements.

At about my eighth year, I became perfectly sure that they were as distinct from atmospheric phenomena as from the members of our animal kingdom. In the delight this discovery afforded me, I tried to communicate it to others. I never succeeded in doing so. Aside from the fact that my speech was almost entirely incomprehensible, as I have said, the extraordinary nature of my vision rendered it suspect. No one thought of pausing to unravel my gestures and my phrases, any more than to admit that I could see through wooden walls, even though I had given proof of this on many occasions. Between me and the others there was an almost insurmountable barrier.

I fell into discouragement and daydreams, I became a sort of little recluse; I caused uneasiness, and felt it myself, among children of my own age. I was not exactly an underdog, for my swiftness put me beyond the reach of childish tricks and gave me the means of revenging myself easily. At the slightest threat, I was off at a distance—I mocked all pursuit. No matter how many of them there were, children never succeeded in surrounding me, much less in holding me prisoner. It was not worth while even to try to seize me by a trick. Weak as I might be at carrying burdens, my leaps were irresistible and freed me at once. I could return at will, overcome my adversary, even more than one, with swift, sure blows. Accordingly I was left in peace. I was looked on as innocent and at the same time a bit magical; but it was a feeble magic, which they scorned.

By degrees I made a life for myself outdoors, wild, meditative, not without its pleasures. Only the affection of my mother humanized me, even though, busy all day long, she found little time for caresses.

4.

I shall try to describe briefly a few scenes from my tenth year, in order to give substance to the explanations which have gone before.

It is morning. A bright glow illumines the kitchen—a pale yellow glow to my parents and the servants, richly various to me. The first breakfast is being served: bread and tea. But I do not take tea. I have been given a glass of Schiedam with a raw egg. My mother is hovering over me tenderly; my father questions me. I try to answer him, I slow down my speech; he understands only a syllable here and there. He shrugs. "He'll never learn to talk!"

My mother looks at me with compassion, convinced that I am a bit simple. The servants and laborers no longer even feel any curiosity about the little violet monster; the Frieslander has long ago gone back to her country. As for my sister, who is two years old, she is playing near me, and I feel a deep affection for her.

Breakfast over, my father goes off to the fields with the laborers; my mother begins to busy herself with her daily tasks. I follow her into the farmyard. The animals come up to her. I watch them with interest; I like them. But, all around, the other Kingdom is in motion, and it attracts me still more; it is the mysterious domain which only I know.

On the brown earth a few shapes are sprawled out; they move, they pause, they palpitate on the surface of the ground. They belong to several species, different in contours, in movement, and above all in the arrangement, design and shadings of the lines which run through them. Taken together, these lines constitute the essential part of their being, and, child though I am, I know it very well. Whereas the mass of their bodies is dull, grayish, the lines are almost always brilliant. They form highly complicated networks, radiating from centers, spreading out until they fade and lose their identity. Their tints and curves are innumerable. These colors vary within a single line, as the form does also, but to a lesser extent. The creature as a whole is distinguished by a rather irregular but very distinct outline; by the radiant centers; by the multicolored lines which intermingle freely. When it moves, the lines tremble, oscillate; the centers contract and dilate, while the outline changes little.

All this I see very well already, though I may be unable to define it; a delightful spell falls over me when I watch the *Moedigen.** One of them, a colossus ten meters long and almost as wide, passes slowly across the farmyard and disappears. This one, with some bands the size of cables, and centers as big as eagles' wings, greatly interests and almost frightens me. I pause for a moment, about to follow it, but then others attract my attention. They are of all sizes: some are no larger than our tiniest insects, while I have seen others

* This is the name which I gave them spontaneously in my childhood and which I have retained, though it corresponds to no quality or form of these creatures.

more than thirty meters long. They advance on the ground itself, as if attached to solid surfaces. When they meet a material object—a wall, or a house—they cross it by molding themselves to its surface, always without any significant change in their outlines. But when the obstacle is of living or once-living matter, they pass directly through it; thus I have seen them appear thousands of times out of trees and beneath the feet of animals and men. They can pass through water also, but prefer to remain on the surface.

These land *Moedigen* are not the only intangible creatures. There is an aerial population of a marvelous splendor, of an incomparable subtlety, variety and brilliance, beside which the most beautiful birds are dull, slow and heavy. Here again there are internal lines and an outline. But the background is not grayish, it is strangely luminous; it sparkles like sunlight, and the lines stand out from it in trembling veins; the centers palpitate violently. The *Vuren*, as I call them, are of a more irregular form than the land *Moedigen* and commonly propel themselves by means of rhythmic dispositions, intertwinings and untwinings which, in my ignorance, I cannot make out and which baffle my imagination.

Meanwhile I am making my way across a recently mowed meadow; the battle of a *Moedig* with another one has drawn my attention. These battles are frequent, and they excite me tremendously. Sometimes the battles are equal; more often an attack is made by the stronger upon the weaker. (The weaker is not necessarily the smaller.) In the present case, the weaker one, after a short defense, takes to flight, hotly pursued by the aggressor. Despite the swiftness of their motions, I follow them and succeed in keeping them in view until the struggle begins again. They fling themselves on each other—firmly, even rigidly, solid to each other. At the shock, their lines phosphoresce, moving toward the point of contact; their centers grow smaller and paler.

At first the struggle remains more or less equal; the weaker puts forth a more intense energy and even succeeds in gaining a truce from its adversary. It profits by this to flee once more, but is rapidly overtaken, strongly attacked and at last seized—that is to say, held fast in a hollow in the outline of the other. This is exactly what it has been trying to avoid, as it counters the stronger one's buffets with blows that are weaker but swifter. Now I see all its lines shudder, its centers throb desperately; and the lines gradually thin out, grow pale; the centers blur. After a few minutes, it is set free: it withdraws slowly, dull, debilitated. Its antagonist, on the contrary, glows more brightly; its lines are more vivid, its centers clearer and livelier.

This fight has moved me profoundly. I think about it and compare it with the fights I sometimes see between *our* animals. I realize confusedly that the *Moedigen,* as a group, do not kill, or rarely kill, that the victor contents itself with *increasing its strength* at the expense of the vanquished.

The morning wears on; it is nearly eight o'clock; the Zwartendam school is about to open. I gain the house in one leap, seize my books, and here I am among my fellows, where no one guesses what profound mysteries palpitate around him, where no one has the least idea of the living things through which all humanity passes and which pass through humanity, leaving no mark of that mutual penetration.

I am a very poor scholar. My writing is nothing but a hasty scrawl, unformed, illegible; my speech remains uncomprehended; my absence of mind is manifest. The master calls out continually, "Karel Ondereet, have you done with watching the flies?"

Alas, my dear master! It is true that I watch the flies in the air, but how much more does my mind accompany the mysterious *Vuren* that pass through the room! And what strange feelings obsess my childish mind, to note everyone's blindness and above all your own, grave shepherd of intellects!

5.

The most painful period of my life was that which ran from my twelfth to my eighteenth year.

To begin with, my parents tried to send me to the academy. I knew nothing there but misery and frustration. At the price of exhausting struggles, I succeeded in expressing the most ordinary things in a partially comprehensible manner: slowing my syllables with great effort, I uttered them awkwardly and with the intonations of the deaf. But as soon as I had to do with anything complicated, my speech regained its fatal swiftness; no one could follow me any longer. Therefore I could not register my progress orally. Moreover, my writing was atrocious, my letters piled up one on the other, and in my impatience I forgot whole syllables and words; it was a monstrous hodgepodge. Besides, writing was a torment to me, perhaps even more intolerable than speech—of an asphyxiating slowness, heaviness! If occasionally, by taking much pain and sweating great drops, I succeeded in beginning an exercise, at once I was at the end of my energy and patience; I felt about to faint. Accordingly I preferred the masters' remonstrances, the anger of my father, punishments, privations, scorn, to this horrible labor.

Thus I was almost totally deprived of the means of expression. Already an object of ridicule for my thinness and my strange color, my odd eyes, once more I passed for a kind of idiot. It was necessary for my parents to withdraw me from school and resign themselves to making a peasant of me.

The day my father decided to give up all hope, he said to me with unaccustomed gentleness, "My poor boy, you see I have done my duty—my whole duty. Never reproach me for your fate."

I was strongly moved. I shed warm tears; never had I felt more bitterly my isolation in the midst of men. I dared to embrace my father tenderly; I muttered, "Just the same, it's not true that I'm a halfwit!" And, in fact, I felt myself superior to those who had been my fellow pupils. Some time ago my intelligence had undergone a remarkable development. I read, I understood, I divined; and I had enormous matter for reflection, beyond that of other men, in that universe visible to me alone.

My father could not make out my words, but he softened to my embrace. "Poor boy!" he said.

I looked at him; I was in terrible distress, knowing too well that the gap between us would never be bridged. My mother, through love's intuition, saw in that moment that I was not inferior to the other boys of my age. She gazed at me tenderly, she spoke artless love words that came from the depths of her being. Nonetheless, I was condemned to give up my studies.

Because of my lack of muscular strength, I was given the care of the horses and the cattle. In this I acquitted myself admirably; I needed no dog to guard the herds, in which no colt or stallion was as agile as I.

Thus, from my fourteenth to my seventeenth year I lived the solitary life of the herdsman. It suited me better than any other. Given over to observation and contemplation, together with some reading, my mind never stopped growing. Incessantly I compared the two orders of creation which lay before my eyes; I drew from them ideas about the constitution of the universe; vaguely I sketched out hypotheses and systems. If it be true that in that period my thoughts were not perfectly ordered, did not make a lucid synthesis—for they were adolescent thoughts, uncoordinated, impatient, enthusiastic—nevertheless they were original, and fruitful. That their value may have depended above all upon my unique constitution, I would be the last to deny. But they did not draw all their strength from that source. I think I may say without pride that in subtlety as in logic they notably surpassed those of ordinary young men.

They alone brought consolation to my melancholy half-pariah's life, without companions, without any real communication with the rest of my household, even my adorable mother.

At the age of seventeen, life became definitely unsupportable to me. I was weary of dreaming, weary of vegetating on a desert island of thought. I fell into languor and boredom. I rested immobile for long hours, indifferent to the whole world, inattentive to anything that happened in my family. What mattered it that I knew of more marvelous things than other men, since in any case this knowledge must die with me? What was the mystery of living things to me, or even the duality of the two living systems crossing through each other without awareness of each other? These things might have intoxicated me, filled me with enthusiasm and ardor, if I could have taught them or shared them in any way. But what would you! Vain and sterile, absurd and miserable, they contributed rather to my perpetual psychic quarantine.

Many times I dreamed of setting down, recording, in spite of everything, by dint of continuous effort, some of my observations. But since leaving school I had completely abandoned the pen, and, already so wretched a scribbler, it was all I could do, with the utmost application, to trace the twenty-six letters of the alphabet. If I had still entertained any hope, perhaps I should have persisted. But who would have taken my miserable lucubrations seriously? Where was the reader who would not think me mad? Where the sage who would not show me the door with irony or disdain?

To what end, therefore, should I consecrate myself to that vain task, that exasperating torment, almost comparable to the requirement, for an ordinary man, to grave his thoughts upon tablets of marble with a huge chisel and a Cyclopean hammer? My penmanship would have had to be steno-graphic—and yet more: of a superswift stenography! Thus I had no courage at all to write, and at the same time I fervently hoped for I know not what unforeseen event, what happy and singular destiny. It seemed to me that there must exist, in some corner of the earth, impartial minds, lucid, searching, qualified to study me, to understand me, to extract my great secret from me and communicate it to others. But where were these men? What hope had I of ever meeting them?

And I fell once more into a vast melancholy, into the desire for immobility and extinction. During one whole autumn, I despaired of the universe. I languished in a vegetative state, from which I emerged only to give way to long groans, followed by painful rebellions of conscience.

I grew thinner still, thin to a fantastic degree. The villagers called me, ironically, *"den Heyligen Gheest,"* the Holy Ghost. My silhouette was tremulous as that of the young poplars, faint as a shadow; and with all this, I grew to a giant's stature.

Slowly, a project was born. Since my life had been thrown into the discard, since my days were without joy and all was darkness and bitterness to me, why wallow in sloth? Supposing that no mind existed which could respond to my own —at least it would be worth the effort to convince myself of that fact. At least it would be worth while to leave this gloomy countryside, to go and search for scientists and philosophers in the great cities. Was I not in myself an object of curiosity? Before calling attention to my extrahuman knowledge, could I not arouse a desire to study my person? Were not the mere physical aspects of my being worthy of analysis —and my sight, and the extreme swiftness of my movements, and the peculiarity of my diet?

The more I thought of it, the more it seemed reasonable to me to hope, and the more my resolution hardened. The day came when it was unshakable, when I confided it to my parents. Neither one nor the other understood much of it, but in the end both gave in to repeated entreaties: I obtained permission to go to Amsterdam, free to return if fortune should not favor me.

One morning, I left.

6.

From Zwartendam to Amsterdam is a matter of a hundred kilometers or thereabouts. I covered that distance easily in two hours, without any other adventure than the extreme surprise of those going and coming to see me run so swiftly, and a few crowds at the edges of the villages and towns I skirted. To make sure of my direction, I spoke two or three times to solitary old people. My sense of orientation, which is excellent, did the rest.

It was about nine o'clock when I reached Amsterdam. I entered the great city resolutely and walked along its beautiful, dreaming canals, where quiet merchant fleets dwell. I did not attract as much attention as I had feared. I walked quickly, among busy people, enduring here and there the gibes of some young street Arabs. Nevertheless, I did not decide to stop. I wandered here and there through the city, until at last I resolved to enter a tavern on one of the quays of the Heerengracht. It was a peaceful spot; the magnificent canal stretched, full of life, between cool rows of trees; and among the *Moedigen* which I saw moving about on its banks it seemed to me that I perceived a new species. After some hesitation, I crossed the sill of the tavern, and addressing myself to the publican as slowly as I could, I begged him to be kind enough to direct me to a hospital.

The landlord looked at me with amazement, suspicion and curiosity; took his huge pipe out of his mouth, put it back in after several attempts, and at last said, "You're from the colonies, I suppose?"

Since it was perfectly useless to contradict him, I answered, "Just so!"

He seemed delighted at his own shrewdness. He asked me another question: "Maybe you come from that part of Borneo where no one has ever been?"

"Exactly right!"

I had spoken too swiftly: his eyes grew round.

"Exactly right," I repeated more slowly.

The landlord smiled with satisfaction. "You can hardly speak Dutch, can you? So, it's a hospital you want. No doubt you're sick?"

"Yes."

Patrons were gathering around. It was whispered already that I was an anthropophagus from Borneo; nevertheless, they looked at me with much more curiosity than aversion. People were running in from the street. I became nervous and uneasy. I kept my composure nonetheless and said, coughing, "I am very sick!"

"Just like the monkeys from that country," said a very fat man benevolently. "The Netherlands kills them!"

"What a funny skin!" added another.

"And how does he see?" asked a third, pointing to my eyes.

The ring moved closer, encircling me with a hundred curious stares, and still newcomers were crowding into the room.

"How tall he is!"

In truth, I was a full head taller than the biggest of them.

"And thin!"

"This anthropophagy doesn't seem to nourish them very well!"

Not all the voices were spiteful. A few sympathetic persons protected me:

"Don't crowd so—he's sick!"

"Come, friend, courage!" said the fat man, remarking my nervousness. "I'll lead you to a hospital myself."

He took me by the arm and set about elbowing the crowd aside, calling, "Way for an invalid!"

Dutch crowds are not very fierce. They let us pass, but they went with us. We walked along the canal, followed by a compact multitude, and people cried out, "It's a cannibal from Borneo!"

At length we reached a hospital. It was the visiting hour. I was taken to an intern, a young man with blue spectacles, who greeted me peevishly. My companion said to him, "He's a savage from the colonies."

"What, a savage!" cried the other.

He took off his spectacles to look at me. Surprise held him motionless for a moment. He asked me brusquely, "Can you see?"

"I see very well."

I had spoken too swiftly.

"It's his accent," said the fat man proudly. "Once more, friend."

I repeated it and made myself understood.

"Those aren't human eyes," murmured the student. "And the color! Is that the color of your race?"

Then I said, with a terrible effort to slow myself down, "I have come to show myself to a scientist."

"Then you're not ill?"

"No."

"And you come from Borneo?"

"No."

"Where are you from, then?"

"From Zwartendam, near Duisburg."

"Why, then, does this man claim you're from Borneo?"

"I didn't want to contradict him."

"And you wish to see a scientist?"

"Yes."

"Why?"

"To be studied."

"So as to earn money?"

"No, for nothing."

"You're not a pauper? A beggar?"

"No!"

"What makes you want to be studied?"

"My constitution—"

But again, in spite of my efforts, I had spoken too swiftly. I had to repeat myself.

"Are you sure you can see me?" he asked, staring at me. "Your eyes are like horn."

"I see very well."

And, moving to left and right, I snatched things up, put them down, threw them in the air and caught them again.

"Extraordinary!" said the young man.

His softened voice, almost friendly, filled me with hope. "See here," he said at last, "I really think Dr. van den Heuvel might be interested in your case. I'll go and inform him. Wait in the next room. And, by the way—I forgot—you're not ill, after all?"

"Not in the least."

"Good. Wait—go in there. The doctor won't be long."

I found myself seated among monsters preserved in alcohol: fetuses, infants with bestial shapes, colossal batrachians, vaguely anthropomorphic saurians.

This is well chosen for my waiting room, I thought. Am I not a candidate for one of these brandy-filled sepulchers?

7.

When Dr. van den Heuvel appeared, emotion overcame me. I had the thrill of the Promised Land—the joy of reaching it, the dread of being banished. The doctor, with his great bald forehead, the analyst's penetrating look, the mouth soft and yet stubborn, examined me in silence. As always, my excessive thinness, my great stature, my horny eyes, my violet color, caused him astonishment.

"You say you wish to be studied?" he asked at length.

I answered forcefully, almost violently, "Yes!"

He smiled with an approving air and asked me the usual question: "Do you see all right, with those eyes?"

"Very well. I can even see through wood, clouds—"

But I had spoken too fast. He glanced at me uneasily. I began again, sweating great drops: "I can even see through wood, clouds—"

"Really! That would be extraordinary. Well, then! What do you see through the door there?" He pointed to a closed door.

"A big library with windows . . . a carved table . . ."

"Really!" he repeated, stunned.

My breast swelled; a deep stillness entered my soul.

The scientist remained silent for a few seconds. Then: "You speak with some difficulty."

"Otherwise I should speak too rapidly! I cannot speak slowly."

"Well, then, speak a little as you do naturally."

Accordingly I told him the story of my entry into Amsterdam. He listened to me with an extreme attention, an air of intelligent observation, which I had never before encountered among my fellows. He understood nothing of what I said, but he showed the keenness of his intellect.

"If I am not mistaken, you speak fifteen to twenty syllables a second, that is to say three or four times more than the human ear can distinguish. Your voice, in addition, is much higher than anything I have ever heard in the way of human voices. Your excessively rapid gestures are well suited to your speech. Your whole constitution is probably more rapid than ours."

"I run," I said, "faster than a greyhound. I write—"

"Ah!" he interrupted. "Let us see your writing."

I scrawled some words on a tablet which he offered me, the first few fairly legible, the rest more and more scrambled, abbreviated.

"Perfect!" he said, and a certain pleasure was mingled with his surprise. "I really think I must congratulate myself on this meeting. Certainly it should be very interesting to study you."

"It is my dearest, my only, desire!"

"And mine, naturally. Science . . ."

He seemed preoccupied, musing. He finished by saying, "If only we could find an easy way of communication."

He walked back and forth, his brows knotted. Suddenly: "What a dolt I am! You must learn shorthand, of course! Hm! . . . Hm!" A cheerful expression spread over his face. "And I've forgotten the phonograph—the perfect confidant! All that's needed is to revolve it more slowly in the reproduction than in the recording. It's agreed: you shall stay with me while you are in Amsterdam!"

The joy of a fulfilled vocation, the delight of ceasing to spend vain and sterile days! Aware of the intelligent personality of the doctor, against this scientific background, I felt a delicious well-being; the melancholy of my spiritual solitude, the sorrow for my lost talents, the pariah's long misery that had weighed me down for so many years, all vanished, evaporated in the sensation of a new life, a real life, a saved destiny!

8.

Beginning the following day, the doctor made all the necessary arrangements. He wrote to my parents; he sent me to a professor of stenography and obtained some phonographs. As he was quite rich and entirely devoted to science, there was no experiment which he could not undertake, and my vision, my hearing, my musculature, the color of my skin, were submitted to scrupulous investigations, from which he drew more and more enthusiasm, crying, "This verges on the miraculous!"

I very well understood, after the first few days, how important it was to go about things methodically—from the simple to the complex, from the slightly abnormal to the wonderfully abnormal. Thus I had recourse to a little legerdemain, of which I made no secret to the doctor: that is, I revealed my abilities to him only one at a time.

The quickness of my perceptions and movements drew his attention first. He was able to convince himself that the subtlety of my hearing was in proportion to the swiftness of my speech. Graduated trials of the most fugitive sounds, which I imitated with ease, and the words of ten or fifteen persons all talking at once, which I distinguished perfectly, demonstrated this point beyond question. My vision proved no less swift; comparative tests between my ability to resolve the movement of a galloping horse, or an insect in flight, and the same ability of an apparatus for taking instantaneous photographs, proved all in favor of my eye.

As for perceptions of ordinary things, simultaneous movements of a group of people, of children playing, the motion of machines, bits of rubble thrown in the air or little balls tossed into an alley, to be counted in flight—they amazed the doctor's family and friends.

My running in the big garden, my twenty-meter jumps, my instantaneous swiftness to pick up objects or put them back, were admired still more, not by the doctor, but by those around him. And it was an ever renewed pleasure for the wife and children of my host, while walking in the fields, to see me outstrip a horseman at full gallop or follow the flight of any swallow; in truth, there was no thoroughbred but I could give it a start of two-thirds the distance, whatever it might be, nor any bird I could not easily overtake.

As for the doctor, more and more satisfied with the results of his experiments, he described me thus: "A human being, endowed in all his movements with a swiftness incomparably superior, not merely to that of other humans, but also to that of all known animals. This swiftness, found in the most minute constituents of his body as well as in the whole organism, makes him an entity so distinct from the remainder of creation that he merits a special place in the animal kingdom for himself alone. As for the curious structure of his eyes, as well as the skin's violet color, these must be considered simply the earmarks of this special condition."

Tests being made of my muscular system, it proved in no

way remarkable, unless for its excessive leanness. Neither did my ears yield any particular information; nor, for that matter, did my skin—except, of course, for its pigmentation. As for my dark hair, a purplish black in color, it was fine as spiderweb, and the doctor made a minute examination of it.

"One would need to dissect you!" he often told me, laughing.

Thus time passed easily. I had quickly learned to write in shorthand, thanks to my intense desire and to the natural aptitude I showed for this method of rapid transcription, into which, by the way, I introduced several new abbreviations. I began to make notes, which my stenographer transcribed; for the rest, we had phonographs built, according to the doctor's special design, which proved perfectly suited to reproduce my voice at a lower speed.

At length my host's confidence in me became complete. During the first few weeks he had not been able to avoid the suspicion—a very natural one—that my peculiar abilities might be accompanied by some mental abnormality, some cerebral derangement. This anxiety once put aside, our relations became perfectly cordial, and I think, as fascinating for one as for the other.

We made analytic tests of my ability to see through a great number of "opaque" substances; and of the dark coloration which water, glass or quartz takes on for me at certain thicknesses. It will be recalled that I can see clearly through wood, leaves, clouds and many other substances; that I can barely make out the bottom of a pool of water half a meter deep; and that a window, though transparent, is less so to me than to the average person and has a rather dark color. A thick piece of glass appears blackish to me. The doctor convinced himself at leisure of all these singularities—astonished above all to see me make out the stars on cloudy nights.

Only then did I begin to tell him that colors too present themselves differently to me. Experience established beyond doubt that red, orange, yellow, green, blue and indigo are perfectly invisible to me, like infrared or ultraviolet to a normal eye. On the other hand, I was able to show that I perceive violet, and beyond violet a range of colors—a spectrum at least double that which extends from the red to the violet.*

* Quartz gives me a spectrum of about eight colors: the longest violet and the seven succeeding colors in the ultraviolet. But there remain about eight more colors which are not refracted by quartz, and which are refracted more or less by other substances.

This amazed the doctor more than all the rest. His study of it was long and painstaking; it was conducted, besides, with enormous cunning. In this accomplished experimenter's hands, it became the source of subtle discoveries in the order of sciences as they are ranked by humanity; it gave him the key to far-ranging phenomena of magnetism, of chemical affinities, of induction; it guided him toward new conceptions of physiology. To know that a given metal shows a series of unknown tints, variable according to the pressure, the temperature, the electric charge, that the most rarefied gases have distinct colors, even at small depths; to learn of the infinite tonal richness of objects which appear more or less black, whereas they present a more magnificent spectrum in the ultraviolet than that of all known colors; to know, finally, the possible variations in unknown hues of an electric circuit, the bark of a tree, the skin of a man, in a day, an hour, a minute—the use that an ingenious scientist might make of such ideas can readily be imagined.

We worked patiently for a whole year without my mentioning the *Moedigen*. I wished to convince my host absolutely, give him countless proofs of my visual faculties, before daring the supreme confidence. At length, the time came when I felt I could reveal everything.

9.

It happened in a mild autumn full of clouds, which rolled across the vault of the sky for a week without shedding a drop of rain. One morning van den Heuvel and I were walking in the garden. The doctor was silent, completely absorbed in his speculations, of which I was the principal subject. At the far end, he began to speak:

"It's a nice thing to dream about, anyhow: to see through clouds, pierce through to the ether, whereas we, blind as we are . . ."

"If the sky were all I saw!" I answered.

"Oh, yes—the whole world, so different . . ."

"Much more different even than I've told you!"

"How's that?" he cried with an avid curiosity. "Have you been hiding something from me?"

"The most important thing!"

He stood facing me, staring at me fixedly, in real distress, in which some element of the mystical seemed to be blended.

"Yes, the most important thing!"

We had come near the house, and I dashed in to ask for a phonograph. The instrument that was brought to me was an advanced model, highly perfected by my friend, and could record a long speech; the servant put it down on the stone table where the doctor and his family took coffee on mild summer evenings. A miracle of exact, fine construction, the device lent itself admirably to recording casual talks. Our dialogue went on, therefore, almost like an ordinary conversation.

"Yes, I've hidden the main thing from you, because I wanted your complete confidence first—and even now, after all the discoveries you've made about my organism, I am afraid you won't find it easy to believe me, at least to begin with."

I stopped to let the machine repeat this sentence. I saw the doctor grow pale, with the pallor of a great scientist in the presence of a new aspect of matter. His hands were trembling.

"I shall believe you!" he said, with a certain solemnity.

"Even if I try to tell you that our order of creation—I mean our animal and vegetable world—isn't the only life on earth, that there is another, as vast, as numerous, as varied, invisible to your eyes?"

He scented occultism and could not refrain from saying, "The world of the fourth state of matter—departed souls, the phantoms of the spiritualists."

"No, no, nothing like that. A world of living creatures, doomed like us to a short life, to organic needs—birth, growth, struggle. A world as weak and ephemeral as ours, a world governed by laws equally rigid, if not identical, a world equally imprisoned by the earth, equally vulnerable to accident, but otherwise completely different from ours, without any influence on ours, as we have no influence on it—except through the changes it makes in our common ground, the earth, or through the parallel changes that we create in the same ground."

I do not know if van den Heuvel believed me, but certainly he was in the grip of strong emotion. "They are fluid, in short?" he asked.

"That's what I don't know how to answer, for their properties are too contradictory to fit into our ideas of matter. The earth is as resistant to them as to us, and the same with most minerals, although they can penetrate a little way into a humus. Also, they are totally impermeable and solid with respect to each other. But they can pass through plants, animals, organic tissues, although sometimes with a certain difficulty; and we ourselves pass through them the same way. If one of them could be aware of us, we should perhaps seem fluid with respect to them, as they seem fluid with respect to us; but probably he could no more *decide* about it than I can—he would be struck by similar contradictions. There is one peculiarity about their shape: they have hardly any thickness. They are of all sizes. I've known some to reach a hundred meters in length, and others are as tiny as our smallest insects. Some of them feed on earth and air, others on air and on their own kind—without killing as we do, however, because it's enough for the stronger to draw strength from the weaker, and because this strength can be extracted without draining the springs of life."

The doctor said brusquely, "Have you seen them ever since childhood?"

I guessed that he was imagining some more or less recent disorder in my body. "Since childhood," I answered vigorously. "I'll give you all the proofs you like."

"Do you see them now?"

"I see them. There are a great many in the garden."

"Where?"

"On the path, the lawns, on the walls, in the air. For there are terrestrial and aerial ones—and aquatic ones too, but those hardly ever leave the surface of the water."

"Are they numerous everywhere?"

"Yes, and hardly less so in town than in the country, in houses than in the street. Those that like the indoors are smaller, though, no doubt because of the difficulty of getting in and out, even though they find a wooden door no obstacle."

"And iron . . . glass . . . brick?"

"All impermeable to them."

"Will you describe one of them, a fairly large one?"

"I see one near that tree. Its shape is extremely elongated, and rather irregular. It is convex toward the right, concave toward the left, with swellings and hollows: it looks something like an enlarged photograph of a big, fat larva. But its structure is not typical of the Kingdom, because structure varies a great deal from one species (if I may use that word) to another. Its extreme thinness, on the other hand, is a common characteristic: it can hardly be more than a tenth of a millimeter in thickness, whereas it's one hundred and fifty centimeters long and forty centimeters across at its widest.

"What distinguishes this, and the whole Kingdom, above all are the lines that cross it in nearly every direction, ending in networks that fan out between two systems of lines. Each system has a center, a kind of spot that is slightly raised above the mass of the body, or occasionally hollowed out. These centers have no fixed form; sometimes they are almost circular or elliptical, sometimes twisted or helical, sometimes divided by many narrow throats. They are astonishingly mobile, and their size varies from hour to hour. Their borders palpitate strongly, in a sort of transverse undulation. In general, the lines that emerge from them are big, although there are also very fine ones; they diverge, and end in an infinity of delicate traceries which gradually fade away. However, certain lines, much paler than the others, are not produced by the centers; they stay isolated in the system and grow without changing their color. These lines have the faculty of moving within the body, and of varying their curves, while the centers and their connected lines remain stable.

"As for the colors of my *Moedig,* I must forego any attempt to describe them to you; none of them falls within the spectrum perceptible to your eye, and none has a name in your vocabulary. They are extremely brilliant in the networks, weaker in the centers, very much faded in the independent lines, which, however, have a very high brilliance— an ultraviolet metallic effect, so to speak. . . . I have some observations on the habits, the diet and the range of the *Moedigen,* but I don't wish to submit them to you just now."

I fell silent. The doctor listened twice to the words recorded by our faultless interpreter; then for a long time he was silent. Never had I seen him in such a state: his face was rigid, stony, his eyes glassy and cataleptic; a heavy film of sweat covered his temples and dampened his hair. He tried to speak and failed. Trembling, he walked all around the garden; and when he reappeared, his eyes and mouth expressed a violent passion, fervent, religious; he seemed more like the disciple of some new faith than like a peaceful investigator.

At last he muttered, "I'm overwhelmed! Everything you have just said seems terribly lucid—and have I the right to doubt, considering all the wonders you've already shown me?"

"Doubt!" I said warmly. "Doubt as hard as you can! Your experiments will be all the more fruitful for it."

"Ah," he said in a dreaming voice, "it's the pure stuff of wonder, and so magnificently superior to the pointless marvels of fairy tales! My poor human intelligence is so tiny before such knowledge! I feel an enormous enthusiasm. Yet something in me doubts . . ."

"Let's work to dispel your doubt—our efforts will pay for themselves ten times over!"

10.

We worked; and it took the doctor only a few weeks to clear up all his uncertainties. Several ingenious experiments, together with the undeniable consistency of all the statements I had made, and two or three lucky discoveries about the *Moedigen's* influence on atmospheric phenomena, left no question in his mind. When we were joined by the doctor's elder son, a young man of great scientific aptitude, the fruitfulness of our work and the conclusiveness of our findings were again increased.

Thanks to my companions' methodical habits of mind, and their experience in study and classification—qualities which I was absorbing little by little—whatever was uncoordinated or confused in my knowledge of the *Moedigen* rapidly became transformed. Our discoveries multiplied; rigorous experiments gave firm results, in circumstances which in ancient times and even up to the last century would have suggested at most a few trifling diversions.

It is now five years since we began our researches. They are far, very far from completion. Even a preliminary report of our work can hardly appear in the near future. In any case, we have made it a rule to do nothing in haste; our discoveries are of too immanent a kind not to be set forth in the most minute detail, with the most sovereign patience and the finest precision. We have no other investigator to forestall, no patent to take out or ambition to satisfy. We stand at a height where vanity and pride fade away. How can there be any comparison between the joys of our work and the wretched lure of human fame? Besides, do not all these things flow from the single accident of my physical organization? What a petty thing it would be, then, for us to boast about them!

No; we live excitedly, always on the verge of wonders, and yet we live in immutable serenity.

I have had an adventure which adds to the interest of my life, and which fills me with infinite joy during my leisure hours. You know how ugly I am; my bizarre appearance is fit only to horrify young women. All the same, I have found a companion who not only can put up with my show of affection, but even takes pleasure in it.

She is a poor girl, hysterical and nervous, whom we met one day in a hospital in Amsterdam. Others find her wretched-looking, plaster-white, hollow-cheeked, with wild eyes. But to me her appearance is pleasant, her company charming. From the very beginning my presence, far from alarming her like all the rest, seemed to please and comfort her. I was touched; I wanted to see her again.

It was quickly discovered that I had a beneficial influence on her health and well-being. On examination, it appeared that I influenced her by animal magnetism: my nearness, and above all the touch of my hands, gave her a really curative gaiety, serenity, and calmness of spirit. In turn, I took pleasure in being near her. Her face seemed lovely to me; her pallor and slenderness were no more than signs of delicacy; for me her eyes, able to perceive the glow of magnets, like those of many hyperesthesiacs, had none at all of the distracted quality that others criticized.

In short, I felt an attraction for her, and she returned it with passion. From that time, I resolved to marry her. I gained my end readily, thanks to the good will of my friends.

This union has been a happy one. My wife's health was re-established, although she remained extremely sensitive and frail. I tasted the joy of being like other men in the essential part of life. But my happiness was crowned six months ago: a child was born to us, and in this child are combined all the faculties of my constitution. Color, vision, hearing, extreme rapidity of movement, diet—he promises to be an exact copy of my physiology.

The doctor watches him grow with delight. A wonderful hope has come to us—that the study of the *Moedig* World, of the Kingdom parallel to our own, this study which demands so much time and patience, will not end when I cease to be. My son will pursue it, undoubtedly, in his turn. Why may he not find collaborators of genius, able to raise it to a new power? Why may he also not give life to seers of the invisible world?

As for myself, may I not look forward to other children, may I not hope that my dear wife may give birth to other sons of my flesh, like unto their father? As I think of it, my heart trembles, I am filled with an infinite beatitude; and I know myself blessed among men.

Olaf Stapledon, by his own account, "attempted several careers, in each case escaping before the otherwise inevitable disaster. First, as a schoolmaster, I swotted up Bible stories on the eve of the Scripture lesson. Then, in a Liverpool ship ping office, I spoiled bills of lading, and in Port Said I innocently let skippers have more coal than they needed. Next I determined to create an Educated Democracy. Workington miners, Barrow riveters, Crewe railwaymen gave me a better education than I could give them. Since then two experiences have dominated me: philosophy and the tragic disorder of our whole terrestrial hive."

Curiously, it was Rosny who wrote of superman as a bewildered misfit. Stapledon's Odd John is almost implausibly aggressive and successful from childhood on—glib speaker, money-making inventor and stock-market operator, organizer, spiritual leader; almost anything you want to name, John can do. But here, in a brief episode from Odd John, *is a less confident view of the fate of* Homo superior *in a world of* Homo sapiens.

a selection from

ODD JOHN

BY OLAF STAPLEDON

"Well," he said, "I had better begin at the beginning. I told you before that when I was in Scotland I used to find myself in telepathic touch with people, and that some of the people seemed queer people, or people in a significant way more like me than you. Since I came home I've been working up the technique for tuning in to the people I want. Unfortunately it's much easier to pick up the thoughts of folk one knows well than of strangers. So much depends on the general form of the mind, the matrix in which the thoughts occur, so to speak. To get you or Pax I have only to think of you. I can get your actual consciousness, and if I want to I can get a good bit of the deeper layers of you, too."

I was seized with horror, but I comforted myself with incredulity.

"Oh, yes, I can," said John. "While I've been talking, half your mind was listening and the other half was thinking about a quarrel you had last night with—"

I cut him short with an expostulation.

"Righto—don't get excited," said John. "*You* haven't much to be ashamed of. And anyhow I don't want to pry. But just now—well, you kept fairly shouting the stuff at me, because while you were attending to me you were thinking about it. You'll probably soon learn how to shut me out at will."

I grunted, and John continued: "As I was saying, it's much harder to get in touch with people one doesn't know, and at first I didn't know any of the people I was looking for. On the other hand, I found that the people of my sort make, so to speak, a much bigger 'noise' telepathically than the rest. At least they do when they want to, or when they don't care. But when they want *not* to, they can shut themselves off completely. Well, at last I managed to single out from the general buzz of telepathic 'noise,' made by the normal species, a few outstanding streaks or themes that seemed to have about them something or other of the special quality that I was looking for."

John paused, and I interjected, "What sort of quality?"

He looked at me for some seconds in silence. Believe it or not, but that prolonged gaze had a really terrifying effect on me. . . .

There was a long silence, then he continued his report. "The first trace of a mentality like my own gave me a lot of trouble. I could only catch occasional glimpses of this fellow, and I couldn't make him take any notice of me. And the stuff that did come through to me was terribly incoherent and bewildering. I wondered whether this was the fault of my technique or whether his was a mind too highly developed for me to understand. I tried to find out where he was, so that I could go and see him. He was evidently living in a large building with lots of rooms and many other people. But he had very little to do with the others. Looking out of his window, he saw trees and houses and a long grassy hill. He heard an almost continuous noise of trains and motor traffic. At least, *I* recognized it as that, but it didn't seem to mean much to him. Clearly, I thought, there's a main line and a main road quite close to where he lives. Somehow I must find that place. So I bought the motor bike.

"Meanwhile I kept on studying him. I couldn't catch any of his thoughts, but only his perceptions, and the way he felt about them. One striking thing was his music. Sometimes when I found him he was outside the house in a sloping field with trees between it and the main road; and he would be playing a pipe, a sort of recorder, but with the octave very oddly divided. I discovered that each of his hands had *five* fingers and a thumb. Even so, I couldn't make out how he managed all the extra notes. The kind of music he played was extraordinarily fascinating to me. Something about it, the mental pose of it, made me quite sure the man was really my sort. I discovered, by the way, that he had the not very helpful name of James Jones.

"Once when I got him he was out in the grounds and near a gap in the trees, so that he could see the road. Presently a bus flashed past. It was a Green Line bus, and it was labelled 'Brighton.' I noticed with surprise that these words apparently meant nothing to James Jones. But they meant a lot to me. I went off on the bike to search the Green Line routes out of Brighton. It took me a couple of days to find the right spot—the big building, the grassy hill, and so on. I stopped and asked someone what the building was. It was a lunatic asylum."

John's narrative was interrupted by my guffaw of relief.

"Funny," he said, "but not quite unexpected. After pulling lots of wires I got permission to see James Jones, who was a relative of mine, I said. They told me at the asylum that there was a family likeness, and when I saw James Jones I knew what they meant. He's a little old man with a big head and huge eyes, like mine. He's quite bald, except for a few crisp white curls above the ears. His mouth was smaller than mine (for the size of him) and it had a sort of suffering sweetness about it, especially when he let it do a peculiar compressed pout, which was a characteristic mannerism of his. Before I saw him they had told me a bit about him. He gave no trouble, they said, except that his health was very bad and they had to nurse him a lot. He hardly ever spoke, and then only in monosyllables. He could understand simple remarks about matters within his ken, but it was often impossible to get him to attend to what was said to him. Yet, oddly enough, he seemed to have a lively interest in everything happening around him. Sometimes he would listen intently to people's voices, but not, apparently, for their significance, simply for their musical quality. He seemed to have an absorbing interest in perceived rhythms of all sorts. He would study the grain of a piece of wood, poring over it by the hour; or the ripples on a duck pond. Most music, ordinary music invented by *Homo sapiens,* seemed at once to interest and outrage him, though when one of the doctors played a certain bit of Bach he was gravely attentive and afterward went off to play oddly twisted variants of it on his queer pipe. Certain jazz tunes had such a violent effect on him that after hearing one record he would sometimes be prostrate for days. They seemed to tear him with some kind of conflict of delight and disgust. Of course the authorities regarded his own pipe playing as the caterwauling of a lunatic.

"Well, when we were brought face to face, we just stood and looked at one another for so long that the attendant found it uncomfortable. Presently James Jones, keeping his eyes on mine, said one word, with quiet emphasis and some surprise, 'Friend!' I smiled and nodded. Then I felt him catch a glimpse of my mind, and his face suddenly lit up with intense delight and surprise. Very slowly, as if painfully searching for each word, he said, 'You—are—not—mad, *not mad!* We two, *not mad!* But these—' slowly pointing at the attendant and smiling—'all mad, quite, quite mad. But kind and clever. He cares for me. I cannot care for self. Too busy with—with . . .' The sentence trailed into silence. Smiling seraphically, he nodded slowly again and again. Then he came forward and laid a hand for an instant on my head. That was the end. When I said yes, we were friends and he and I saw things the same way, he nodded again; but when he tried to speak, an expression of almost comic perplexity came over his face. Looking into his mind, I saw that it was already a welter of confusion. He perceived, but he could not find any mundane significance in what he perceived. He saw the two human beings that confronted him, but he no longer connected my visible appearance with human personality, with the mind that he was still striving to communicate with. He didn't even see us as physical objects at all, but just as color and shape, without any meaning.

"I asked him to play to me. He could not understand. The attendant put the pipe into his hand, closing the fingers over it. He looked blankly at it. Then with a sudden smile of enlightenment he put it to his ear, like a child listening to a shell. The attendant took it again and played a few notes on it, but in vain. Then I took it and played a little air that I had heard him play before I found him. His attention was held. Perplexity cleared from his face. To our surprise he spoke, slowly but without difficulty. 'Yes, John Wainwright,' he said, 'you heard *me* play that the other day. I knew some *person* was listening. Give me my pipe.'

"He took it, seated himself on the edge of the table, and played, with his eyes fixed on mine."

John startled me with one sharp gasp of laughter. "God! it was music," he said. "If you could have heard it! I mean if you could have *really* heard it, and not merely as a cow might! It was lucid. It straightened out the tangles of my mind. It showed me just precisely the true, appropriate attitude of the adult human spirit to its world. Well, he played on, and I went on listening, hanging on to every note, to remember it. Then the attendant interrupted. He said this sort of noise always upset the other patients. It wasn't as if it was real *music*, but such crazy stuff. That was why J. J. was really only allowed to play out of doors.

"The music stopped with a squawk. J. J. looked with a kindly but tortured smile at the attendant. Then he slid back into insanity. So complete was his disintegration that he actually tried to eat the mouthpiece."

Remembering Isaac Asimov's remark about building a mechanical mind that is better than a man (see page 44), you will not be surprised to find that our next superman is not exactly human. Superman, after all, need not be made in our image or even be born on our planet. Nor, in fact, need he be confined to one body.

Poul Anderson, a shy, studious man who at thirty-six still looks like an undergraduate, began writing science fiction at the University of Minnesota, where he took a degree in physics. One of the most prolific and versatile s.f. writers, he is the author of two hundred stories and twenty novels. In 1956, when he was guest of honor at the annual World Science Fiction Convention in Detroit, the program included a panel of magazine editors, each of whom announced what he was going to publish in his next issue. Every one of them sooner or later got around to saying, ". . . and a long novelette by Poul Anderson."

"Call Me Joe," first published in Astounding, *April 1957, is remarkable for the author's ingenious and legitimate use of ideas drawn from stories by other writers. (The background of this story derives from two totally different stories about Jupiter—"Bridge," by James Blish, which became part of that writer's "Okie" trilogy, and "Desertion," by Clifford Simak, which became part of his prize-winning novel* City.) *It is also noteworthy, as you are about to see, for the dedicated, almost finicking care of the technical detail work, contrasting with the raw power of the story itself.*

CALL ME JOE

BY POUL ANDERSON

The wind came whooping out of eastern darkness, driving a lash of ammonia dust before it. In minutes, Edward Anglesey was blinded.

He clawed all four feet into the broken shards which were soil, hunched down and groped for his little smelter. The wind was an idiot bassoon in his skull. Something whipped across his back, drawing blood, a tree yanked up by the roots and spat a hundred miles. Lightning cracked, immensely far overhead where clouds boiled with night.

As if to reply, thunder toned in the ice mountains and a red gout of flame jumped and a hillside came booming down, spilling itself across the valley. The earth shivered.

Sodium explosion, thought Anglesey in the drumbeat noise. The fire and the lightning gave him enough illumination to find his apparatus. He picked up tools in muscular hands, his tail gripped the trough, and he battered his way to the tunnel and thus to his dugout.

It had walls and roof of water, frozen by sun-remoteness and compressed by tons of atmosphere jammed onto every square inch. Ventilated by a tiny smoke hole, a lamp of tree oil burning in hydrogen made a dull light for the single room.

Anglesey sprawled his slate-blue form on the floor, panting. It was no use to swear at the storm. These ammonia gales often came at sunset, and there was nothing to do but wait them out. He was tired, anyway.

It would be morning in five hours or so. He had hoped to cast an axhead, his first, this evening, but maybe it was better to do the job by daylight.

He pulled a dekapod body off a shelf and ate the meat raw, pausing for long gulps of liquid methane from a jug. Things would improve once he had proper tools; so far, everything had been painfully grubbed and hacked to shape with teeth, claws, chance icicles, and what detestably weak and crumbling fragments remained of the spaceship. Give him a few years and he'd be living as a man should.

He sighed, stretched, and lay down to sleep.

Somewhat more than one hundred and twelve thousand miles away, Edward Anglesey took off his helmet.

He looked around, blinking. After the Jovian surface, it was always a little unreal to find himself here again, in the clean, quiet orderliness of the control room.

His muscles ached. They shouldn't. He had not really been fighting a gale of several hundred miles an hour, under three gravities and a temperature of 140 absolute. He had been here, in the almost non-existent pull of Jupiter V, breathing oxynitrogen. It was Joe who lived down there and filled his lungs with hydrogen and helium at a pressure which could still only be estimated, because it broke aneroids and deranged piezoelectrics.

Nevertheless, his body felt worn and beaten. Tension, no doubt—psychosomatics. After all, for a good many hours now he had, in a sense, been Joe, and Joe had been working hard.

With the helmet off, Anglesey held only a thread of identification. The esprojector was still tuned to Joe's brain but no longer focused on his own. Somewhere in the back of his mind, he knew an indescribable feeling of sleep. Now and then, vague forms or colors drifted in the soft black—dreams? Not impossible that Joe's brain should dream a little when Anglesey's mind wasn't using it.

A light flickered red on the esprojector panel, and a bell whined electronic fear. Anglesey cursed. Thin fingers over the controls of his chair, he slewed around and shot across to the bank of dials. Yes, there—K tube oscillating again! The circuit blew out. He wrenched the face plate off with one hand and fumbled in a drawer with the other.

Inside his mind, he could feel the contact with Joe fading. If he once lost it entirely, he wasn't sure he could regain it. And Joe was an investment of several million dollars and quite a few highly skilled man-years.

Anglesey pulled the offending K tube from its socket and threw it on the floor. Glass exploded. It eased his temper a bit, just enough so he could find a replacement, plug it in, switch on the current again. As the machine warmed up, once again simplifying, the Joeness in the back alleys of his brain strengthened.

Slowly, then, the man in the electric wheel chair rolled out of the room, into the hall. Let somebody else sweep up the broken tube. To hell with it. To hell with everybody.

Jan Cornelius had never been farther from Earth than some comfortable Lunar resort. He felt much put upon that the Psionics Corporation should tap him for a thirteen-month exile. The fact that he knew as much about esprojectors and their cranky innards as any other man alive was no excuse. Why send anyone at all? Who cared?

Obviously the Federation Science Authority did. It had seemingly given those bearded hermits a blank check on the taxpayer's account.

Thus did Cornelius grumble to himself, all the long hyperbolic path to Jupiter. Then the shifting accelerations of approach to its tiny inner satellite left him too wretched for further complaint. And when he finally, just prior to disembarkation, went up to the greenhouse for a look at Jupiter, he said not a word. Nobody does, the first time.

Arne Viken waited patiently while Cornelius stared. *It still gets me too,* he remembered. *By the throat. Sometimes I'm afraid to look.*

At length Cornelius turned around. He had a faintly

Jovian appearance himself, being a large man with an imposing girth. "I had no idea," he whispered. "I never thought . . . I had seen pictures, but . . ."

Viken nodded. "Sure, Dr. Cornelius. Pictures don't convey it."

Where they stood, they could see the dark broken rock of the satellite, jumbled for a short way beyond the landing slip and then chopped off sheer. This moon was scarcely even a platform, it seemed, and cold constellations went streaming past it, around it. Jupiter lay across a fifth of that sky, softly ambrous, banded with colors, spotted with the shadows of planet sized moons and with whirlwinds as broad as Earth. If there had been any gravity to speak of, Cornelius would have thought, instinctively, that the great planet was falling on him. As it was, he felt as if sucked upward, his hands were still sore where he had grabbed a rail to hold on.

"You live here . . . all alone . . . with this?" He spoke feebly.

"Oh, well, there are some fifty of us all told, pretty congenial," said Viken. "It's not so bad. You sign up for four-cycle hitches—four ship arrivals—and believe it or not, Dr. Cornelius, this is my third enlistment."

The newcomer forbore to inquire more deeply. There was something not quite understandable about the men on Jupiter V. They were mostly bearded, though otherwise careful to remain neat; their low-gravity movements were somehow dreamlike to watch; they hoarded their conversation, as if to stretch it through the year and a month between ships. Their monkish existence had changed them—or did they take what amounted to vows of poverty, chastity, and obedience because they had never felt quite at home on green Earth?

Thirteen months! Cornelius shuddered. It was going to be a long, cold wait, and the pay and bonuses accumulating for him were scant comfort now, four hundred and eighty million miles from the sun.

"Wonderful place to do research," continued Viken. "All the facilities, hand-picked colleagues, no distractions—and, of course . . . " He jerked his thumb at the planet and turned to leave.

Cornelius followed, wallowing awkwardly. "It is very interesting, no doubt," he puffed. "Fascinating. But really,

Dr. Viken, to drag me way out here and make me spend a year-plus waiting for the next ship—to do a job which may take me a few weeks . . ."

"Are you sure it's that simple?" asked Viken gently. His face swiveled around, and there was something in his eyes that silenced Cornelius. "After all my time here, I've yet to see any problem, however complicated, which when you looked at it the right way didn't become still more complicated."

They went through the ship's air lock and the tube joining it to the station entrance. Nearly everything was underground. Rooms, laboratories, even halls, had a degree of luxuriousness—why, there was a fireplace with a real fire in the common room! God alone knew what *that* cost! Thinking of the huge chill emptiness where the king planet laired, and of his own year's sentence, Cornelius decided that such luxuries were, in truth, biological necessities.

Viken showed him to a pleasantly furnished chamber which would be his own. "We'll fetch your luggage soon, and unload your psionic stuff. Right now, everybody's either talking to the ship's crew or reading his mail."

Cornelius nodded absently and sat down. The chair, like all low-gee furniture, was a mere spidery skeleton, but it held his bulk comfortably enough. He felt in his tunic, hoping to bribe the other man into keeping him company for a while. "Cigar? I brought some from Amsterdam."

"Thanks." Viken accepted with disappointing casualness, crossed long, thin legs and blew grayish clouds.

"Ah . . . are you in charge here?"

"Not exactly. No one is. We do have one administrator, the cook, to handle what little work of that type may come up. Don't forget, this is a research station, first, last, and always."

"What is your field, then?"

Viken frowned. "Don't question anyone else so bluntly, Dr. Cornelius," he warned. "They'd rather spin the gossip out as long as possible with each newcomer. It's a rare treat to have someone whose every last conceivable reaction hasn't been— No, no apologies to me. 'S all right. I'm a physicist, specializing in the solid state at ultrahigh pressures." He nodded at the wall. "Plenty of it to be observed—there!"

"I see." Cornelius smoked quietly for a while. Then: "I'm supposed to be the psionics expert, but, frankly, at present I've no idea why your machine should misbehave as reported."

"You mean those, uh, K tubes have a stable output on Earth?"

"And on Luna, Mars, Venus—everywhere, apparently, but here." Cornelius shrugged. "Of course, psibeams are always persnickety, and sometimes you get an unwanted feedback when— No. I'll get the facts before I theorize. Who are your psimen?"

"Just Anglesey, who's not a formally trained esman at all. But he took it up after he was crippled, and showed such a natural aptitude that he was shipped out here when he volunteered. It's so hard to get anyone for Jupiter V that we aren't fussy about degrees. At that, Ed seems to be operating Joe as well as a Ps.D. could."

"Ah, yes. Your pseudojovian. I'll have to examine that angle pretty carefully, too," said Cornelius. In spite of himself, he was getting interested. "Maybe the trouble comes from something in Joe's biochemistry. Who knows? I'll let you into a carefully guarded little secret, Dr. Viken: psionics is not an exact science."

"Neither is physics," grinned the other man. After a moment, he added more soberly: "Not my brand of physics, anyway. I hope to make it exact. That's why I'm here, you know. It's the reason we're all here."

Edward Anglesey was a bit of a shock the first time. He was a head, a pair of arms, and a disconcertingly intense blue stare. The rest of him was mere detail, enclosed in a wheeled machine.

"Biophysicist originally," Viken had told Cornelius. "Studying atmospheric spores at Earth Station when he was still a young man—accident, crushed him up, nothing below his chest will ever work again. Snappish type, you have to go slow with him."

Seated on a wisp of stool in the esprojector control room, Cornelius realized that Viken had been soft-pedaling the truth.

Anglesey ate as he talked, gracelessly, letting the chair's tentacles wipe up after him. "Got to," he explained. "This stupid place is officially on Earth time, GMT. Jupiter isn't. I've got to be here whenever Joe wakes, ready to take him over."

"Couldn't you have someone spell you?" asked Cornelius.

"Bah!" Anglesey stabbed a piece of prot and waggled it at the other man. Since it was native to him, he could spit out English, the common language of the station, with unmeasured ferocity. "Look here. You ever done therapeutic esping? Not just listening in, or even communication, but actual pedagogic control?"

"No, not I. It requires a certain natural talent, like yours." Cornelius smiled. His ingratiating little phrase was swallowed without being noticed by the scored face opposite him. "I take it you mean cases like, oh, re-educating the nervous system of a palsied child?"

"Yes, yes. Good enough example. Has anyone ever tried to suppress the child's personality, take him over in the most literal sense?"

"Good God, no!"

"Even as a scientific experiment?" Anglesey grinned. "Has any esprojector operative ever poured on the juice and swamped the child's brain with his own thoughts? Come on, Cornelius, I won't snitch on you."

"Well . . . it's out of my line, you understand." The psionicist looked carefully away, found a bland meter face and screwed his eyes to that. "I have, uh, heard something about . . . Well, yes, there were attempts made in some pathological cases to, uh, bull through . . . break down the patient's delusions by sheer force—"

"And it didn't work," said Anglesey. He laughed. "It *can't* work, not even on a child, let alone an adult with a fully developed personality. Why, it took a decade of refinement, didn't it, before the machine was debugged to the point where a psychiatrist could even 'listen in' without the normal variation between his pattern of thought and the patient's—without that variation setting up an interference scrambling the very thing he wanted to study. The machine has to make automatic compensations for the differences between individuals. We still can't bridge the differences between species.

"If someone else is willing to co-operate, you can very gently guide his thinking. And that's all. If you try to seize control of another brain, a brain with its own background of experience, its own ego, you risk your very sanity. The other brain will fight back instinctively. A fully developed, matured, hardened human personality is just too complex for outside control. It has too many resources, too much hell the subconscious can call to its defense if its integrity is threatened. Blazes, man, we can't even master our own minds, let alone anyone else's!"

Anglesey's cracked-voice tirade broke off. He sat brooding at the instrument panel, tapping the console of his mechanical mother.

"Well?" said Cornelius after a while.

He should not, perhaps, have spoken. But he found it hard to remain mute. There was too much silence—half a billion miles of it, from here to the sun. If you closed your mouth five minutes at a time, the silence began creeping in like fog.

"Well," gibed Anglesey. "So our pseudojovian, Joe, has a physically adult brain. The only reason I can control him is that his brain has never been given a chance to develop its own ego. I *am* Joe. From the moment he was 'born' into consciousness, I have been there. The psibeam sends me all his sense data and sends him back my motor-nerve impulses. Nevertheless, he has that excellent brain, and its cells are recording every trace of experience, even as yours and mine; his synapses have assumed the topography which is my 'personality pattern.'

"Anyone else, taking him over from me, would find it was like an attempt to oust me myself from my own brain. It couldn't be done. To be sure, he doubtless has only a rudimentary set of Anglesey-memories—I do not, for instance, repeat trigonometric theorems while controlling him—but he has enough to be, potentially, a distinct personality.

"As a matter of fact, whenever he wakes up from sleep—there's usually a lag of a few minutes, while I sense the change through my normal psi faculties and get the amplifying helmet adjusted—I have a bit of a struggle. I feel almost a . . . a resistance until I've brought his mental currents completely into phase with mine. Merely dreaming has been enough of a different experience to . . ." Anglesey didn't bother to finish the sentence.

"I see," murmured Cornelius. "Yes, it's clear enough. In fact, it's astonishing that you can have such total contact with a being of such alien metabolism."

"I won't for much longer," said the esman sarcastically,

"unless you can correct whatever is burning out those K tubes. I don't have an unlimited supply of spares."

"I have some working hypotheses," said Cornelius, "but there's so little known about psibeam transmission—is the velocity infinite or merely very great, is the beam strength actually independent of distance? How about the possible effects of transmission—oh, through the degenerate matter in the Jovian core? Good Lord, a planet where water is a heavy mineral and hydrogen is a metal! What do we know?"

"We're supposed to find out," snapped Anglesey. "That's what this whole project is for. Knowledge. Bull!" Almost, he spat on the floor. "Apparently what little we have learned doesn't even get through to people. Hydrogen is still a gas where Joe lives. He'd have to dig down a few miles to reach the solid phase. And I'm expected to make a scientific analysis of Jovian conditions!"

Cornelius waited it out, letting Anglesey storm on while he himself turned over the problem of K-tube oscillation.

"They don't understand back on Earth. Even here they don't. Sometimes I think they refuse to understand. Joe's down there without much more than his bare hands. He, I, we started with no more knowledge than that he could probably eat the local life. He has to spend nearly all his time hunting for food. It's a miracle he's come as far as he has in these few weeks—made a shelter, grown familiar with the immediate region, begun on metallurgy, hydrurgy, whatever you want to call it. What more do they want me to do, for crying in the beer?"

"Yes, yes," mumbled Cornelius. "Yes, I . . ."

Anglesey raised his white bony face. Something filmed over in his eyes.

"What—" began Cornelius.

"Shut up!" Anglesey whipped the chair around, groped for the helmet, slapped it over his skull. "Joe's waking. Get out of here."

"But if you'll let me work only while he sleeps, how can I—"

Anglesey snarled and threw a wrench at him. It was a feeble toss, even in low gee. Cornelius backed toward the door. Anglesey was turning in the esprojector. Suddenly he jerked.

"Cornelius!"

"Whatisit?" The psionicist tried to run back, overdid it, and skidded in a heap to end up against the panel.

"K tube again." Anglesey yanked off the helmet. It must have hurt like blazes, having a mental squeal build up uncontrolled and amplified in your own brain, but he said merely: "Change it for me. Fast. And then get out and leave me alone. Joe didn't wake up of himself. Something crawled into the dugout with me—I'm in trouble down there!"

It had been a hard day's work, and Joe slept heavily. He did not wake until the hands closed on his throat.

For a moment then he knew only a crazy smothering wave of panic. He thought he was back on Earth Station, floating in null gee at the end of a cable while a thousand frosty stars haloed the planet before him. He thought the great I beam had broken from its moorings and started toward him, slowly, but with all the inertia of its cold tons, spinning and shimmering in the Earthlight, and the only sound himself screaming and screaming in his helmet trying to break from the cable the beam nudged him ever so gently but it kept on moving he moved with it he was crushed against the station wall nuzzled into it his mangled suit frothed as it tried to seal its wounded self there was blood mingled with the foam his blood *Joe roared*.

His convulsive reaction tore the hands off his neck and sent a black shape spinning across the dugout. It struck the wall, thunderously, and the lamp fell to the floor and went out.

Joe stood in darkness, breathing hard, aware in a vague fashion that the wind had died from a shriek to a low snarling while he slept.

The thing he had tossed away mumbled in pain and crawled along the wall. Joe felt through lightlessness after his club.

Something else scrabbled. The tunnel! They were coming through the tunnel! Joe groped blind to meet them. His heart drummed thickly and his nose drank an alien stench.

The thing that emerged, as Joe's hands closed on it, was only about half his size, but it had six monstrously taloned feet and a pair of three-fingered hands that reached after his eyes. Joe cursed, lifted it while it writhed, and dashed it to the floor. It screamed, and he heard bones splinter.

"Come on, then!" Joe arched his back and spat at them, like a tiger menaced by giant caterpillars.

They flowed through his tunnel and into the room, a dozen

of them entered while he wrestled one that had curled itself around his shoulders and anchored its sinuous body with claws. They pulled at his legs, trying to crawl up on his back. He struck out with claws of his own, with his tail, rolled over and went down beneath a heap of them and stood up with the heap still clinging to him.

They swayed in darkness. The legged seething of them struck the dugout wall. It shivered, a rafter cracked, the roof came down. Anglesey stood in a pit, among broken ice plates, under the wan light of a sinking Ganymede.

He could see now that the monsters were black in color and that they had heads big enough to accommodate some brain, less than human but probably more than apes. There were a score of them or so, they struggled from beneath the wreckage and flowed at him with the same shrieking malice.

Why?

Baboon reaction, thought Anglesey somewhere in the back of himself. See the stranger, fear the stranger, hate the stranger, kill the stranger. His chest heaved, pumping air through a raw throat. He yanked a whole rafter to him, snapped it in half, and twirled the iron-hard wood.

The nearest creature got its head bashed in. The next had its back broken. The third was hurled with shattered ribs into a fourth, they went down together. Joe began to laugh. It was getting to be fun.

"Yeee-ow! Ti-i-i-iger!" He ran across the icy ground, toward the pack. They scattered, howling. He hunted them until the last one had vanished into the forest.

Panting, Joe looked at the dead. He himself was bleeding, he ached, he was cold and hungry and his shelter had been wrecked—but he'd whipped them! He had a sudden impulse to beat his chest and howl. For a moment he hesitated. Why not? Anglesey threw back his head and bayed victory at the dim shield of Ganymede.

Therefore he went to work. First build a fire, in the lee of the spaceship—which was little more by now than a hill of corrosion. The monster pack cried in darkness and the broken ground, they had not given up on him, they would return.

He tore a haunch off one of the slain and took a bite. Pretty good. Better yet if properly cooked. Heh! They'd made a big mistake in calling his attention to their existence! He finished breakfast while Ganymede slipped under the western ice mountains. It would be morning soon. The air was almost still, and a flock of pancake-shaped sky-skimmers, as Anglesey called them, went overhead, burnished copper color in the first pale dawn streaks.

Joe rummaged in the ruins of his hut until he had recovered the water-smelting equipment. It wasn't harmed. That was the first order of business, melt some ice and cast it in the molds of ax, knife, saw, hammer he had painfully prepared. Under Jovian conditions, methane was a liquid that you drank and water was a dense hard mineral. It would make good tools. Later on he would try alloying it with other materials.

Next— yes. To hell with the dugout, he could sleep in the open again for a while. Make a bow, set traps, be ready to massacre the black caterpillars when they attacked him again. There was a chasm not far from here, going down a long way toward the bitter cold of the metallic-hydrogen strata: a natural icebox, a place to store the several weeks' worth of meat his enemies would supply. This would give him leisure to— Oh, a hell of a lot!

Joe laughed exultantly and lay down to watch the sunrise.

It struck him afresh how lovely a place this was. See how the small brilliant spark of the sun swam up out of eastern fog banks colored dusky purple and veined with rose and gold; see how the light strengthened until the great hollow arch of the sky became one shout of radiance; see how the light spilled warm and living over a broad fair land, the million square miles of rustling low forests and wave-blinking lakes and feather-plumed hydrogen geysers; and see, see, see how the ice mountains of the west flashed like blued steel!

Anglesey drew the wild morning wind deep into his lungs and shouted with a boy's joy.

"I'm not a biologist myself," said Viken carefully. "But maybe for that reason I can better give you the general picture. Then Lopez or Matsumoto can answer any questions of detail."

"Excellent." Cornelius nodded. "Why don't you assume I am totally ignorant of this project? I very nearly am, you know."

"If you wish," laughed Viken.

They stood in an outer office of the xenobiology section.

No one else was around, for the station's clocks said 1730 GMT and there was only one shift. No point in having more, until Anglesey's half of the enterprise had actually begun gathering quantitative data.

The physicist bent over and took a paperweight off a desk. "One of the boys made this for fun," he said, "but it's a pretty good model of Joe. He stands about five feet tall at the head."

Cornelius turned the plastic image over in his hands. If you could imagine such a thing as a feline centaur with a thick prehensile tail . . . The torso was squat, long-armed, immensely muscular; the hairless head was round, wide-nosed, with big deep-set eyes and heavy jaws, but it was really quite a human face. The over-all color was bluish gray.

"Male, I see," he remarked.

"Of course. Perhaps you don't understand. Joe is the complete pseudojovian—as far as we can tell, the final model, with all the bugs worked out. He's the answer to a research question that took fifty years to ask." Viken looked sidewise at Cornelius. "So you realize the importance of your job, don't you?"

"I'll do my best," said the psionicist. "But if . . . well, let's say that tube failure or something causes you to lose Joe before I've solved the oscillation problem. You do have other pseudos in reserve, don't you?"

"Oh, yes," said Viken moodily. "But the cost . . . We're not on an unlimited budget. We do go through a lot of money, because it's expensive to stand up and sneeze this far from Earth. But for that same reason our margin is slim."

He jammed hands in pockets and slouched toward the inner door, the laboratories, head down and talking in a low, hurried voice. "Perhaps you don't realize what a nightmare planet Jupiter is. Not just the surface gravity—a shade under three gees, what's that?—but the gravitational potential, ten times Earth's. The temperature. The pressure. Above all, the atmosphere, and the storms, and the darkness!

"When a spaceship goes down to the Jovian surface, it's a radio-controlled job; it leaks like a sieve, to equalize pressure, but otherwise it's the sturdiest, most utterly powerful model ever designed; it's loaded with every instrument, every servomechanism, every safety device the human mind has yet thought up to protect a million-dollar hunk of precision equipment. And what happens? Half the ships never reach the surface at all. A storm snatches them and throws them away, or they collide with a floating chunk of Ice Seven—small version of the Red Spot—or, so help me, what passes for a flock of *birds* rams one and stoves it in! As for the fifty per cent which do land, it's a one-way trip. We don't even try to bring them back. If the stresses coming down haven't sprung something, the corrosion has doomed them anyway. Hydrogen at Jovian pressure does funny things to metals.

"It cost a total of about five million dollars to set Joe, one pseudo, down there. Each pseudo to follow will cost, if we're lucky, a couple of million more."

Viken kicked open the door and led the way through. Beyond was a big room, low-ceilinged, coldly lit and murmurous with ventilators. It reminded Cornelius of a nucleonics lab; for a moment he wasn't sure why, then he recognized the intricacies of remote control, remote observation, walls enclosing forces which could destroy the entire moon.

"These are required by the pressure, of course," said Viken, pointing to a row of shields. "And the cold. And the hydrogen itself, as a minor hazard. We have units here duplicating conditions in the Jovian, uh, stratosphere. This is where the whole project really began."

"I've heard something about that. Didn't you scoop up airborne spores?"

"Not I." Viken chuckled. "Totti's crew did, about fifty years ago. Proved there was life on Jupiter. A life using liquid methane as its basic solvent, solid ammonia as a starting point for nitrate synthesis: the plants use solar energy to build unsaturated carbon compounds, releasing hydrogen; the animals eat the plants and reduce those compounds again to the saturated form. There is even an equivalent of combustion. The reactions involve complex enzymes and—well, it's out of my line."

"Jovian biochemistry is pretty well understood, then."

"Oh, yes. Even in Totti's day they had a highly developed biotic technology: Earth bacteria had already been synthesized and most gene structures pretty well mapped. The only reason it took so long to diagram Jovian life processes was the technical difficulty, high pressure and so on."

"When did you actually get a look at Jupiter's surface?"

"Gray managed that, about thirty years ago. Set a televisor ship down, a ship that lasted long enough to flash him quite a series of pictures. Since then, the technique has improved. We know that Jupiter is crawling with its own weird kind of life, probably more fertile than Earth. Extrapolating from the airborne micro-organisms, our team made trial syntheses of metazoans and—"

Viken sighed. "Damn it, if only there were intelligent native life! Think what they could tell us, Cornelius, the data, the— Just think back how far we've gone since Lavoisier, with the low-pressure chemistry of Earth. Here's a chance to learn a high-pressure chemistry and physics at least as rich with possibilities!"

After a moment, Cornelius murmured slyly, "Are you certain there *aren't* any Jovians?"

"Oh, sure, there could be several billion of them." Viken shrugged. "Cities, empires, anything you like. Jupiter has the surface area of a hundred Earths, and we've only seen maybe a dozen small regions. But we do know there aren't any Jovians using radio. Considering their atmosphere, it's unlikely they ever would invent it for themselves—imagine how thick a vacuum tube has to be, how strong a pump you need! So it was finally decided we'd better make our own Jovians."

Cornelius followed him through the lab into another room. This was less cluttered, it had a more finished appearance; the experimenter's haywire rig had yielded to the assured precision of an engineer.

Viken went over to one of the panels which lined the walls and looked at its gauges. "Beyond this lies another pseudo," he said. "Female, in this instance. She's at a pressure of two hundred atmospheres and a temperature of 194 absolute. There's a . . . an umbilical arrangement, I guess you'd call it, to keep her alive. She was grown to adulthood in this, uh, fetal stage—we patterned our Jovians after the terrestrial mammal. She's never been conscious, she won't ever be till she's 'born.' We have a total of twenty males and sixty females waiting here. We can count on about half reaching the surface. More can be created as required. It isn't the pseudos that are so expensive, it's their transportation. So Joe is down there alone till we're sure that his kind *can* survive."

"I take it you experimented with lower forms first," said Cornelius.

"Of course. It took twenty years, even with forced-catalysis techniques, to work from an artificial airborne spore to Joe. We've used the psibeam to control everything from pseudo insects on up. Interspecies control is possible, you know, if your puppet's nervous system is deliberately designed for it and isn't given a chance to grow into a pattern different from the esman's."

"And Joe is the first specimen who's given trouble?"

"Yes."

"Scratch one hypothesis." Cornelius sat down on a workbench, dangling thick legs and running a hand through thin sandy hair. "I thought maybe some physical effect of Jupiter was responsible. Now it looks as if the difficulty is with Joe himself."

"We've all suspected that much," said Viken. He struck a cigarette and sucked in his cheeks around the smoke. His eyes were gloomy. "Hard to see how. The biotics engineers tell me *Pseudocentaurus sapiens* has been more carefully designed than any product of natural evolution."

"Even the brain?"

"Yes. It's patterned directly on the human, to make psibeam control possible, but there are improvements—greater stability."

"There are still the psychological aspects, though," said Cornelius. "In spite of all our amplifiers and other fancy gadgets, psi is essentially a branch of psychology, even today —or maybe it's the other way around. Let's consider traumatic experiences. I take it the . . . the adult Jovian fetus has a rough trip going down?"

"The ship does," said Viken. "Not the pseudo itself, which is wrapped up in fluid just like you were before birth."

"Nevertheless," said Cornelius, "the two-hundred-atmospheres pressure here is not the same as whatever unthinkable pressure exists down on Jupiter. Could the change be injurious?"

Viken gave him a look of respect. "Not likely," he answered. "I told you the J ships are designed leaky. External pressure is transmitted to the, uh, uterine mechanism through a series of diaphragms, in a gradual fashion. It takes hours to make the descent, you realize."

"Well, what happens next?" went on Cornelius. "The ship lands, the uterine mechanism opens, the umbilical connection disengages, and Joe is, shall we say, born. But he has an adult brain. He is not protected by the only half-developed infant brain from the shock of sudden awareness."

"We thought of that," said Viken. "Anglesey was on the psibeam, in phase with Joe, when the ship left this moon. So it wasn't really Joe who emerged, who perceived. Joe has never been much more than a biological waldo. He can only suffer mental shock to the extent that Ed does, because it *is* Ed down there!"

"As you will," said Cornelius. "Still, you didn't plan for a race of puppets, did you?"

"Oh, heavens, no," said Viken. "Out of the question. Once we know Joe is well established, we'll import a few more esmen and get him some assistance in the form of other pseudos. Eventually females will be sent down, and uncontrolled males, to be educated by the puppets. A new generation will be born normally—well, anyhow, the ultimate aim is a small civilization of Jovians. There will be hunters, miners, artisans, farmers, housewives, the works. They will support a few key members, a kind of priesthood. And that priesthood will be esp-controlled, as Joe is. It will exist solely to make instruments, take readings, perform experiments, and tell us what we want to know!"

Cornelius nodded. In a general way, this was the Jovian project as he had understood it. He could appreciate the importance of his own assignment.

Only, he still had no clue to the cause of that positive feedback in the K tubes.

And what could he do about it?

His hands were still bruised. *Oh, God,* he thought with a groan, for the hundredth time, *does it affect me that much? While Joe was fighting down there, did I really hammer my fists on metal up here?*

His eyes smoldered across the room, to the bench where Cornelius worked. He didn't like Cornelius, fat cigar-sucking slob, interminably talking and talking. He had about given up trying to be civil to the Earthworm.

The psionicist laid down a screwdriver and flexed cramped fingers. *"Whuff!"* He smiled. "I'm going to take a break."

The half-assembled esprojector made a gaunt backdrop for his wide soft body, where it squatted toad fashion on the bench. Anglesey detested the whole idea of anyone sharing this room, even for a few hours a day. Of late he had been demanding his meals brought here, left outside the door of his adjoining bedroom-bath. He had not gone beyond for quite some time now.

And why should I?

"Couldn't you hurry it up a little?" snapped Anglesey.

Cornelius flushed. "If you'd had an assembled spare machine, instead of loose parts—" he began. Shrugging, he took out a cigar stub and relit it carefully; his supply had to last a long time. Anglesey wondered if those stinking clouds were blown from his mouth of malicious purpose. *I don't like you, Mr. Earthman Cornelius, and it is doubtless quite mutual.*

"There was no obvious need for one, until the other esmen arrive," said Anglesey in a sullen voice. "And the testing instruments report this one in perfectly good order."

"Nevertheless," said Cornelius, "at irregular intervals it goes into wild oscillations which burn out the K tube. The problem is why. I'll have you try out this new machine as soon as it is ready, but, frankly, I don't believe the trouble lies in electronic failure at all—or even in unsuspected physical effects."

"Where, then?" Anglesey felt more at ease as the discussion grew purely technical.

"Well, look. What exactly is the K tube? It's the heart of the esprojector. It amplifies your natural psionic pulses, uses them to modulate the carrier wave, and shoots the whole beam down at Joe. It also picks up Joe's resonating impulses and amplifies them for your benefit. Everything else is auxiliary to the K tube."

"Spare me the lecture," snarled Anglesey.

"I was only rehearsing the obvious," said Cornelius, "because every now and then it is the obvious answer which is hardest to see. Maybe it isn't the K tube which is misbehaving. Maybe it is you."

"What?" The white face gaped at him. A dawning rage crept red across its thin bones.

"Nothing personal intended," said Cornelius hastily. "But you know what a tricky beast the subconscious is. Suppose, just as a working hypothesis, that way down underneath, you don't *want* to be on Jupiter. I imagine it is a rather terrifying environment. Or there may be some obscure Freudian element involved. Or, quite simply and naturally, your subconscious may fail to understand that Joe's death does not entail your own."

"Um-m-m." *Mirabile dictu,* Anglesey remained calm. He rubbed his chin with one skeletal hand. "Can you be more explicit?"

"Only in a rough way," replied Cornelius. "Your conscious mind sends a motor impulse along the psibeam to Joe.

Simultaneously, your subconscious mind, being scared of the whole business, emits the glandular-vascular-cardiac-visceral impulses associated with fear. These react on Joe, whose tension is transmitted back along the beam. Feeling Joe's somatic fear symptoms, your subconscious gets still more worried, thereby increasing the symptoms. Get it? It's exactly similar to ordinary neurasthenia, with this exception, that since there is a powerful amplifier, the K tube, involved, the oscillations can build up uncontrollably within a second or two. You should be thankful the tube does burn out—otherwise your brain might do so!"

For a moment Anglesey was quiet. Then he laughed. It was a hard, barbaric laughter. Cornelius started as it struck his eardrums.

"Nice idea," said the esman. "But I'm afraid it won't fit all the data. You see, I like it down there. I like being Joe."

He paused for a while, then continued in a dry impersonal tone: "Don't judge the environment from my notes. They're just idiotic things like estimates of wind velocity, temperature variations, mineral properties—insignificant. What I can't put in is how Jupiter looks through a Jovian's infrared-seeing eyes."

"Different, I should think," ventured Cornelius after a minute's clumsy silence.

"Yes and no. It's hard to put into language. Some of it I can't, because man hasn't got the concepts. But . . . oh, I can't describe it. Shakespeare himself couldn't. Just remember that everything about Jupiter which is cold and poisonous and gloomy to us is *right* for Joe."

Anglesey's tone grew remote, as if he spoke to himself. "Imagine walking under a glowing violet sky, where great flashing clouds sweep the earth with shadow and rain strides beneath them. Imagine walking on the slopes of a mountain like polished metal, with a clean red flame exploding above you and thunder laughing in the ground. Imagine a cool wild stream, and low trees with dark coppery flowers, and a water-fall—methanefall, whatever you like—leaping off a cliff, and the strong live wind shakes its mane full of rainbows! Imagine a whole forest, dark and breathing, and here and there you glimpse a pale-red wavering will-o'-the-wisp, which is the life radiation of some fleet, shy animal, and . . . and . . ."

Anglesey croaked into silence. He stared down at his

clenched fists, then he closed his eyes tight and tears ran out between the lids. "Imagine being *strong!*"

Suddenly he snatched up the helmet, crammed it on his head and twirled the control knobs. Joe had been sleeping, down in the night, but Joe was about to wake up and—roar under the four great moons till all the forest feared him?

Cornelius slipped quietly out of the room.

In the long brazen sunset light, beneath dusky cloud banks brooding storm, he strode up the hill slope with a sense of day's work done. Across his back, two woven baskets balanced each other, one laden with the pungent black fruit of the thorn tree and one with cable-thick creepers to be used as rope. The ax on his shoulder caught the waning sunlight and tossed it blindingly back.

It had not been hard labor, but weariness dragged at his mind and he did not relish the household chores yet to be performed, cooking and cleaning and all the rest. Why couldn't they hurry up and get him some helpers?

His eyes sought the sky resentfully. Moon Five was hidden; down here, at the bottom of the air ocean, you saw nothing but the sun and the four Galilean satellites. He wasn't even sure where Five was just now, in relation to himself. *Wait a minute, it's sunset here, but if I went out to the viewdome I'd see Jupiter in the last quarter, or would I, oh, hell, it only takes us half an Earth day to swing around the planet anyhow—*

Joe shook his head. After all this time, it was still damnably hard, now and then, to keep his thoughts straight. *I, the essential I, am up in heaven, riding Jupiter Five between cold stars. Remember that. Open your eyes, if you will, and see the dead control room superimposed on a living hillside.*

He didn't, though. Instead, he regarded the boulders strewn wind-blasted gray over the tough mossy vegetation of the slope. They were not much like Earth rocks, nor was the soil beneath his feet like terrestrial humus.

For a moment Anglesey speculated on the origin of the silicates, aluminates, and other stony compounds. Theoretically, all such materials should be inaccessibly locked in the Jovian core, down where the pressure got vast enough for atoms to buckle and collapse. Above the core should lie thousands of miles of allotropic ice, and then the metallic-hydrogen layer. There should not be complex minerals this far up, but there were.

Well, possibly Jupiter had formed according to theory, but had thereafter sucked enough cosmic dust, meteors, gases and vapors down its great throat of gravitation to form a crust several miles thick. Or more likely the theory was altogether wrong. What did they know, what *could* they know, the soft pale worms of Earth?

Anglesey stuck his—Joe's—fingers in his mouth and whistled. A baying sounded in the brush, and two midnight forms leaped toward him. He grinned and stroked their heads; training was progressing faster than he'd hoped, with these pups of the black caterpillar beasts he had taken. They would make guardians for him, herders, servants.

On the crest of the hill, Joe was building himself a home. He had logged off an acre of ground and erected a stockade. Within the grounds there now stood a leanto for himself and his stores, a methane well, and the beginnings of a large, comfortable cabin.

But there was too much work for one being. Even with the half-intelligent caterpillars to help, and with cold storage for meat, most of his time would still go to hunting. The game wouldn't last forever, either; he had to start agriculture within the next year or so—Jupiter year, twelve Earth years, thought Anglesey. There was the cabin to finish and furnish; he wanted to put a waterwheel, no, methane wheel, in the river to turn any of a dozen machines he had in mind, he wanted to experiment with alloyed ice and—

And, quite apart from his need of help, why should he remain alone, the single thinking creature on an entire planet? He was a male in this body, with male instincts—in the long run, his health was bound to suffer if he remained a hermit, and right now the whole project depended on Joe's health.

It wasn't right!

But I am not alone. There are fifty men on the satellite with me. I can talk to any of them, any time I wish. It's only that I seldom wish it, these days. I would rather be Joe.

Nevertheless . . . I, the cripple, feel all the tiredness, anger, hurt, frustration, of that wonderful biological machine called Joe. The others don't understand. When the ammonia gale flays open his skin, it is I who bleed.

Joe lay down on the ground, sighing. Fangs flashed in the mouth of the black beast which humped over to lick his face. His belly growled with hunger, but he was too tired to fix a meal. Once he had the dogs trained . . .

Another pseudo would be so much more rewarding to educate.

He could almost see it, in the weary darkening of his brain. Down there, in the valley below the hill, fire and thunder as the ship came to rest. And the steel egg would crack open, the steel arms—already crumbling, puny work of worms!—lift out the shape within and lay it on the earth.

She would stir, shrieking in her first lungful of air, looking about with blank mindless eyes. And Joe would come and carry her home. And he would feed her, care for her, show her how to walk—it wouldn't take long, an adult body would learn those things very fast. In a few weeks she would even be talking, be an individual, a soul.

Did you ever think, Edward Anglesey, in the days when you also walked, that your wife would be a gray four-legged monster?

Never mind that. The important thing was to get others of his kind down here, female *and* male. The station's niggling little plan would have him wait two more Earth years, and then send him only another dummy like himself, a contemptible human mind looking through eyes which belonged rightfully to a Jovian. It was not to be tolerated!

If he weren't so tired . . .

Joe sat up. Sleep drained from him as the realization entered. *He* wasn't tired, not to speak of. Anglesey was. Anglesey, the human side of him, who for months had slept only in cat naps, whose rest had lately been interrupted by Cornelius—it was the human body which drooped, gave up, and sent wave after soft wave of sleep down the psibeam to Joe.

Somatic tension traveled skyward; Anglesey jerked awake.

He swore. As he sat there beneath the helmet, the vividness of Jupiter faded with his scattering concentration, as if it grew transparent; the steel prison which was his laboratory strengthened behind it. He was losing contact. Rapidly, with the skill of experience, he brought himself back into phase with the neural currents of the other brain. He willed sleepiness on Joe, exactly as a man wills it on himself.

And, like any other insomniac, he failed. The Joe body

was too hungry. It got up and walked across the compound toward its shack.

The K tube went wild and blew itself out.

The night before the ships left, Viken and Cornelius sat up late.

It was not truly a night, of course. In twelve hours the tiny moon was hurled clear around Jupiter, from darkness back to darkness, and there might well be a pallid little sun over its crags when the clocks said witches were abroad in Greenwich. But most of the personnel were asleep at this hour.

Viken scowled. "I don't like it," he said. "Too sudden a change of plans. Too big a gamble."

"You are only risking—how many?—three male and a dozen female pseudos," Cornelius replied.

"And fifteen J ships. All we have. If Anglesey's notion doesn't work, it will be months, a year or more, till we can have others built and resume aerial survey."

"But if it does work," said Cornelius, "you won't need any J ships, except to carry down more pseudos. You will be too busy evaluating data from the surface to piddle around in the upper atmosphere."

"Of course. But we never expected it so soon. We were going to bring more esmen out here, to operate some more pseudos—"

"But they aren't *needed*," said Cornelius. He struck a cigar to life and took a long pull on it, while his mind sought carefully for words. "Not for a while, anyhow. Joe has reached a point where, given help, he can leap several thousand years of history—he may even have a radio of sorts operating in the fairly near future, which would eliminate the necessity of much of your esping. But without help, he'll just have to mark time. And it's stupid to make a highly trained human esman perform manual labor, which is all that the other pseudos are needed for at this moment. Once the Jovian settlement is well established, certainly, then you can send down more puppets."

"The question is, though," persisted Viken, "can Anglesey himself educate all those pseudos at once? They'll be helpless as infants for days. It will be weeks before they really start thinking and acting for themselves. Can Joe take care of them meanwhile?"

"He has food and fuel stored for months ahead," said Cornelius. "As for what Joe's capabilities are—well, hm-m-m, we just have to take Anglesey's judgment. He has the only inside information."

"And once those Jovians do become personalities," worried Viken, "are they necessarily going to string along with Joe? Don't forget, the pseudos are not carbon copies of each other. The uncertainty principle assures each one a unique set of genes. If there is only one human mind on Jupiter, among all those aliens—"

"One *human* mind?" It was barely audible. Viken opened his mouth inquiringly. The other man hurried on.

"Oh, I'm sure Anglesey can continue to dominate them," said Cornelius. "His own personality is rather—tremendous."

Viken looked startled. "You really think so?"

The psionicist nodded. "Yes. I've seen more of him in the past weeks than anyone else. And my profession naturally orients me more toward a man's psychology than his body or his habits. You see a waspish cripple. I see a mind which has reacted to its physical handicaps by developing such a hellish energy, such an inhuman power of concentration, that it almost frightens me. Give that mind a sound body for its use and nothing is impossible to it."

"You may be right, at that," murmured Viken after a pause. "Not that it matters. The decision is taken, the rockets go down tomorrow. I hope it all works out."

He waited for another while. The whirring of ventilators in his little room seemed unnaturally loud, the colors of a girlie picture on the wall shockingly garish. Then he said slowly, "You've been rather close-mouthed yourself, Jan. When do you expect to finish your own esprojector and start making the tests?"

Cornelius looked around. The door stood open to an empty hallway, but he reached out and closed it before he answered with a slight grin, "It's been ready for the past few days. But don't tell anyone."

"How's that?" Viken started. The movement, in low gee, took him out of his chair and halfway across the table between the men. He shoved himself back and waited.

"I have been making meaningless tinkering motions," said Cornelius, "but what I waited for was a highly emotional moment, a time when I can be sure Anglesey's entire attention will be focused on Joe. This business toworrow is exactly what I need."

"Why?"

"You see, I have pretty well convinced myself that the trouble in the machine is psychological, not physical. I think that for some reason, buried in his subconscious, Anglesey doesn't want to experience Jupiter. A conflict of that type might well set a psionic-amplifier circuit oscillating."

"Hm-m-m." Viken rubbed his chin. "Could be. Lately Ed has been changing more and more. When he first came here, he was peppery enough, and he would at least play an occasional game of poker. Now he's pulled so far into his shell you can't even see him. I never thought of it before, but . . . yes, by God, Jupiter must be having some effect on him."

"Hm-m-m." Cornelius nodded. He did not elaborate—did not, for instance, mention that one altogether characteristic episode when Anglesey had tried to describe what it was like to be a Jovian.

"Of course," said Viken thoughtfully, "the previous men were not affected especially. Nor was Ed at first, while he was still controlling lower-type pseudos. It's only since Joe went down to the surface that he's become so different."

"Yes, yes," said Cornelius hastily. "I've learned that much. But enough shop talk—"

"No. Wait a minute." Viken spoke in a low, hurried tone, looking past him. "For the first time, I'm starting to think clearly about this. Never really stopped to analyze it before, just accepted a bad situation. There *is* something peculiar about Joe. It can't very well involve his physical structure, or the environment, because lower forms didn't give this trouble. Could it be the fact that Joe is the first puppet in all history with a potentially human intelligence?"

"We speculate in a vacuum," said Cornelius. "Tomorrow, maybe, I can tell you. Now I know nothing."

Viken sat up straight. His pale eyes focused on the other man and stayed there, unblinking. "One minute," he said.

"Yes?" Cornelius shifted, half rising. "Quickly, please. It is past my bedtime."

"You know a good deal more than you've admitted," said Viken. "Don't you?"

"What makes you think that?"

"You aren't the most gifted liar in the universe. And then, you argued very strongly for Anglesey's scheme, this sending down the other pseudos. More strongly than a newcomer should."

"I told you, I want his attention focused elsewhere when—"

"Do you want it that badly?" snapped Viken.

Cornelius was still for a minute. Then he sighed and leaned back.

"All right," he said. "I shall have to trust your discretion. I wasn't sure, you see, how any of you old-time station personnel would react. So I didn't want to blabber out my speculations, which may be wrong. The confirmed facts, yes, I will tell them; but I don't wish to attack a man's religion with a mere theory."

Viken scowled. "What the devil do you mean?"

Cornelius puffed hard on his cigar; its tip waxed and waned like a miniature red demon star. "This Jupiter Five is more than a research station," he said gently. "It is a way of life, is it not? No one would come here for even one hitch unless the work was important to him. Those who re-enlist, they must find something in the work, something which Earth with all her riches cannot offer them. No?"

"Yes," answered Viken. It was almost a whisper. "I didn't think you would understand so well. But what of it?"

"Well, I don't want to tell you, unless I can prove it, that maybe this has all gone for nothing. Maybe you have wasted your lives and a lot of money, and will have to pack up and go home."

Viken's long face did not flicker a muscle. It seemed to have congealed. But he said calmly enough, "Why?"

"Consider Joe," said Cornelius. "His brain has as much capacity as any adult human's. It has been recording every sense datum that came to it, from the moment of 'birth'— making a record in itself, in its own cells, not merely in Anglesey's physical memory bank up here. Also, you know, a thought is a sense datum, too. And thoughts are not separated into neat little railway tracks; they form a continuous field. Every time Anglesey is in rapport with Joe, and thinks, the thought goes through Joe's synapses as well as his own— and every thought carries its own associations, and every associated memory is recorded. Like if Joe is building a hut,

the shape of the logs might remind Anglsey of some geometric figure, which in turn would remind him of the Pythag-
orean theorem—"

"I get the idea," said Viken in a cautious way. "Given time,
Joe's brain will have stored everything that ever was in Ed's."

"Correct. Now, a functioning nervous system with an en-
grammatic pattern of experience, in this case a *nonhuman*
nervous system—isn't that a pretty good definition of a personality?"

"I suppose so. Good Lord!" Viken jumped. "You mean
Joe is—taking over?"

"In a way. A subtle, automatic, unconscious way." Cornelius drew a deep breath and plunged into it. "The pseudojovian is so nearly perfect a life form: your biologists en-
gineered into it all the experience gained from nature's
mistakes in designing *us*. At first, Joe was only a remote-con-
trolled biological machine. Then Anglesey and Joe became
two facets of a single personality. Then, oh, very slowly, the
stronger, healthier body . . . more amplitude to its thoughts
. . . do you see? Joe is becoming the dominant side. Like
this business of sending down the other pseudos—Anglesey
only thinks he has logical reasons for wanting it done. Actually, his 'reasons' are mere rationalizations for the instinctive
desires of the Joe facet.

"Anglesey's subconscious must comprehend the situation,
in a dim reactive way; it must feel his human ego gradually
being submerged by the steamroller force of *Joe's* instincts
and *Joe's* wishes. It tries to defend its own identity, and is
swatted down by the superior force of Joe's own nascent
subconscious.

"I put it crudely," he finished in an apologetic tone, "but
it will account for that oscillation in the K tubes."

Viken nodded, slowly, like an old man. "Yes, I see it," he
answered. "The alien environment down there . . . the
different brain structure. . . . Good God! Ed's being swallowed up in Joe! The puppet master is becoming the puppet!"
He looked ill.

"Only speculation on my part," said Cornelius. All at once,
he felt very tired. It was not pleasant to do this to Viken,
whom he liked. "But you see the dilemma, no? If I am right,
then any esman will gradually become a Jovian—a monster
with two bodies, of which the human body is the unimportant

auxiliary one. This means no esman will ever agree to control a pseudo—therefore, the end of your project."

He stood up. "I'm sorry, Arne. You made me tell you what I think, and now you will lie awake worrying, and I am maybe quite wrong and you worry for nothing."

"It's all right," mumbled Viken. "Maybe you're not wrong."

"I don't know." Cornelius drifted toward the door. "I am going to try to find some answers tomorrow. Good night."

The moon-shaking thunder of the rockets, crash, crash, crash, leaping from their cradles, was long past. Now the fleet glided on metal wings, with straining secondary ram-jets, through the rage of the Jovian sky.

As Cornelius opened the control-room door, he looked at his telltale board. Elsewhere a voice tolled the word to all the stations, *One ship wrecked, two ships wrecked,* but Anglesey would let no sound enter his presence when he wore the helmet. An obliging technician had haywired a panel of fifteen red and fifteen blue lights above Cornelius' esprojector, to keep him informed, too. Ostensibly, of course, they were only there for Anglesey's benefit, though the esman had insisted he wouldn't be looking at them.

Four of the red bulbs were dark and thus four blue ones would not shine for a safe landing. A whirlwind, a thunderbolt, a floating ice meteor, a flock of mantalike birds with flesh as dense and hard as iron—there could be a hundred things which had crumpled four ships and tossed them tattered across the poison forests.

Four ships, hell! Think of four living creatures, with an excellence of brain to rival your own, damned first to years in unconscious night and then, never awakening save for one uncomprehending instant, dashed in bloody splinters against an ice mountain. The wasteful callousness of it was a cold knot in Cornelius' belly. It had to be done, no doubt, if there was to be any thinking life on Jupiter at all; but then let it be done quickly and minimally, he thought, so that the next generation could be begotten by love and not by machines!

He closed the door behind him and waited for a breathless moment. Anglesey was a wheel chair and a coppery curve of helmet, facing the opposite wall. No movement, no awareness whatsoever. Good! It would be awkward, perhaps ruinous, if Anglesey learned of this most intimate peering. But he needn't, ever. He was blindfolded and ear-plugged by his own concentration.

Nevertheless, the psionicist moved his bulky form with care, across the room to the new esprojector. He did not much like his snooper's role, he would not have assumed it at all if he had seen any other hope. But neither did it make him feel especially guilty. If what he suspected was true, then Anglesey was all unawares being twisted into something not human; to spy on him might be to save him.

Gently, Cornelius activated the meters and started his tubes warming up. The oscilloscope built into Anglesey's machine gave him the other man's exact alpha rhythm, his basic biological clock. First you adjusted to that, then you discovered the subtler elements by feel, and when your set was fully in phase you could probe undetected and—

Find out what was wrong. Read Anglesey's tortured subconscious and see what there was on Jupiter that both drew and terrified him.

Five ships wrecked.

But it must be very nearly time for them to land. Maybe only five would be lost in all. Maybe ten would get through. Ten comrades for—Joe?

Cornelius sighed. He looked at the cripple, seated blind and deaf to the human world which had crippled him, and felt a pity and an anger. It wasn't fair, none of it was.

Not even to Joe. Joe wasn't any kind of soul-eating devil. He did not even realize, as yet, that he *was* Joe, that Anglesey was becoming a mere appendage. He hadn't asked to be created, and to withdraw his human counterpart from him would very likely be to destroy him.

Somehow, there were always penalties for everybody when men exceeded the decent limits.

Cornelius swore at himself, voicelessly. Work to do. He sat down and fitted the helmet on his own head. The carrier wave made a faint pulse, inaudible, the trembling of neurones low in his awareness. You couldn't describe it.

Reaching up, he turned to Anglesey's alpha. His own had a somewhat lower frequency, it was necessary to carry the signals through a heterodyning process. Still no reception. Well, of course he had to find the exact wave form, timbre was as basic to thought as to music. He adjusted the dials slowly, with enormous care.

Something flashed through his consciousness, a vision of clouds roiled in a violet-red sky, a wind that galloped across horizonless immensity—he lost it. His finger shook as he tuned back.

The psibeam between Joe and Anglesey broadened. It took Cornelius into the circuit. He looked through Joe's eyes, he stood on a hill and stared into the sky above the ice mountains, straining for sign of the first rocket, and simultaneously he was still Jan Cornelius, blurrily seeing the meters, probing about for emotions, symbols, any key to the locked terror in Anglesey's soul.

The terror rose up and struck him in the face.

Psionic detection is not a matter of passive listening in. Much as a radio receiver is necessarily also a weak transmitter, the nervous system in resonance with a source of psionic-spectrum energy is itself emitting. Normally, of course, this effect is unimportant; but when you pass the impulses, either way, through a set of heterodyning and amplifying units, with a high negative feedback . . .

In the early days, psionic psychotherapy vitiated itself because the amplified thoughts of one man, entering the brain of another, would combine with the latter's own neural cycles according to the ordinary vector laws. The result was that both men felt the new beat frequencies as a nightmarish fluttering of their very thoughts. An analyst, trained into self-control, could ignore it; his patient could not, and reacted violently.

But eventually the basic human wave timbres were measured, and psionic therapy resumed. The modern esprojector analyzed an incoming signal and shifted its characteristics over to the "listener's" pattern. The *really* different pulses of the transmitting brain, those which could not possibly be mapped onto the pattern of the receiving neurones—as an exponential signal cannot very practicably be mapped onto a sinusoid—those were filtered out.

Thus compensated, the other thought could be apprehended as comfortably as one's own. If the patient were on a psibeam circuit, a skilled operator could tune in without the patient being necessarily aware of it. The operator could either probe the other man's thoughts or implant thoughts of his own.

Cornelius' plan, an obvious one to any psionicist, had depended on this. He would receive from an unwitting Anglesey-Joe. If his theory was right and the esman's personality was being distorted into that of a monster, his thinking would be too alien to come through the filters. Cornelius would receive spottily or not at all. If his theory was wrong, and Anglesey was still Anglesey, he would receive only a normal human stream of consciousness and could probe for other troublemaking factors.

His brain roared!

What's happening to me?

For a moment, the interference which turned his thoughts to saw-toothed gibberish struck him down with panic. He gulped for breath, there in the Jovian wind, and his dreadful dogs sensed the alienness in him and whined.

Then, recognition, remembrance, and a blaze of anger so great that it left no room for fear. Joe filled his lungs and shouted it aloud, the hillside boomed with echoes:

"Get out of my mind!"

He felt Cornelius spiral down toward unconsciousness. The overwhelming force of his own mental blow had been too much. He laughed, it was more like a snarl, and eased the pressure.

Above him, between thunderous clouds, winked the first thin descending rocket flare.

Cornelius' mind groped back toward the light. It broke a watery surface, the man's mouth snapped after air and his hands reached for the dials, to turn his machine off and escape.

"Not so fast, you." Grimly, Joe drove home a command that locked Cornelius' muscles rigid. "I want to know the meaning of this. Hold still and let me look!" He smashed home an impulse which could be rendered, perhaps, as an incandescent question mark. Remembrance exploded in shards through the psionicist's forebrain.

"So. That's all there is? You thought I was afraid to come down here and be Joe, and wanted to know why? But I *told* you I wasn't!"

I should have believed, whispered Cornelius.

"Well, get out of the circuit, then." Joe continued growling it vocally. "And don't ever come back in the control room, understand? K tubes or no, I don't want to see you again. And I may be a cripple, but I can still take you apart cell by cell. Now sign off—leave me alone. The first ship will be landing in minutes."

You a cripple—you, Joe Anglesey?

"What?" The great gray being on the hill lifted his barbaric head as if to sudden trumpets. "What do you mean?"

Don't you understand? said the weak, dragging thought. *You know how the esprojector works. You know I could have probed Anglesey's mind in Anglesey's brain without making enough interference to be noticed. And I could not have probed a wholly nonhuman mind at all, nor could it have been aware of me. The filters would not have passed such a signal. Yet you felt me in the first fractional second. It can only mean a human mind in a nonhuman brain.*

You are not the half-corpse on Jupiter Five any longer. You're Joe—Joe Anglesey.

"Well, I'll be damned," said Joe. "You're right."

He turned Anglesey off, kicked Cornelius out of his mind with a single brutal impulse, and ran down the hill to meet the spaceship.

Cornelius woke up minutes afterward. His skull felt ready to split apart. He groped for the main switch before him, clashed it down, ripped the helmet off his head and threw it clanging on the floor. But it took a little while to gather the strength to do the same for Anglesey. The other man was not able to do anything for himself.

They sat outside sick bay and waited. It was a harshly lit barrenness of metal and plastic, smelling of antiseptics—down near the heart of the satellite, with miles of rock to hide the terrible face of Jupiter.

Only Viken and Cornelius were in that cramped little room. The rest of the station went about its business mechanically, filling in the time till it could learn what had happened. Beyond the door, three biotechnicians, who were also the station's medical staff, fought with death's angel for the thing which had been Edward Anglesey.

"Nine ships got down," said Viken dully. "Two males, seven females. It's enough to start a colony."

"It would be genetically desirable to have more," pointed out Cornelius. He kept his own voice low, in spite of its underlying cheerfulness. There was a certain awesome quality to all this.

"I still don't understand," said Viken.

"Oh, it's clear enough—now. I should have guessed it before, maybe. We had all the facts, it was only that we couldn't make the simple, obvious interpretation of them. No, we had to conjure up Frankenstein's monster."

"Well," Viken's words grated, "we have played Frankenstein, haven't we? Ed is dying in there."

"It depends on how you define death." Cornelius drew hard on his cigar, needing anything that might steady him. His tone grew purposely dry of emotion.

"Look here. Consider the data. Joe, now: a creature with a brain of human capacity, but without a mind—a perfect Lockean *tabula rasa* for Anglesey's psibeam to write on. We deduced, correctly enough—if very belatedly—that when enough had been written, there would be a personality. But the question was, whose? Because, I suppose, of normal human fear of the unknown, we assumed that any personality in so alien a body had to be monstrous. Therefore it must be hostile to Anglesey, must be swamping him—"

The door opened. Both men jerked to their feet.

The chief surgeon shook his head. "No use. Typical deep-shock traumata, close to terminus now. If we had better facilities, maybe . . ."

"No," said Cornelius. "You cannot save a man who has decided not to live any more."

"I know." The doctor removed his mask. "I need a cigarette. Who's got one?" His hands shook a little as he accepted it from Viken.

"But how could he—decide—anything?" choked the physicist. "He's been unconscious ever since Jan pulled him away from that . . . that thing."

"It was decided before then," said Cornelius. "As a matter of fact, that hulk in there on the operating table no longer has a mind. I know. I was there." He shuddered a little. A stiff shot of tranquilizer was all that held nightmare away from him. Later he would have to have that memory exorcised.

The doctor took a long drag of smoke, held it in his lungs a moment, and exhaled gustily. "I guess this winds up the project." he said. "We'll never get another esman."

"I'll say we won't." Viken's tone sounded rusty. "I'm going to smash that devil's engine myself."

"Hold on a minute!" exclaimed Cornelius. "Don't you understand? This isn't the end. It's the beginning!"

"I'd better get back," said the doctor. He stubbed out his cigarette and went through the door. It closed behind him with a deathlike quietness.

"What do you mean?" Viken said it as if erecting a barrier.

"Won't you understand?" roared Cornelius. "Joe has all Anglesey's habits, thoughts, memories, prejudices, interests. Oh, yes, the different body and the different environment— they do cause some changes, but no more than any man might undergo on Earth. If you were suddenly cured of a wasting disease, wouldn't you maybe get a little boisterous and rough? There is nothing abnormal in it. Nor is it abnormal to want to stay healthy—no? Do you see?"

Viken sat down. He spent a while without speaking.

Then, enormously slow and careful: "Do you mean Joe is Ed?"

"Or Ed is Joe. Whatever you like. He calls himself Joe now, I think—as a symbol of freedom—but he is still himself. What *is* the ego but continuity of existence?

"He himself did not fully understand this. He only knew— he told me, and I should have believed him—that on Jupiter he was strong and happy. Why did the K tube oscillate? A hysterical symptom! Anglesey's subconscious was not afraid to stay on Jupiter—it was afraid to come back!

"And then, today, I listened in. By now, his whole self was focused on Joe. That is, the primary source of libido was Joe's virile body, not Anglesey's sick one. This meant a different pattern of impulses—not too alien to pass the filters, but alien enough to set up interference. So he felt my presence. And he saw the truth, just as I did.

"Do you know the last emotion I felt as Joe threw me out of his mind? Not anger any more. He plays rough, him, but all he had room to feel was joy.

"I *knew* how strong a personality Anglesey has! Whatever made me think an overgrown child brain like Joe's could override it? In there, the doctors—bah! They're trying to salvage a hulk which has been shed because it is useless!"

Cornelius stopped. His throat was quite raw from talking. He paced the floor, rolled cigar smoke around his mouth but did not draw it any farther in.

When a few minutes had passed, Viken said cautiously,

"All right. You should know—as you said, you were there. But what do we do now? How do we get in touch with Ed? Will he even be interested in contacting us?"

"Oh, yes, of course," said Cornelius. "He is still himself, remember. Now that he has none of the cripple's frustration, he should be more amiable. When the novelty of his new friends wears off, he will want someone who can talk to him as an equal."

"And precisely who will operate another pseudo?" asked Viken sarcastically. "I'm quite happy with this skinny frame of mine, thank you!"

"Was Anglesey the only hopeless cripple on Earth?" asked Cornelius quietly.

Viken gaped at him.

"And there are aging men, too," went on the psionicist, half to himself. "Someday, my friend, when you and I feel the years close in, and so much we would like to learn—maybe we too would enjoy an extra lifetime in a Jovian body." He nodded at his cigar. "A hard, lusty, stormy kind of life, granted—dangerous, brawling, violent—but life as no human, perhaps, has lived it since the days of Elizabeth the First. Oh, yes, there will be small trouble finding Jovians."

He turned his head as the surgeon came out again.

"Well?" croaked Viken.

The doctor sat down. "It's finished," he said.

They waited for a moment, awkwardly.

"Odd," said the doctor. He groped after a cigarette he didn't have. Silently, Viken offered him one. "Odd. I've seen these cases before. People who simply resign from life. This is the first one I ever saw that went out smiling—smiling all the time."

7.

MARVELOUS INVENTIONS

Mark Twain, perhaps the only authentic literary genius America has produced, was a literary volcano from his thirty-seventh to his seventy-fourth year. He wrote novels, travel books, essays, diatribes, letters, memoirs. He wrote realistic contemporary fiction, historical fiction (probably his weakest line, though he loved it best), satiric fantasy, and science fiction. His A Connecticut Yankee in King Arthur's Court *is a rigorously worked-out story of extrapolation, on a theme L. Sprague de Camp was later to use in* Lest Darkness Fall: *What happens when a modern man, thrown back in time, tries to change history?*

And here is a story, first published in Century, *November 1898, in which Twain forecast an invention whose large staring eye you have probably turned off in order to read this book.*

FROM THE LONDON TIMES OF 1904

BY MARK TWAIN

CHICAGO, April 1, 1904.

I resume by cable-telephone where I left off yesterday. For many hours, now, this vast city—along with the rest of the globe, of course—has talked of nothing but the extraordinary episode mentioned in my last report. In accordance with your instructions, I will now trace the romance from its beginnings down to the culmination of yesterday—or today; call it which you like. By an odd chance, I was a personal actor in a part of this drama myself. The opening scene plays in Vienna. Date, one o'clock in the morning, March 31, 1898. I had spent the evening at a social entertainment. About midnight I went away, in company with the military attachés of the British, Italian, and American embassies, to finish with a late smoke. This function had been appointed to take place in the house of Lieutenant Hillyer, the third attaché mentioned in the above list. When we arrived there we found several visitors in the room: young Szczepanik;* Mr. K., his financial backer; Mr. W., the latter's secretary; and Lieutenant Clayton of the United States army. War was at that time threatening between Spain and our country, and Lieutenant Clayton had been sent to Europe on military business. I was well acquainted with young Szczepanik and his two friends, and I knew Mr. Clayton slightly. I had met him at West Point years before, when he was a cadet. It was when General Merritt was superintendent. He had the reputation of being an able officer, and also of being quick-tempered and plain-spoken.

This smoking-party had been gathered together partly for business. This business was to consider the availability of the telelectroscope for military service. It sounds oddly enough now, but it is nevertheless true that at that time the invention was not taken seriously by anyone except its inventor. Even his financial supporter regarded it merely as a curious and interesting toy. Indeed, he was so convinced of this that he had actually postponed its use by the general world to the end of the dying century by granting a two years' exclusive lease of it to a syndicate, whose intent was to exploit it at the Paris World's Fair.

When we entered the smoking-room we found Lieutenant Clayton and Szczepanik engaged in a warm talk over the telelectroscope in the German tongue. Clayton was saying:

"Well, you know *my* opinion of it, anyway!" And he brought his fist down with emphasis upon the table.

"And I do not value it," retorted the young inventor, with provoking calmness of tone and manner.

Clayton turned to Mr. K., and said:

* Pronounced (approximately) *Zepa*nik.

"*I* cannot see why you are wasting money on this toy. In my opinion, the day will never come when it will do a farthing's worth of real service for any human being."

"That may be; yes, that may be; still, I have put the money in it, and am content. I think, myself, that it is only a toy; but Szczepanik claims more for it, and I know him well enough to believe that he can see farther than I can—either with his telelectroscpe or without it."

The soft answer did not cool Clayton down; it seemed only to irritate him the more; and he repeated and emphasized his conviction that the invention would never do any man a farthing's worth of real service. He even made it a "brass" farthing, this time. Then he laid an English farthing on the table, and added:

"Take that, Mr. K., and put it away; and if ever the telelectroscope does any man an actual service—mind, a *real* service—please mail it to me as a reminder, and I will take back what I have been saying. Will you?"

"I will." And Mr. K. put the coin in his pocket.

Mr. Clayton now turned toward Szczepanik, and began with a taunt—a taunt which did not reach a finish; Szczepanik interrupted it with a hardy retort, and followed this with a blow. There was a brisk fight for a moment or two; then the attachés separated the men.

The scene now changes to Chicago. Time, the autumn of 1901. As soon as the Paris contract released the telelectroscope, it was delivered to public use, and was soon connected with the telephonic systems of the whole world. The improved "limitless-distance" telephone was presently introduced, and the daily doings of the globe made visible to everybody, and audibly discussable, too, by witnesses separated by any number of leagues.

By and by Szczepanik arrived in Chicago. Clayton (now captain) was serving in that military department at the time. The two men resumed the Viennese quarrel of 1898. On three different occasions they quarreled, and were separated by witnesses. Then came an interval of two months, during which time Szczepanik was not seen by any of his friends, and it was at first supposed that he had gone off on a sightseeing tour and would soon be heard from. But no; no word came from him. Then it was supposed that he had returned to Europe. Still, time drifted on, and he was not heard from.

Nobody was troubled, for he was like most inventors and other kinds of poets, and went and came in a capricious way, and often without notice.

Now comes the tragedy. On the 29th of December, in a dark and unused compartment of the cellar under Captain Clayton's house, a corpse was discovered by one of Clayton's maid-servants. It was easily identified as Szczepanik's. The man had died by violence. Clayton was arrested, indicted, and brought to trial, charged with this murder. The evidence against him was perfect in every detail, and absolutely unassailable. Clayton admitted this himself. He said that a reasonable man could not examine this testimony with a dispassionate mind and not be convinced by it; yet the man would be in error, nevertheless. Clayton swore that he did not commit the murder, and that he had had nothing to do with it.

As your readers will remember, he was condemned to death. He had numerous and powerful friends, and they worked hard to save him, for none of them doubted the truth of his assertion. I did what little I could to help, for I had long since become a close friend of his, and thought I knew that it was not in his character to inveigle an enemy into a corner and assassinate him. During 1902 and 1903 he was several times reprieved by the governor; he was reprieved once more in the beginning of the present year, and the execution-day postponed to March 31.

The governor's situation has been embarrassing, from the day of the condemnation, because of the fact that Clayton's wife is the governor's niece. The marriage took place in 1899, when Clayton was thirty-four and the girl twenty-three, and has been a happy one. There is one child, a little girl three years old. Pity for the poor mother and child kept the mouths of grumblers closed at first; but this could not last forever—for in America politics has a hand in everything—and by and by the governor's political opponents began to call attention to his delay in allowing the law to take its course. These hints have grown more and more frequent of late, and more and more pronounced. As a natural result, his own party grew nervous. Its leaders began to visit Springfield and hold long private conferences with him. He was now between two fires. On the one hand, his niece was imploring him to pardon her husband; on the other were the leaders, insisting that he stand to his plain duty as chief magistrate of the State, and place no further bar to Clayton's execution. Duty won in the struggle, and the governor gave his word that he would not again respite the condemned man. This was two weeks ago. Mrs. Clayton now said:

"Now that you have given your word, my last hope is gone, for I know you will never go back from it. But you have done the best you could for John, and I have no reproaches for you. You love him, and you love me, and we both know that if you could honorably save him, you would do it. I will go to him now, and be what help I can to him, and get what comfort I may out of the few days that are left to us before the night comes which will have no end for me in life. You will be with me that day? You will not let me bear it alone?"

"I will take you to him myself, poor child, and I will be near you to the last."

By the governor's command, Clayton was now allowed every indulgence he might ask for which could interest his mind and soften the hardships of his imprisonment. His wife and child spent the days with him; I was his companion by night. He was removed from the narrow cell which he had occupied during such a dreary stretch of time, and given the chief warden's roomy and comfortable quarters. His mind was always busy with the catastrophe of his life, and with the slaughtered inventor, and he now took the fancy that he would like to have the telelectroscope and divert his mind with it. He had his wish. The connection was made with the international telephone-station, and day by day, and night by night, he called up one corner of the globe after another, and looked upon its life, and studied its strange sights, and spoke with its people, and realized that by grace of this marvelous instrument he was almost as free as the birds of the air, although a prisoner under locks and bars. He seldom spoke, and I never interrupted him when he was absorbed in this amusement. I sat in his parlor and read and smoked, and the nights were very quiet and reposefully sociable, and I found them pleasant. Now and then I would hear him say, "Give me Yedo"; next, "Give me Hong-Kong"; next, "Give me Melbourne." And I smoked on, and read in comfort, while he wandered about the remote under-world, where the sun was shining in the sky, and the people were at their daily work. Sometimes the talk that came from those far regions through the microphone attachment interested me, and I listened.

Yesterday—I keep calling it yesterday, which is quite natural for certain reasons—the instrument remained unused, and that, also, was natural, for it was the eve of the execution-day. It was spent in tears and lamentations and farewells. The governor and the wife and child remained until a quarter past eleven at night, and the scenes I witnessed were pitiful to see. The execution was to take place at four in the morning. A little after eleven a sound of hammering broke out upon the still night, and there was a glare of light, and the child cried out, "What is that, papa?" and ran to the window before she could be stopped, and clapped her small hands, and said: "Oh, come and see, mama—such a pretty thing they are making!" The mother knew—and fainted. It was the gallows!

She was carried away to her lodging, poor woman, and Clayton and I were alone—alone, and thinking, brooding, dreaming. We might have been statues, we sat so motionless and still. It was a wild night, for winter was come again for a moment, after the habit of this region in the early spring. The sky was starless and black, and a strong wind was blowing from the lake. The silence in the room was so deep that all outside sounds seemed exaggerated by contrast with it. These sounds were fitting ones; they harmonized with the situation and the conditions: the boom and thunder of sudden storm-gusts among the roofs and chimneys, then the dying down into moanings and wailings about the eaves and angles; now and then a gnashing and lashing rush of sleet along the window-panes; and always the muffled and uncanny hammering of the gallows-builders in the courtyard. After an age of this, another sound—far off, and coming smothered and faint through the riot of the tempest—a bell tolling twelve! Another age, and it tolled again. By and by, again. A dreary, long interval after this, then the spectral sound floated to us once more—one, two, three; and this time we caught our breath: sixty minutes of life left!

Clayton rose, and stood by the window, and looked up into the black sky, and listened to the thrashing sleet and the piping wind; then he said: "That a dying man's last of earth should be—this!" After a little he said: "I must see the sun again—the sun!" and the next moment he was feverishly calling: "China! Give me China—Peking!"

I was strangely stirred, and said to myself: "To think that it is a mere human being who does this unimaginable miracle —turns winter into summer, night into day, storm into calm, gives the freedom of the great globe to a prisoner in his cell, and the sun in his naked splendor to a man dying in Egyptian darkness!"

I was listening.

"What light! what brilliancy! what radiance! . . . This is Peking?"

"Yes."

"The time?"

"Mid-afternoon."

"What is the great crowd for, and in such gorgeous costumes? What masses and masses of rich color and barbaric magnificence! And how they flash and glow and burn in the flooding sunlight! What *is* the occasion of it all?"

"The coronation of our new emperor—the Czar."

"But I thought that that was to take place yesterday."

"This *is* yesterday—to you."

"Certainly it is. But my mind is confused, these days; there are reasons for it. . . . Is this the beginning of the procession?"

"Oh, no; it began to move an hour ago."

"Is there much more of it still to come?"

"Two hours of it. Why do you sigh?"

"Because I should like to see it all."

"And why can't you?"

"I have to go—presently."

"You have an engagement?"

After a pause, softly: "Yes." After another pause: "Who are these in the splendid pavilion?"

"The imperial family, and visiting royalties from here and there and yonder in the earth."

"And who are those in the adjoining pavilions to the right and left?"

"Ambassadors and their families and suites to the right; unofficial foreigners to the left."

"If you will be so good, I—"

Boom! That distant bell again, tolling the half-hour faintly through the tempest of wind and sleet. The door opened, and the governor and the mother and child entered—the woman in widow's weeds! She fell upon her husband's breast in a passion of sobs, and I—I could not stay; I could not bear it. I went into the bedchamber, and closed the door. I sat there waiting—waiting—waiting, and listening to the rattling sashes and the blustering of the storm. After what seemed a long, long time, I heard a rustle and movement in the parlor, and knew that the clergyman and the sheriff and the guard were come. There was some low-voiced talking; then a hush; then a prayer, with a sound of sobbing; presently, footfalls—the departure for the gallows; then the child's happy voice: "Don't cry *now*, mama, when we've got papa again, and taking him home."

The door closed; they were gone. I was ashamed: I was the only friend of the dying man that had no spirit, no courage. I stepped into the room, and said I would be a man and would follow. But we are made as we are made, and we cannot help it. I did not go.

I fidgeted about the room nervously, and presently went to the window, and softly raised it—drawn by that dread fascination which the terrible and the awful exert—and looked down upon the courtyard. By the garish light of the electric lamps I saw the little group of privileged witnesses, the wife crying on her uncle's breast, the condemned man standing on the scaffold with the halter around his neck, his arms strapped to his body, the black cap on his head, the sheriff at his side with his hand on the drop, the clergyman in front of him with bare head and his book in his hand.

"I am the resurrection and the life—"

I turned away. I could not listen; I could not look. I did not know whither to go or what to do. Mechanically, and without knowing it, I put my eye to that strange instrument, and there was Peking and the Czar's procession! The next moment I was leaning out of the window, gasping, suffocating, trying to speak, but dumb from the very imminence of the necessity of speaking. The preacher could speak, but I, who had such need of words—

"And may God have mercy upon your soul. Amen."

The sheriff drew down the black cap, and laid his hand upon the lever. I got my voice.

"Stop, for God's sake! The man is innocent. Come here and see Szczepanik face to face!"

Hardly three minutes later the governor had my place at the window, and was saying:

"Strike off his bonds and set him free!"

Three minutes later all were in the parlor again. The reader will imagine the scene; I have no need to describe it. It was a sort of mad orgy of joy.

A messenger carried word to Szczepanik in the pavilion, and one could see the distressed amazement dawn in his face as he listened to the tale. Then he came to his end of the line, and talked with Clayton and the governor and the others; and the wife poured out her gratitude upon him for saving her husband's life, and in her deep thankfulness she kissed him at twelve thousand miles' range.

The telelectrophonoscopes of the globe were put to service now, and for many hours the kings and queens of many realms (with here and there a reporter) talked with Szczepanik, and praised him; and the few scientific societies which had not already made him an honorary member conferred that grace upon him.

How had he come to disappear from among us? It was easily explained. He had not grown used to being a world-famous person, and had been forced to break away from the lionizing that was robbing him of all privacy and repose. So he grew a beard, put on colored glasses, disguised himself a little in other ways, then took a fictitious name, and went off to wander about the earth in peace.

Such is the tale of the drama which began with an inconsequential quarrel in Vienna in the spring of 1898, and came near ending as a tragedy in the spring of 1904.

MARK TWAIN.

CHICAGO, April 5, 1904.

To-day, by a clipper of the Electric Line, and the latter's Electric Railway connections, arrived an envelop from Vienna, for Captain Clayton, containing an English farthing. The receiver of it was a good deal moved. He called up Vienna, and stood face to face with Mr. K., and said:

"I do not need to say anything; you can see it all in my face. My wife has the farthing. Do not be afraid—she will not throw it away."

M.T.

CHICAGO, April 23, 1904.

Now that the after developments of the Clayton case have run their course and reached a finish, I will sum them up. Clayton's romantic escape from a shameful death steeped all this region in an enchantment of wonder and joy—during the proverbial nine days. Then the sobering process followed, and men began to take thought, and to say: "But *a man was killed,* and Clayton killed him." Others replied: "That is true: we have been overlooking that important detail; we have been led away by excitement."

The feeling soon became general that Clayton ought to be tried again. Measures were taken accordingly, and the proper representations conveyed to Washington; for in America, under the new paragraph added to the Constitution in 1899, second trials are not State affairs, but national, and must be tried by the most august body in the land—the Supreme Court of the United States. The justices were therefore summoned to sit in Chicago. The session was held day before yesterday, and was opened with the usual impressive formalities, the nine judges appearing in their black robes, and the new chief justice (Lemaitre) presiding. In opening the case, the chief justice said:

"It is my opinion that this matter is quite simple. The prisoner at the bar was charged with murdering the man Szczepanik; he was tried for murdering the man Szczepanik; he was fairly tried, and justly condemned and sentenced to death for murdering the man Szczepanik. It turns out that the man Szczepanik was not murdered at all. By the decision of the French courts in the Dreyfus matter, it is established beyond cavil or question that the decisions of courts are permanent and cannot be revised. We are obliged to respect and adopt this precedent. It is upon precedents that the enduring edifice of jurisprudence is reared. The prisoner at the bar has been fairly and righteously condemned to death for the murder of the man Szczepanik, and, in my opinion, there is but one course to pursue in the matter: he must be hanged."

Mr. Justice Crawford said:

"But, your Excellency, he was pardoned on the scaffold for that."

"The pardon is not valid, and cannot stand, because he was pardoned for killing a man whom he had not killed. A man cannot be pardoned for a crime which he has not committed; it would be an absurdity."

"But, your Excellency, he did kill a man."

"That is an extraneous detail; we have nothing to do with it. The court cannot take up this crime until the prisoner has expiated the other one."

Mr. Justice Halleck said:

"If we order his execution, your Excellency, we shall bring about a miscarriage of justice; for the governor will pardon him again."

"He will not have the power. He cannot pardon a man for a crime which he has not committed. As I observed before, it would be an absurdity."

After a consultation, Mr. Justice Wadsworth said:

"Several of us have arrived at the conclusion, your Excellency, that it would be an error to hang the prisoner for killing Szczepanik, but only for killing the other man, since it is proven that he did not kill Szczepanik."

"On the contrary, it is proved that he *did* kill Szczepanik. By the French precedent, it is plain that we must abide by the finding of the court."

"But Szczepanik is still alive."

"So is Dreyfus."

In the end it was found impossible to ignore or get around the French precedent. There could be but one result: Clayton was delivered over to the executioner. It made an immense excitement; the State rose as one man and clamored for Clayton's pardon and retrial. The governor issued the pardon, but the Supreme Court was in duty bound to annul it, and did so, and poor Clayton was hanged yesterday. The city is draped in black, and, indeed, the like may be said of the State. All America is vocal with scorn of "French justice," and of the malignant little soldiers who invented it and inflicted it upon the other Christian lands.

The stories of Jules Verne are among those which cannot be properly appreciated unless the reader first comes to them at a certain age. If you are past twenty and have not yet read Verne, I pity you: your opportunity is lost.

In an article called "The Watery Wonders of Captain Nemo," Theodore L. Thomas has written:

Years after reading the novel, people remember things from it that are not there. . . . Recently, a United States Patent Office official received an interesting inquiry. Was it true that a patent examiner had rejected the patent application of an inventor of a new periscope because of the periscope described by Jules Verne in *Twenty Thousand Leagues Under the Sea?* Well, the fact is that Verne is totally silent on the subject of periscopes in the novel; the *Nautilus* had no periscope. Another misremembered description concerns the storage batteries used aboard the *Nautilus*. There are none. . . . The novel leaves readers with the impression that it is a storehouse of advanced technology, and the impression grows as the reader ages.

Verne's method, in fact, was to deluge his reader with vague generalities and with page upon page of science ripped bodily out of textbooks: but he did know how to tell a fascinating story. Here, for proof, is the episode of the walk on the ocean floor, from Twenty Thousand Leagues *(1870).*

a selection from

TWENTY THOUSAND LEAGUES UNDER THE SEA

BY JULES VERNE

At the Captain's call two of the ship's crew came to help us to dress in these heavy and impervious clothes, made of India rubber without seam, and constructed expressly to resist considerable pressure. One would have thought it a suit of armor, both supple and resisting. This formed trousers and waistcoat. The trousers were finished off with thick boots, weighted with heavy leaden soles. The texture of the waistcoat was held together by bands of copper, which crossed the chest, protecting it from the great pressure of the water, and leaving the lungs free to act; the sleeves ended in gloves, which in no way restrained the movement of the hands. There was a vast difference noticeable between these consummate apparatuses and the old cork breastplates, jackets and other contrivances in vogue during the eighteenth century.

Captain Nemo and one of his companions (a sort of Hercules, who must have possessed great strength), Conseil and myself were soon enveloped in the dresses. There remained nothing more to be done but enclose our heads in the metal box. But before proceeding to this operation, I asked the Captain's permission to examine the guns we were to carry.

One of the *Nautilus* men gave me a simple gun, the butt end of which, made of steel, hollow in the center, was rather large. It served as a reservoir for compressed air, which a valve, worked by a spring, allowed to escape into a metal tube. A box of projectiles, in a groove in the thickness of the butt end, contained about twenty of these electric balls, which, by means of a spring, were forced into the barrel of the gun. As soon as one shot was fired, another was ready.

"Captain Nemo," said I, "this arm is perfect, and easily handled; I ask only to be allowed to try it. But how shall we gain the bottom of the sea?"

"At this moment, Professor, the *Nautilus* is stranded in five fathoms, and we have nothing to do but to start."

"But how shall we get off?"

"You shall see."

Captain Nemo thrust his head into the helmet, Conseil and I did the same, not without hearing an ironical "Good sport!" from the Canadian. The upper part of our dress terminated in a copper collar, upon which was screwed the metal helmet. Three holes, protected by thick glass, allowed us to see in all directions, by simply turning our heads in the interior of the headdress. As soon as it was in position, the Rouquayrol apparatus on our backs began to act; and, for my part, I could breathe with ease.

With the Ruhmkorff lamp hanging from my belt, and the gun in my hand, I was ready to set out. But to speak the truth, imprisoned in these heavy garments and glued to the deck by my leaden soles, it was impossible for me to take a step.

But this state of things was provided for. I felt myself being pushed into a little room next to the wardrobe room. My companions followed, towed along in the same way. I heard a watertight door, furnished with stopper plates, close upon us, and we were wrapped in profound darkness.

After some minutes, a loud hissing was heard. I felt the cold mount my feet to my chest. Evidently from some part of the vessel they had, by means of a tap, given entrance to the water, which was invading us, and with which the room was soon filled. A second door cut in the side of the *Nautilus* then opened. We saw a faint light. In another instant our feet trod the bottom of the sea.

And now, how can I retrace the impression left upon me by that walk under the waters? Words are impotent to relate such wonders! Captain Nemo walked in front, his companion followed some steps behind. Conseil and I remained near each other, as if an exchange of words had been possible through our metallic cases. I no longer felt the weight of my clothing, or of my shoes, of my reservoir of air or my thick helmet, in the midst of which my head rattled like an almond in its shell.

The light, which lit the soil thirty feet below the surface of the ocean, astonished me by its power. The solar rays shone through the watery mass easily and dissipated all color, and I clearly distinguished objects at a distance of a hundred and fifty yards. Beyond that the tints darkened into fine gradations of ultramarine and faded into vague obscurity. Truly this water which surrounded me was but another air denser than the terrestrial atmosphere, but almost as transparent. Above me was the calm surface of the sea.

We were walking on fine, even sand, not wrinkled as on a flat shore, which retains the impression of the billows. This dazzling carpet, really a reflector, repelled the rays of the sun with wonderful intensity, which accounted for the vibration which penetrated every atom of liquid. Shall I be believed when I say that, at the depth of thirty feet, I could see as if I were in broad daylight?

For a quarter of an hour I trod on this sand sown with the impalpable dust of shells. The hull of the *Nautilus,* resembling a long shoal, disappeared by degrees; but its lantern, when darkness should overtake us in the waters, would help to guide us on board by its distinct rays.

. . . The ground was still on the incline; its declivity seemed to be getting greater and to be leading us to greater depths. It must have been about three o'clock when we reached a narrow valley, between high perpendicular walls, situated about seventy-five fathoms deep. Thanks to the perfection of our apparatus, we were forty-five fathoms below the limit which nature seems to have imposed on man as to his submarine excursions.

I say seventy-five fathoms, though I had no instrument

by which to judge the distance. But I knew that even in the clearest waters the solar rays could not penetrate farther. And accordingly the darkness deepened. At ten paces not an object was visible. I was groping my way, when I suddenly saw a brilliant white light. Captain Nemo had just put his electric apparatus into use; his companion did the same, and Conseil and I followed their example. By turning a screw I established a communication between the wire and the spiral glass, and the sea, lit by our four lanterns, was illuminated for a circle of thirty-six yards.

Captain Nemo was still plunging into the dark depths of the forest, whose trees were getting scarcer at every step. I noticed that vegetable life disappeared sooner than animal life. The medusae had already abandoned the arid soil, from which a great number of animals, zoophytes, articulata, molluscs, and fishes still obtained sustenance.

As we walked, I thought the light of our Ruhmkorff apparatus could not fail to draw some inhabitant from its dark couch. But if they did approach us, they at least kept at a respectful distance from the hunters. Several times I saw Captain Nemo stop, put his gun to his shoulder and after some moments drop it and walk on. At last, after about four hours, this marvelous excursion came to an end. A wall of superb rocks in an imposing mass rose before us, a heap of gigantic blocks, an enormous, steep granite shore, forming dark grottoes, but presenting no practicable slope; it was the prop of the Island of Crespo. It was the earth! Captain Nemo stopped suddenly. A gesture of his brought us all to a halt, and, however desirous I might be to scale the wall, I was obliged to stop. Here ended Captain Nemo's domains. And he would not go beyond them. Farther on was a portion of the globe he might not trample upon.

The return began. Captain Nemo had returned to the head of his little band, directing their course without hesitation. I thought we were not following the same route to return to the *Nautilus*. The new road was very steep, and consequently very painful. . . . For one hour a plain of sand lay stretched before us. Sometimes it rose to within two yards and some inches of the surface of the water. I then saw our image clearly reflected, drawn inversely, and above us appeared an identical group reflecting our movements and our actions—in a word, like us in every point, except that they walked with their heads downward and their feet in the air.

Another effect I noticed was the passage of thick clouds which formed and vanished rapidly; but on reflection I understood that these seeming clouds were due to the varying thickness of the reeds at the bottom, and I could even see the fleecy foam which their broken tops multiplied on the water, and the shadows of large birds passing above our heads, whose rapid flight I could discern on the surface of the sea.

On this occasion, I was witness to one of the finest gunshots which ever made the nerves of a hunter thrill. A large bird of great breadth of wing, clearly visible, approached, hovering over us. Captain Nemo's companion shouldered his gun and fired when it was only a few yards above the waves. The creature fell stunned, and the force of its fall brought it within the reach of the dextrous hunter's grasp. It was an albatross of the finest kind.

Our march had not been interrupted by this incident. For two hours we followed these sandy plains, then fields of algae very disagreeable to cross. Candidly, I could do no more when I saw a glimmer of light, which, for a half mile, broke the darkness of the waters. It was the lantern of the *Nautilus*. . . .

I had remained some steps behind, when I presently saw Captain Nemo coming hurriedly toward me. With his strong hand he bent me to the ground, his companion doing the same to Conseil. At first I knew not what to think of this sudden attack, but I was soon reassured by seeing the Captain lie down beside me and remain immovable.

I was stretched on the ground, just under shelter of a bush of algae, when, raising my head, I saw some enormous mass, casting phosphorescent gleams, pass blusteringly by.

My blood froze in my veins as I recognized two formidable sharks . . . It was a couple of tintoreas, terrible creatures, with enormous tails and a dull glassy stare, the phosphorescent matter ejected from holes pierced around the muzzle. Monstrous brutes which would crush a whole man in their iron jaws. I did not know whether Conseil stopped to classify them; for my part, I noticed their silver bellies, and their huge mouths bristling with teeth, from a very unscientific point of view, and more as a possible victim than as a naturalist.

Happily the voracious creatures do not see well. They

passed without seeing us, brushing us with their brownish fins, and we escaped by a miracle from a danger certainly greater than meeting a tiger full face in the forest. Half an hour after, guided by the electric light, we reached the *Nautilus*. The outside door had been left open, and Captain Nemo closed it as soon as we had entered the first cell. He then pressed a knob. I heard the pumps working in the midst of the vessel, I felt the water sinking from around me, and in a few moments the cell was entirely empty. The inside door then opened, and we entered the vestry.

There our diving dress was taken off, not without some trouble; and, fairly worn out from want of food and sleep, I returned to my room, in great wonder at this surprising excursion at the bottom of the sea.

Among those who wrote about television before it came into existence were Hugo Gernsback, Theodore Sturgeon and John W. Campbell, Jr. (who said it would never be popular); after it happened, most stories in which it appeared took the form of virtuous yelps of disapproval, like "The Pedestrian," by Ray Bradbury (whose television credits cannot be listed here for lack of space).

Almost alone among the new crop of s.f. writers, Will Stanton does not view with alarm our habit of sitting glassy-eyed in front of an electronic box. On the contrary, he suggests that with a little more refinement, and a certain amount of luck, TV may become preferable to, and indistinguishable from, "real life."

YOU ARE WITH IT!

BY WILL STANTON

"The deep freeze has been acting up again." Kay Dobbs slid into the breakfast nook across from her husband. "I wish you'd call the man as soon as you get to the office."

Stanley Dobbs folded his paper to the editorial page. "All right."

"Tell him it hasn't worked right since the last time he was here." She reached across and folded back a corner of the paper to examine an advertisement for handbags. "Did you remember to call your friend about the speaker for the P.T.A.?"

"I'll do it first thing."

"Better phone the phone company too. Find out about that long-distance call they charged us for."

"Yes, I'd better do that."

"I think it makes more of an impression coming from a man," Kay said.

Stanley backed his car out to the street. Kay waved goodbye from the picture window. It was the custom in Belle Acres for wives to wave goodbye from their picture windows.

At the end of the block Stanley joined a small stream of commuters winding their way down to the station. Here, along with the members of other tributaries, they were picked up by the train much like a river picking up silt to be deposited at the end of its run.

Stanley was reviewing his schedule for the day as he stepped into his office and closed the door. Immediately he was aware of certain changes. In fact, the office bore slight resemblance to the room he had left the night before. It was more like a half-lighted stage with billows of mist rising from various points on the floor. In the center, seated at a small round table, was a solitary figure in evening clothes. When he spoke his voice had a hollow, artificial quality, rather like an actor rehearsing in the bottom of a well.

"How do you do?" he remarked in a faintly bogus British accent. "Won't you join me? For the next ninety minutes I am to be your host."

"How do you do?" said Stanley. He hesitated and then walked over, placed his hat and briefcase on the table and sat down.

"You are now where no mortal has ever been." The Host was projecting his voice as if addressing a vast audience. "You are just over the horizon. The exact spot? Well, you won't find it on any map, nor the date on any calendar."

"It's the seventeenth," said Stanley. "Tuesday."

"It is twenty-five hours past midnight on the thirty-first of

November," said the Host. "You are about to start your perilous journey into the unknown."

Stanley looked at his watch. "I did have a couple of phone calls to make—"

The Host smiled. "Perhaps I have been needlessly mystifying you," he remarked in a more conversational tone. "This, as you may have guessed, is a new sort of television program. It is a combination of adventure, supernatural and audience participation. A chap from Duke University suggested it."

Stanley nodded politely. "It sounds very interesting."

"It is more than interesting," said the Host. "It is voodoo, black magic and witchcraft brought into every home through the marvels of modern communication. For the first time a member of the viewing audience will actually be able to take part in the violence and terror that have brought happiness to so many."

"I'm afraid I haven't been keeping up with TV lately," Stanley admitted. "Since we put in the new patio we've been sitting out there a great deal."

"When the time comes you will know what to do," the Host assured him. "You are not being asked to play a part—you are going to live the part. Mr. Stanley Dobbs—You Are With It!" The last words were picked up by echoing voices and repeated in tones that faded with the light until Stanley found himself alone in the dark and the silence.

As the lights came on again Stanley discovered he was standing beneath the marquee of a night club. The doorman bowed. "The Commissioner was here looking for you," he said.

Nodding absently, Stanley went inside and sat down at a quiet table in the corner. There was a good crowd present, eating, drinking and listening to the music of Arabella and her All-Girl Orchestra.

After a moment he was joined by the proprietress—Big Yvette. "We haven't seen you for quite a while," she observed.

He shrugged. "You know how it is."

"Yes, I know." Big Yvette placed her hand on his. "I worry about you."

"I have a job to do," Stanley said.

"I suppose we shouldn't complain about that," she said, "with so much unemployment and all."

A waiter approached the table. He was carrying a bottle of

Napoleon brandy. "Compliments of Arabella and her All-Girl Orchestra," he explained.

"Oh." Abruptly he realized that the music had stopped.

"They're backstage," the waiter told him.

"I'd like to thank them," Stanley said. He went back and entered the dressing room.

The orchestra leader looked up with a cry of delight. "Darling, we've missed you." She put her arms around his neck.

"I just wanted to thank you," he said, "before I left."

"Before you left?"

He nodded. "I have a job to do."

"Oh." There was disappointment in her voice. "We were hoping you could come up to our place after the show."

"Our place?" he repeated.

"We share an apartment." She indicated the other members of the band. "We've taken the top floor of the U.N. Hilton."

"Let's just say I'll make it if I can," he said. "You know I'd like to."

Her arms tightened around his neck. "You really mean it?"

He looked down into her eyes. Turning his head, he looked into the eyes of Francine and Iris and Millie-Jo and Ursula and Gretchen and Dee and Carlotta and the rest. "I mean it," he said.

Outside the club he caught a taxi. "I got a message for you," the driver told him, "from the Big Boy himself. He said to lay off."

"He did?" said Stanley, coolly lighting a cigarette. "I heard the Big Boy was knocked off last week."

"He was," the driver said. "But I been in bed with a cold. This is the first chance I had to deliver the message."

"Let me out at the next corner," Stanley said. He paid the driver. "Better take care of that cold," he said.

"They say summer colds are the worst kind," the driver said.

Stanley went into a vacant garage and down three flights of stairs and rapped on the door. It was opened by a man whose face was known to no more than three or four persons in the entire country.

"Good evening, Chief," Stanley said, following him into the luxuriously appointed office.

"I don't believe you have met the Contessa." The Chief gestured toward a beautiful young woman sitting at one side of the room in an ermine wrap. "She will accompany you as far as Budapest. After that you will be on your own."

Stanley bowed. The Chief unrolled a map. "We have learned that the secret police are holding the Professor in a fortress at this spot. It will be your job to get him out of the country unharmed. You will follow our standard procedure in dealing with the guards. As for the electric fence, the dogs and the mine fields, you will no doubt wish to use your own methods."

"It seems pretty much routine," Stanley said. "I should think one of your regular operatives could handle the job."

"The Professor himself presents no particular problem," the Chief conceded. "However, smuggling his cyclotron out of the country may prove more difficult. I think it only fair to warn you that it may involve considerable risk."

Stanley shrugged. "That's what I get paid for."

"So you do." The Chief put down the map and picked up his pipe. "Is that the real reason you do it?" he inquired casually. "For the money?"

Stanley smiled a tight, cryptic little smile. "There are certain persons who criticize what we call the American way of life. I don't happen to be among them. And when something threatens that way of life—" he paused to smile again—"I do what has to be done."

The Chief nodded. "How soon can you leave?" he asked.

The next morning Stanley was late coming down to breakfast. "You'll have to hurry or you'll miss your train," his wife said.

Stanley swallowed his juice. "If I have to hurry I'll hurry," he said, "I've done it before."

"I wish you didn't have to work late so often," Kay said, "I didn't even hear you come in."

"I didn't notice the time."

"I don't suppose you remembered to call the deep-freeze man? Well, we're going to have to do something about the water softener too."

"All right."

"I've made out a list," she said. "I've put it in your breast pocket. For one thing I think you ought to call several boarding kennels. You know how busy they're going to be at vacation time, and last year I'm sure they didn't remember to give Mr. Toidy his grated carrots."

"I'll make a point of that," he said.

"I simply can't stand it when an animal doesn't receive proper care," she said. "It does something to me."

Stanley was a little late getting to the office, but the truck was waiting. He climbed up in the cab beside the driver. "Do you know that old warehouse down on Sixth?" he asked.

The driver nodded. "Sure, but it won't be open this time of night."

"I've got a tip that they're running a brewery there," Stanley said. "How much speed can you get out of this truck?"

"Could be fifty—maybe fifty-five," the driver said. He revved up the engine. "It ought to be enough to break through the doors."

"It's worth a try," Stanley said.

They rammed the doors and came to a halt in the middle of the warehouse. On both sides of them were rows of barrels. There was no one in sight.

Stanley seized an ax and handed one to the driver. "I'll take this side and you take that one," he said. Raising the ax, he drove it into the top of the first barrel. Then he went on to the next. He and the driver reached the end of their rows at the same time. He leaned his ax against the wall. "How's it going?" he asked.

The driver wiped his forehead. "All the barrels on this side got dishes in them," he said.

"Same here," Stanley said. "It looks like somebody gave me a wrong steer."

"Well," said the driver, "you can't win them all."

Stanley rolled down his sleeves. "There's just one other possibility," he said.

In the gambling room Stanley moved from table to table, killing time. One of the dealers beckoned. "The Boss wants to see you," he said. "Upstairs."

Stanley nodded. Upstairs the door was opened by a hard-faced man, who motioned him inside. The Boss was seated at the head of a long table. On either side were assembled all the notorious names of the underworld.

"We've been expecting you," the Boss remarked in a silky

tone. He moved his hand to indicate the others. "I believe you may know some of these gentlemen."

"I believe so." Stanley nodded. "Abdul . . . Agasis . . . Albrecht . . . Alvarado . . . Andradi . . . Antorski . . . Aristides . . . Aspasian . . ."

"Yes," said the Boss, "now, then——"

"Bakunin . . . Baldini . . . Bauman . . ." Stanley continued strolling beside the table. "Beckhold . . . Bernardo . . . Bjornstrom . . . Black Eagle . . ."

"Let's get down to business," the Boss said. "You'll find a package at the end of the table."

Stanley gave it a casual glance. "What's in it?"

"What does it look like?"

Stanley opened the package. "It looks like two and a half million dollars," he said, "in small bills." He tossed it back on the table.

"It's yours," the Boss said. "Take it. Go on a vacation somewhere."

"Perhaps I forgot to tell you," Stanley said. "I have a job to do."

The Boss studied him, his eyes narrowed. "We'll double it."

Stanley returned the stare. "There is such a thing as the American Dream," he remarked softly, "and when any group or organization threatens to destroy it, well——" he smiled briefly—"there are a few of us who do what we can."

"So?" The Boss's voice was dangerously low. "You would really like to believe we would all allow you to leave here alive?"

"Say that again." Stanley was playing for time. He shot a lightning glance around the room, calculating the odds. He had got out of tighter corners, and the element of surprise was on his side. He closed his eyes for a moment, his mind rapidly formulating a plan.

When he woke up, Kay was in the kitchen. He could smell the coffee. "Did you remember to check with the man about the garage door?" she asked when he was at the table.

"He wasn't in."

"I wish you didn't have to spend so much time at the office," Kay said.

He reached for the marmalade. "I have a job to do."

"I know, but you don't have to kill yourself."

He put marmalade on a piece of toast. "That's true."

"The insurance is due today," she said.

At the door of his office he paused for a moment and then went in. The Lieutenant looked up from his desk. "Sorry to bother you," he said, "but this one really has us stopped."

"Is that so?" Stanley sat on the corner of the desk. "Fill me in."

The Lieutenant lifted his hand helplessly. "What is there to tell? The man was found on the steps of Grant's Tomb. Young, well dressed, no signs of violence, no identification, no witnesses. The autopsy showed him to be in perfect health—if he'd been alive, that is."

"I see. Then you don't have any idea what killed him?"

The Lieutenant got to his feet, pacing across the room. "I've stopped having ideas," he said. "Maybe we killed him. Society—maybe that did it. There seems to be a new sickness now—no goals, no ideals, nothing to live for. Maybe one of these days we'll all just stop living."

"Well, Lieutenant," Stanley remarked, "I don't see why you don't just throw in the sponge. Enjoy yourself while you can."

The Lieutenant gave him an irritated glance. "Don't talk crazy. I'm getting paid to do a job."

"You say there was no identification on the body?"

The Lieutenant shook his head wearily. "No wallet, no keys, no letters—nothing but this." He picked up a slip of paper from the desk. "This was in his breast pocket. It appears to be some kind of code, but the boys in the cipher room haven't been able to break it yet." He tossed it across the desk.

Stanley picked it up and started to read. " 'Deep fr.— board ken.—P.T.A.—phone phone co.—gar. Dr.—pay ins—' " His eyes traveled to the bottom of the paper; there seemed to be about forty entries. Somewhere in the back of his mind was an elusive wisp of meaning.

"Does it mean anything?" the Lieutenant asked quickly.

"The pieces are all here," he said slowly, "or most of the pieces. If I can put them together—"

"Sorry, gentlemen, I'm afraid it's all over."

The two men looked up, startled, to see a shadowy figure in the doorway. It was the Host.

"All over?" The Lieutenant stared. "What do you mean?"

"The show," replied the Host. "At the last minute the sponsor changed his mind."

"The sponsor?" Stanley said.

"Actually the sponsor's wife, I believe, but that is neither here nor there. At any rate, you are now free to return to your normal everyday lives."

Stanley turned slowly toward the Lieutenant. "Our normal, everyday lives."

"Quite right," said the Host briskly. "And now if you will turn in any props you may have—"

Stanley reached in his pocket and drew out the pistol.

"Is it loaded?" the Host inquired. "You'd better empty it."

"Yes," Stanley said, "perhaps that would be best." When the gun was empty he dropped it on the desk.

The Lieutenant looked thoughtfully at the figure on the floor. "Sometimes we have to do things we don't like," he observed. "It's all part of the job."

"I know." Stanley picked up the slip of paper from the desk. He folded it carefully, then leaned over the body and tucked the paper in the breast pocket.

"There *is* such a thing as the American Dream," the Lieutenant continued softly, "and when someone threatens to destroy it—"

"We do what has to be done," Stanley said. He put the gun back in his pocket. "I guess that wraps it up."

The Lieutenant frowned. "There's still one detail. I hate to ask you, but we have to get telephotos of a certain office. The only place they can be taken from is the top floor of the U.N. Hilton. It will mean being confined there for a week or more—"

Stanley shrugged. "As you said, Lieutenant, it's all part of the job." He turned then, and walked slowly into the night.

The weapon to end war is an old and bitter joke; poison gas and nuclear bombs, although "too frightful to use in war," have been used. But suppose someone should invent an anti-weapon—a device that would keep all other modern instruments of destruction from being used. What then?

Here is a queerly impressive picture of the creative mind at work, a vivid and plausible glimpse of the next war, and a question whose answer is not as obvious as it seems.

CEASE FIRE

BY FRANK HERBERT

Snow slanted across the frozen marshland, driven in fitful gusts. It drifted in a low mound against the wooden observation post. The antennae of the Life Detector atop the O.P. swept back and forth in a rhythmic half circle like so many frozen sticks brittle with rime ice.

The snow hid all distance, distorted substance into gray shadows without definition. A suggestion of brightness to the north indicated the sun that hung low on the horizon even at midnight in this season.

Out of possible choices of a place for a world-shattering invention to be born, this did not appear in the running.

A rifle bullet spanged against an abandoned tank northeast of the O.P., moaned away into the distance. The bullet only emphasized the loneliness, the isolation of the O.P. set far out ahead of the front lines on the Arctic battlefields of 1972. Behind the post to the south stretched the long reaches of the Canadian Barren Grounds. An arm of the Arctic Ocean below Banks Island lay hidden in the early snowstorm to the north.

One operator—drugged to shivering wakefulness—stood watch in the O.P. The space around him was barely six feet in diameter, crammed with equipment, gridded screens glowing a pale green with spots that indicated living flesh: a covey of ptarmigan, a possible Arctic fox. Every grid point on the screens held an aiming code for mortar fire.

This site was designated O.P. 114 by the Allied command. It was no place for the sensitive man who had found himself pushed, shunted and shamed into this position of terror. The fact that he did occupy O.P. 114 only testified to the terrible urgencies that governed this war.

Again a rifle bullet probed the abandoned tank. Corporal Larry Hulser, crouched over the O.P.'s screens, tried to get a track on the bullet. It had seemed to come from the life-glow spot he had identified as probably an Arctic fox.

Much too small for a human, he thought. Or is it?

The green glow of the screens underlighted Hulser's dark face, swept shadows upward where they merged with his black hair. He chewed his lip, his eyes darting nervously with the fear he could never hide, the fear that made him the butt of every joke back at the barracks.

Hulser did not look like a man who could completely transform his society. He looked merely like an indefinite lump of humanity encased in a Life Detector shield, crouching in weird green shadows.

In the distant days of his youth, one of Hulser's chemistry professors had labeled him during a faculty tea "a mystic—sure to fail in the modern world."

The glow spot Hulser had identified as a fox shifted its position.

Should I call out the artillery? Hulser wondered. No. This could be the one they'd choose to investigate with a flying detector. And if the pilot identified the glow as a fox . . . Hulser cringed with the memory of the hazing he had taken on the wolf he'd reported two months earlier.

"Wolfie Hulser!"

I'm too old for this game, he thought. Thirty-eight is too old. If there were only some way to end—

Another rifle bullet spanged against the shattered tank. Hulser tried to crouch lower in the tiny wooden O.P. The bullets were like questing fingers reaching out for unrecognized metal—to identify an O.P. When the bullets found their mark, a single 200-mm. mortar shell followed, pinpointed by echo phones. Or it could be as it had been with Breck Wingate, another observer.

Hulser shivered at the memory.

They had found Wingate slumped forward across his instruments, a neat hole through his chest from side to side just below the armpits. Wind had whistled through the wall of the O.P. from a single bullet hole beside Wingate. The enemy had found him and never known.

Hulser glanced up nervously at the plywood walls, all that shielded him from the searching bullets—a wood shell designed to absorb the metal seekers and send back the sound of a bullet hitting a snowdrift. A rolled wad of plot paper filled a hole made on some other watch near the top of the dome.

Again Hulser shivered.

And again a bullet spanged against the broken tank. Then the ground rumbled and shook as a mortar shell zeroed the tank.

Discouraging us from using it as an O.P., thought Hulser.

He punched the backtrack relay to give the mortar's position to his own artillery, but without much hope. The enemy was beginning to use the new "shift" shells that confused backtrack.

The phone beside his L.D. screens glowed red. Hulser leaned into the cone of silence, answered, "O.P. one fourteen. Hulser."

The voice was Sergeant Chamberlain's. "What was that mortar shooting at, Wolfie?"

Hulser gritted his teeth, explained about the tank.

Chamberlain's voice barked through the phone, "We shouldn't have to call for an explanation of these things! Are you sure you're awake and alert?"

"Yeah, Sarge."

"O.K. Keep your eyes open, Wolfie!"

The red glow of the phone died.

Hulser trembled with rage. *Wolfie!*

He thought of Sergeant Mike Chamberlain: tall, overbearing, the irritating nasal twang in his voice. And he thought of what he'd like to do to Chamberlain's narrow, small-eyed face and its big nose. He considered calling back and asking for "Schnozzle" Chamberlain.

Hulser grinned tightly. That'd get him! And he'd have to wait another four hours before he could do anything about it.

But the thought of the certain consequences of arousing Chamberlain's anger wiped the grin from Hulser's face.

Something moved on his central screen. The fox. Or was it a fox? It moved across the frozen terrain toward the shattered tank, stopped halfway.

A fox investigating the strange odors of cordite and burned gas? he wondered. Or is it the enemy?

With this thought came near panic. If any living flesh above a certain minimum size—roughly fifty kilos—moved too close to an O.P. without the proper I.F.F., the hut and all in it exploded in a blinding flash of thermite—everything incinerated to prevent the enemy from capturing the observer's Life Detector shield.

Hulser studied the grid of his central screen. It reminded

him of a game he'd played as a boy: two children across a room from each other, ruled graph paper hidden behind books in their laps; each player's paper contained secretly marked squares; four in a row—a battleship; three in a row —a destroyer; two in a . . .

Again the glow on his screen moved toward the tank crater.

He stared at the grid intersection above the glowing spot, and far away in his mind a thought giggled at him: Call and tell 'em you have a battleship on your screen at O-6-C. That'd get you a Section Eight right out of this man's Army!

Out of the Army!

His thoughts swerved abruptly to New Oakland, to Carol Jean. To think of her having our baby back there and—

Again the (fox?) moved toward the tank crater.

But his mind was hopelessly caught now in New Oakland. He thought of all the lonely years before Carol: working five days a week at Planetary Chemicals . . . the library and endless pages of books (and another channel of his mind commented. You scattered your interests too widely!) . . . the tiny cubbyhole rooms of his apartment . . . the tasteless—

Now, the (fox?) darted up to the tank crater, skirted it.

Hulser's mind noted the movement, went right on with its reverie: Then Carol! Why couldn't we have found each other sooner? Just one month together and—

Another small glowing object came on the screen near the point where he'd seen the first one. It too darted toward the tank crater.

Hulser was back in the chill present, a deadly suspicion gnawing at him: The enemy has a new type of shield, not as good as ours. It merely reduces image size!

Or is it a pair of foxes?

Indecision tore at him.

They could have a new shield, he thought. We don't have a corner on the scientific brains.

And a piece of his mind wandered off in a new direction— the war within the war: the struggle for equipment superiority. A new weapon, a new shield; a better weapon, a better shield. It was like a terrible ladder dripping with maimed flesh.

They could have a new shield, his mind repeated.

And another corner of his mind began to think about the shields—the complex flicker-lattice that made human flesh transparent to—

Abruptly he froze. In all clarity, every diagram in place, every equation, every formula complete—all spread out in his mind was the instrument he knew could end this war. Uncontrolled shivering took over his body. He swallowed in a dry throat.

His gaze stayed on the screen before him. The two glow spots joined, moved into the tank crater. Hulser bent into the cone of silence at his phone. "This is O.P. one fourteen. I have two greenies at co-ordinates oh-six-C-sub T-R. I think they're setting up an O.P.!"

"Are you sure?" It was Chamberlain's nasal twang.

"Of course I'm sure!"

"We'll see."

The phone went dead.

Hulser straightened, wet his lips with his tongue. Will they send a plane for a sky look? They don't really trust me.

A rending explosion at the tank crater answered him.

Immediately, a rattle of small-arms fire sprang up from the enemy lines. Bullets quested through the gray snow.

It was an enemy O.P.! Now they know we have an observer out here!

Another bullet found the dome of the O.P.

Hulser stared at the hole in terror. What if they kill me? My idea will die with me! The war will go on and on and—He jerked toward the phone, screamed into it, "Get me out of here! Get me out of here! Get me out of here!"

When they found him, Hulser was still mumbling the five words.

Chamberlain's lanky form crouched before the O.P.'s crawl hole. The three muffled figures behind him ignored the O.P., their heads turning, eyes staring off into the snow, rifles at the ready. The enemy's small-arms fire had stopped.

Another one's broke, thought Chamberlain. I thought shame might make him last a little while longer!

He dragged Hulser out into the snow, hissed, "What is it, you? Why'd you drag us out into this?"

Hulser swallowed, said, "Sarge, please believe me. I know how to detonate enemy explosives from a distance without even knowing where the explosives are. I can—"

"Detonate explosives from a distance?" Chamberlain's

eyes squinted until they looked like twin pieces of flint. Another one for the head shrinkers unless we can shock him out of it, he thought. He said, "You've gone off your rocker, you have. Now, you git down at them instruments and—"

Hulser paled. "No, Sarge! I have to get back where—"

"I could shoot your head off right where you—"

Fear, frustration, anger—all of the complex pressure-borne emotions in Hulser—forced the words out of him: "You big-nosed, ignorant lump. I can end this war! You hear?" His voice climbed. "Take me back to the lieutenant! I'm gonna send your kind back under the rocks you—"

Chamberlain's fist caught Hulser on the side of the head, sent him tumbling into the snow. Even as he fell, Hulser's mind said, But you told him, man! You finally told him!

The sergeant glanced back at his companions, thought, If the enemy heard him, we've had it! He motioned one of the other men in close. "Mitch, take the watch on this O.P. We'll have to get Hulser back."

The other nodded, ducked through the crawl hole.

Chamberlain bent over Hulser. "You stinkin' coward!" he hissed. "I've half a mind to kill you where you sit! But I'm gonna take you in so's I can have the personal pleasure of watchin' you crawl when they turn the heat on you! Now you git on your feet! An' you git to walkin'!"

Major Tony Lipari—"Tony the Lip" to his men—leaned against the canvas-padded wall of his dugout, hands clasped behind his head. He was a thin, oily-looking man with black hair parted in the middle and slicked to his head like two beetle wings. In civilian life he had sold athletic supplies from a wholesale house. He had once worn a turban to an office party, and it had been like opening a door on his appearance. Somewhere in his ancestry there had been a Moor.

The major was tired (Casualty reports! Endless casualty reports!) and irritable, faintly nervous.

We don't have enough men to man the O.P.s now! he thought. Do we have to lose another one to the psych boys?

He said, "The lieuten—" His voice came out in a nervous squeak, and he stopped, cleared his throat. "The lieutenant has told me the entire story, Corporal. Frankly, it strikes me as utterly fantastic."

Corporal Hulser stood at attention before the major. "Do I have the Major's permission to speak?"

Lipari nodded. "Please do."

"Sir, I was a chemist—I mean as a civilian. I got into this branch because I'd dabbled in electronics and they happened to need L.D. observers more than they needed chemists. Now, with our shields from—" He broke off, suddenly overwhelmed by the problem of convincing Major Lipari.

He's telling me we need L.D. observers! thought Lipari. He said, "Well, go on, Hulser."

"Sir, do you know anything about chemistry?"

"A little."

"What I mean is, do you understand Redox equations and substitution reactions of—"

"Yes, yes. Go on!"

Hulser swallowed, thought, He doesn't understand. Why won't he send me back to someone who does? He said, "Sir, you're aware that the insulation layer of our L.D. shields is a typical kind of protection for—"

"Certainly! Insulates the wearer from the electric charge of the suit!"

Hulser goggled at the major. "Insulates . . . Oh, no, sir. Begging the Major's pardon, but—"

"Is this necessary, Corporal?" asked Lipari. And he thought, If he'd only stop this act and get back to work! It's so obvious he's faking! If—

"Sir, didn't you get the—"

"I had a full quota of L.D.-shield orientation when they called me back into the service," said Lipari. "Infantry's my specialty, of course. Korea, you know. But I understand how to operate a shield. Go on, Corporal." He kicked his chair away from the wall.

"Sir, what that insulation layer protects the wearer from is a kind of pseudo-substitution reaction in the skin. The suit's field can confuse the body into producing nitrogen bubbles at—"

"Yes, Hulser! I know all that! But what's this have to do with your wonderful idea?"

Hulser took a deep breath. "Sir, I can build a projector on the principle of the L.D. suits that will produce an artificial substitution reaction in any explosive. I'm sure I can!"

"You're sure?"

"Yes, sir. For example, I could set up such a reaction in Trinox that would produce fluorine and ionized hydrogen—"

in minute quantities, of course, but sufficient that any nearby field source would detonate—"

"How would you make sure there was such a field in the enemy's storage area?"

"Sir! Everybody wears L.D. shields of one kind or another! They're field generators. Or an internal-combustion motor . . . or . . . or just anything! If you have an explosive mixture collapsing from one system into another in the presence of fluorine and hydrogen—" he shrugged—"it'd explode if you looked cross-eyed at it!"

Lipari cleared his throat. "I see." Again he leaned back against the wall. The beginnings of an eyestrain headache tugged at his temples. Now the put-up-or-shut-up, he thought. He said, "How do we build this wonderful projector, Corporal?"

"Sir, I'll have to sit down with some machinists and some E-techs and—"

"Corporal, I'll decide who sits down with whom among my men. Now, I'll tell you what you do. You just draw up the specifications for your projector and leave them with me. I'll see that they get into the proper hands through channels."

"Sir, it's not that simple. I have all of the specs in my head now, yes, but in anything like this you have to work out bugs that—"

"We have plenty of technical experts who can do that," said Lipari. And he thought, Why doesn't he give up? I gave him the chance to duck out gracefully! Scribble something on some paper, give it to me. That's the end of it!

"But, sir—"

"Corporal! My orderly will give you paper and pencil. You just—"

"Sir! It can't be done that way!"

Lipari rubbed his forehead. "Corporal Hulser, I am giving you an order. You will sit down and produce the plans and specifications for your projector. You will do it now."

Hulser tasted a sourness in his mouth. He swallowed. And that's the last we'd ever hear of Corporal Larry Hulser, he thought. Tony the Lip would get the credit.

He said, "Sir, after you submit my plans, what would you do if someone asked, for example, how the polar molecules of—"

"You will explain all of these things in your outline. Do I make myself clear, Corporal?"

"Sir, it would take me six months to produce plans that could anticipate every—"

"You're stalling, Corporal!" Major Lipari pushed himself forward, came to his feet. He lowered his voice. "Let's face it, Hulser. You're faking! I know it. You know it. You just had a bellyful of war and you decided you wanted out."

Hulser shook his head from side to side.

"It's not that simple, Corporal. Now, I've shown you in every way I can that I understand this, that I'm willing to—"

"Begging the Major's pardon, but—"

"You will do one of two things, Corporal Hulser. You either produce the diagrams, sketches or whatever to prove that you *do* have a worthy idea or you will go back to your unit. I'm done fooling with you!"

"Sir, don't you under—"

"I could have you shot under the Articles of War!"

And Lipari thought, That's what he needs—a good shock!

Bitter frustration almost overwhelmed Hulser. He felt the same kind of anger that had goaded him to attack Sergeant Chamberlain. "Major, enough people know about my idea by now that at least some of them would wonder if you hadn't shot the goose that laid the golden egg!"

Lipari's headache was full-blown now. He pushed his face close to Hulser's. "I have some alternatives to a firing squad, Corporal!"

Hulser returned Lipari's angry glare. "It has occurred to me, *sir,* that this project would suddenly become 'our' project, and then 'your' project, and somewhere along the line a mere corporal would get lost!"

Lipari's mouth worked wordlessly. Presently he said, "That did it, Hulser! I'm holding you for a general court! There's one thing I can do without cooking any goose but yours!"

And that ends the matter as far as I'm concerned, thought Lipari. What a day!

He turned toward the door of his dugout. "Sergeant!"

The door opened to admit Chamberlain's beanpole figure. He crossed the room, came to attention before Lipari, saluted. "Sir?"

"This man is under arrest, Sergeant," said Lipari. "Take him back to area headquarters under guard and have him held for a general court. On your way out send in my orderly."

Chamberlain saluted. "Yes, sir." He turned, took Hulser's arm. "Come along, Hulser."

Lipari turned away, groped on a corner shelf for his aspirin. He heard the door open and close behind him. And it was not until this moment that he asked himself, Could that crackpot actually have had a workable idea? He found the aspirin, shrugged the thought away. Fantastic!

Hulser sat on an iron cot with his head in his hands. The cell walls around him were flat, riveted steel. It was a space exactly the length of the cot, twice as wide as the cot. At his left, next to the foot of the bed, was a barred door. To his right, at the other end of the floor space, were a folding washbasin with water closet under. The cell smelled foul despite an overriding stink of disinfectant.

Why don't they get it over with? he asked himself. Three days of this madhouse! How long are they—

The cell door rattled.

Hulser looked up. A wizened figure in a colonel's uniform stood on the other side of the bars. He was a tiny man, grayhaired, eyes like a curious bird, a dried parchment skin. In the proper costume he would have looked like a medieval sorcerer.

A youthful M.P. sergeant stepped into view, unlocked the door, stood aside. The colonel entered the cell.

"Well, well," he said.

Hulser came to his feet, saluted.

"Will you be needing me, sir?" asked the M.P. sergeant.

"Eh?" The colonel turned. "Oh. No, Sergeant. Just leave that door open and—"

"But, sir—"

"Nobody could get out of this cell block, could they, Sergeant?"

"No, sir. But—"

"Then just leave the door open and run along."

"Yes, sir." The sergeant saluted, frowned, turned away. His footsteps echoed down the metal floor of the corridor.

The colonel turned back to Hulser. "So you're the young man with the bright idea."

Hulser cleared his throat. "Yes, sir."

The colonel glanced once around the cell. "I'm Colonel Page of General Savage's staff. Chemical warfare."

Hulser nodded.

"The General's adjutant suggested that I come over and talk to you," said Page. "He thought a chemist might—"

"Page!" said Hulser. "You're not the Dr. Edmond Page who did the work on pseudolithium?"

The colonel's face broke into a pleased smile. "Why, yes, I am."

"I read everything about your work that I could get my hands on," said Hulser. "It struck me that if you'd just . . ." His voice trailed off.

"Do go on," said Page.

Hulser swallowed. "Well, if you'd just moved from organic chemistry into inorganic . . ." He shrugged.

"I might have induced direct chemical rather than organic reactions?" asked Page.

"Yes, sir."

"That thought didn't occur to me until I was on my way over here," said Page. He gestured toward the cot. "Do sit down."

Hulser slumped back to the cot.

Page looked around, finally squeezed past Hulser's knees, sat down on the lid of the water closet. "Now, let's find out just what your idea is."

Hulser stared at his hands.

"I've discussed this with the General," said Page. "We feel that you may know what you're talking about. We would deeply appreciate a complete explanation."

"What do I have to lose?" asked Hulser.

"You may have reason for feeling bitter," said Page. "But after reading the charges against you I would say that you've been at least partly responsible for your present situation." He glanced at his wrist watch. "Now tell me exactly how you propose to detonate munitions at a distance—this projector you've talked about."

Hulser took a deep breath. This is a chemist, he thought. Maybe I can convince him. He looked up at Page, began explaining.

Presently the colonel interrupted. "But it takes enormous amounts of energy to change the atomic—"

"I'm not talking about changing atomic structure in that sense, sir. Don't you see it? I merely set up an artificial condition *as though* a catalyst were present. A pseudo catalyst. And this brings out of the static mixture substances that are already there: ionized hydrogen from moisture—fluorine from the actual components in the case of Trinox. White phosphorus from Ditrate. Nitric oxide and rhombic sulfur from common gunpowder."

Page wet his lips with his tongue. "But what makes you think that, in a nonorganic system, the presence of the pseudo catalyst—" He shook his head. "Of course! How stupid of me! You'd first get a polar reaction—just as I did with pseudolithium. And that would be the first step into—" His eyes widened and he stared at Hulser. "My dear boy, I believe you've opened an entirely new field in nonorganic chemistry!"

"Do you see it, sir?"

"Of course I see it!" Page got to his feet. "You'd be creating an artificial radical with unstable perimeter. The presence of the slightest bit of moisture in that perimeter would give you your ionized hydrogen and—" he clapped his hands like a small boy in glee—"kapowie!"

Hulser smiled.

Page looked down at him. "Corporal, I do believe your projector might work. I confess that I don't understand about field lattices and these other electronic matters, but you apparently do."

"Yes, sir."

"How did you ever stumble onto this?" asked Page.

"I was thinking about the lattice effect in our Life Detector systems, when suddenly there it was: the complete idea!"

Page nodded. "It was one of those things that had to remain dormant until the precisely proper set of circumstances." Page squeezed past Hulser's knees. "No, no. Stay right there. I'm going to get up a meeting with Colonel Allenby of the L.D. section, and I'll get in someone with more of a mechanical bent—probably Captain Stevens." He nodded. "Now, Corporal, you just stay right here until—" His glance darted around the cell, and he laughed nervously. "Don't you worry, young man. We'll have you out of here in a few hours."

Hulser was to look back on the five weeks of the first phase in "Operation Big Boom" as a time of hectic unreality. Corps ordered the project developed in General Savage's reserve area after a set of preliminary plans had been shipped outside. The thinking was that there'd be less chance of a security leak that close to a combat zone, and that the vast barrens of the reserve area offered better opportunity for a site free of things that could detonate mysteriously and lead to unwanted questions.

But Corps was taking no chances. They ringed the area with special detachments of M.P.s. Recording specialists moved in on the project, copied everything for shipment stateside.

They chose an open tableland well away from their own munitions for the crucial test. It was a barren, windy place: gray rocks poking up from frozen earth. The long black worm of a power cable stretched away into the distance behind the test shelter.

A weasel delivered Hulser and Page to the test site. The projector box sat on the seat between them. It was housed in a green container two feet square and four feet long. A glass tube protruded from one end. A power connection, sealed and with a red "Do not connect" sign, centered the opposite end. A tripod mounting occupied one side at the balance point.

The morning was cold and clear with a brittle snap to the air. The sky had a deep-cobalt quality, almost varnished in its intensity.

About fifty people were gathered for the test. They were strung out through the shelter—a long shed open along one side. An empty tripod stood near the open side and almost in the center. On both sides of the tripod technicians sat before recording instruments. Small black wires trailed away ahead of them toward an ebony mound almost a mile from the shed and directly opposite the open side.

General Savage already was on the scene, talking with a stranger who had arrived that morning under an impressive air cover. The stranger had worn civilian clothes. Now he was encased in an issue parka and snow pants. He didn't look or act like a civilian. And it was noted that General Savage addressed him as "sir."

The General was a brusque, thick-bodied man with the overbearing confidence of someone secure in his own ability. His face held a thick-nosed, square-jawed, bulldog look. In fatigues without insignia he could have been mistaken for a sergeant. He looked the way a hard, old-line sergeant is expected to look. General Savage's men called him "Me Tarzan," mainly because he took snow baths, mother naked, in subzero weather.

A white-helmeted security guard ringed the inside of the

test shed. Hulser noted that they wore no side arms, carried no weapons except hand-held bayonets. He found himself thinking that he would not have been surprised to see them carrying crossbows.

General Savage waved to Page as the colonel and Hulser entered the shed. Colonel Page returned the gesture, stopped before a smooth-cheeked lieutenant near the tripod.

"Lieutenant," said Page, "have all explosives except the test stack been removed from the area?"

The lieutenant froze to ramrod attention, saluted. "Yes, sir, Colonel."

Page took a cigarette from his pocket. "Let me have your cigarette lighter, please, Lieutenant."

"Yes, sir." The lieutenant fumbled in a pocket, withdrew a chrome lighter, handed it to Page.

Colonel Page took the lighter in his hand, looked at it for a moment, hurled both lighter and cigarette out into the snow. The lighter landed about sixty feet away.

The lieutenant paled, then blushed.

The colonel said, "Every cigarette lighter, every match. And check with everyone to see that they took those special pills at least four hours ago. We don't want any *internal* combustion without a motor around it."

The lieutenant looked distraught. "Yes, sir."

"And, Lieutenant, stop the last weasel and have the driver wait to cart the stuff you collect out of our area."

"Yes, sir." The lieutenant hurried away.

Page turned back to Hulser, who had mounted the projector on its tripod, now stood beside it.

"All ready, sir," said Hulser. "Shall I connect the cable?"

"What do you think?" asked Page.

"We're as ready as we'll ever be."

"O.K. Connect it, then stand by with the switch in your hands."

Hulser turned to comply. And now, as the moment of the critical test approached, he felt his legs begin to tremble. He felt sure that everyone could see his nervousness.

A tense stillness came over the people in the shed.

General Savage and his visitor approached. The General was explaining the theory of the projector. His visitor nodded.

Seen close up, the other man gave the same impression of hard competence that radiated from General Savage—only more competent, harder. His cheekbones were like two ridges of tan rock beneath cavernous sockets, brooding dark eyes.

General Savage pointed to the black mound of explosives in the distance. "We have instruments in there with the explosives, sir. The wires connect them with our recorders here in the shed. We have several types of explosives to be tested, including kerosene, gasoline, engine oil. Everything we could lay our hands on except atomics. But if these things blow, then we'll know the projector also will work on atomics."

The visitor spoke, and his voice came out with a quality like a stick dragged through gravel. "It was explained to me that—the theory being correct—this projector will work on any petroleum fuel, including coal."

"Yes, sir," said Savage. "It is supposed to ignite coal. We have a few lumps in a sack to one side. You can't see it because of the snow. But our instruments will tell us which of these things are affected—" he glanced at Hulser—"if any."

Colonel Page returned from checking the recording instruments.

Savage turned to the colonel. "Are we ready, Ed?"

"Yes, General." He glanced at Hulser, nodded. "Let's go, Larry. Give it power."

Hulser depressed the switch in his hand, involuntarily closed his eyes, then snapped them open and stared at the distant explosives.

A low humming arose from the projector.

Page spoke to the General. "It'll take a little time for the effect to build u–"

As he started to say "up" the mound of explosives went *up* in a giant roaring and rumbling. Colonel Page was left staring at the explosion, his mouth shaped to say "p."

Steam and dust hid the place where the explosives had been.

The gravel voice of the visitor spoke behind Hulser. "Well, there goes the whole shooting match, General. And I *do* mean shooting!"

"It's what we were afraid of, sir," said Savage. "But there's no help for it now." He sounded bitter.

Hulser was struck by the bitterness in both voices. He turned, became conscious that the lieutenant whom Page had reprimanded was beating at a flaming breast pocket, face livid. The people around him were laughing, trying to help.

Page had hurried along the line of recorders, was checking each one.

The significance of the lieutenant's antics suddenly hit Hulser. *Matches! He forgot his spare matches after losing his cigarette lighter!* Hulser glanced to where the colonel had thrown the lighter, saw a black patch in the snow.

Page returned from checking the recorders. "We can't be sure about the coal, but as nearly as we can determine, it touched off everything else in the stack!" He put an arm on Hulser's shoulder. "This young genius has won the war for us."

The (civilian?) snorted.

Savage turned, scowled at Hulser.

But Hulser was staring out at the explosion crater, a look of euphoria on his face.

The technicians were moving out into the area now, probing cautiously for unexploded fragments.

The General and his visitor exchanged a glance that could have meant anything.

Savage signaled his radio operator to call for transportation.

Presently, a line of weasels came roaring up to the test site.

Savage took Hulser's arm in a firm grip. "You'd better come with us. You're a valuable piece of property now."

Hulser's mind came back to the curious conversation between Savage and the visitor after the explosion, and he was struck by the odd sadness in the General's voice. Could he be an old war dog sorry to see it end? Somehow, on looking at the General, that didn't fit.

They sped across the barrens to the base, Hulser uncomfortable between the General and his visitor. Apparently no one wanted to discuss what had just happened. Hulser was made uncomfortable by the lack of elation around him. He looked at the back of the driver's neck, but that told him nothing.

They strode into the General's office, an oblong room without windows. Maps lined the walls. A low partition separated one space containing two barren tables from another space containing three desks, one set somewhat apart. They crossed to the separate desk.

Savage indicated his visitor. "This is Mr. Sladen." There was a slight hesitation on the "Mr."

Hulser suppressed a desire to salute, shook hands. The other man had a hard grip in an uncalloused hand.

Sladen's gravelly baritone came out brusque and commanding. "Brief him, General. I'll go get my people and their gear together. We'll have to head right back."

Savage nodded. "Thank you, sir. I'll get right at it."

Sladen cast a speculative look at Hulser. "Make sure he understands clearly what has just happened. I don't believe he's considered it."

"Yes, sir."

Sladen departed.

Hulser felt an odd sinking sensation in his stomach.

Savage said, "I'm not rank happy, Hulser, and we haven't much time. We're going to forget about military formality for a few minutes."

Hulser nodded without speaking.

"Do you know what has just happened?" asked Savage.

"Yes, sir. But what puzzles me is that you people don't seem pleased about our gaining the whip hand so we can win this war. It's—"

"It's not certain that we have the whip hand." Savage sat down at his desk, picked up a book bound in red leather.

"You mean the enemy—"

"Bright ideas like yours just seem to float around in the air, Hulser. They may already have it, or they could be working on it. Otherwise, I'd have seen that your brainstorm was buried. It seems that once human beings realize something can be done, they're not satisfied until they've done it."

"Have there been any signs that the enemy—"

"No. But neither have *they* seen any signs of *our* new weapon . . . I hope. The point is: we do have it and we're going to use it. We'll probably overwhelm them before they can do anything about it. And that'll be the end of *this* war."

"But if explosives are made obsolete, that'll mean an end to all wars," protested Helser. "That's what I'm concerned about!"

The General sneered. "Nothing, my bright-eyed young friend, has thus far made war impossible! When this one's over, it'll be just a matter of time until there's another war, both sides using your projector."

"But, sir—"

"So the next war will be fought with horse cavalry, swords, crossbows and lances," said Savage. "And there'll be other little *improvements!*" He slammed the red book onto his desk, surged to his feet. "Elimination of explosives only makes espionage, poisons, poison gas, germ warfare—all of these—a necessity!"

"How can you—"

"Don't you understand, Hulser? You've made the military use of explosives impossible. That means gasoline. The internal-combustion motor is out. That means jet fuels. Airplanes are out. That means gunpowder. Everything from the smallest sidearm to the biggest cannon is out!"

"Certainly, but—"

"But we have other alternatives, Hulser. We have the weapons King Arthur used. And we have some *modern* innovations: poison gases, curare-tipped crossbow bolts, bacterial—"

"But the Geneva Convention—"

"Geneva Convention be damned! And that's just what will happen to it as soon as a big enough group of people decide to ignore it!" General Savage hammered a fist on his desk. "Get this! Violence is a part of human life. The lust for power is a part of human life. As long as people want power badly enough, they'll use any means to get it—fair or foul! Peaceful or otherwise!"

"I think you're being a pessimist, sir."

"Maybe I am. I *hope* I am. But I come from a long line of military people. We've seen some things to make us pessimists."

"But the pressures for peace—"

"Have thus far not been strong enough to prevent wars, Hulser." The General shook his head. "I'll tell you something, my young friend: When I first saw the reference to your ideas in the charges against you, I had the sinking sensation one gets when going down for the third time. I hoped against hope that you were wrong, but I couldn't afford *not* to investigate. I hoped that Major Lipari and Sergeant Chamberlain had you pegged for—"

The General stopped, glared at Hulser. "There's another bone I have to pick with you! Your treatment of two fine soldiers was nothing short of juvenile! If it wasn't for the Liparis and the Chamberlains, you'd be getting thirty lashes every morning from your local slave keeper!"

"But, sir—"

"Don't 'But, sir' me, Hulser! If there was time before you leave, I'd have you deliver personal apologies to both of them!"

Hulser blushed, shook his head. "I don't know. All I really know is that I was sure my idea would work, and that Lipari and Chamberlain didn't understand. And I knew if I was killed, or if my idea wasn't developed, the enemy might get it first."

Savage leaned back against his desk, passed a hand across his eyes. "You were right, of course. It's just that you were bucking the system, and you're not the right kind to buck the system. Your kind usually fails when you try."

Hulser sighed.

"You're now a valuable piece of property, my lad. So don't feel sorry for yourself. You'll be sent home where you can be around when your wife has that child."

Hulser looked surprised.

"Oh, yes, we found out about her," said Savage. "We thought at first you were just working a good dodge to get home to her." He shrugged. "You'll probably have it fairly soft now. You'll be guarded and coddled. You'll be expected to produce another act of *genius!* The Lord knows, maybe you *are* a genius."

"You wait and see, sir. I think this will mean an end to all wars."

The General suddenly looked thoughtful. "Hulser, a vastly underrated and greatly despised writer—in some circles—once said, 'There is nothing more difficult to take in hand, more perilous to conduct, or more uncertain in its success, than to take the lead in the introduction of a new order of things.' That's a very deep statement, Hulser. And there you are, way out in front with 'a new order of things.' I hope for the sake of that child you're going to have—for the sake of all children—that we don't have another war." He shrugged. "But I don't hold out too—"

Sladen popped back into the office. "Our air cover's coming up, General. We'll have to take him like he is. Send his gear along later, will you?"

"Certainly, sir." Savage straightened, stuck out his right hand, shook with Hulser. "Good luck, Hulser. You take what I said to heart. It's the bitter truth that men of war have to live with. You weren't attacking the source of the problem with your bright idea. You were attacking one of the symptoms."

Savage's left hand came up from his desk with the red book. "Here's a gift for that child you're going to have." He pressed the book into Hulser's hands. "The next generation will need to understand this book."

Hulser had time to say, "Thank you, sir." Then he was propelled out the door by Sladen.

It was not until he was on the plane winging south that Hulser had an opportunity to examine the book. Then he gripped it tightly in both hands, stared out the window at the sea of clouds. The book was a limited edition copy, unexpurgated, of the works of Niccolo Machiavelli, the master of deceit and treachery.

SUGGESTED READING

If you have enjoyed reading this anthology, as I hope, you may want to look up some of the stories and books mentioned in it. Here they are:

Aldiss, Brian W. *Galaxies Like Grains of Sand*. Signet Books (paperback), New York, 1960.

Asimov, Isaac. *I, Robot*. Gnome Press, New York, 1950.

Bierce, Ambrose. *The Collected Writings of Ambrose Bierce*. Citadel Press, New York, 1946.

Blish, James. *Earthman, Come Home*. Putnam, New York, 1955.

———. *They Shall Have Stars*. Faber, London, 1956; Avon (paperback), New York, 1957, as *Year 2018!*.

———. *A Clash of Cymbals*. Faber, London, 1959; Avon (paperback), New York, 1958, as *The Triumph of Time*.

Bradbury, Ray. "The Pedestrian," in *Golden Apples of the Sun*. Doubleday, New York, 1953.

de Camp, L. Sprague. *Lest Darkness Fall*. Henry Holt & Co., New York, 1941.

Derleth, August (ed.) *Beyond Time and Space*. Pellegrini and Cudahy, New York, 1950.

Gernsback, Hugo. *Ralph 124C41+*. Frederick Fell, Inc., New York, 1950.

Heinlein, Robert A. "By His Bootstraps," in *Famous Science Fiction Stories*. Modern Library, New York, 1957.

———. "Coventry," in *Revolt in 2100*. Shasta, Chicago, 1953.

———. "Lifeline," in *The Man Who Sold the Moon*. Shasta, Chicago, 1950.

———. *Methuselah's Children*. Gnome Press, New York, n.d.

————. "Requiem," in *Famous Science Fiction Stories*. Modern Library, New York, 1957.

————. "Universe," in *The Best of Science Fiction*. Crown Publishers, New York, 1946.

Leinster, Murray. *Sidewise in Time*. Shasta, Chicago, 1950.

Lewis, C. S. *Out of the Silent Planet*. Macmillan, New York, 1943.

————. See also *Perelandra*, Macmillan, New York, 1944; and *That Hideous Strength*, Macmillan, New York, 1946.

O'Brien, Fitz-James. *Collected Stories*. Boni, New York, 1925 (eight stories).

————. *The Diamond Lens*. Rudge, New York, 1932 (thirteen stories).

Poe, Edgar Allen. *The Complete Tales and Poems of Edgar Allan Poe*. Random House (Modern Library [G40]), New York.

Pratt, Fletcher (ed.). *World of Wonder*. Twayne Publishers, New York, 1952.

Reynolds, Mack and Brown, Fredric (eds.). *Science Fiction Carnival*. Shasta, Chicago, 1953.

Simak, Clifford. *City*. Gnome Press, New York, 1952.

Stapledon, Olaf. *Odd John*, in *Portable Novels of Science*. Viking Press, New York, 1945.

Sturgeon, Theodore. "Ether Breather," in *Without Sorcery*. Prime, Philadelphia, 1948.

Twain, Mark. *A Connecticut Yankee in King Arthur's Court*. Modern Library, New York, 1949.

Verne, Jules. *From the Earth to the Moon and a Trip Around It*. Lippincott, New York, 1958.

————. *Twenty Thousand Leagues Under the Sea*. Doubleday (Dolphin Series [C167]), New York, 1960.

Wells, H. G. *Seven Science Fiction Novels of H. G. Wells*. Dover Publications, New York, 1949.

————. *Twenty-eight Science Fiction Stories*. Dover Publications, New York, 1952.

Here is another list, of books about science fiction. Some, but not all, are mentioned in this anthology.

Amis, Kingsley. *New Maps of Hell*. Harcourt, Brace, New York, 1960.

Bailey, J. O. *Pilgrims Through Space and Time*. Argus, New York, 1947.

Davenport, Basil. *Inquiry into Science Fiction*. Longmans, Green, New York, 1955.

de Camp, L. Sprague. *Science Fiction Handbook*. Hermitage, New York, 1953.

Knight, Damon. *In Search of Wonder*. Advent, Chicago, 1956.

Kornbluth, Cyril, *et al. The Science Fiction Novel*. Advent, Chicago, 1959.

Lewis, C. S. *An Experiment in Criticism*. Cambridge University Press, New York, 1961.

Nicolson, Marjorie Hope. *Voyages to the Moon*. Macmillan, New York, 1948.